PYRAMIDS OF THRUSH CREEK

To Janet

Henry Young

Feb. 22 2015

PYRAMIDS OF THRUSH CREEK

HENRY YOUNDT

TATE PUBLISHING
AND ENTERPRISES, LLC

Pyramids of Thrush Creek

Published by Tate Publishing & Enterprises, LLC
127 E. Trade Center Terrace | Mustang, Oklahoma 73064 USA
1.888.361.9473 | www.tatepublishing.com

Tate Publishing is committed to excellence in the publishing industry. The company reflects the philosophy established by the founders, based on Psalm 68:11,
"The Lord gave the word and great was the company of those who published it."

Cover design by Charito Sim
Interior design by Jomel Pepito

Published in the United States of America
ISBN: 978-1-63449-868-5
1. Fiction / Christian / General
2. Fiction / Action & Adventure
14.12.08

Mystery

1

1994.

He wasn't afraid. He was well aware of the dangers, but he had other things on his mind as his glistening blue kayak slipped quietly along the secluded stream. *Could there be a supernatural being that created the universe? Is there any physical evidence to support such a belief? If it were true, there would have to be evidence.* With a life vest drawn snug across his chest and muscles bulging from his bare arms, Roger Koralsen paddled a slow, steady pace. Someone watching from a distance could have recognized his regular Sunday morning routine.

A brisk breeze mussed his dark wavy hair and sent ripples across the smooth water. His brown eyes danced over the serene landscape as the drumming of a woodpecker rolled across the quiet valley. He loved the solitude of this section of Thrush Creek, hidden deep in the mountains of central Pennsylvania. It was here that he felt close to the yearning deep inside him, that longing for something he couldn't quite identify.

Despite the dangers of kayaking alone, he was on the water almost every Sunday morning unless the weather was impossible. His paddle strokes quickened a bit as he approached the remains of a four-foot-high dam. A thirty-foot opening had been blasted out of the dam years earlier. But that was only after the tragedy.

He steered his kayak through the center of the opening and rode over the series of knee-high waves that followed. Then, as always, he made a 180-degree left turn into the eddy and drifted up behind the ten-foot section of dam jutting out from the left bank. His eye immediately caught something unusual. On the riverbank, just behind the dam, someone had built a small pyramid of rounded grapefruit-sized stones. Three stones formed the triangular base with one stone on the top.

Roger knew a triangle of anything could be a distress signal. But this was so small and inconspicuously placed that it was not likely to be intended as a distress signal. Someone might arrange three canoes into a triangle to attract the attention of an air-borne rescue team. But this small pyramid of stones in a cove behind the dam would not be noticed by anyone unless they turned into the eddy, as Roger had done. Still, the reason for its existence aroused his curiosity.

For no particular reason, he reached out with his paddle and knocked the stone off the top of the pyramid. Something silver glistened in the sunlight between the other stones. He pulled up on shore, got out of his boat, bent over, and picked up the item— a silver necklace with a plain heart-shaped pendant. He flipped the heart over and held it so the sunlight hit it at an angle. On the back of the heart, he could see the engraved initials R.K. & M.D. He straightened up quickly and glanced all around as he recognized the familiar object. This was the necklace he had given to Michelle, his high school sweetheart, the year they both graduated from high school. *Who could have put this here? Why?*

Two weeks after graduation, Michelle had drowned in this very area doing the very same thing he was now doing, kayaking alone. But that was before the low-head dam was destroyed. A skilled white-water boater, Michelle was well aware of the dangerous hydraulic below a low-head dam. She was quite familiar with the river. She and Roger had frequently canoed it together, and they always portaged around the dam. She knew the location of the dam and would have avoided getting too close to it. No one really knew what happened that day in 1987. Her boat was found tumbling in the hydraulic. Her body was never recovered.

Now, almost seven years later, here was her necklace, under a small pyramid. *What could this mean?* If someone found it along the river, why would they bury it in a pyramid? Did someone, who knew his routine, purposely put it there for him to find? If so, then why?

He felt someone was trying to make him relive all the pain of those years following Michelle's death, trying to force him back to the booze and wild parties. If he went back there, it would cost him his career as a teacher.

Roger stood there examining the necklace in the palm of his hand. Then he clutched it and dangled it from his fingers, glancing around to see who might be watching. There was no sign of anyone, although there was no shortage of places a person could be hiding. He paced up and down along the riverbank, looking for a note or any clue to the meaning of what he had found. He roamed into the shadowy woods, then back to his kayak, feeling frustrated because he had found nothing and saw no one.

Though only six miles from town, this area seemed quite remote. The hillsides on both sides of the creek were covered with trees. The right bank was steep and bordered with brier thickets. The left bank, where Roger stood, was heavily posted with No Trespassing signs. Not a single building was in sight anywhere. The only signs of civilization were the remains on the old dam and the No Trespassing signs.

Having no idea how long he had been there, Roger glanced at his watch. He had to get going. He slipped the necklace into his pocket and stood for a moment, staring at the four stones that had formed the pyramid. Then he raised his hands toward the forest and shouted to whoever might be hiding there, "What do you want? Why are you doing this to me?" There was no answer.

Even the birds were silent. He slowly pushed his kayak into the water, climbed in, and headed downstream.

About four miles ahead, he would come to a small church sitting high up on the left bank, with a lawn running down to the water's edge. Beyond the church lay the quaint little town of Thrush Glen. He needed to be there about the time the morning worship service ended. His friend Rick Beck, who attended the church regularly, would then shuttle him back upriver to his SUV. Roger would then return to the church and pick up his boat.

Roger had known Rick forever, it seemed. They had become best friends in first grade and remained close through high school. They had reconnected after college and now, for the last two years, they shared an apartment on the edge of town.

Questions about the necklace and pyramid swirled in Roger's head as his paddle blades stirred the water. He felt a thirst come over him that he knew would not be quenched by his water bottle. It wasn't just Michelle's sudden death that had previously driven him to alcohol, but also the lingering questions about what had become of her body. He had to remain strong. But he couldn't walk away from this. He had to find an explanation for the necklace in his pocket.

Just ahead, to the right, a great blue heron stood motionless. As the kayak approached, the heron took to flight. It flew downstream a hundred yards or more and landed in the shallow water near the edge of the creek. There it stood, cautiously looking about till the kayak got too close again. The whole process was repeated over and over as the heron led Roger onward, not that he wouldn't have followed the creek anyway. Following the flow of water was his passion, his pastime, his therapy. A pair of kingfishers darted from tree to tree and then disappeared.

As the church came into view, Roger could see a number of people standing outside the door chatting. He paddled up to the bank and got out. As Roger hauled his boat up onto the lawn, Rick Beck and George Lauger strolled down toward the creek.

George, another classmate from high school, was an average kind of guy, medium height, medium build, with medium brown hair. Roger had nothing against George. He just never found him to be very friendly.

"Nice day to be out on the river, aye?" Rick shouted as they approached.

"Sure is. Couldn't ask for anything better."

George stood, gazing up the creek with his back to the other two. "Did ya see much wild life?" he asked without turning.

"Just the normal." Roger rubbed his hand over his pocket to be sure the necklace was still there. "You won't believe what I found."

"You hungry?" Rick asked. "George 'n' I decided we're stopping at the deli for cheesesteaks. If you're not hungry, you'll just have to wait in the car while we eat."

"Oh, I think I could handle a cheesesteak!" Roger shot back. "Why are you just standing there looking at the water? Let's get going."

"I guess that means he's hungry," George quipped as the three turned and headed for the parking lot.

As Rick pulled out of parking lot, Roger leaned forward against the driver's seat, stuck his right hand up between George and Rick and opened his fist. "Look what I found along the creek today. It's Michelle's! Someone hid it in a little pile of stones, kind of like a—"

"Whoa! Back up!" Rick butted in. "How do you know it's Michelle's?"

"I bought it for her. I engraved our initials on it. See?" Roger turned the heart over in the palm of his hand.

"So it really is Michelle's?" George turned to look back at Roger.

"Just listen to me. This is too weird." Roger went on to recount how he found the necklace at the dam, hidden in a small pyramid of stones.

"That is really weird," George agreed as he examined the necklace. "Is this how you found it, or did you clean it up?"

"No. I just put it in my pocket"

"It doesn't look like something that's been lying on the ground or in the river for five years," George observed.

"Six years, almost seven now."

"Wow, almost seven years." Rick drummed his fingers on the steering wheel. "It doesn't seem that long."

"You're right," Roger continued. "This is too clean to have been outdoors all that time. And that pyramid was not there last week. Someone did this just within the last week. And I think they intended for me to find it."

"Do you think somebody found it right after the accident and kept it all these years?" Rick asked.

"I don't know. But obviously somebody knows something about Michelle." Roger clenched his fist. "And I'm going to find out who they are and what they know."

"Does anyone know for sure if Michelle was wearing the necklace when she drowned?" George's eyebrows furrowed.

"She wore it all the time." Roger rubbed his thumb gently over the pendant. "And it wasn't in any of her stuff we went through after her death. Her mother let me go through all her stuff and take anything I wanted. It wasn't there."

"Who would do something like this?" Rick glanced in the mirror.

"I have no idea." Roger leaned back in his seat. "Only one person keeps coming to my mind. And I don't know why. I have no reason to connect him to anything. He's just the creepiest person I know—the father of one of my students. He never looks you straight in the face. It seems like he has a grudge against everyone, but he won't say why. He makes all these little sarcastic comments, but he won't repeat or explain anything. He saw Michelle's picture on my desk and says, 'You ought to be over her by now.' I said, 'She was a great person. I'll never forget her. And

I don't want to.' He says, 'Some people just can't seem to cope with a tough situation.' Like he thought I wasn't coping with it. He's weird! His son is a good student though. Seems to be a well-adjusted kid and everything. I had no problems to discuss with the parents. We didn't have any conflict. But the father is really creepy."

George pondered for a bit and then said, "I wonder if we could get a list of everyone who helped search for Michelle after the accident." Glancing over his shoulder at Roger, he added, "I'll see what I can find."

As Rick turned into Joe's Deli & Grill, Roger said firmly, "Look, you guys don't say a word about this to anyone. If someone is trying to send me a message or mess with my head or anything like that, he'll have to strike again. Let's just keep our eyes and ears open and our mouths shut."

"Good strategy," George affirmed. "I won't say a thing."

"Agreed!" Rick slammed to a stop in the first parking space.

Roger inhaled deeply as they entered the small deli. The aroma of chopped steak sizzling on the grill made him realize how hungry he was. Rick stepped up to the counter. "I'll have a cheesesteak, fries, and a Pepsi." He pulled a ten dollar bill out of his wallet.

"Make that two of everything," Roger chimed in.

"Make it three," George added as he passed Rick a ten dollar bill. "I'll go find us a table. Outside, I suppose?"

"Sure." Roger handed another ten to Rick.

The girl at the cash register rang up the order. "Twenty-five oh two."

Rick handed her the three tens. She took two pennies out of a small dish by the register, then handed Rick five one dollar bills. Rick turned toward Roger with a perplexed look as he glanced at the five bills fanned out in his hand.

Roger nodded toward a jar on the counter with a poster about starving children. "Put the extra two in that jar, then it'll come out even." Rick dropped two dollars into the jar, handed one to Roger, put one on the tray with the food, and stuck the other one in his wallet. Then they headed outside to the picnic table where George was seated.

Rick set the tray on the table and flicked the dollar bill toward George. "There's your change."

"This looks like a pretty good meal for nine bucks," George said as he picked up the dollar bill.

"Yeah, it is." Roger's mind was obviously on something other than the meal. "We're missing a dollar. We each paid nine dollars. Three times nine is twenty-seven. We put two in the jar. That only makes twenty-nine. We gave the girl thirty."

"Well, Rick, you're the bean counter." George quipped.

"I know she gave me the right change," Rick turned to Roger. "Ya know, Roger, I think you should be an accountant. They say a good accountant can make the numbers come out any way he wants."

George glanced at Rick with a grin and added, "Yeah, I'm not sure that he should be teaching math to fourth graders."

"Seriously," Roger insisted, "what happened to the other dollar?"

2

"Good morning, Mr. Koralsen," a young voice called out.

Roger looked up from his papers to see fourth-grader Destiny Morris entering the classroom. "Good morning, Destiny. Did you have a nice weekend?"

"Yeah." Destiny smiled. "I went canoeing with my dad on Saturday."

Roger's hand stopped flipping papers. "Oh? Where did you go?"

"Well, we started at an iron bridge."

"On Thrush Creek?"

"Yeah, I think that was the name."

"Where did you take out?"

"At a churchyard."

"And at one point you went through an old broken dam, right?"

"Yeah, that was fun! It was like a rapids. The waves were splashing in over the edges, and I was getting all wet."

"Did you see anything interesting?"

"Well, we saw a lot of birds and stuff. And a big fish jumped out of the water right in front of us. That was really neat."

"Did you stop anywhere along the creek to fish or play or anything?"

"No. But we had to dump the water out of the canoe after we went through the dam. Mostly, we just kept going."

Before Roger could get any more information, their conversation was interrupted by another group of students entering the classroom. The end of the school year was approaching, and the students were becoming increasingly hyperactive. They were eager for summer vacation, and so was their teacher. Although he had a busy schedule, Roger's mind was constantly being interrupted with thoughts of Michelle and the question of how her necklace found its way into the pyramid along Thrush Creek.

On Wednesday evening, Roger was correcting homework in the room he and Rick called the library. Although the room was a bit short on bookshelves, the guys preferred to call it the library rather than a family room. This room, separated from the kitchen by a peninsular bar cabinet, was outfitted with a mixed motif featuring motorcycles, whitewater sports, big trucks, and Penn State memorabilia. It was a place where a man could relax and choose the world in which he wanted to lose himself.

As Roger's mind wavered between checking papers and pondering the mystery surrounding Michelle, someone knocked on the back door. *Another interruption—George Lauger!*

George proudly presented Roger with a list of persons who had helped in the search for Michelle's body. "Where did you get this?" Roger snatched the list from George's hand.

"I put it together from fire company records and stuff I saved. Anything that was printed, newspapers, and whatever, I saved it. I've got lots of pictures too."

"I didn't know you had all that stuff."

"You're not the only one who cared about Michelle."

Roger heard that comment loud and clear but made no reply.

"It's probably not a complete list," George went on. "There were some people out there who didn't seem to be part of any organized group. In fact, most anyone in Thrush Glen could have been out there helping. But this is a list of those I know were there."

"Let's see. Is there a Bobby Billmant on here?" Roger mumbled as he scanned over the list.

"Bobby Billmant? That must be the creepy parent you were talking about."

"Yeah. You know him?"

"Sort of. He was treasurer of the fire company for a short while. Nobody else wanted the job, and he volunteered. So they gave it to him. But they soon found out that nobody trusted him. Some people think he was embezzling, but the records were so poorly kept that nobody could prove anything. So they forced him to resign."

"That sounds like Bobby. And I see you've got him on the list. But so is almost everyone else I know and some that I don't know."

"Yeah," George agreed. "It doesn't mean much. But then again, whoever did this is probably on that list."

"Melvin Morris helped," Roger observed. "He and his daughter, Destiny, were canoeing out there on Saturday. But I can't believe he would do something like that."

"Well, you can keep that list for what it's worth. I've got to run along. My mom is expecting me home for dinner this evening."

After George left, Roger spent hours reading the list of names over and over and wondering, *If someone found the necklace during the search, why would they keep it for almost seven years, then bury it in a pyramid of stones?*

That Sunday, Rick agreed to skip church and join Roger for a canoe trip down Thrush Creek, though he insisted that they time the trip an hour later so that he wouldn't arrive at the church at the same time everyone else was leaving. Rick normally played guitar in the worship band on Sunday mornings, and he didn't want the other musicians to see his real reason for taking the morning off. But if there was someone who knew something about what had become of Michelle's body, he wanted to do all he could to help Roger track down that person.

Rick felt the warm sun on his shoulders as they put the canoe into the water. But still, each breath of the fresh spring air held a crispness that heightened the anticipation of the day ahead. The mountainsides radiated a dozen shades of green and the sound of water gurgling over rocks beckoned them to join the flow of the river. Roger steadied the boat as Rick got seated in the bow. They paddled briskly out to the middle of the creek and headed downstream with paddle blades flashing in perfect unison.

"Ya know?" Rick said, breaking their rhythm. "Something just doesn't make sense to me. You saw four stones piled up in a simple little pyramid and you noticed a triangular pattern. You assumed that since there was a pattern, someone must have intentionally arranged them that way. You even considered that the triangular pattern might have some special meaning. You didn't assume that the currents of a flooded creek could have randomly deposited them in that position. You assumed a person did it."

"Of course," Roger butted in eagerly. "That seems like a reasonable assumption, doesn't it? And obviously it was right. What are you getting at?"

"But yet," Rick continued thoughtfully, "when you study the complex patterns formed by the chemicals in our DNA, you conclude that there was no intentional plan for that. We're not talking about a simple triangle here. We're talking about a complex code that contains the blueprint for the human body, or any other living thing. Those codes, you believe, came about by the random process of nature."

"Well, not exactly." Roger paused at the end of his J-stroke. "As you know, the process is called natural selection. And it's not a random process. Yes, the mutations occur at random. But the changes that make the organism inferior die out while those that improve the organism get passed on. So as the name suggests, there is a selection process which is responsible for continual improvement. It's not random. And the complex DNA code doesn't prove that there's a God."

"No, it doesn't prove it. But it certainly suggests a plan."

"Not when you understand the whole process."

"Okay. But how did this process of improvement get started?" Rick pressed on. He knew Roger was enjoying this debate. "You believe that four chemicals could have come together randomly to form the first amino acids. And you believe that some number of different amino acids randomly came together to form the first proteins. And that somehow developed into the first living cell, which just happened to have its blueprint recorded in a DNA code so it could reproduce itself. All that happened without any planning. However, you see four stones on a pile and you say, 'Ah, there's a pattern. There must have been a plan or a purpose. Some intelligent mind has been at work here.' Does that make sense?"

"Well," Roger replied slowly. "I think it does. Those stones weren't in the water where the current could move them around. They were put there in one week's time, and there was no flood water during that week. On the other hand, the chemicals for the amino acids were in solution. For billions of years, these chemicals were randomly coming in contact with each other. Sooner or later the right ones had to link up and form an amino acid. That's not as farfetched as you make it sound."

"It sounds like pretty long odds to me." Rick gazed downriver.

"It is long odds. But that doesn't mean it didn't happen."

"Well, for me, it's easier to believe that the process was guided by some kind of intelligent being."

"Well, for me, it's not. And where did the intelligent being come from?"

"Yeah, no matter how we explain it, we always get back to something that always existed. And that blows my mind. I just wish I could prove to you that God exists."

"I wish too you could," Roger agreed. "I wish we could prove it one way or the other and put an end to this eternal debate."

"Wouldn't that rock the world?" Rick turned in his seat, rocking the canoe and unintentionally dramatizing his point. "That would affect everyone on the planet one way or the other."

"That certainly would rock," Roger agreed. "That's an important issue to a lot of people. A lot of people would have to change their beliefs. But how can we prove a negative? How can anybody prove that God does not exist, especially when this God is supposed to be a supernatural spirit rather than a physical being?"

"If we could come up with some solid proof, we'd be famous."

"Right now, I'm more interested in tracking down that person who had Michelle's necklace."

"I'm with you there. Maybe by the time we solve that mystery, the answer to the other question will become obvious."

"It *should* be obvious!" Roger paused in midstroke. "Think about it, Rick. If there were a god who manipulates things on this earth, the evidence wouldn't be that hard to see."

"Maybe it's not." Rick planted his paddle and pulled forward. "We just have to open our eyes."

"But to be scientific," Roger countered, "you can't just look for evidence that supports one side of an argument. You have to look at all the evidence and see what it suggests."

"So," Rick scanned the river ahead, "we keep looking at the evidence until it sinks in."

"One thing we can agree on." Roger gazed at the mountainside. "No matter how it came about, this is a fantastic world we live in. Just look around at all the trees and plants, blue sky, fresh air. I love it out here."

"You're right about that!"

"I don't see how anyone can see all this and not be affected by it somehow."

"Yeah, this is just as good as sitting in church." They paddled along quietly enjoying the serenity of the environment.

"You hear that bird?" Roger asked. "It sounds like it's saying, 'Cheeseburger, cheeseburger.'" They listened quietly as a rich melodious voice called out again from somewhere up on the wooded hillside.

"You mean that one?"

"Yeah, that. You know what kind of bird that is?"

"No."

"That's a blue jay."

"A blue jay? You're kidding."

"No. It is. A lot of people don't realize that blue jays have quite a variety of beautiful calls. Everyone knows about the '*jay, jay*' they scream when they're alarmed. But that's not the only call they have."

"I didn't know that." Rick always enjoyed Roger's nature trivia. "It's like a completely different voice. I know some birds, like the cardinal, have different calls, but it's always the same voice."

"Yeah," Roger paused as the blue jay sang out again, "it's like the blue jay has a singing voice and a screaming voice."

"Just like some rock stars." Rick chuckled. Blue jays, wood thrushes, and other birds continued singing as they made their way downstream without making a sound other that an occasional paddle bumping against the gunnels.

As they approached the remains of the old dam, Roger said, "Now after we get through that series of waves, we'll make an eddy turn to the left. We'll drift up behind the dam. Then, if you want to, we can go back out and try to surf one of the waves."

"Aye, aye, Captain. Sounds good to me."

They rode through the waves, made a 180-degree turn then let the eddy draw them up behind the dam. "There it is again!" Roger exclaimed, pointing his paddle toward the small pyramid of grapefruit-size stones hidden behind the dam. "Someone rebuilt it." He turned the canoe and pushed the bow up onto the shore. They climbed out and walked over to the pyramid. Roger picked up the top stone to expose a key ring with a car key. He picked it up, slowly examining it. The key ring was a souvenir from Washington, DC. It had a polished metal plate attached with "Washington, DC" engraved on one side. "Michelle" was engraved on the other side.

"Is it hers?" Rick asked.

"You bet!" Roger was certain. "She bought this on our class trip to Washington. And that's the key to her Toyota. She left her car at the iron bridge. I was going to meet her at the church later that day. Her purse and some other personal things were in her dry bag. The dry bag was still tucked in the bow of her kayak when they retrieved it. But her keys were missing. Her keys would have been in her pocket. Whoever found this found her body."

"Why would someone not report finding a body?" Rick wondered out loud. "What kind of pervert would do something like this? It's bizarre. It's insane!"

"If I ever get my hands on that low-down sewer varmint, he'll wish he'd never messed with me!"

"Just keep your cool, Roger. Don't react the way he wants you to."

"Let's look around and see what else we can find," Roger said in a calmer tone.

As they scouted in eerie silence, they soon noticed that although the area was heavily posted, there was a slightly worn foot path following the edge of the creek. And someone was maintaining the No Trespassing signs. Any sign in bad condition was replaced with a new one right over top of the old one. They were all signed with the name Robert Stoner.

"Ah, look here." Rick pointed to a fishing lure tangled in some tree branches hanging over the water about thirty yards below the dam. "Someone fishes from here. You can see where they stand, the grass is worn off." About fifteen yards above the dam, they noticed another spot that was worn from someone standing along the creek, presumably fishing.

"Ya know, you can't see the pyramid from either of these spots." Rick observed. "From down below it's hidden by a big clump of bushes. And from up here, it's behind the dam."

"So what does that mean?"

"I don't know if it means anything. It's just something I noticed."

As they started back toward the dam, Roger said, "Let's get out of here. This place is starting to freak me out."

They got into the canoe and shoved off. Roger turned the boat downstream, completely forgetting about surfing a wave.

After returning from canoeing and a quick stop for a burger, Rick and Roger stopped by to update George on the day's events. The door to George's woodworking shop was open. The two walked in to find George studying a stack of cherry boards.

"What? Are you working on Sunday?" Roger grinned.

"No," George responded. "I'm just trying to figure out where I went wrong. Yesterday I started working on some bookcases for a client. But I ran out of lumber. I was using number one common lumber. That has knots and defects in it. Number one common is supposed to yield 67 percent good material. In other words, I could expect to lose 33 percent when I cut out all the defects. I need forty-five square feet of nice wood for the project. So I added 33 percent to that and bought sixty square feet of rough lumber. Now I have all the defects cut out, and I only have forty square feet. I'm short five feet."

"You started with sixty square feet and ended up with forty." Roger sounded like a schoolteacher. "That's 33 percent waste, isn't it?"

"Right," George agreed. "I added 33 percent to what I needed and I had 33 percent waste. So, why am I short five feet?"

Rick chuckled. "I guess the five feet of lumber went to the same place that Roger's missing dollar went last week."

"Okay, you can make fun of me." Roger had received his share of ribbing from Rick over that mistake. And he had accepted it in good humor.

"I thought you guys are so smart," George quipped. "You're always arguing about the origin of the universe or some other intellectual issue. I thought you'd be able to help me with a simple math problem."

Rick realized that Roger, always eager to be one up on George, was about to explain his mistake. *But before we help him, we ought to have a little fun. If I start it, I'm sure Roger will play along.* "That's not my department." Rick winked at Roger. "That's teaching. I'm just a bean counter."

"But today is Sunday," Roger shot back. "I don't work on Sundays."

"Oh, now he's becoming religious?" Rick turned to George with raised eyebrows.

"I don't care if it comes from an accountant or a teacher," George sounded desperate. "I just need somebody to explain where I'm screwing up."

3

An attractive petite young teacher paused at the doorway of Roger's empty classroom. Roger was busy packing his personal belongings into a box to take home for the summer. She cleared her throat to get his attention then sauntered toward him with an enticing smile on her glossy red lips. Roger sensed that she had been trying to corner him alone for some time. But he was always busy and always surrounded by so many other people. All year, it seemed he hadn't had the opportunity to really get to know her. "What you up to, Mr. Roger?" she asked with a twinkle in her dark brown eyes.

"Hi, Ms. Keller," he replied with only a brief glance.

"You're not my student. You can call me Kathy."

"Hi, Kathy. I'm just packing up my stuff."

"You're all ready for a summer vacation, I guess?" She seemed to be admiring his physique.

"I can't believe the school year is over already." He finally smiled back at her. "It seems like just last month you were introduced as a new teacher."

She snuggled up beside him, shoulder to biceps, and asked, "Would you like to go along for a drink to celebrate my first year of teaching?"

"Well, actually," he paused, enjoying her closeness and the smell of her perfume, "I don't drink. But I could go for a cappuccino or a root-beer float or whatever."

"I'm sorry. I didn't know you don't drink."

"I did enough of that in college—getting sick, barfing my guts out, then getting up the next morning with a hangover and trying to make sense of everything. I don't need to do that anymore."

"Oh. You can't take just one drink and stop?"

"No, that's not what I meant. I can drink responsibly if I want to." Roger chuckled. He wasn't sure that was actually true. "But why do I have to drink at all? Just because somebody decided that's the socially acceptable thing to do, now I'm expected to do it? That's a bunch of bull crap."

"I'm not trying to make you drink." She seemed to accept his candor and his independent spirit. "I just thought you might want to go out and celebrate."

"Well, here's my real concern." Roger turned, his eyes met hers. "In just a few years these fourth graders are going to start thinking they're grown-ups. They'll want to start doing the things grown-ups do. It's hard to convince teenagers that something is okay for adults, but not for them. The things we do are so much more important than what we say."

"That's very noble of you. I guess I never thought of it that way before."

"Kathy, you go to church, don't you? What do *they* say about booze?"

"Well, I guess they'd say it's bad. But I don't think I've ever heard them actually say that."

"I wonder why that is," Roger mused. "It seems that in the past, a lot of churches held a legalistic view on alcohol. Now, I guess they realized that view wasn't biblical. So now they don't want to talk about it at all. There are a lot of good reasons to stay away from alcohol, even though the Bible condones drinking."

"I thought you don't go to church."

"I don't."

Kathy hesitated, fumbling with the edge of her sweater. "Well, root-beer floats would be fine. It's been years since I've had one of those. I'll feel like I'm fourteen again."

"Shall we go then?" Roger picked up his box and turned toward the door.

"Can I help you carry anything?"

"Okay. If you want to, you can grab that planter of Venus flytraps."

"You have a lot of interesting things for your students," Kathy commented as she picked up the planter and fell in step beside Roger.

"Well, I try to make learning fun." Roger smiled broadly. "Do you have big plans for the summer?"

"Ah…no, not really. I'm still trying to find a summer job. What are your plans?"

"I'd like to spend a week or two canoe-camping in the wilderness—maybe the Allagash wilderness in Maine or someplace like that. But I haven't gotten a definite plan together yet. I've been looking at maps and buying gear. But I haven't found enough people to go along."

"How many do you need?"

"Well, if you're going into a wilderness area where you are totally dependent on yourself and what you bring with you, it's good to have a group of at least three boats. The smaller the group, the greater the risks."

"More power to ya!" Kathy replied as they strode across the parking lot toward Roger's red Ford Explorer. "I don't like camping. I hate bugs and snakes and all kinds of little critters. But it's strange. I always enjoy listening to people talk about their camping experiences."

As they drove toward town, they discussed job opportunities and the old-fashioned community of Thrush Glen with its rustic charm. As they entered town on Main Street, Roger nodded toward a family-owned hardware store on the right. "Have you ever been in there?" he asked.

"Nope."

"It's quite a place. You should check it out sometime. You can buy anything from seed corn to work clothes or hunting rifles."

"Stuff I really need." Kathy chuckled.

A few doors down, on the left, was a small grocery store built in 1890, and probably looking much the same as it did then. Next door to that was a quaint little shop with a faded sign that read "Elsie's Flower Shoppe." The bank was on the corner of Main Street and Church Street. Across the street from the bank was the general store and post office.

"There's another unique place." Roger grinned. "You can buy groceries or clothing or just about anything and pick up your mail at the same time."

"Thank goodness, my mail is delivered." Kathy seemed unimpressed. In the middle of the next block was the theater, which looked like it belonged in the 1920s, and next door was Betsy's Ice Cream Parlor.

The ice cream parlor was an old building with a creaky wooden floor. It held the aroma of aged wood with just a tinge of furniture polish. Two large ceiling fans hung from the beams supporting the high ceiling. Each side wall had a row of booths separated by high backs, and over each booth hung a Tiffany lamp. An antique nickelodeon player piano stood along the end wall, playing tunes from the roaring twenties. The nostalgia was from an era that neither of them had known, but still the romantic atmosphere seeped into their veins. Kathy brushed close beside Roger as they made their way to a booth. As she got seated, he snuggled in beside her.

As they sat in their booth sipping root-beer floats, Roger glanced up to see Bobby Billmant approaching. "Well, what's this?" Bobby said as he came near their booth. "A teenage couple having root-beer floats. Well, ain't that lovely."

"Yeah, we're just trying—" Roger stopped in midsentence as Bobby walked right on by without even looking directly at them.

"He's really strange," Kathy said softly.

"So you have his daughter in your class, don't you?" Roger glanced over his shoulder to be sure Bobby was gone.

"Yeah. And you have his son."

"That's right. He's fine. But I don't know what's up with the dad. He makes all these weird comments, and I never know how I'm supposed to take it."

"I had a puzzle on my desk." Kathy glanced over her shoulder. "Kind of like a Rubik's Cube. But instead of being in the shape of a cube, it was a triangular pyramid. It's a lot easier to solve than the cube. More on a third-grade level. But anyway, at our parent-teacher conference, he seemed kind of mesmerized by it. Like the shape had some special meaning or something. But he wouldn't really say what it was. He just gives you this blank stare, like you don't know if he's plotting some sort of evil scheme or what."

"It seems like he's just trying to push people's buttons." Roger stirred his float.

"Yeah." Kathy nodded. "But he kind of scares me. He's an ex-Marine, ya know. To me, that means he wouldn't have any trouble hurting someone if he wanted to. And I just don't know what's going on inside his head."

"I wouldn't want to get into a fight with him."

"It seems that beard is like a mask, and there's no expression in his eyes. So you just can't read his face at all."

"Do you know if he goes fishing or canoeing or anything?" Roger cocked his head.

"I don't have a clue. Why?"

"No reason. I was just curious."

Before Roger knew it, he was making strange noises trying to suck up the last drop of root beer with a straw.

When they arrived back at the school, Roger pulled his car up beside hers. Without realizing it, he found himself asking, "Would you like to go out for dinner sometime? Maybe go see a movie or something?"

"Sure. That would be great," she answered without hesitation. "Like when?"

"Ah…I don't know," Roger stammered. "I'll call you sometime."

"Okay." Kathy smiled as she got out of his car. "I'll see ya."

As Roger drove home, his mind was working on an idea that had started to formulate while he was telling Kathy about his camping plans. Instead of taking a group on a wilderness camping trip, he could spend time camping alone along Thrush Creek. He could find a secluded spot overlooking the area of the dam and secretly monitor whatever activity might go on there. He would have plenty of time to relax and observe nature, read, write, or draw and all the while keep an eye out for any activity in the area.

As he unpacked his things, he noticed a spider in the planter of Venus flytraps. He wondered if it had been there while Kathy was carrying it and imagined her reaction if she had seen it. He watched as the spider crawled across an open pair of leaves and came in contact with the small hairlike sensors. The leaves quickly snapped together, trapping the spider inside. *What an amazing plant*, he thought. Within the next few days, the plant would secrete enzymes, which would digest the spider, and the nutrients would be absorbed by the plant. He thought about the three unique features of the plant: the ability to sense the movement of a living organism on its leaves, the ability to move its leaves, and the ability to digest its prey.

All three of these features had to work together to produce one benefit, supplying the plant with added nutrition. In his mind, he compared it to the little pyramid of four stones along Thrush Creek. The three unique features of the plant were the base stones, which together supported the top stone, the beneficial nutrients. Take away any one of the base stones and the top would tumble down. He wondered how these three unique features evolved. *Which one came first? No single feature by itself would provide any benefit to the plant. What are the odds of the three features evolving simultaneously? How could the process on natural selection produce such a plant?* He knew what Rick's answer would be, but there had to be a more scientific explanation. However, if the three features had developed toward a future benefit, that certainly would lend credence to Rick's view of things. He made a mental note to do some research on the question as soon as he had time.

But first he had to get prepared for overnight camping on Thrush Creek. He would stay only one night on his first trip. He would go out tomorrow, Thursday, and return sometime on Friday. So he only needed enough food and water for a day or day and a half at the most. He spent the rest of the evening organizing an assortment of camping gear, extra clothes, food, drinks, binoculars, camera, sketch pad, pencils, and journal. Around ten thirty, he went to bed with an air of anticipation for what the next day would bring.

As Roger lay in bed, his mind kept returning to the items he had found in the pyramids. He felt as though his life was again beginning to revolve around that terrible event of June 20, 1987. He remembered how he had gone out to the creek to meet Michelle. She expected to be off the water by about three o'clock, and he was going to shuttle her back to her car at the iron bridge. He got to the creek a half hour early and waited and waited under a gray sky. An hour went by, then two. He began thinking about going to a phone and calling for help. But he was afraid that as soon as he left, she might show up and wonder why he wasn't there. Finally, around five o'clock, he drove to a nearby convenience store and called 911.

He remembered talking to the dispatcher and getting so choked up he could hardly get the words out. Township police chief Theodore Miller was first to arrive. He was tall, broad-shouldered, and muscular and brought an air of calmness and reassurance. Roger remembered how he had immediately sensed that he was talking with someone who cared deeply about the situation he was facing. In the weeks to come, Chief Miller would become a personal friend, affectionately known as Chief Theodore. Even before the water rescue team arrived, the police chief radioed one of his officers and sent him to the iron bridge to see if Michelle's car was there.

Then the water rescue team arrived and headed up the creek in their motorized inflatable boat, searching for the missing boater. In less than an hour, they found her kayak, trapped in the hydraulic below Good's Dam. Then the endless search for Michelle began.

Roger remembered how he had prayed and prayed for a miracle, that somehow, some way, Michelle would be alive and well. He remembered the indirect message he heard from everyone at her memorial service, that Michelle was now in a better place and her death was somehow an answer to everyone's prayers for her safety and well-being. Roger just couldn't see it that way. Chief Theodore seemed to be the only person who didn't impose that message on Roger. The chief always made Roger feel that he was okay, no matter what emotions he was experiencing.

He thought about the many times he'd ended up so drunk that he had no memory of what he'd done. He had to avoid being drawn back into that. But he couldn't ignore the mystery that now surrounded Michelle's disappearance.

Thoughts of Michelle, the search, Michelle's parents and friends, and Chief Theodore kept swirling around in Roger's head till eventually he drifted off to sleep.

4

The next morning, Roger loaded everything into his SUV, with his kayak on the roof, and headed out to the creek. Instead of putting in at the iron bridge, he took a small dirt road to an access area several miles downstream from the bridge. That way he would be able to paddle back upstream to his car on Friday and wouldn't need to make arrangements with anyone for shuttle service. Paddling upstream, of course would be more difficult, but by staying out of the main current and using the slack water and eddies he figured he would be able to cover that distance in two or three hours.

The morning sky was overcast and it drizzled from time to time as Roger made his way downstream. He didn't really mind the dreary weather; in fact, he enjoyed the exhilarating feel of the drizzle in his face. It was certainly better than the blazing hot sun. By the time he reached the last bend before the dam, the sky was beginning to clear. Roger glance at the sky, thinking the sun might break through.

Before rounding the bend, Roger pulled up onto a pebbled beach to the right, still out of sight from the dam. He dragged his kayak up into the thick patch of ferns and huckleberries above the beach. Then he continued another hundred feet, pushing through the thick wet bushes and butterfly weed till he reached the pine forest. Here, on a bit of a knoll between the creek and the mountain, he found a spot where he had a good view downstream to the area of the dam and beyond. Even without binoculars, he could easily monitor the area around the dam. He could set up his tent under the pine trees. It wasn't altogether level, but it would do. Waist-high bushes would provide enough of a blind to keep his campsite hidden.

He then returned to the kayak and picked up his dry bag. He slipped his arms through the shoulder straps, picked up a small camping stove and folding beach chair, and then fought his way through the wet bushes again, back to the pine trees. After setting up his tent, Roger positioned his chair so he could see downstream and so that the sun, what little there was, would help dry his clothes. He did not want to attract anyone's attention by building a campfire.

By lunch time, the sun was shining warmly and his clothes were comfortably dry. He ate the cold lunch he had packed that morning. So far he had seen chipmunks, squirrels, geese, an osprey, chickadees, and a rose-breasted grosbeak, but not one person. The afternoon was much the same. At one point he got out his sketch pad and looked around at all the scenery. It was all beautiful, but nothing inspired him to start drawing. It seemed his mind didn't want to focus on the beauties of nature around him. After sketching a pyramid of four rounded stones, he put his pad away again.

For about the fifteenth time, he picked up his binoculars and scanned the area of the dam and the surrounding hillsides. But this time, the afternoon sun was coming through between the tall pines at just the right angle to expose something he had missed before. About a half mile below the dam, halfway up the mountainside, there was what appeared to be a small building. He could see only part of the roof and gable end. The rest of the building was hidden behind trees. Gnawing on beef jerky, he watched carefully, but he did not see any activity in that area nor anywhere along the creek.

In the evening, he lit his little propane camping stove and heated some water for soup and hot chocolate. He paced about the campsite eating dried apricots and a granola bar, all the while keeping an eye on the creek. As darkness fell and the night-loving insects began their chorus, he took the binoculars and carefully examined the area of the building, looking for light. But it was as dark as the rest of the mountainside. As the sky darkened, he gazed at the stars. The big dipper was hidden by the trees to his north, but to the south, he could pick out Sagittarius and Scorpius. In the blackness of the forest, the sky became a dazzling array of lights gleaming and twinkling from the vastness of space. Eventually, his neck grew tired from looking up, so he went into his tent and crawled into his sleeping bag. *What could the Allagash offer that I don't have right here?* he wondered as he closed his eyes.

When he opened his eyes again, the morning light was filtering through his nylon tent and a Carolina wren was singing, "Tea kettle, tea kettle." He crawled out of the tent, stretched, and strolled around the campsite breathing the fresh morning air. He could hear the soothing sound of water running over rocks and a dense mist was rising from Thrush Creek. He lit the stove and made a cup of instant coffee. Then he started frying bacon and eggs.

As the mist began to clear from the creek, he could make out the form of a person down by the dam. Looking through the binoculars, he could see that the man was fishing from the shore a short distance above the dam. As Roger ate his breakfast he kept checking to see if the fisherman was still there. As the sun rose, the mist gradually disappeared. Roger looked through the binoculars again. The man was wearing all camouflage except for black combat boots and a black belt with a holster and pistol. He was tall, slender, and rugged-looking, with a roughly trimmed beard.

Roger watched as the man occasionally reeled in a fish, then cast out his line and continued fishing. About midmorning Roger noticed two canoes coming down the creek. With the help of the binoculars, he recognized Destiny Morris and her father in the one boat. He did not know the pair in the other boat. As the two canoes rounded the bend, Roger looked down toward the dam again. The fisherman was gone. The boats moved along steadily, through the dam and eventually out of sight. The fisherman reemerged and continued fishing.

A while later, four teenage boys approached in a canoe and two kayaks. As soon as they rounded the bend, the fisherman disappeared again. And when they were out of sight, he reappeared and continued fishing. Roger wondered, *Is this disappearing fisherman the person who has been leaving items for me to find?*

He ate a light lunch, then packed up all his things and headed back to his kayak. He stowed his gear in the boat then took the binoculars and went back up to the knoll one more time. The fisherman was still fishing. *If this guy is trying to send me some kind of message*, Roger thought, *maybe he'll have something to say when I come down the creek.*

He went back down and put his boat in the water. But as he paddled around the bend, the fisherman disappeared. He paddled down the creek and came gliding slowly in to the shore just above the dam. He got out and stretched as if he had been cramped up in a small boat for half a day. He touched his toes and twisted from side to side, keeping a sharp eye out for any sign of the disappearing fisherman. He paced about flexing his legs and taking the opportunity to look down over the dam to see if the pyramid had been rebuilt. The stones were scattered about, just as he and Rick had left them the week before. He did a couple of knee bends, then casually began strolling into the woods.

He had only gone about fifty feet when a gunshot rang out from close range and a chunk of bark exploded off the side of a tree not more than six feet in front of him. Roger turned around slowly with his hands raised to shoulder height. "Now that's a message I understand," he said out loud. He walked quickly back to his boat, climbed in, and shoved off.

With adrenaline rushing through his arteries, paddling upstream was no problem at all. It seemed like only a short time till he was approaching a class two rapids, which was about a quarter mile from where he left his car. He paddled into an eddy at the bottom of the rapids and glided up to the rock which created the eddy. He rested there a moment, quietly enjoying the scenery while turbulent water rushed by on both sides. Then he ferried across the main current to catch the tail end of another eddy. That one advanced him another fifty feet upstream. He zigzagged his way around rocks and through some minor currents till he reached a large circulating eddy along the shore.

He pulled up along the shore to rest a few minutes. He thought about all the paddling skills he had learned from Max, how to read the water and use the currents to your best advantage, how to paddle efficiently, and lots of other skills he used all the time. He was lucky to have had the opportunity to spend so much time paddling with a person like Max. And now, the skills he'd learned from Max would come into play. From the top to this eddy, he would have a short but swift section of water to cross before entering the placid water above the rapids. This was where the stream's current accelerated as it funneled into the narrow channel of the rapids.

He started gathering speed as he paddled up the eddy. Then he turned into the main current, and paddling furiously, he inched his way upstream till he broke free of the swift current. From here it was an easy stretch of flat water back to his starting point.

This little trip provided a bit of everything, he thought as he slipped along quietly. He had exercised his muscles and tested his paddling skills. He also had time for rest and relaxation. There was both quietness and excitement. He had time to contemplate on the items he found in the pyramid. But he felt no closer to understanding what it meant.

5

"So he actually shot at you," Rick commented after hearing Roger recount the events of the last two days.

"I don't know that he actually tried to hit me," Roger continued. "I think it was probably a warning shot."

"Still, that's serious," Rick raised his eyebrows. "Do you think we ought to call the police?"

"I was trespassing. And we can't prove that he even saw me or intentionally shot toward me. Let's not run to the police just yet. We can always do that later. I've been keeping a journal with dates and times of everything that happened that might be related. So if we decide to contact the police later, we'll still have good reliable information to give them."

"We ought to find out more about this landowner though," Rick argued. "What was that name on the No Trespassing signs?"

"Stoner. Robert Stoner."

"I wonder if that's the guy you saw and if that building is where he lives."

"Yeah, I wonder too."

"We'll have to see what George can find out about the property."

"Why George?" Roger's eyes narrowed.

"He's good at tracking down information like that. Ask him anything, and he'll find the answer somewhere."

"I don't know. I'm not so sure I want him involved."

"He's a smart guy. While you and I were racking up college debt, he was working his tail off getting established in business."

"He does really seem to like his woodworking."

"Right," Rick continued. "And of the three of us, he's the only one who is self-employed and owns the house he lives in."

"That's one of those little facts that always annoy me."

Later that afternoon, when Rick and Roger dropped in on George, they found him at the kitchen table working on a puzzle. The puzzle consisted of nine square pieces with pictures of birds. Each bird was positioned so that half of the bird fell on one piece and half on the adjacent piece. There were four species of birds with three identical pictures of each. The goal was to arrange the pieces in a three by three square with all the bird halves matched together properly.

"I've been working at this almost every evening this week." George leaned back in his chair. "I just can't get it."

"It's only nine pieces," Roger quipped. "How hard can it be?"

"Here! You try it." George pushed the pieces toward Roger. "I'll bet you fifty bucks you can't put it together in less than an hour."

"God, help me," Roger said softly as he started randomly picking up pieces and positioning them in a three-by-three grid, matching the bird halves as he went. Within a few minutes he had eight pieces arranged so that everything matched. But the last piece, which had to go in the middle of the bottom row, created a bird with two tails and no head. Roger studied for about thirty seconds then took the piece from the top right corner, placed it in the middle of the bottom row and put the remaining piece on the top right corner. "There," he said. "I did it."

"Leapin' lords! I can't believe it!" George reached toward Roger for a high five. "I spent hours on that!"

"Beginner's luck, I suppose," Roger said, trying to be modest.

"I think it was an answer to a prayer," Rick kept a poker face.

"What are you talking about?" Roger shot back.

Rick glanced at George with a mischievous twinkle in his eye. "He did say, 'God, help me,' didn't he?"

"Yes, he did," George agreed with a smirk.

"You know that wasn't a prayer. It was just an expression." Roger seemed to be taking it seriously. "I'm surprised you're not accusing me of using God's name in vain."

"Well, apparently, God thought it was a prayer," Rick responded, still grinning. "And he decided to help you. Think about it. What are the odds of just picking up those pieces and laying them out in the proper order like that?"

"Yeah, what are the odds, anyway?" Roger adjusted a piece that was slightly out of line. "Let's figure it out."

"You need a calculator?" George got to his feet.

"Well, let's see," Roger continued. "We have nine pieces that can go in nine positions, and each one can be turned four directions. What's nine to the fourth power?"

"Here you go." George slid a pocket calculator across the table.

"What's this?" Roger complained as he examined the calculator. "It has no scientific functions. You mean a rich guy like you can't afford a scientific calculator?"

"You have to do it the old-fashioned way," George replied. "Press nine times nine times nine times nine. I hope you don't get carpal tunnel from all that repetitive motion."

"Six thousand five hundred sixty one." Roger looked up from the calculator. "That's not so impossible. If the odds were like a million to one, you might convince me that God helped me. But six or seven thousand to one—I can chalk that up to luck."

"Six thousand something?" Rick looked puzzled. "I thought it would be much higher than that."

"Me too," George agreed. "Are you sure that's right?"

"That's nine to the fourth power," Roger punched the numbers again.

"I don't follow your logic," Rick peered over Roger's shoulder. "What makes you say it's nine to the fourth power?"

"I'm not sure I can explain it," Roger replied. "How would *you* figure it out?"

"I don't know," Rick shrugged.

"Well," George quipped, "I still say it was a prayer."

"Okay then," Roger turned toward George. "My next prayer is that you actually pay me the fifty bucks. Remember? Just before I said, 'God, help me,' you said you bet fifty bucks I couldn't do it in less than an hour."

"Right, I did. Sorry, I don't have that much cash right now."

"Yeah, yeah. I hear ya. You do have a credit card, right?"

"You take credit cards?"

"No, but Red Lobster does. We'll all go to Red Lobster, put it on your card, and call it even."

"That'll be more than fifty bucks."

"Including your meal. But what's a few bucks among friends?"

George wasn't sure how sincere Roger was in using the term *friends*. But it felt good to be included. "Okay. It's a deal," he replied.

"Deal," Roger confirmed. "I'll drive."

During the forty-five minute drive, Roger retold his story in detail for George's benefit. They rehashed all the frustrating questions over and over. Who was this disappearing fisherman? Who was Robert Stoner? Was he really the landowner? Who could have acquired Michelle's personal items? Why would they bury them in a small pyramid along the creek?

On Sunday morning, Roger set out to do a little exploring by land, instead of his usual trip down the river. He wanted to see if he could find a road or a lane or maybe just a trail leading to the building he had spotted in the vicinity of the old broken dam. And perhaps he would find a mailbox with a name on it. He started at a concrete bridge about a mile and a half below the dam, intending to drive the whole way around three sides of the area till he returned to the river farther upstream.

As he rounded the first bend after leaving the bridge, he noticed a narrow unpaved lane leading into the woods. No Trespassing signs were posted on trees on both sides of the lane. But there was no mailbox along the road and no utility lines going into the woods. He made a mental note and continued on, checking the utility lines and watching for a mailbox or any kind of trail into the forest. He followed the winding Lumber Mill Road up the mountainside till he reached Ridge Road. He turned left and followed Ridge Road as it snaked northward along the top of the ridge. On the left side of the road, about every hundred yards, there would be a tree with one of the same signs he had seen along the river. He stopped several times to check the signature. They were all signed with the name Robert Stoner.

After about three miles, he turned left onto a gravel road, which took him down the mountainside and back to the river. He had not seen a mailbox or any utility lines going into the area. He pulled off at the spot where he had gotten onto the river on Thursday and got out of his car. He stood, leaning against the side of his car, watching the flow of the river and listening to the sound of the water while gray clouds spilled over the ridge and whisked across the blue sky. *Life should be like a river, ever flowing forward*, he thought. *But mine is becoming a whirlpool, circling round and round.* Eventually he headed back his winding path toward the concrete bridge, double-checking the whole area. It seemed the lane at the bridge was the only thing leading in toward the vicinity of the building.

Roger pulled off by the bridge and began walking up the deserted country road to take a closer look at the lane and check the name on the signs. As he approached the lane, he heard the sound of a vehicle coming out. He quickly stepped into the shadows of the woods and stood behind a large oak tree. He peered around the tree as the vehicle emerged. It was a township police cruiser, and Chief Theodore Miller was at the wheel.

Roger knew that Chief Theodore went to church on Saturdays, and he normally took the Sunday morning shift so the other two officers could attend church if they wanted to. So it was not unusual to see him on patrol on a Sunday morning. But what was he doing out here in this little lane in the woods?

Maybe I made a mistake by not reporting the gunshot incident. If there was some kind of problem or disturbance that brought the police out here, the information about what happened on Friday could be important. And I might be able to get information from Chief Theodore to answer some of my questions.

After the police cruiser pulled out and disappeared around the bend, Roger proceeded to check the name on the signs. They too were signed by Robert Stoner. He peered in the lane to where it faded into the darkness of the forest but noticed nothing unusual. He walked quickly back to his car and headed home.

After reviewing the morning's events with Rick, Roger said, "Maybe it's time I talk to Chief Theodore about this whole thing."

"I don't know about that." Rick stared at the floor. "I think your first idea was pretty good. Keep our eyes and ears open and our mouths shut."

"Why? Don't you trust Chief Theodore?"

"Well, to be honest, I'm not sure how far I could trust him."

"What! Why not?"

"I should keep my mouth shut. But working at the bank and doing people's taxes on the side, I find things out—things I should keep confidential." Rick raised his eyes to meet Roger's. "But I know I can trust you. There's something I have to tell you about the chief."

"Like what?"

"Well, first of all, his salary hardly supports his lifestyle. And of course, you know he buys a lot of groceries and stuff for some poor folks."

"Yeah, everyone seems to know that."

"But no one seems to know who those poor folks are."

"So?"

"He pays cash for all that stuff, doesn't have any record of how much he spends, and doesn't use it as a tax write-off. He buys a lot of other stuff with cash too."

"What's wrong with that?"

"Nothing. But here's the thing. His paycheck is deposited electronically, and he never makes cash withdrawals. So I'm wondering where all his cash comes from. His wife doesn't have a job. He doesn't report any other income."

"You actually think Chief Theodore is doing something dishonest?"

"I can't prove anything. I've been keeping an eye on this for some time. I don't know what's going on. But I wouldn't trust him."

"I'd like to know what he was doing out there in the woods." Roger socked his fist into his hand.

"Me too," Rick agreed. "Let's keep our eyes open, and you keep on recording everything in your journal. We'll figure it out sooner or later."

6

Kathy glanced about the softly lit room and noted the rustic outdoor theme. *Well, they certainly didn't blow their budget on decorating.* There was a gentle din of Friday evening dinner guests visiting and waitresses taking orders while hits from the sixties played in the background. She gazed across the table into Roger's eyes. "Am I boring you?" she half-whispered.

He jolted back to the present. "No, no. I'm sorry. I guess I've got a lot on my mind."

"I noticed that. Would you like to talk about it?"

"No. I don't want to trouble you with it. How's your vacation going so far? Did you find a job yet?"

"No. But I did apply at the library today."

"That's right. You told me that earlier."

"And how's your vacation going, Mr. Roger? Are you still planning to run off to the Allagash wilderness?"

"No. I guess I'll have to give that up for this year. But I did go out camping overnight on Thrush Creek last week. I think I may do it again tomorrow—camp overnight and come back Sunday, about noon."

"You should have a great time. They're calling for nice weather the next couple days."

"What about you, Kathy? You got any big plans coming up?"

"Next weekend I'm going to Washington. There's a whole busload of us going down for an antiabortion demonstration."

Now here's something that could lead an interesting discussion. Roger took a sip from his glass of Pepsi. "Are you demonstrating against abortion itself or against the court decision that made it legal?"

"What do you mean?"

"Well, who's your audience? Are you trying to influence law makers and judges, or are you trying to influence ordinary citizens who have abortions and the doctors who perform them?"

"I don't know. We're going to Washington. So I guess we're trying to influence the government."

"Did you ever consider what would happen if you were successful and actually overturned Roe v. Wade?

"Yeah. We'd save about one point three million babies a year."

"Okay. But beside that?"

"What do you mean 'beside that'? You don't think that's enough?"

"Well, first of all, the number of illegal abortions would rebound. So you wouldn't save as many babies as you might think. Now the fact is, illegal abortions are just as immoral as legal ones. But you have added health risks. By making it illegal, you create a financial opportunity for unqualified and unscrupulous people who are willing to break the law to make a buck. In my opinion, that's not a good thing."

"The law needs to be enforced." Kathy scowled. "If they don't enforce the law, it won't mean anything. But with proper enforcement, we could save a lot of babies."

"But that's almost impossible to do without invading people's privacy," Roger continued. "And here's the other thing that would happen. Most of the babies that you do save from abortion would be born into homes where they are not wanted. A lot of them would be neglected, mistreated, and abused."

"They can be adopted. There are lots of people who want to adopt children."

"We already have more unwanted children than what are being adopted."

"That's because the government makes it so difficult and expensive to adopt a child."

"We keep hearing the horror stories in the news about children being left in deplorable conditions, children being abused and raped, stories about frustrated parents punishing a baby because it won't stop crying. The more they hurt the child, the more it cries. The more it cries, the more they injure the child, till finally the child dies. Some of the babies you save would suffer a fate much worse than abortion."

"Roger, I never would have thought that you would be proabortion."

"I'm not! I just accept the fact that forcing my opinions on everyone else would make a bad situation worse. But I'm not proabortion. In fact, I bet I'm more pro-life than you are."

"How's that?"

"Well, what do you say about a high-risk pregnancy, where the mother's life is in danger? Is abortion okay then?"

"Yeah, but that's the only time."

"I thought you'd say that. But where does that come from? Where do we get the idea that we should kill the offspring to save the parent? Look at nature. The most important thing we have to do is to pass life on to the next generation. The offspring is always more important than the parent. Look at the salmon. They spawn, they die. It's okay. Life has been passed to the next generation. Take the honeybee. The queen mates, and then she kills the drones. They're dispensable. Their life has been passed to the next generation. Killing the offspring to save the parent goes against nature."

"So, Mr. Know-it-all, what do *you* think we should do about abortion?"

"I think that if everyone who claims to be a Christian would really believe what they say they believe, you'd have a different strategy on this issue."

"What are you trying to say?"

"Most Christians say they believe there is an almighty God who has the power to change people's hearts, to change the way they think and view things. If they really believe that, why are they fooling around trying to change the law? They should be convincing people to believe in God so he can change their hearts. That way, the babies you save from abortion would be born into homes where they are wanted and loved and cared for. Isn't that the kind of results we all want?"

"But we do try to win converts to Christ. Of course, then we're accused of being intolerant and not respecting other people's views."

"I'm not accusing you of that. I just enjoy debating this kind of stuff."

"And at the same time that we're trying to get converts, we're trying to fix the law. We're working on both fronts."

"But you can't do both." Roger's voice was getting louder. "Trying to force your beliefs down everyone else's throats is no way to win friends and influence people. You're making enemies of the very people you should be trying to convert. Instead of reaching out to help those in need, you're building barriers. That strategy makes no sense—unless you recognize that there is no God who can change people's hearts."

Kathy paused briefly. She knew Roger loved to argue, and she enjoyed an intellectual challenge too. But this wasn't what she considered part of a romantic evening. "Have you seen *Schindler's List*?" she asked.

"No, I haven't."

"I haven't either. But I'd like to."

"George drove the whole way to Harrisburg to see it. He said it was really worthwhile."

Kathy smiled at his change in tone. "It's finally coming to the theater in this little town."

"We'll have to go see it."

Early Saturday morning, as Roger was finishing breakfast and Rick was reading the newspaper, the back door opened and George yelled out, "You guys up?"

"Who could that be, so early in the morning?" Roger yelled back. "Come on in."

George strolled into the kitchen and dropped a piece of paper on the table in front of Roger. "Here's what I found out about that land along Thrush Creek." He walked to the other side of the table and sat down. "It's owned by an old lady in Philadelphia by the name of Eva Stoner. Her husband, Robert, passed away in 1974. So he hasn't signed his name on any No Trespassing signs recently."

"Seventy-four? That's twenty years ago. Those signs were definitely put up since that," Rick said as he came into the kitchen.

"So," Roger slid his cereal bowl aside, "I suppose they were put up by someone who doesn't actually own the land."

"The Stoners," George continued, "bought the land from the man Robert worked for, a Philadelphia businessman by the name of Earl Keelson. In the early nineteen hundreds, the land belonged to a local lumber company called Good Lumber. When Mr. Good died, his daughter, Sadie Miller, sold the business and the land to the Keelsons."

"Did you say Miller?" Rick raised his eyebrows. "Any connection to our police chief?"

"I knew you'd ask that. I've already checked it out. Yes, Sadie Miller was Chief Theodore's grandmother. But that land hasn't been in his family since before he was born."

"Did you find anything about the building?" Roger glanced at George.

"Robert Stoner did build some kind of cabin or cottage on the property sometime around 1950."

"So," Roger rose from his chair, "we still don't know who this disappearing fisherman is. But we know he's not Robert Stoner."

"And," Rick added, "we don't know what the police chief was doing out there on a Sunday morning."

"And is any of this related to what you guys found in those pyramids?" George glanced from Rick to Roger.

"If that fisherman is keeping people out of the area," Roger rubbed his chin thoughtfully, "that kind of narrows down the list of people who could have put the pyramids there. It would have to be him or someone he allows on the property or someone who accesses the area by canoe or kayak."

"Who does that eliminate?" Rick rubbed his chin, mimicking Roger.

"I don't know," Roger was too deep in thought to notice Rick's mockery. "Maybe nobody at this point. I'm going out camping again tonight. I'll do some more surveillance, see if I can learn anything new."

"By the way," George looked at Roger. "I ran into my high school math teacher yesterday."

"Mr. Wagner?"

"Yeah. I asked him about that bird puzzle we were working on last week. He said the odds are like twenty-three billion to one."

"How'd he come up with that?" Roger wasn't ready to accept twenty-three billion without some evidence.

"I don't know. He took nine factorial times something or other."

"So you're telling me I was wrong."

"You said if it was more than a million to one you'd have to believe that God helped you." George waited for Roger's reaction.

"I don't think that's actually what I said," Roger snapped. "And you haven't proven that twenty-three billion is the correct number."

"I think you did say something like that," Rick argued.

"Well, you guys are taking that whole thing way too seriously!" Roger dropped his cereal bowl in the sink with a clatter.

"Okaaay." George was looking for a more agreeable subject. "So what are you guys planning to do the rest of the day?"

"Well, I just need to get my camping stuff together sometime," Roger replied. "I'll probably head out right after lunch."

"I'm meeting up with a bunch of bikers." Rick glanced out the window. "We'll probably spend most of the day riding around the countryside."

"You want to go along canoeing?" Roger hoped George wouldn't accept the offer.

"Nah," George replied. "I wanna mow my mom's lawn before the sun gets too hot. And mine should be mowed sometime today too."

As George walked behind the mower, breathing the fresh morning air and feeling the warm sunshine on his shoulders, he thought about the information he had given Roger. He hoped it would be helpful. It seemed a little ironic that the two college graduates looked to him for this kind of research. *Why do I do it? It doesn't make any sense. Why should I be helping them? I had to bust my romp to earn a living while they were having a good time in college.* But he enjoyed doing it, and it felt good to know that they relied on him.

After lunch, he laid down on the couch to relax. He thought back to the struggles he and his mother had faced in his teen years. Now he owned a house with a woodworking shop out back. The income from his little woodworking business was more than enough to pay the mortgage and put food on the table. And it was growing. He wasn't rich, but as far as he was concerned, life was good.

Soon he drifted off to sleep, and in a dream he walked into an elaborate, sparkling-clean men's room. There was no one there except the janitor, who had just finished cleaning all the porcelain and polishing the chrome. "Everything's nice and clean for you, sir," the janitor said with a slight bow.

George nodded and smiled as he recognized the face of Dr. Martin Luther King. It seemed strange to see the civil rights leader serving as a janitor. Stranger still was the realization that there was no racial difference between himself and Dr. King. George looked at himself in the mirror. He had not been transformed into a person of a different race, and Dr. King still bore his dark skin and African-American features. Yet somehow, all racial differences were gone. They were simply two men acknowledging each other politely. It was a strange, but wonderful, feeling.

"I should be the one cleaning the restroom for you, Dr. King," George managed to say.

"We should all be serving each other," Dr. King spoke with gentle authority. "But we're not here to discuss who cleans the bathroom. We're here to talk about the past and the future."

"The past and the future?"

"You and I have both had a painful past," Dr. King continued. "We've both suffered from circumstances that were beyond our control. All my trials are over now, but you still have more to come. Don't let yourself become a prisoner to the past. Keep looking forward. Keep serving others, and you will be greatly rewarded."

"I will?"

"Yes. The good things that you are enjoying now are only the beginning of what's intended for you. But it's an elusive reward. The moment you start seeking the reward, you start losing it."

George opened his eyes and looked around. He was in his living room. He felt a bit disappointed to realize that it was only a dream. But he had a renewed feeling of anticipation for what the future might bring.

7

After a light lunch, Roger headed out to Thrush Creek. Because it was easier to pack camping gear into an open canoe, he decided to take his canoe rather than the kayak. He had his canoe equipped with a butt thwart, which positioned the paddler just aft of center, and made the canoe ideal for solo paddling. Since Rick was providing shuttle service after church the next day, there would be no need to paddle back upstream to his car. It would be an all down-river trip, and the canoe would work fine for that. He left his SUV at the iron bridge, and with the afternoon sun in his face and a slight tailwind, he headed down the creek. It was that lackadaisical time of day when most intelligent life seemed to be taking a siesta.

With lazy, uneven strokes, he slowly made his way downstream, occasionally drifting with the current and enjoying the calm of the afternoon. As he paddled quietly across the flat water just above the class two rapids, a pileated woodpecker flew across the creek and landed on the trunk of a large dead tree. The woodpecker quickly moved around to the opposite side of the tree and out of sight. On the side facing the creek, just above where the woodpecker landed, was a large, somewhat rectangular hole, typical of a pileated woodpecker's nest.

Roger put down his paddle and grabbed the binoculars he had hanging around his neck. Even before he got the binoculars to his eyes, he could see two small heads popping out of the hole, begging to be fed. Through the binoculars he could see that the babies already had red crests on their heads. They would probably soon be old enough to leave the nest. The crow-sized adult, still behind the tree, cocked her head to peer around the tree at the unfamiliar object in the water. Roger remained motionless. Although she regarded him as a danger, the instinct to care for her offspring eventually overpowered the fear for her own safety. She came around the tree, inserted her beak into the mouth of a baby and began giving it the food she had swallowed earlier. She spent a few seconds feeding one, then a few seconds feeding the other. Then it was over, and the adult flew away into the forest.

Suddenly Roger realized that the current and tailwind working together were driving him toward the rapids much more quickly than he had anticipated. In fact, he was only seconds away from crashing broadside into a rock protruding out of the water at the beginning of the rapids. He grabbed his paddle, planted the end of the blade against the rock, and gave a shove, pushing the canoe away from the rock. But just as his push reached maximum force, the blade slipped off the rock. Immediately his whole upper body was leaning far out over the gunnel, heading face first toward the water with no way to recover. The canoe was tilting almost to the point of capsizing, and water was pouring in over the edge. As Roger plunged into the water, the boat righted itself, but already it was completely swamped.

As Roger got his head up out of the water, he noticed the tee grip of his paddle had snagged the strap of his binoculars, which were still hanging around his neck. He immediately realized the danger. If the binoculars got snagged on a stationary object, he could be strangled or pulled underwater. First he freed the paddle and dropped it in the water. Then he quickly pulled the strap up over his head and tossed the binoculars into the canoe, hoping they would somehow stay there. But that was only one danger eliminated.

He was now floating through a class two rapids on the downstream side of a swamped canoe—a very dangerous place to be. If the current washed him against a rock, the canoe would come down right on top of him. The current pushing against a sixteen-foot canoe could exert tons of pressure, pinning him to the rock, holding him underwater, or even crushing him to death. He started to swim, trying to get clear of the canoe. Before he had time to get very far, he noticed that the current was taking him directly toward a large rock. He turned his legs toward the rock with knees partially bent. When his feet hit the rock, he pushed with his legs, shoving himself sideways and clearing the rock just as the canoe lodged firmly against it with a scraping thud. His paddle had floated out of reach, but he decided to let it go. He might be able to retrieve it later. He started swimming toward the left bank, but the current was pushing him to the right. So he turned and swam toward the right bank. Eventually he reached calmer water that was about knee deep. He got to his feet, staggered up to the right bank, climbed out, and flopped in the tall grass to catch his breath.

Roger lay there panting and visualizing a rescue team searching for his body. He thought about Michelle. *Did a similar sort of thing cause her accident? What were her last minutes like?* He promised himself that he would never go canoeing or kayaking alone again. Even though he was a skilled boater and this section of the creek had nothing more difficult than a class two rapids, the dangers were still very real. Accidents could happen anytime anywhere. And the dangers were increased dramatically by being alone.

After resting a few minutes, Roger made his way about two hundred feet up along the edge of the creek to where his canoe was stuck on a rock, close to the opposite shore. He continued on another hundred feet so he could swim across the calm water above rapids without danger of getting swept into the rapids again.

Finally he stood by his canoe, catching his breath from the swim and the hike back down the left shore. The canoe was lodged against a rock about fifteen feet off shore. The water between the shore and the rock was about shin-deep with a moderate current. The strongest current ran just beyond the canoe. The upstream face of the rock tapered gradually into the water. The canoe, which was still basically upright, had slid up on that tapered face so that the downstream gunnel was four to six inches above the waterline. The midsection of the upstream gunnel was three to four inches below the water and a considerable current was rushing in at the center, swirling around and exiting closer to the bow and stern. Since the water exiting the canoe had to overcome the force of the downstream current, the water level inside the boat was at least two inches higher than outside. Somehow his binoculars had found their way into the stern where they were somewhat protected from being washed overboard.

Roger retrieved his binoculars, untied his spare paddle, and headed for shore with those two items. Then he returned and retrieved his dry bag. His folding chair, which hadn't been tied in, was the only thing missing. Now he was ready for the hardest part, getting the canoe out of the water.

First he tried lifting on the downstream edge so the water could pour out on the low side as he rolled the canoe over. But the canoe wouldn't budge. Then he tried the upstream edge. But that too was firmly pinned to the rock. Then he got a firm grip on the bow and heaved with all his might in every direction. But it wouldn't move a bit. "God, help me," he muttered as he plopped his butt down on the bow and left his feet dangle in the water. He sat there, resting and trying to think of some clever way to extricate his boat by himself and feeling very lucky that he was not trapped between the canoe and the rock. *What would Max do?* he wondered. He finally concluded that he would have to leave his boat there and hike back to his car. Tomorrow he could return, bringing Rick and George along. Perhaps, with the strength of all three, they could roll the boat over and retrieve it from the creek.

As he stood up to leave, Roger noticed that the current running into the canoe had subsided significantly. He knew the creek had come up about six inches from rain two days ago and the water level was probably still receding a bit. But to see such a change in so little time was certainly unusual. Then he realized that at some time the wind had changed direction. Now there was a stiff breeze blowing upstream. If the wind was pushing back on the flat water above the rapids, that could affect the flow of water through the rapids, but only temporarily.

As he walked around to the downstream side of the canoe, he noticed that the water level inside the boat had dropped and was now even with the water outside. He got a firm grip on the gunnel and heaved with all his might. Water started pouring out of the opposite side as Roger slowly rolled his side upward. The farther he lifted it, the lighter it became till he rolled it completely upside down. Then he pulled the stern up onto the rock and waded out to the bow. He lifted the bow two feet above the water and flipped it right side up. Finally, his canoe was floating on top of the water again. If Max had seen this, he would have been proud. Of course, Max wouldn't have approved of him being out here alone in the first place.

He waded to shore, towing the boat behind him. As he pulled the boat up on shore, he realized how hungry and thirsty he was. The sun was quite warm, so there was no need to change into dry clothes. After a drink and a snack, he repacked his gear and headed downstream. About a half mile down the creek, Roger spied his paddle floating in slack water along the right bank. As he pulled alongside the paddle, he reached out and snagged it with the tee grip of the spare paddle and pulled it into the boat. He continued on his way feeling very lucky that things had not turned out worse. By the time he reached his campsite, his clothes were almost dry.

He set up his campsite under the pines on the knoll overlooking the area of the dam, just as he had done the week before. It was about seven o'clock when he was finished setting up camp. He lit his stove to heat a can of beef stew. Initially, he thought a whole can of beef stew would be more than enough. But for the rest of the evening, as he paced back and forth watching the river, he found himself munching on whatever he could find in his pack—a banana, a small box of raisins, a peppermint patty, a granola bar, a pack of butterscotch crumpets, a bag of pretzels, and a couple slices of beef jerky. He had not seen any activity anywhere along the creek or around the cottage. As darkness fell, he sat on a rock sipping a cup of hot chocolate. Then he crawled into his sleeping bag, thankful to be alive.

The next morning, Roger was up at daybreak. As he dressed himself inside the tent, he discovered he had quite a few sore muscles from the previous day's activity. He emerged from the tent, dressed in camouflage, and did a few stretching exercises. Then he fried up a pan full of bacon and eggs for breakfast. As soon as he finished eating, he began taking down his tent and packing up. By eight o'clock, he was heading down the creek to his next stakeout.

After passing through the remains of the old dam, Roger made the eddy turn, as always, and drifted up behind the dam. He paused a few moments looking for a new pyramid or any other sign of human activity. Seeing nothing, he peeled into the main current and rode the waves one more time as he headed downstream. By eight forty-five, he was pulling ashore under the concrete bridge.

He hiked up the road to the lane he had discovered the week before. His heart pounded as he walked slowly and quietly between the No Trespassing signs into the unpaved lane. About 150 feet in, just out of sight from the road, two large boulders blocked vehicles from going any farther. He could see where the lane had once been excavated, but now trees fifteen to twenty years old were growing in the old lane. He could easily see a warn footpath continuing up the lane. Roger looked around for a safe place to hide and watch the area. About fifty feet off the lane, on the uphill side, was a patch of laurel. He crawled into the laurel and found a comfortable, well-shrouded place to sit. Here he would stay for the next couple hours and see what he could see. Maybe it would be only wildlife, maybe nothing at all.

A few minutes later, a yellow jacket buzzed by his head and landed on the ground three feet to his left. It quickly disappeared into a small hole. A few seconds later two yellow jackets emerged from the hole and flew away, paying no attention to Roger. *I guess if I don't bother them, they won't bother me*, Roger thought to himself. It seemed to be a very busy nest. The arrivals and departures every five to ten seconds were a bit unnerving. He considered moving to another location but reasoned that if they hadn't attacked him while he was crawling in, they wouldn't attack while he's sitting still.

After almost an hour, Roger heard footsteps. A man was coming down the foot path. He looked like a star of an old western movie, with a cowboy hat, denim shirt, blue jeans, and cowboy boots. He had a gun belt, with a full row of bullets, slung low around his hips. The man stopped by the boulders in the lane and leaned against a tree. Facing out the lane with his left shoulder to the tree, he stood with his legs crossed so that his weight was on his right foot and the toe of his left boot was resting on the ground. He appeared to be waiting for somebody.

Roger slowly brought the binoculars to his eyes and studied the man's face. Was this the disappearing fisherman? This man's beard seemed to be trimmed more neatly than the fisherman's, but other than that, Roger didn't know what the fisherman's face looked like. This man's gun was a western-type revolver made of blue steel with a carved walnut handle. The fisherman had worn a modern-looking semiautomatic pistol. This man appeared to be the same height and build as the fisherman, and Roger assumed it could possibly be the same person.

Roger had to remain as still and quiet as possible. His heart thumped even harder as he thought about the bees. This would be a terrible time for them to attack. A crazy thought went through his head. *What if the pounding of my heartbeat vibrates through the ground and agitates the hundreds yellow jackets in the nest?*

Eventually Roger heard a car on the road. It slowed down and stopped. He heard it coming in the lane, and momentarily the township police cruiser came, backing into view. It stopped in front of the boulders, and Chief Theodore Miller stepped out. The cowboy walked out from behind the boulders, and the two chatted briefly. Then the chief opened the trunk of the cruiser, and the cowboy handed him what appeared to be a large wad of cash. Chief Miller folded it over and stuck it in his pocket without looking at it. Then the two lifted four grocery bags and a six-pack of beer out of the trunk and set them on the ground. The chief closed the trunk, got in the cruiser, and left. The cowboy picked up two bags and headed back up the foot path.

When the cowboy was safely out of sight, Roger quietly crawled out of the laurel, trying not to disturb the yellow jackets. He came down to the lane and took a quick look in the two remaining grocery bags. There was bread, milk, various canned foods, and a few fresh vegetables. Seeing nothing really unusual, Roger hurried out the lane, then jogged down the road to his canoe hidden under the bridge.

8

Rick and George were waiting by the creek, enjoying the warm noonday sunshine when Roger arrived at the churchyard. As the bow of the canoe plowed into the bank, Rick grabbed it by the deck plate and pulled it up onto the grass. He turned and looked inquisitively at Roger. "Well, now I know where Chief Theodore gets his cash," Roger blurted out, still resting against the butt thwart.

"Okay, let's hear it," George turned his full attention to Roger.

Roger stood up and stepped out of the canoe as he began telling how he hid in the laurel and watched the chief deliver groceries to a man dressed like a cowboy. He told about the wad of cash, at least an inch thick, that the cowboy handed to the chief.

"I guess you couldn't see what denomination the bills were?" Rick ran his fingers through his hair.

"No. I was a little too far away for that."

"If it was ones and fives," Rick observed, "it could have been just enough to cover the cost of the groceries. But if it was twenties and fifties, it could have been hundreds or even a thousand or more."

"So we don't know if that's where the chief gets all his cash." George turned toward Rick. "But we know that's where some of it comes from."

"And," Rick added, "we know his grocery purchases for the poor aren't charitable donations after all. He's getting paid to do that."

"What about this cowboy character?" George cocked his head toward Roger. "Is he just some poor old hermit living out here in the woods? Or is something else going on here?"

"I don't know," Roger paced with his chin in his hand. "I think it's probably the same guy I saw fishing. But I can't be sure. They're the same height and build. They both wear a gun, but it's not the same gun."

"How old?" George glanced at Roger.

"Forties or fifties, I'd say."

"If he had permission from Mrs. Stoner to live on her property," Rick speculated, "he would probably put her name on the No Trespassing signs, rather than her deceased husband's name."

"He probably bought new signs and just copied the name from the old ones." Roger rolled his canoe over on the grass.

"And if he's living out here in seclusion," George gazed absently at the canoe, "where does he get the cash to pay Chief Theodore?"

"I think it's pretty safe to assume that something illegal is going on here." Rick glanced over his shoulder to be sure that no one was eavesdropping. "But what it is or how serious it is, I haven't got a clue."

"And does it have anything to do with the items we found in the pyramids?" Roger added as the three started walking toward the parking lot.

"We won't know that until we figure out what's going on," Rick replied.

"Right," Roger snapped his fingers. "We've got to somehow find out what's happening in there."

"How are we going to do that?" George questioned.

Roger sensed a change in George. He seemed more eager to help. "I'm thinking about just walking up that lane and see what we can see," Roger eyed the other two. "We can take a bag of groceries along. And if we see the guy, we say, 'Hey, we brought you some groceries.'"

The other two stared back at Roger without comment.

"What do you think?" Roger continued. "Anybody willing to go along?"

"You're crazy!" Rick put his hand on Roger's shoulder and gave a shove. "If you keep snooping around there, you're going to get shot."

"What do you suggest we do?" Roger stopped and faced Rick.

"Well, I haven't figured that out yet." Rick shrugged his shoulders.

"Give it some time, Roger," George advised. "Don't go doing something stupid. We'll figure this all out sooner or later."

"I've got to find out what's going on in there! This is killing me!" It wasn't just simple curiosity Roger was dealing with. He felt that the cottage, the place, and that man was somehow connected to the girlfriend he had lost seven years ago.

"I really think you should get a summer job." Rick's tone was serious. "You need something else to occupy your mind."

"You're probably right. I could always go back to driving truck for my dad again. But driving truck gives you too much time to think and not enough time to do anything. I like having time for extra reading and studying over the summer."

"If you really want a job, you can find something else," George added. "I think it would do you some good."

"You guys want to go for cheesesteaks again?" Rick opened the car door.

"Sounds good to me," Roger nodded.

"Me too." George rubbed his stomach.

On Wednesday morning, as Roger scanned the Help Wanted section of the newspaper, his mind was on something else. He kept wondering what was going on at that little cottage in the woods above Thrush Creek. *Who put Michelle's personal items into the pyramid of stones? Who was this cowboy-fisherman? And what was he doing out there?* He just had to find some answers. He had to. It was either follow through with his plan or go out to a bar and get trashed.

A squirrel stood motionless on his hind legs, watching cautiously as Roger walked to his car and opened the door. It scurried halfway up a tree and chattered as the car door closed with a thud. *Even the squirrels think I'm crazy*, Roger thought as he started the engine. He drove to the grocery store and picked up a loaf of bread, four cans of soup, a few bananas, a box of oatmeal cookies, and a bag of potato chips. He set the bag of groceries on the passenger seat and headed out to Thrush Creek. He drove slowly down the road toward the concrete bridge looking for any sign of human activity. He stopped and backed cautiously into the lane, stopping in front of the big boulders, just as the chief had done. Then he opened the door and stepped out boldly and picked up his bag of groceries. Still seeing no one, he closed the car door, leaving it unlocked in case he had to make a quick getaway. With eyes and ears alert for anything, he started walking up the narrow trail shrouded by bushes and young trees.

He had only gone about thirty yards when he heard a dog start barking somewhere ahead. He stopped and listened. Half a minute later, a German shepherd came into view, trotting toward Roger with its head low and tail straight out the back. Roger turned and looked back at his car. The dog broke into a gallop, barking ferociously. Roger dropped the groceries and ran for the car. He zigzagged between the boulders and around the back corner of his car. As he grabbed the door handle, he saw the dog leaping directly over the large boulder. Roger jumped into his car and slammed the door, almost catching the dog's nose. The German shepherd planted his huge paws against the door, barking and snapping at the window. The dog scratched at the car door as Roger started the engine. Roger drove out the lane with the dog running alongside, jumping up at the window and barking at Roger through the glass. He pulled out on the road and tramped on the accelerator. As he sped away, he looked in the mirror and saw the dog standing at the end of the lane, still barking. "Hey, I brought you some groceries," Roger shouted with a laugh.

Roger decided to keep the adventure to himself since Rick and George had already advised him to stay away from the area. And he knew they were right. He knew he was becoming obsessed with this whole thing and needed to get involved with something else. But when Rick came home from work that afternoon, he walked into the house and immediately asked, "Where did you get all the scratches on your car door?" So reluctantly, Roger told Rick what he had done.

"Well, it was a good effort anyway," Rick grinned. "You didn't find any answers, but you left him a bag of groceries. I'm sure he'll appreciate that."

"Yeah," Roger chuckled, "he'll probably think Chief Theodore was there to deliver and the dog chased him away."

"I'm trying to imagine his next conversation with the chief." Rick mocked, "What groceries? What are you talking about? I wasn't here."

"Maybe we'll confuse them into revealing more clues," Roger speculated.

"But did you learn anything from this?" Rick sounded like his father. "Did you get it out of your system now, or am I going to have to keep telling you not to go there?"

"I think I learned my lesson." Roger stared at the floor.

"I hope so." Rick sank into his recliner. "However, if you'd like to go out and canoe the river again on Saturday, I'd be all for that."

"You mean you want to go along?" Roger's face brightened.

"Right. I've got the whole day free. We can go out early and spend half the day watching the river from your campsite. I'll take my scope along. Maybe we can see something you couldn't see with binoculars."

"Sounds like a plan. We'll pack lunch and eat at the campsite. We can stay there till two or three o'clock and still have plenty of time to be back before dark."

"I'm looking forward to it. I really need some R & R."

Kathy twisted the wet cloth in her hand, wringing the water out. She had no idea how long she had been scrubbing her bathtub. Her mind was on something else entirely. She was wondering how Roger really felt toward her. She had seduced him into a relationship, which seemed to be mostly physical. She knew Roger was enjoying their private time as much as she was. *But does he really care for me? Have I secured a spot in his heart?* She had to find a way to make him forget that high school girlfriend, that memory of the perfect female. *If she were alive today, she'd prove to be as imperfect as the rest of us. But how do I compete with a memory like that?* She walked out of the sparkling bathroom and into the bedroom where she flopped on the bed and stared at the ceiling.

That Friday was the twentieth of June. Seven years had passed since Michelle's accident on the river. Roger spent part of the morning reviewing his journals and looking at photos from the event and reading anything related to it. But he uncovered no new insights to the mystery. Then he decided to do something he had never done before. In midafternoon, he drove downtown to Elsie's Flower Shop.

Pearl Billmant, Bobby's wife, was finishing a flower arrangement as Roger entered the antiquated shop. "Good afternoon, Mr. Koralsen," Pearl greeted him with a friendly smile. "How may I help you?"

"Good afternoon. I'd like seven red roses, please."

"Okay. Seven red roses coming right up." Pearl opened the glass door to the refrigerated display case. "Is Ms. Keller having a birthday?"

"No, these aren't for Kathy."

"You are still going out with her, I hope."

"Yeah, she and I still see each other occasionally. But these roses are for…well, you see, today it's seven years since Michelle passed away. And I never did anything like this before."

"Well, I think that's a lovely thing to do. It's always good to remember our loved ones who have been taken from us. It doesn't mean that you're living in the past or that you're not coping with the loss. It's just a nice way to show respect for someone you loved. And I think it does some good for the person who gives the flowers as well."

"Have you lost someone close?" Roger asked intuitively.

"Yeah. Actually it was more of a loss for my husband. His twin brother, Richard, was killed in an accident on our wedding day. They were really close. I guess Rich had a little too much to drink at the reception and no one stopped him from driving home. It was a horrible accident. Bobby hasn't been the same since."

"That's too bad. Is he blaming himself for what happened?"

"I think he blames everybody, including himself. He won't talk about it. He just keeps building a shell around himself. He won't let himself develop a close relationship with anyone, not even me."

"That must be difficult. How long ago?"

"Fifteen years."

"Bobby was one of those who came out to help search for Michelle seven years ago. Did he ever talk about that?"

"Not that I recall."

"Does he have any memorabilia or pictures or anything from the search?"

"Not that I know of. Why?"

"Well," Roger didn't want to be too explicit, "he made some strange comments to me about Michelle. And some unusual things have happened. I just thought maybe he knows something."

"Don't pay any attention to the things he says. He makes strange comments to everyone. It's just part of building that shell around himself."

"Well, thanks for telling me about that." Roger pulled his wallet out of his pocket.

"If this was my business, I'd give you the roses free." Pearl punched the buttons of an old-fashioned cash register. "But I just work here."

Roger paid for the flowers, and as he was leaving, Pearl said, "Have a nice afternoon. I'm sure Michelle will appreciate the roses."

Roger thought about that statement as he drove toward the iron bridge. He didn't believe in life after death. So as far as he was concerned, Michelle couldn't possibly know or appreciate what he was doing. *So why am I doing it?* He wanted to honor Michelle. But she couldn't see what he was doing. Nobody else was going to be there to see it. He was the only one who would know. So the only logical explanation was that he was doing this for himself. Maybe Pearl was right; giving flowers does something good for the person who gives them. *It's kind of like feeding birds,* he thought. *We tell ourselves we want to help the birds. But the truth is they don't need our help. We just enjoy seeing them come to our feeders and we enjoy thinking that we're helping them. But we're really doing it for ourselves, not the birds.*

When Roger arrived at the bridge, he parked in the spot where Michelle had parked seven years before. A mourning dove cooed softly as he took the roses and walked out onto the bridge to the middle of the creek. *If God designed everything to be so wonderful, why would a bird have such a depressing song?* The dove continued cooing as Roger dropped the roses one by one into the water. He watched each one till it floated out of sight, then he dropped the next one, hoping that one of them would somehow find its way to Michelle, wherever she may be. With each rose, his vision became more blurred, and his memory clearer.

He remembered Michelle's hearty laughter. Not only had she been a happy, care-free person, but she had a genuine concern for those around her. She made everyone happy. She knew how to have a good time, but she also knew how to empathize with anyone who was going through tough times. He remembered the party she threw for George's sixteenth birthday.

Before that, George was very withdrawn and never attended social activities. George's father had skipped town several years before, and life had become a full time struggle for George and his mother. If George's mother would have planned a party, there probably would have been very few kids showing up. George was not a popular kid. But since Michelle planned the party and she was going to be there, all the boys wanted to be there. Since lots of boys would be there, all the girls wanted to be there too. Michelle tried hard not to take the spotlight away from George. She drew attention to some of his accomplishments and exposed his talents. Everyone had a good time, but for George, it was a turning point. He started getting a lot of requests to make things from wood. He was asked to help on projects requiring artistic ability. And he got involved socially.

When the last rose had drifted out of sight, Roger walked back to his car and headed home with a feeling that he was facing a new future. He was ready to start looking seriously for something to fill his time and his mind. Maybe it would be a summer job or maybe it would be some kind of volunteer work. He had the rest of his life ahead of him, and he was ready for anything, maybe even ready to fall in love again.

9

Rick shivered in the cool morning air as he and Roger got seated in the canoe and headed out from the iron bridge. Morning mist was rising from the river, but the rising red sun promised a hot, humid day. A woodpecker drummed in the distance as the canoe reached midstream. Rick looked back at Roger with a grin and said, "Now if you want to watch any woodpeckers, just let me know so I can watch out for rocks while you gawk at the birds."

"Okay," Roger chuckled. "It's good to know you're looking out for me."

A Canada goose swam along in front of them as they made their way down the mist-covered creek. They followed quietly along, steering around rocks and trying to take advantage of the best currents. Finally the goose took to the air, circled around, and headed back upstream. As they crossed the flat water above the rapids, Roger stopped paddling and pointed out the woodpecker hole in the dead tree. "It looks like the young have left the nest." Roger rested his paddle on the gunnels as they drifted slowly by.

"I was kind of hoping I'd get to see them," Rick gazed at the hole. "It seems I'm never at the right place at the right time."

"You see what you're missing when you're out there riding your cycle on the highway?" Roger resumed paddling.

"Yeah, but I still like my Harley. I like the sound of those pipes and the feel of acceleration when I twist the throttle."

"Your Harley sounds fine. But when it comes to the sound of pipes, I prefer a Caterpillar diesel."

"You never will get truck driving out of your blood, will you? Those two summers, working your way through college, scarred you for life."

"Every time I visit my dad and see his trucks, I get the urge to get behind the wheel again. But I know I've chosen a better vocation."

"Yeah." Rick studied the rapids ahead. "A schoolteacher can have a tremendous impact on a lot of young lives. But now come down off your pedestal and steer me through this rapids."

They both turned their attention to paddling as they navigated their way into the rapids. Using J-strokes and forward sweeps, Roger steered the boat around the rocks and into the swiftest current. The canoe accelerated with the current and sped them on their way, bobbing over the waves.

When they reached the bend above the dam, they beached the canoe and carried it up into the huckleberry bushes, out of sight from the creek. Roger hoisted the dry bag containing their lunch and gear onto his shoulders and headed up toward the pine trees. Rick picked up the two camping chairs and followed. As soon as they got to the campsite, they set their things down and gazed downriver.

In the morning sunlight, they could see someone fishing just above the dam. Roger quickly opened the dry bag and found his binoculars. Rick started setting up the telescope as Roger watched the man through the binoculars. "He's wearing a camouflage tee shirt and blue jeans…and he's got a gun on his belt. He has a beard, but I can't see his face well enough to say for sure that it's the same guy I saw giving cash to Chief Theodore."

"Give me a minute," Rick squinted into the scope. "I'll give you a close up look at his face." In no time, he had the scope focused on the fisherman. He stepped aside and nodded to Roger. "There you go. Take a look through this."

Peering through the scope, Roger said softly, "Okay, now turn your face this way, cowboy. Yeah, come on, just like that. That's him, all right! I'm sure of it now." They took turns watching through the scope, but before long, the man reeled in his line, pulled a stringer of fish out of the water and headed into the woods.

"So now we know that the fisherman and the cowboy are the same person," Rick unfolded his chair. "But what the heck does that mean?"

"Well, it means that we only know about one person out here. And he's probably living in that building." Roger pulled a small cooler out of the dry bag. "I've got some sodas in here. Just help yourself. We've got plenty of snacks. So don't go hungry."

"So what are the possibilities?" Rick slouched in his chair with his face to the sun and his arms dangling by his sides. "Is he some kind of hermit or a fugitive or what else might he be?"

"If he's a fugitive, why would our police chief be helping him?" Roger furrowed his eyebrows. "Could he be in the witness protection program?"

"Why would someone in the witness protection program be handing wads of cash to the police?" Rick looked at Roger, then gazed at the sky again. "Let's just suppose he's a hermit who doesn't want any involvement in society. He finds the remains of a human body. He doesn't want the attention that will come if he reports it. So he digs a hole and buries it. He takes the necklace and key ring. Sometime later he builds a pyramid as a memorial to the victim and puts the personal items inside it."

"So why does the maniac always carry a gun and shoot at intruders?" Roger kicked Rick's chair leg. "Why does he have a vicious dog? If he doesn't want to have anything to do with society, why does he have regular contacts with the police chief? I think he's some kind of outlaw. But you could still be right about him finding human remains and burying them to avoid attention. Although if he wanted to avoid attention, would he build a memorial to the deceased?"

"So what kind of criminal activity might he be involved in, way out here in the woods?"

"Marijuana," Roger replied without hesitation. "I bet if we could search that whole mountainside, we'd find a big healthy patch of pot somewhere in those woods."

"The police do aerial searches for that, don't they?" Rick sat up straight and scanned the landscape.

"But if the police are in on the deal, they could easily avoid finding it," Roger returned to the telescope and started scanning the hillside.

"It would probably be hard to see that from this angle," Rick put the binoculars up to his eyes. "But if he took out enough trees..."

"It would be great if we could come up with some hard evidence." Roger kept studying the landscape. "When we don't have enough facts, we can come up with all kinds of theories."

They spent the next half hour scanning the whole mountainside with binoculars and telescope but found nothing. "Maybe we should get someone to fly us over the area sometime," Rick suggested.

"Yeah, we should! See what we can see from up there. I'm not so much concerned about catching a criminal. But I sure would like to know what he knows about Michelle."

"Let's see if we can see any more of that building." Rick refocused the telescope. "Can't see much of it—just part of the roof and the gable with some kind of small window or louvered vent. Here, take a look."

"Yeah, I didn't see that before." Roger peered through the scope. "It looks like an attic vent."

"I guess you need vents if you want to dry marijuana in the attic," Rick quipped.

"I was thinking," Roger continued, "that he could look out through those louvers and see this whole section of the creek. He could see me come down through every Sunday morning and make the turn into the eddy. He would know right where to put that pyramid to attract my attention."

"If he's raising marijuana, why would he want to attract your attention?"

"We don't know if he's raising marijuana."

"Right. It's like you said, 'When we don't have enough facts, we can come up with all kinds of theories.'"

Roger finally got a can of soda from the cooler and sat down with a large bag of potato chips. They spent the rest of the morning snacking, watching the river, and speculating on all their theories. By noon, they had eaten their fill of chips, pretzels, apples, cheese and crackers, sardines, beef jerky, cookies, and candy.

Near the bushes at the edge of the campsite, Roger started a small pile of empty containers and other garbage. "You're not going to leave that stuff there, are you?" Rick nodded toward the pile.

"No way! When we're done, we'll put all that back into the empty potato chip bag and take it home. So we have to empty that bag."

"We're getting there." Rick took a handful of chips.

"There's two more sardines in here." Roger picked up the can.

"You can have 'em. I've had my fill."

"Yeah, there's a limit to how many of those you can eat at one time. If you don't want them, I'm throwing them out." With that, Roger tossed the can onto the garbage pile.

He returned and reached into his dry bag. "I brought some light reading along in case you get bored." He handed Rick a copy of *Playboy.*

"What! I thought you're an outdoors man." Rick held the magazine in both hands, gazing at the cover. "You mean you're so bored with the natural environment that you have to bring something like this along to entertain yourself?"

"Nah. I just picked that up a few days ago. I guess I kind of needed something to help get my mind off all this other..."

Rick was no longer listening. His mind had gone back to age seventeen, when his mother had discovered such a magazine hidden in his room. He remembered the man-to-man talk his father had with him after the incident. Afterward, he had promised himself that he would always keep away from this kind of thing. He remembered how upset his mother had become over the thought that her son would indulge himself in such filth. "A tool of the devil," she called it. *It is a tool of the devil*, he thought. *A very enjoyable one*. But he was determined that he would not let himself be drawn into it. It had been eight years since he had leafed through a magazine like this. And much as he wanted to, he was not about to give in now.

"Well, are you going to open it or not?" Roger eyed Rick with a grin. "Or are you just enjoying the cover so much that you can't turn the page?"

"Are there any good articles in here?" Rick grinned back at Roger.

"Heck, yeah!" Roger chuckled. "There's a real good article right in the center."

Rick's pulse accelerated as he turned directly to the centerfold. They lost track of time as they passed the magazine back and forth, commenting on the various pictures. Eventually they were interrupted by a rustling sound from the direction of their garbage pile.

They both looked up to see a possum sniffing at the sardine cans. The possum, with several babies clinging to her back, went right to feasting on the leftover sardines. "Apparently the smell of those sardines was enough to bring her out in broad daylight," Roger said softly. They watched as the possum devoured the sardines and then poked around in the garbage pile till she found an apple core.

"I've heard people refer to them as cute." Rick frowned. "I just don't see it. To me, she just looks like an extra ugly rodent."

"They're not rodents," Roger responded in a split second. "They're marsupials. They're more closely related to kangaroos than rodents."

"I know that. I was just referring to the shape of her body and general appearance. They're shaped similar to rodents, except rodents are cute."

"Marsupials come in all shapes and sizes from kangaroos to marsupial mice, from wombats to Tasmanian wolves." Roger had obviously flipped into teaching mode. "They resemble other species, but they're not related."

"So how do you think that happened?" Rick sensed the opportunity for another good debate. "How did such similar features evolve in different family lines? Did those wolflike traits evolve twice, once in the marsupial family line and once in the canine family line? Did the rodent-like body evolve twice?"

"Apparently, they did."

"But what are the odds that random mutations and natural selection would produce such similar results in two families that aren't related? What could cause the results to be so similar?"

"I don't know." Roger shook his head slowly. "Maybe some environmental factor influenced the outcome."

"To me, it suggests that the process may have been controlled by some form of intelligence." Rick was on the edge of his seat. "Just like a mechanical engineer can put a Caterpillar engine in a Peterbilt or a Kenworth or some other truck, a genetic engineer could put a marsupial reproductive system in an animal that looks like a mouse or one that looks like a wolf or kangaroo. He could mix and match things however he wants."

"Yeah, if you want to believe a fairy tale."

"Or to look at it another way, whatever process he used to develop a body type in one family line, he could repeat in another family line and get similar results."

"When you look at all the evidence," Roger sounded sure of himself, "there's a pretty good case for natural selection."

"I don't think you're looking at all the evidence." Rick rose to his feet. "Look how everything functions in the ecosystem. There seems to be a purpose for everything. Plants supply oxygen that we need. We supply carbon dioxide that they need. Flowers produce nectar for the bees. Bees pollinate the flowers in return. Things have a purpose other than their own survival. But if there is no intelligent planner, then nothing can have any purpose at all."

"Actually, nothing *has* any purpose at all!" Roger seemed to be enjoying this mental match as much as Rick was. "They function in the ecosystem as they do because, as they evolved, they adapted to the environment. So each species became dependent on other species in the ecosystem. That doesn't mean there was a master plan for all of this. This is just the way it evolved."

"And you really think that the rodent body style evolved twice?" Rick stopped pacing and faced Roger. "And the wolflike features, you think they evolved twice?"

"I suppose they did." Roger leaned back in his chair.

"Well," Rick resumed pacing, "I guess it's like you said earlier, 'When you don't have enough facts, you can come up with all kinds of theories.'"

"Scientists keep coming up with more evidence. Maybe someday we'll have enough to prove the theory."

"I just can't believe that all this came about by chance. I think that somehow God controlled it. He may have used the evolution process. He may have taken millions of years to do it. I don't know if he used genetic engineering or how he manipulated the process. Or maybe he just spoke the words and everything came into being instantly. But somehow, he planned it and he did it."

"Like you said," Roger grinned, "when you don't have enough facts, you can come up with all kinds of theories."

10

By three o'clock, Rick and Roger had cleaned up the campsite, packed the canoe, and were heading downstream. Rick was unusually quiet. It didn't matter whether he watched the ripples in the water or if his eye followed the curve of the landscape or if he focused on the rocks protruding from the water. Everywhere he looked, he saw some shape that reminded him of some part of one of the pictures he had viewed several hours earlier. He just couldn't get those pictures out of his mind. After eight years of keeping himself clean, he had given in to his weakness. *I'm such a failure.* He prayed silently for forgiveness. Still, everywhere he looked, the pictures kept appearing.

After riding the waves below the remains of the old dam, they made the eddy turn and came up behind the dam. There, floating in the quiet water by the shore was a red rose. "What the heck?" Rick pointed with his paddle. "Is that one of the roses you dropped yesterday?"

"It looks like it." Roger steered the canoe into the shore.

"Maybe this is where Michelle is," Rick half-whispered.

"I doubt it. The divers searched this area so thoroughly." Roger climbed out of the boat. "I don't see how she could have been here and they missed finding her. Her body must have been washed downstream somewhere."

"Maybe this is where the fisherman buried her."

"We don't even know that he found her and buried her." Roger picked up the rose and examined it.

"But you yourself said that whoever found her keys found her body."

"And we don't know who that was or what he did with the body." Roger rolled the stem between his thumb and finger, slowly turning the rose. The petals were still neatly curled and not fully open. One leaf had been torn off, leaving a crescent shaped fragment attached to the stem. But the flower was still in perfect condition.

The stones that had formed the pyramid lay strewn at Roger's feet. With the edge of his sneaker, he pushed three stones together in a triangular pattern. He laid the rose across the three stones. Then he put the top stone back in place, forming a pyramid with the rose protruding from one side and the stem sticking out the opposite side. "There, mister pyramid builder," he grinned mischievously. "Now it's your turn. Now you can try to figure out what this means."

"What does it mean?" Rick studied Roger's face.

"I have no idea." Roger chuckled as they both turned toward the canoe.

Rick squinted into the sun as they headed downstream again, allowing the swirling currents to lead them toward that unreachable spot where the afternoon sun glared off the water. Jet trails in the blue sky led his eye to the unknown beyond the horizon while the green mountainsides beckoned his heart to explore their vastness. And somewhere in this big picture there had to be a clue—a clue that would lead them to understand the things he and Roger had found in the small pyramid. As they slowly made their way downstream, Roger kept the boat close to the left bank, looking for any signs of human activity.

"Look at the soap suds." Rick pointed with his paddle. A small stream of water was trickling down the mountainside to the creek. Just before entering the creek, it dropped over a two-foot ledge, creating a small waterfall. The waterfall was only about four inches wide, but at its base was a heap of suds.

"That's interesting." Roger gave his paddle a powerful reverse sweep. He turned the boat one-hundred-eighty degrees and snuggled up to the bank. They climbed out and pulled the canoe up onto the bank. With paddles in hand, they slowly and quietly explored their way up the small stream into a ravine. Here and there they found tin cans and beer bottles partially submerged in the mud.

"Do you think we should go back?" Roger glanced over his shoulder after they had gone about a thousand feet.

"There doesn't seem to be anyone around." Rick scanned the area ahead. "What's that?" He pointed at a three-inch pipe protruding from the right bank of the stream just ahead. A small amount of water was flowing from the pipe into the stream.

"It's probably a drain pipe from that cottage," Roger said softly. "The cottage is probably just up over the edge of this ravine."

"We can't be *that* close to it. We haven't gone that far up the mountainside. Do you think he's running raw sewage right out into the stream?"

"A little cottage in the woods built in the early fifties? I guess anything's possible." Roger surveyed the area as they approached the pipe. "But it might not be sewage. He probably has an outhouse. This might be the drain from the kitchen sink or the overflow from a spring or something like that."

"The water looks clean."

"It looks like this is where he dumps his garbage," Roger continued in a low undertone as he pointed ahead. On the right side of the ravine was a pile of tin cans, jars, and bottles. "Let's see what we can learn from his garbage."

They quietly made their way to the garbage pile and started checking its contents. "He eats Campbell's vegetable soup and Bush's Baked Beans." Rick held up a can and then quietly put it down. "He drinks Budweiser."

"Budweiser. That matches the brand Chief Theodore delivered. But so what? It looks like he uses a lot of flashlight batteries."

"You never found any utility wires coming in here, did you? If he doesn't have electricity, I suppose he would use a lot of batteries."

"This seems to be all stuff that won't burn. He probably burns all his paper and stuff like that."

A blue jay started screaming, "*Jay-jay!*"

"Oh crap!" Roger said softly, "he's letting everyone know we're here." With his paddle, Roger quietly extricated a few small jars from the pile. His eyes narrowed as he read the labels. "Now there's something I certainly didn't expect to see."

"What's this?" Rick picked up a pressurized can and turned it to read the label. "Starting fluid?" He pressed the button, spraying out a mist.

"Starting fluid." Roger glanced at the can. "They use that to start diesel engines in cold weather."

"Maybe he has a diesel generator." Rick cocked his head.

"It's diethyl ether." Roger sounded like a teacher again. "Some people inhale it to get high."

"Ether? Didn't they use that as an anesthetic at one time?"

"Yeah. In its pure form, it was a pretty good anesthetic. Starting fluid, of course, isn't that pure. It often leaves them feeling pretty sick and hung over. But if you breathe enough of the stuff, it will incapacitate you."

They heard a dog bark, and both looked up to see the German shepherd trotting down the ravine toward them. "Maybe the blue jay was warning us that the dog is coming." Rick felt more scared than he sounded.

"We can't outrun him!" Roger gripped his paddle with both hands. "We'll have to fend him off with our paddles!"

With a paddle in his left hand and the can of starting fluid in his right, Rick started spraying a cloud of ether in the direction of the dog as they retreated slowly backward, down the ravine.

The dog, growling and barking as he came, trotted right through the ether without hesitating. Roger was swinging his paddle with both hands. Rick was jabbing at the dog as he continued spraying ether directly toward the dog's face. The dog darted from side to side, dodging the paddle blades and trying to avoid the strange odor of the starting fluid.

In little more than a minute, the can of ether was empty. Rick hurled the empty can at the dog and then gripped his paddle with both hands. Roger managed to land a blow to the side of the dog's head with the edge of his paddle. But the German shepherd seemed undaunted. They continued backing down the ravine, swinging and poking at the dog. Gradually the distance between them and the dog increased. It seemed the dog, being perhaps a little subdued by the ether, was no longer determined to attack them. He seemed to be content with driving them out of the area. As they neared the creek, the dog stopped advancing. He stood his ground, barking at them as they got their canoe into the water. They paddled as fast as they could toward the far side of the creek.

"If I never see that dog again, I'll be quite happy." Roger sighed he turned the boat downstream.

"I won't argue with you on that. I wonder why that guy threw out the can of starting fluid with that much left."

"He must not need it anymore."

"Maybe his generator broke down."

"Or," Roger added, "he used it to get high one time and didn't like the after affects. Now he just drinks Budweiser."

"Well, the next time you buy groceries for him," Rick grinned as he glanced at Roger's serious expression, "be sure to include a six-pack of Bud."

"Okay," Roger laughed as the tension drained from his face. "But you have to go along to protect me from that man-eating dog."

As they passed under the concrete bridge, Roger let out a sigh of relief. "I always feel safer after I pass this bridge. I'm finally out of his territory."

"You mean the dog or the man?"

"Both!"

"Well, at least we got a few more facts for you to put in your journal," Rick spoke without turning as he kept pulling forward with powerful strokes. "Tomorrow we can bring George up to speed on everything and see what he can get out of it. Sooner or later, we'll figure this thing out."

"Yeah," Roger agreed absently, "we'll figure it out if we don't get ourselves killed."

As they paddled along quietly, Roger's mind eventually went back to their discussion about the ecosystem. He pondered Rick's assertion that everything has a purpose beyond its own survival. He felt he had countered Rick's argument quite well. Evolution made perfect sense. But one thing still troubled him. The Venus flytrap.

He couldn't explain how natural selection could have simultaneously produced the ability to detect an insect, the ability to close the leaves, forming a trap, and the ability to produce enzymes to digest the insect. He knew Rick would claim that this was proof of a plan by an intelligent being. But was there any other explanation of how this plant came into existence? He had to find time to do some research. But right now, the mystery surrounding Michelle seemed more important.

11

Roger had a large pizza ready to come out of the oven by the time Rick and George returned from the Sunday morning church service. His journal was lying on the kitchen table next to a basket of warm bread sticks and a bag of potato chips. He'd missed his Sunday morning trip down Thrush Creek, but hopefully this change in routine would yield some new insight to the mystery.

"It smells good," George said after he took a deep breath. He got seated at the table, grabbed a bread stick, and then opened the journal.

"I hope you can find something in there that Rick and I might have overlooked." Roger glanced at George as he set the pizza on the table.

They reviewed all the events since May 25, when Roger had found Michelle's necklace hidden in the pyramid. As the pizza gradually disappeared, they discussed everything they had learned, from the history of the property to Chief Miller's finances to Bobby Billmant's strange behavior. They rehashed all their theories and speculations.

"Did you ever feel like someone was watching you, then you look around, and there is somebody just staring at you?" Rick's eyes narrowed as he glanced from George the Roger.

"Yeah, I know what you mean." Roger studied Rick's face.

"I'll never forget," George gazed into space, "when I was in shop class in high school. I was sanding a cabinet with a portable belt sander. My eyes were focused on my work. I didn't see anyone around me. But I could just feel someone watching me. The feeling was so strong that I became self-conscious. I started trying to be smooth and professional-looking in the way I handled the sander. Finally I looked up. As soon as I raised my head, there was a bright flash, and there was Michelle, watching me through her camera. She was taking pictures for the year book."

"I remember that picture." Roger closed his eyes as he visualized the page in the year book.

"How is that possible?" Rick was looking directly at Roger. "How can we feel someone watching us? We can't possibly feel the light rays going from our body to their eyes."

"It can't be anything physical," George replied before Roger had a chance. "Our spirits must somehow connect with the other person's spirit and give us a sense of what's going on."

"I think it's mental telepathy," Roger countered as his mind assembled his argument. "As our brains function, they produce fluctuating electrical currents known as brain waves. This results in an electromagnetic field around us. I believe this enables one brain to communicate directly with another, without the use of the five physical senses."

Now George was studying Rick's face. "Why are you asking about that, Rick?"

"When we came down the river yesterday," Rick hesitated, "I just felt like Michelle was watching us."

"I feel that way almost every time I come down through there," Roger added flatly.

"I could just feel her looking down from above," Rick turned toward Roger. "But that would mean that George's explanation must be the correct one because her brain is no longer producing brain waves. Even though her body is dead, her spirit lives on. So there must be some sort of spiritual connection."

"Well, I'm sure George knows more than I about spiritual connections, if there is such a thing. But I wasn't sensing that she was necessarily looking down from above."

"What's your explanation?" George nodded toward Roger.

"I keep coming back to one thing." Roger paused, glancing at the other two. "Her body was never found. Maybe she's still—"

"Don't go there, Roger!" Rick was right in his face. "You know she can't possibly be alive. Remember how long it took you to get closure on that issue the first time. You don't want to go through that all again, do you?"

"If you start thinking those kinds of things again," George's voice was sincere, "it'll only lead to a lot of pain and misery. You've been doing so well, starting to date again and everything. Don't go back there."

"He's right." Rick leaned back. "You've made a lot of progress over the last couple of years. Don't go back."

"There is no reasonable explanation of how she could have survived and still be out there somewhere," George went on. "Just don't let that idea into your head."

"I'm sorry I brought up the subject." Rick punched Roger on the shoulder.

"Well then," Roger concluded, "our feeling that Michelle is watching must be just our imagination. When we came down the creek yesterday, we both imagined the same thing. Imagine that!"

"Mental telepathy." Rick smirked. "Our brains are both functioning and producing brain waves. So I thought what you thought. Imagine that!"

"At least my brain is functioning," Roger quipped. "Sometimes I wonder about yours."

George strolled into the next room and picked up the TV remote control, which was lying on top of the *Playboy* magazine. "What's this?" he asked holding the magazine up to Rick.

"Oh, that's Roger's." Rick grinned sheepishly.

"Enjoy!" Roger smiled broadly.

"I don't want to look at that!" George declared, flinging the magazine at Roger. "All that would do is make me dissatisfied with my nonexistent sex life."

Roger caught the magazine in a defensive reflex. "There are plenty of young ladies who would love to go out with you, George."

"And if I ever find the kind of lady I want to marry, she probably won't look like any of the girls in that magazine. So why would I want to make myself dissatisfied?"

"You're right." Roger agreed as he dropped the magazine into the waste can. Sometimes it was just impossible to argue with George's practical wisdom.

George flopped into an easy chair and started surfing channels. Soon they were all snoring while the Minnesota Twins played the New York Yankees.

The next morning, Roger awoke to a very vivid dream. He heard Rick's alarm clock buzzing in the next room. As Rick got up and got ready for work, Roger lay in bed reviewing the dream in his mind. He had seen Michelle and the disappearing fisherman fishing together at the old dam on Thrush Creek. The man, wearing his gun, was fishing from his normal spot above the dam. Michelle was fishing in the eddy below the dam, from the very spot where Roger had found the pyramid. As he fished, the man kept an eye on Michelle. As Michelle fished, or pretended to, she was rolling some stones around with her feet. She arranged three stones into a triangle then, pretending to be working on her fishing line. She squatted down, slipped off her necklace, and dropped it between the stones. She placed the fourth stone on top, then stood up with her fishing rod in hand and walked back to the man. Soon they both walked into the woods and disappeared.

Roger couldn't get the dream out of his mind. What if it was true? What if the fisherman had abducted Michelle and was holding her hostage in the little cottage for the last seven years? What if Michelle was the one who built the pyramids? The triangles were a distress signal after all, placed where the fisherman would not notice, but where Roger couldn't miss them. Maybe it was Michelle who was watching him from behind the louvered vent and knew his routine. No wonder he always felt like Michelle was watching him on the river.

Everything seemed to make sense. It was Chief Theodore who determined that there was no sign of foul play. But now it seemed that he was somehow in on the crime. In the months following Michelle's disappearance, Roger had often felt that the chief knew more than he was telling, but he assumed that was just normal for police work.

If the dream was true, Roger had to do something. But what? His friends had warned him not to think that Michelle was still alive. He couldn't talk to them; they wouldn't listen. They wouldn't even let him explain. He couldn't go to the local police. How would the state police respond if he came in and told them he dreamed about a crime and he wanted them to check it out? *They'd probably think I'm crazy. Maybe I am crazy. I shouldn't be letting these thoughts into my head.*

His mind kept going over the scenario again and again as he got dressed and ate breakfast. He couldn't come up with one logical reason why this couldn't be true. It seemed it was up to him, and only him, to do something. But what? He had to either rescue Michelle or prove that she wasn't there. He had to march right into that little cottage and check it out. "This is crazy!" he said out loud. For the first time in his life he wished he had a gun. But if he went in carrying a gun, the man would probably shoot to kill. There would be no warning shot like the last time. *Going in with a gun may be more dangerous than going unarmed. And what about the dog?*

Roger went up to his room and picked up a four-and-a-half-foot-long walking stick he had made years before. The top end was heavy and gnarled. *This would make a pretty good club.* He gripped it by the narrow end and took several swings at an imaginary dog. He took the walking stick along down to the kitchen.

He got a tablet and started writing a note. "Rick, if I'm not here when you get home, call the state police." He ripped the sheet off, crumpled it into a ball, and threw it in the waste can. *This is insane. I'm losing my mind.* He paced the floor, thinking about Michelle. What if she was waiting in that cottage and hoping to be rescued? *I have to do it! If it turns out not to be true, and I get home before Rick, I'll destroy the note and nobody will know.*

He started writing again.

> Rick,
>
> If I'm not here when you get home, call the state police. I'm going in to the cottage. I have reason to believe that Michelle never drowned but was abducted and is being held there as a hostage.
>
> Roger

He picked up his walking stick and paced back and forth. He reread the note he left on the table. He thought about how the German shepherd had attacked them at the dump and how they had fought him off with canoe paddles. His fists tightened around the stick as he recalled one of the items he had seen in the dump—baby food jars. "I'll kill that freakin' rapist!" With no more hesitation, he got in his car and headed out.

When he arrived, Roger backed quietly in the lane between the No Trespassing signs and stopped in front of the barricade of boulders. He got out, picked up his walking stick, and closed the door as quietly as he could. He leaned against the side of his car, peering into the forest. Tall oaks and wild cherry trees formed a tight canopy that completely blocked out the sky. Most of the tree trunks were wide enough to easily hide a man or two. He could visualize the German shepherd charging toward him. A breeze was coming toward him from the direction of the cottage, so he felt there may be a chance of approaching the cottage without being detected by the dog. He remembered the warning shot he had received down by the dam. Looking up the trail to where it disappeared into the confusion of the forest, he let out a sigh. "God, help me," he said softly as he started walking.

He walked slowly, carefully placing each step, trying not to rustle any leaves or snap a twig. The trail ran laterally along the mountain then curved right and headed up the slope. It was a long, slow walk. Roger stopped frequently to peer into the army of trees and listen to the eerie silence. He was thinking he must be getting close to the cottage when suddenly he heard a rustling about ten feet in front of him. He stopped and gripped his stick with both hands. His heart was pounding. A skunk emerged casually from the bushes and headed up the trail ahead of Roger. Roger followed at a distance. The skunk waddled along slowly, seeming quite unconcerned about Roger's presence.

Before long, the cottage came into view. It was a plain rectangular building made of concrete block and was badly in need of a fresh coat of whitewash. The lower half of the wall was heavily covered with moss. The windows appeared to have curtains inside. There was a front porch with a rocking chair and a swing. The front door was closed and had no window in it. The skunk meandered out onto unmown lawn and started foraging for grub worms. After a long pause, Roger stepped carefully into the open.

Then the German shepherd came around the far corner of the cottage. He barked twice and headed straight toward Roger with his head down and tail straight out behind him. The dog seemed unconcerned about the skunk, which was almost directly between him and Roger. The skunk raised his head and watched the dog approaching. His tail went up, and at a distance of about five feet, he shifted his rear end and planted his hind feet. The dog recoiled, coughing and gagging. He retreated a few paces, wiped his face on the grass, then shook himself violently. The skunk continued hunting for food as he meandered toward the dog. The dog retreated blindly to the corner of the building, wiped his face again and rolled in the grass. He sneezed and shook himself again. As the skunk grew closer, the dog turned and found his way under the woodshed, which was to the left of the cottage. The skunk continued feeding between the porch and the woodshed.

Roger could hardly breathe the pungent air as he started across the lawn. There was a good breeze coming from the left, so as he approached the cottage, the air became much more breathable. As he stepped up onto the porch, he shifted his stick to one hand and held it like a walking stick. He stepped up to the steel door and knocked loudly. "Hello. Is anybody home?"

12

From inside the cottage, an excited female voice answered, "Roger, is that you?"

He recognized the voice instantly. His heart raced even faster. "Yes, Michelle. It's me!" His voice came out louder than he expected.

"Just a minute." The reply sounded sweet and calm.

He could hear her talking to someone inside. "Put that down, Jasper. He's a friend! He can help us. Put it down! You need his help." Seconds passed like the end of winter. Finally he heard footsteps coming to the door. As the door knob turned, visions of Michelle flooded his mind. He remembered her friendly blue eyes, golden curls, and athletic figure. He propped his walking stick against the wall and prepared to give his high school sweetheart a big hug.

But when the door swung open, the woman standing there was considerably older and a bit heavier. Dull blond hair hung loosely down past the middle of her back. She had a little girl in her arms and a young boy clung to his mother's leg, pressing his head against her thigh. But her blue eyes radiated with a familiar friendliness.

Roger extended his arms as they stepped toward each other. But the little girl turned away and threw her arms around her mother's neck. The boy ducked behind his mother. This was obviously not the right time for a hug. Michelle stepped back and smiled. "Roger, come in!"

"Michelle! I can't believe it." Roger stepped cautiously inside.

"These are my children." Michelle pushed the boy out from behind her. "This is Earl. He's five. And this is Abigail. She's almost three."

"Wow." Roger took only a brief glance at the boy. "He's big." Turning to the girl, he added, "And you're as cute as your mother." He glanced about the room as his eyes adjusted to the dim light.

Straight ahead, along the back wall was an old-fashioned, wood-burning kitchen stove. The smell of stale wood smoke lingered in the room. There was a sink and a few cabinets against the left wall. In the middle of the left half of the room was a small rectangular table with rounded corners. *Right from the fifties*, he observed. It had a green Formica top with a chrome apron around the edges and chrome legs. In the middle of the table, there stood a beer bottle serving as a vase. And in it, he couldn't help but notice a single red rose with one leaf torn in the shape of a crescent.

Reclining on a couch, along the right wall, was the fisherman-cowboy. He had pillows tucked behind him, supporting his left arm, which was badly swollen. His right hand lay across his stomach, clutching a semiautomatic pistol.

"This is Jasper." Michelle flashed her eyes to the side. "He was bitten by a snake this morning. He needs help. I just don't know what to do."

Roger gazed at the man on the couch. A kitchen chair was placed in front of the couch to serve as a nightstand. On it was a glass of water, a blue handkerchief, and a portable CD player. The rugged voice of Johnny Cash was singing, "The old account was settled long ago. And the record's clear today 'cause he washed my sins away." Roger's desire to kill the man seemed to dissipate a bit as he observed his helpless condition and Michelle's concern for him. "I have my car down in the lane," Roger offered halfheartedly. "If you can make it that far, I can drive you to the hospital."

"I can't go there." The reply was quite slurred. "Somebody would figure out who I am. They'd save my life just to send me back to prison. I ain't goin' back. I'm gonna die a free man."

The sooner, the better, Roger thought to himself.

"But, honey, you need help," Michelle pleaded as she sat down on the edge of the couch. "Let him take you."

"No way," Jasper said firmly. "I'd rather die out here in God's country than spend one more day in prison."

"You probably won't die." Roger tried to sound sincere. "Copperhead bites are seldom fatal to a healthy adult."

"This wasn't no copperhead." Jasper's eyes glared. "This was a rattler!"

Roger hesitated and then replied calmly, "It couldn't have been. There are no rattlesnakes in this area. You'd have to go at least fifty miles north before you get into rattlesnake country."

"That's what I always thought. But this was a rattler! I heard him buzzin' before I reached down. But I just thought it was some kind of insect. I never thought about a rattlesnake till he bit me. I got a good look at him, though. I saw his rattles! This was a rattler!"

"Don't get yourself all worked up," Michelle urged as she picked up the handkerchief and wiped the saliva from the corners of his mouth. "Just stay calm."

"Look, Princess," Jasper said softly. "You're the one who needs to get out of here—you and the kids."

"No. We're staying with you." Michelle's voice was gentle but firm.

"Listen to me." Jasper put his hand on her waist. "You know the police chief has been helping us. He ain't doin' that because he wants to. He ain't doin' it for the money. He's doing it because me and Bobby know a lot of stuff about him that he don't want anybody to know. Now with this yet...If people find out what's going on here, his whole life falls apart—his job, his family, his reputation. It all comes to an end, and he goes to prison."

"I don't care about all that." She leaned over and put her head on his shoulder.

"He'll do anything to keep this quiet. Anything!" Jasper continued softly, obviously trying not to alarm the children. "But when it comes to you, he only has one choice. He has to get rid of you. Princess, you gotta take the kids and run for your life!"

"But I can't just leave you here to die," Michelle protested, sitting up and looking into his face.

"Don't worry about me. Think about what's best for the kids."

Michelle sobbed, leaning over him and hugging him with both arms. She buried her face against his neck so the children wouldn't see her tears.

"You've been too good to me." Jasper hugged her with his one good arm. "You've given me much more than I deserve. You've given me the best seven years of my life. And all I give you is trouble, big trouble."

"Don't say that," Michelle spoke softly. From where Roger stood, he could barely hear her. "We had a lot of good times together. You were good to me. You just needed the chance to show all the good that was inside you."

"I know you've been wanting to escape ever since I brought you here." Jasper brushed her hair out of her face. "Now don't waste any more time. Take the children and go into hiding. Bobby is coming tomorrow afternoon. He'll find me lying here and see that you're gone. He'll inform the chief. Then all hell's gonna break loose. You have one day to get ahead of them."

"There's got to be some other way." Michelle wiped her eyes.

"Bobby will do whatever it takes to protect the chief. But when the chief is out of the picture, he'll run. He won't hang around here, and he won't be concerned about you. You're no threat to him. He doesn't need to defend his reputation. So as soon as the chief is locked up or dead, you can go back to your friends and family. But you've got to go into hiding now!"

Michelle stood up, with tears running down her cheeks. She picked up Abigail, who had been standing by the couch. She hugged her, then laid her on Jasper's chest and said, "Take care of her while I pack our things." Then she walked into the kitchen area and disappeared around the corner. Jasper put his right arm around the child as she laid her head on his left shoulder and began sucking her thumb.

Earl had pulled a chair out from the kitchen table and was sitting there, quietly watching everything. Roger stood in the middle of the room with his mouth open. "Young man," Jasper looked at Roger, "I tried to keep you out of here. But you're involved in this now too. You gotta take my family and go someplace where no one will ever find you."

"I'll do everything I can for them."

"You know a good place to go?" Jasper eyed Roger.

"Well," Roger paused and thought about his options, "I've been wanting to go to the Allagash Wilderness, in Maine. That would be a good place to get away from everybody."

"Have you been there before?"

"No."

"Have you talked to anyone about going there?"

"Yes, lots of people."

"Don't go there," Jasper advised. "Go someplace where you know your way around, where you won't see people you know, and there won't be forest rangers tracking your movements."

"West Branch of the Susquehanna," Roger responded decisively. "Clearfield, Karthaus, Keating—I've canoed it numerous times. Canoe campers come and go. No one keeps track of them."

"That sounds like a better choice, closer to home too. You can be there in a couple hours."

"Is Chief Theodore operating alone?" Roger peered down at the man on the couch. "Or is the rest of his police force in on this too?"

"He has a lot of connections in high places," Jasper sounded sincere. "But I don't think anybody else knows about this. I know he has ways to make things happen. He's dangerous. If I were you, I wouldn't trust anybody."

Roger could hear Michelle moving about in the next room, opening and closing drawers. Soon she came out, with three plastic shopping bags stuffed with clothes. Her eyes were swollen and red, and her lips were pressed tightly together. "We don't even have a suitcase," she said as she set the bags next to the door.

"You got a gun, young man?" Jasper's eyes were piercing.

"No. I never needed one."

"You should have a gun. I'll let you take one of mine."

"I don't need it." Roger paused a second. "I walked in here without a gun, didn't I?"

"That's right." Michelle turned from her conversation with Earl. "How did you get past the dog? I was praying for God to send an angel to protect you from that ugly beast."

"You were expecting him?" Jasper mumbled.

"I didn't need an angel," Roger chuckled. "A skunk took care of that detail."

"A skunk!" Michelle smiled as she turned and handed Earl two empty bags. "Go upstairs and put all your clothes in these bags and bring them down here."

As the boy started up the stairs, Jasper nodded to Roger, "Get me that gun down off the shelf." He pointed to a shelf about a foot from the ceiling to the right of the stove. On the shelf was a leather holster with a bullet belt wrapped around it. In the holster was the blue steel, .38-caliber revolver with a walnut handle.

As Roger reached for the gun, Michelle took the little girl by the hand. "Come, Abby, let's get your clothes packed." Roger handed the gun, holster and all, to Jasper.

Jasper just pulled the revolver out of the holster, leaving the rest in Roger's hand and said, "Try that on." Roger wrapped the belt around his waist, buckled it and slid it down to his hips. "Here, I'll show you how this works." Jasper flipped the cylinder out to the side and ejected six live rounds.

"I know how it works." Roger ran his fingers over the row of bullets around his waist. "I just never used one."

Jasper reloaded the gun and shoved it into the holster. "There, how does that feel?"

Roger's eyes narrowed. "It fits okay, I guess."

Jasper eyed Roger, noticing the confusion on his face. "No, I mean how does it make *you* feel?"

Roger reconsidered the question. He had never thought about how attaching a deadly weapon to his body might affect the way he felt about himself. "Oh. I feel kind of like king of the mountain."

Jasper grinned knowingly as Roger paced about the room as if he were trying out a new pair of shoes. His hand swung gently by his side, feeling the location on the gun handle. "But I don't have a permit to carry a hand gun," he said as he unbuckled the belt.

Jasper chuckled weakly. "Do you think I do?"

Roger wrapped the belt around the holster and stuffed it into one of Michelle's bags of clothing. "I saw that," Michelle said as she entered the room with Abigail trailing behind. She put the little girl's bag of clothes by the door with her own and went over to Jasper. "How are you feeling, hon?" She sat down on the edge of the couch, took the handkerchief, and wiped his beard, which was drenched with saliva.

"My lips are really tingling. And I feel like I can't catch my breath. I don't know how much longer I have. I know God is punishing me for all the evil I've done."

"*You* believe in God?" Roger couldn't hide the amusement and doubt in his voice.

"Of course! Don't you?"

"I used to," Roger hesitated. "But I see things a bit differently now."

Michelle glanced at Roger with a look of shock and disbelief. Roger opened his mouth, but no words came out. Earl came down the steps with two bags of clothes and entered the room. "Put those by the door, son." Michelle gestured toward the collection of bags.

"When God punishes you," Jasper stared at Roger, "you'll know that he's real." Roger noticed the sound of a clock ticking somewhere. Jasper put his hand on Michelle's knee. "That duffel bag under the bed, there's about twenty grand in there. Take that with you. I won't need that anymore. I'll just lay here and listen to Johnny Cash till I fall asleep."

Michelle patted his cheek gently. "The duffle bag," she said as she got up and went back to the bed room.

"Come here, son." Jasper beckoned toward Earl with his finger. Earl walked over to his father. Jasper reached out with his right hand and hugged the boy. "You and Mommy and Abby are going to go with this man." His voice broke slightly. "I'm going to stay here. I want you to be a good boy and help Mommy take care of Abby. Okay?"

"Okay." Earl seemed unaware of the seriousness of the situation. His dad patted him on the head as he walked away.

Michelle returned with the duffel bag. She zipped it open, pulled the gun and holster out of her clothes bag and put it in with the money. She zipped it shut again and pushed it toward Roger. "There! You're in charge of that," she said in a disgusted tone.

Jasper reached over and turned up the volume on the CD player. He glanced at Roger as Johnny Cash's voice boomed out, "My God is real, for I can feel Him in my soul."

"Okay, children," Michelle glanced around the room, "I guess we're ready to go." She went over to Jasper and hugged him passionately. Roger turned his back and started counting clothing bags as Michelle pressed her lips into Jasper's wet beard.

"I'm sorry I brought you so much trouble," he said softly and kissed her again. "You deserve much better."

"I'm going to miss you," she replied trying to control her sobs. She stood up, bent over, and kissed him one last time, then turned her back and wiped her tears with the back of her hand.

Roger picked up the duffel bag and a bag of clothes with one hand and two bags of clothes with the other. "Earl, can you carry a bag?" He nudged the boy on the behind with one of his bags.

Earl picked up a bag of clothes and headed out the door. Michelle picked up the two remaining bags and said, "Come on, Abby. You're a big girl. You can walk."

Abigail grabbed her mother's pinky and followed her out the door. Roger pulled the door shut with his elbow as Jasper reached over to the CD player and cranked it up a few more decibels.

13

As Michelle stepped off the porch, Roger noticed the German shepherd coming out from under the woodshed and starting toward the group. “Ruger, stay!” Michelle commanded sharply. The dog immediately sat down and watched as the group headed across the lawn.

“He stinks like a skunk.” Abby held her nose.

“Is Ruger gonna stay with Daddy?” Earl glanced up at his mother.

“I suppose so,” Michelle didn’t seem at all concerned about the dog.

“Ruger. So that’s his name?” Roger looked back at the dog.

“That’s right,” Michelle answered without turning. “If you use his name, he listens pretty well most of the time.”

“How long will he stay there?”

“I don’t know.” Michelle shrugged. “When we’re out of sight, he’ll probably forget the command and go about his business. If he comes after us, I’ll simply give him the command again. No need to worry.”

“I hate that dog!” Roger took another glance over his shoulder.

“I don’t really like him either.” Michelle showed no sign of fear.

Roger noticed the boy glancing at his mother several times. *He has something on his mind.* As they started down the shadowy path through the woods, he finally spoke. “Mommy, is Daddy a bad man?”

“No!” Michelle seemed surprised. “Your daddy is not a bad person. But a long time ago, he did some really bad things.”

“Is that why God is mad at him?” the boy sounded concerned.

“God isn’t mad at him.” Michelle’s voice was firm but tender. “In fact, God loves your daddy very much.” Roger glanced at Michelle and rolled his eyes. She ignored it.

“Then why did the snake bite him?” Earl continued.

“The snake bit him because he put his hand too close to the snake. The snake was afraid of him. So it bit him.”

“That’s right,” Roger agreed. “It’s as simple as that.”

Michelle glanced at Roger and rolled her eyes.

“Who are the bad people?” Earl had a worried look on his face.

“I don’t know who all the bad people are.” Michelle turned to face her son. “But God knows. And he’ll take care of us.”

“Is the chief a bad man?”

“Yes, the chief is bad. But Roger is a good person,” she caught Roger’s eye, “and he’s going to help us stay away from the chief.”

“Yeah, the chief is bad.” Roger smiled. “That’s going to come as a shock to a lot of people.”

“We’re all going for a ride in a car.” Michelle’s enthusiasm didn’t sound quite authentic. “You children have never had a ride in a car before!”

“I’m scared,” Abby’s voice was authentic.

“It’s nothing to be scared of,” Michelle reassured her. “Roger drives in a car every day. Don’t you, Roger? Tell them what it’s like to ride in a car.”

“Hmm, where do I start?” Roger stammered. “Well, first we get in our seats and fasten our seatbelts.”

“Maybe we can skip the seatbelts this time.” Michelle seemed to have it all planned out already. “Roger will sit in the front seat because he’s driving. We’ll all sit in the back seat. I’ll hold Abby on my lap. And, Earl, you can sit beside me. Then he’ll take us out on the road, and we can look out the windows and see a lot of new places that you've never seen before."

"Where are we going?" Earl looked at his mother.

Michelle paused, "I don't know. Roger, where are we going to go?"

"Good question!" Roger thought for a moment. "I guess we'll have to go to my place first. Rick and I have an apartment on the other side of town. We'll have to go there to get my equipment and supplies. We can stay there overnight and head out before daylight. Do you agree with Jasper, that we need to go into hiding? Couldn't we just call the state police?"

"Jasper knows what he's talking about. We'd better take his advice."

"He's a fugitive," Roger countered. "I wouldn't expect him to trust anybody. But we're not fugitives."

"I'll feel safer in the wilderness than being around a lot of people," Michelle sounded earnest.

"Okay," Roger agreed. "I'm thinking West Branch. We'll find a secluded spot, set up a campsite, and stay in hiding till the chief is behind bars. What do you think?"

"I'm fine with that."

"We'll hammer out the details when we get back to my place."

"So do we have to go through town? What if someone recognizes me?" Michelle glanced at Roger.

"The windows are tinted. They won't be able to see you that well. By the way, who is Bobby?"

"I don't know his last name. And that may not even be his real first name. Apparently he's some kind of gang leader or crime boss from a larger city, maybe Harrisburg. But he gets advice from Jasper. And Jasper coordinates things between Bobby and the chief."

"So it's not Bobby Billmant. You would have recognized him."

"I couldn't say. I never met Bobby face-to-face. At first, Jasper would lock me in the attic whenever anybody came to talk with him. But now, since we have the children, they just meet out in the woods somewhere to discuss their plans. As far as I know, Bobby could be anybody."

Abigail stopped by the side of the path, picked a cluster of lavender flowers, and held them up to her mother.

"Wild geraniums, how lovely!" Michelle smiled. "My hands are full. Can you put them in my bag?"

The little girl tucked the flowers in between some of the clothes in Michelle's bag, and they all resumed the pace of a three-year-old.

"By the way, Roger, thanks for the rose. I knew it was from you as soon as Jasper told me where he found it. And I knew it meant you had figured out that I was still alive."

"Well, actually I hadn't figured it out," Roger confessed. "I dropped seven roses off the iron bridge on Friday as a memorial to you. I thought it was the seventh anniversary of your death. One of the roses drifted into the eddy behind the dam, and I found it there on Saturday. I don't know why I put it in the pyramid."

"Then what made you come looking for me?"

"Last night I had a dream. I dreamt that you and Jasper were fishing by the dam. You were at the eddy, and he was above the dam. You were rolling stones around with your feet so he wouldn't see what you were doing. You made a triangle then squatted down and dropped your necklace in and put the stone on top. Then you went back to Jasper."

"That's amazingly accurate!" Michelle shook her head in amazement. "But the kids were there too."

"They weren't in my dream."

"Mommy, I'm hungry," Earl interrupted loudly.

"Wow! It is almost noon," Roger responded, glancing at his watch. "We'll get you something to eat as soon as we get to my house. Do you like pizza?"

"Pizza takes too long," Earl complained. "I'm hungry now."

"I have a frozen pizza I can stick in the microwave, and it'll be ready in no time," Roger smiled at the boy.

"He has no idea what you're talking about." Michelle flashed a quick smile at Roger. "For us, making pizza meant building a fire and making the pizza from scratch."

"Sorry." Roger frowned. "That thought never occurred to me."

"Son, you just have to wait till we get to Roger's house," Michelle continued. "You'll be amazed at how fast he can get food ready."

"Can't you walk a little faster?" Earl gave Abby a nudge from behind. Abby stepped in front of her mother and held up her arms.

"I can take another bag if you want to carry her," Roger offered as he set his bags on the ground. Michelle set her one bag against his two and Roger grabbed the handles of all three.

"I can carry two bags," Earl bragged. "One bag makes me go crooked."

"Wow, you're quite a little man," Roger commented as Earl took the other bag from his mother. "But it helps to have a balanced load, doesn't it?"

Michelle picked up Abigail, and the group got underway at a faster pace.

"I suppose I'm carrying a bag full of dirty money and an illegal fire arm," Roger shot a quick glance at Michelle. "Maybe we should have left that behind."

"It's not all dirty money. I think a good bit of it came from Harold. I don't know where the rest came from."

"Who's Harold?"

"He's Jasper's brother. He's a businessman in Philadelphia. Jasper says he likes to keep his hands clean. I think he tries to stay above the law, but he doesn't mind benefiting from the crimes of Bobby and his gang."

"So Bobby is connected to Harold and Chief Theodore?" Roger furrowed his eyebrows.

"I think they're all three pretty much independent." Michelle sounded uncertain. "But Jasper somehow directs things so they benefit each other. He's kind of like the top of the pyramid."

"And Harold gave Jasper a lot of money?"

"Yeah. Every once in a while he leaves a bag of cash under a big flat rock somewhere up close to Ridge Road. That's what Jasper was picking up when the snake bit him."

"So his brother leaves a bag of cash under a rock. When Jasper goes to pick it up, he's bitten by a snake that's not native to this area. Doesn't that sound a little fishy?" Roger cocked his head, glancing at Michelle.

"Harold wouldn't have done that." Michelle shook her head. "He keeps his hands clean."

"Who do you think would have planted a snake next to the money?" Roger questioned.

"The same person who gave you the dream."

"I guess for you, that's a logical conclusion. But that's not what you said to your son a little while ago."

Roger felt Michelle studying his face from the corner of her eye for a few seconds before she asked, "So what made you stop believing in God?"

"Well, first of all, it doesn't make sense that a loving, all-powerful God would create so much suffering and pain for so many people. When I got a better understanding of science and the universe and how this all came into being, that just seemed like a better theory than the idea of an almighty God."

"I can't believe you're serious, Roger."

"I know some Christians try to make evolution sound like a ridiculous theory. But it's really based on sound scientific evidence."

"We'll talk more about that some other time." Michelle's tone closed the topic.

"Were you able to get any news about friends and family over the last seven years?" Roger asked.

"Very little." She paused. "I'd see you going down the river. But other than that, I don't know what's going on in the world. How is my family?"

"You haven't heard anything about them, I guess?"

"No."

"Well, about five years ago, your parents got divorced."

"I'm not totally surprised by that."

"I didn't expect that you would be. Your mother is living in New York City. Last I heard, your father was somewhere in California. Your sister and her husband are still living in Bellefonte."

"So at least some of my family is not far from this area."

"My arms are tired," Earl complained.

"Well, no wonder," Roger turned to the boy. "You're not tall enough to let your arms hang straight down like I do. You have to bend your elbows. That takes a lot of muscles."

"You've been doing a good job, son," Michelle said encouragingly.

"We're not far from the car now." Roger glanced down the trail. "Why don't we just let those two bags here for now? It won't take me long to jog back and get them. That'll give the rest of you a few minutes to get familiar with the car before we start driving."

"Okay." Michelle agreed. "Earl, just leave them here in the path."

Earl dropped the two bags and let out a big sigh. In no time, he was a few paces ahead of the rest of the group.

"So, Roger, what are you doing with your life?" Michelle leaned slightly toward him.

"I'm a schoolteacher. I teach fourth grade at Sunset Township Elementary School."

"Wow, I'm impressed. I thought you might be driving truck for your dad."

"I did some of that while I was working my way through college. And I enjoyed it. But teaching gives me more of a feeling of accomplishing something worthwhile."

"I've been trying to teach Earl to read. He knows the alphabet, and he can count. And he's starting to read a little. But he has so much to learn about the world outside our little castle."

"If he needs any extra tutoring, I can help get him ready for school."

"This is going to be a huge adjustment for both of them," Michelle said as they rounded a slight bend and got their first look at the car in the distance. Earl stopped and stared down the path at the unfamiliar object.

"It's okay, son. Just keep walking." Michelle turned to Roger and added, "He has a few toys, but I guess he has never seen a real car before.

When they arrived at the car, Roger opened the back and put his bags in as the children watched with cautious curiosity. They ran around looking at the car from all sides when Roger opened all four doors. Michelle sat in the back seat and watched as the children continued to inspect the car.

"I'll be back shortly," Roger said and set out jogging up the trail. As he arrived at the remaining two bags of clothes, he met the German shepherd coming down the trail toward him. He had no stick, no paddle, no weapon of any kind. If the dog attacked him, he'd be in serious trouble. And as a result, Michelle and her children would be in even greater danger. He pointed his finger at the dog, "Ruger, stay!" Ruger hesitated, looking at Roger and seeming uncertain as to whether he should obey or attack. Roger took a bold step toward the dog, shaking his finger as he pointed and shouted sternly, "Ruger! Stay!" The dog sat down. Roger picked up the bags of clothes and headed back toward the car, keeping one eye over his shoulder.

When he returned to the car, Michelle was sitting in the back, on the passenger side, with Abby on her lap. Earl was seated beside his mother, beaming with excitement. Roger stowed the last two bags, closed the hatch, and got into the driver's seat. "Are we all ready?" he asked as he put the key in the ignition.

Earl was standing up, looking over Roger's shoulder, watching every move as they drove slowly out the lane and pulled onto the road. Then Roger tramped on the accelerator, causing Earl to fall back into his seat, giggling with excitement. The children were mesmerized by the passing scenery as they wound their way up the mountainside.

"When we get to my place, we can call 911 and send an ambulance for Jasper," Roger glanced in the rearview mirror.

"I don't think we should." Michelle caught Roger's eye in the mirror. "He doesn't want that. If he's still conscious, he'll shoot it out with anyone who tries to come in. Just let him go peacefully."

Roger turned right on Ridge Road, which snaked its way leisurely along the top of the mountain. The children cringed in fright as a motorcycle roared past them in the opposite direction. "What was that?" Earl asked.

"A motorcycle." Michelle smiled. "It's like a little car with just two wheels."

"It hurt my ears." Earl held his hands over his ears.

"Me too." Abby snuggled against her mother.

"Look at that!" Earl pointed at a two-story house with white siding.

"That's a house where people live." Michelle seemed to anticipate his curiosity.

"It's not like our house," the boy observed.

"You'll see a lot of different kinds of houses. Everybody's house is different. When we get to town, there will be houses everywhere."

"Look, Mommy," Abby pointed at three horses grazing in a pasture.

"Horses." Michelle sounded almost as intrigued as the children. "Roger, they've never seen horses before."

Roger pulled to the side of the road and put the right side windows down. Earl seemed stunned at seeing the glass move all by itself. But his attention was diverted when one of the horses came trotting over to the car and put her head over the fence.

Roger got out, walked up to the horse and rubbed her nose. "Do you want to pet the horse?" he asked, looking in at the children. They both shook their heads quickly. "I guess we'd better keep moving." Roger got back in the car. As he pulled away, both windows went up again.

Roger noticed the puzzlement on Earl's face and opened his mouth to begin explaining the button on the door. But before he started speaking, he changed his mind and decided to keep that secret for a while.

As they made their way into town, the children watched in awe as the sights of everyday civilization passed by on both sides. Whenever they passed people on the sidewalks, Michelle made sure her face was behind Abby's head, so she wouldn't be recognized.

"It looks like there's an accident ahead." Roger glanced over his shoulder. "There's a police car up there with its lights flashing."

Earl was standing up looking through the windshield at the flashing lights as they approached the scene.

"Everybody get down!" Roger commanded suddenly. "It's Chief Theodore directing traffic!" Michelle quickly put Abigail on the floor, and then pulled Earl down as she lay over on the seat. They stayed hunkered down as they passed the accident scene and turned left onto Church Street.

"Okay," Roger let out a sigh of relief. "We're out of his sight."

They all got back into comfortable positions for the final two blocks. Then Roger turned left into his driveway and pulled to the back of the house.

14

"Rick and I have the back part of the house." Roger opened the door from the back porch into the kitchen. "The landlord and his wife live in the front half." The children stopped inside the door and looked around cautiously as Roger flipped the light switch and the room the instantly brightened. "Come on into the library and make yourselves comfortable." He walked into the next room and flipped another light switch.

The children stayed put. From the smell of the room, to the lights and kitchen appliances, it was all so strangely different, intriguing and just a bit scary. Michelle prodded the children into the library. "Wow, look at all the books Roger has," she commented, trying to direct the children to the bookshelf. Earl stood, mesmerized, gazing at a photo of Roger standing in front of a shiny green truck.

"Help yourself to whatever looks interesting," Roger called from the kitchen. "I'll get lunch ready."

Michelle picked up a colorful magazine and got seated. One child stood on each side as their mother leafed through the magazine, explaining all sorts of strange pictures. Earl was so engrossed in the pictures that he seemed to have forgotten all about his terrible hunger. He was oblivious to what Roger was doing in the kitchen. He looked up when the microwave began beeping. But the sound meant nothing to him. This new world was so full of new sounds, sights and smells that he just couldn't investigate every new thing.

"Pizza's ready," Roger called out. Michelle got the children to the table as Roger continued setting out chips, pretzels, and other snack foods. "Soda or water?" Roger asked, as he opened the refrigerator.

"Soda." Earl peered into the strange white cabinet that seemed to be lit from the inside.

"I see he knows what soda is." Roger grinned.

"Yeah, the chief used to bring us some soda from time to time. But that was a rare treat." Michelle pulled Earl away from the fridge and turned him toward the table.

It wasn't long till the children had satisfied their hunger and were distracted by the many strange, new things around them. Earl had discovered how to turn the lights on and off, and Michelle could hardly keep him away from the light switch.

Roger turned to Michelle. "Is it okay if I call George and see if he can come over?"

"Sure!" Michelle's face lit up. "I'm not afraid of our friends. We just have to keep this from the public till we get to a safe place."

"Rick will be home around four," Roger said as he picked up the phone. Abby watched curiously as Roger spoke into the phone. "Hi, George, it's Roger."

Pause.

"Can you come over?"

Pause.

"There's been a new development in our case. You've got to get over here as soon as you can."

Pause.

"You'll see when you get here. You won't believe it. But you gotta come right away."

Pause.

"Okay. See ya." Abby watched him hang up the phone turn to her mother. "He's coming right over. Do you think the kids would like to watch a video?"

Michelle raised her eyebrows. "That should really blow their minds. They've never dreamed of anything like that."

Roger turned on the VCR and started a nature video featuring baby animals. The children were awestruck by the picture and sound coming from the device. But soon they forgot the strange apparatus and were totally absorbed by the baby animals.

Before long, the door opened, and George walked into the kitchen. Michelle jumped out of her chair and ran to meet him. "George!" she cried as she threw her arms around him.

Roger grinned as George's mouth dropped open and his eyes glanced about in disbelief. "Mi-Michelle?" he stammered.

"Yeah! It's me." She squeezed him tighter. Roger realized that he himself hadn't actually hugged her yet.

"What?" George exclaimed as he slowly put his arms around her and gently returned her embrace. "Where were you?"

"Oh, I've been alive and well," she replied as she released him and drew back with a smile.

"The disappearing fisherman was holding her hostage in that little cottage." Roger was eager to fill in the details.

"The who?" Michelle giggled, turning toward Roger.

"Oh, we call him the disappearing fishermen because he always disappears whenever somebody comes down the creek." Roger chuckled.

"What? You had him under surveillance?" Michelle's eyes were wide with surprise.

"From time to time," Roger tried to sound nonchalant.

"And you were a hostage?" George asked, still trying to absorb it all.

"Yeah, for seven years," Michelle paused briefly. "Oh, come meet my children."

"Children?" George half-whispered. "He raped you?"

"Don't jump to conclusions," Michelle quipped as she turned and led the way into the library. "That's Earl, and this is Abigail." She pointed to the children who were still totally engrossed in the video.

"This is unbelievable!" George shook his head. "So how did you escape?"

"Well," Michelle replied, stepping back into the kitchen. "This morning Jasper was bitten by a rattlesnake."

"Who's Jasper?" George's eyes darted from Michelle to Roger.

"The disappearing fisherman," Roger replied.

"We need to go over this whole thing from the beginning." George's brow furrowed. "But shouldn't Rick be here too?"

"He should be home by four." Roger gazed at Michelle watching her children.

"Maybe if we call him, he could skip out a little early." George cocked his head toward the phone.

"We have to keep this whole thing secret till Michelle and the kids and I go into hiding," Roger explained. "As soon as Chief Theodore finds out that Michelle escaped, he'll try to hunt us down and get rid of us."

"What?" George glanced from Roger to Michelle and back to Roger. "Can't we just call the police? State police, that is."

"The chief has connections." Roger looked George straight in the eye. "We don't know how far this corruption goes. We don't know who we can trust. Our best bet is to take off into the wilderness till the chief is behind bars."

"We need to sit down and plan our strategy," Michelle added with a note of concern in her voice. The children weren't the only ones facing a new world on uncertainties.

"I think we need Rick to be in on this," George asserted.

"Go ahead, call him." Roger nodded toward the phone.

George took the phone and dialed Rick's work number.

"Hello, Rick Beck speaking."

"Hi, Rick, it's George."

"Hey, George. What's up?"

"Is there any chance you could get off a little early this afternoon?"

"Maybe, if it's important. What do you have in mind?"

"Are you at a place where we can talk confidentially?"

"Yeah, go ahead. What's going on?"

"We have to keep this absolutely quiet for now. I'm at your place with Roger."

"Yeah?"

"And you won't believe this. Michelle is here with us."

"What!"

"Michelle is alive and well. She is here with us right now."

"Don't say any more. I'll be right home."

The children's video had ended, and they came into the kitchen to see what the adults were doing. "You kids want some candy?" Roger held out a dish of M&Ms.

"They know what that is." Michelle smirked as each child took a handful.

"You want to watch another video?" Roger asked. "I think we have Winnie the Pooh around here somewhere."

Both faces lit up at the mention of the familiar name. "They'll enjoy that," Michelle replied. "They have a book of Winnie the Pooh."

But finding Winnie the Pooh in a bachelor's apartment turned out to be no easy task. By the time Roger found the video and got it started, Rick was arriving. Michelle met him at the door with a big hug.

"I can't believe this!" Rick bonged the side of his head with the heel of his hand. "What happened to you?"

"I was abducted."

"The disappearing fisherman had her locked up in that cottage," George added.

Michelle laughed. "That nickname cracks me up. His name is Jasper."

"Why don't you just start at the beginning," Roger suggested, "and tell us the whole story, or at least the stuff we need to know."

"If you're comfortable talking about it, that is," George added.

"Well," Michelle sat up straight and rested her arms on the table, "that day I was kayaking. I was getting ready to portage around the dam. I was standing with my back to the woods, pulling my boat out of the water. I heard something behind me, but before I could turn around, his arms were around me. He was so strong, I couldn't do anything. He had a rag with some smelly stuff over my face. He told me later it was ether."

Rick and Roger glanced at each other and both said, "Starting fluid."

Michelle looked puzzled. "We found it in your dump," Roger added. "Go on."

"The next thing I knew, I was lying on the couch in the cottage, and Jasper was taking care of me. I still had all my clothes on. I was feeling sick and groggy, but I didn't seem to have any injuries. He was being so kind and thoughtful, and he kept apologizing for what he did. If he wouldn't have apologized, I would never have guessed that he was the same person who grabbed me down at the creek.

"I guess the reality of what was happening hadn't sunk in yet. At that point I wasn't really afraid of him. He seemed to be trying to help me, and my mind was still foggy. But as soon as I was feeling better, he sent me up to the attic and told me to make myself comfortable. There was a mattress on the floor, with a sheet and blanket and a pillow. Then he locked me in the attic and left."

"That must have been terrible." George sounded like he was about to cry.

"That's when it really hit me that I was a hostage and he wasn't going to let me go." Michelle cleared her throat. "Then I was really scared. I had to find a way to escape. There were vents, with metal louvers, in both ends of the attic. I thought maybe I could break out, but they were too strong. If I would have had a hammer or a rock or something, maybe I could have. But all I had was my bare hands. I lay on my back and kicked at the louvers. I kicked at the roof, hoping to find a weak spot. I was angry, and I was panicking. I lay there kicking and crying till I was completely exhausted."

The three guys sat motionless, gazing at Michelle as she continued. "As I lay there catching my breath, I realized that God was with me. Up to that point, I hadn't even thought about praying, at least not consciously. I started thinking more rationally and analyzing my situation. Jasper was much stronger than me, and he had a gun. There was no way I could win a physical battle. The only weapons I had were my intellect and my feminine charm. Somehow, I had to use them to my best advantage."

Roger shifted uneasily. Michelle took a deep breath. "With all my kicking, I had managed to bend some of the louvers a little bit. That made it easier to see out. From there I could see down to the dam and on up the river. I saw Jasper down there cleaning up the crime scene. Then he took my kayak and pushed it out into the creek just above the dam. That made me really angry. It drifted over the dam, and you know the rest of that story."

"Of course, we all thought you drowned," Rick said softly.

"I saw you searching for me," Michelle continued. "I wanted so much to scream and get your attention. But I was too far away. Jasper is the only one who would have heard me. Over the next few months, I spent a lot of time lying on my mattress, looking out through the louvers. I watched them blow up the dam. The attic became my little private space, a place I could go to be alone."

"So who is this Jasper?" George looked into Michelle's eyes. "What's he doing living out there in the woods?"

"He's an escaped convict. I don't know from where or when. He wouldn't talk about that."

"But he treated you okay?" George put his hand on Michelle's arm.

"He was always kind and gentle, except for when he first grabbed me down at the dam. Even then, he didn't injure me other than a few minor bruises. And he has apologized over and over for that." She hesitated and wiped her eyes with the back of her hand. "I'm sorry," she sobbed as Roger passed her a box of tissues. She blew her nose and tried to regain her composure. "Sorry," she sobbed, "I don't even know if my husband is dead or alive."

Rick and George raised their eyebrows and glanced at Roger as Rick silently mouthed the word, "Husband?"

Roger shrugged his shoulders, looking just as puzzled as the other two.

Adventure

15

Roger paced the kitchen floor after Rick and George had been briefed on Michelle's escape and her precarious situation. "Time is slipping away. We have to get our plans together," he said emphatically. "This guy they call Bobby is coming to see Jasper tomorrow afternoon. And I don't think the plans we've talked about so far are going to work at all."

"Why not?" Michelle turned in her chair to look at Roger.

"As soon as someone finds my car parked along the river, the chief will know right where to look for us. If he catches up with us out there in the lonely back country, he can do whatever he wants, and there will be no witnesses. I think we'd be better off surrounded be lots of people. That way he wouldn't be able to touch us without incriminating himself."

Michelle's eyes dropped and stared into the kitchen table. "Roger, all he would have to do is hire a hit man who isn't afraid to gun somebody down in public. He has lots of connections, remember? High places and low. Jasper thought we should disappear into the wilderness. I think that's what we should do."

Roger turned on his heel. "But I don't have enough supplies and equipment for four people!"

"Roger, stop pacing and sit down." Rick returned to the table with notepad and pencil. "Let's go over this one step at a time."

Roger sat down opposite from Rick, propped his elbows on the table, and rested his chin on his thumbs.

"Okay," Rick began, "let's start with the question, 'Where?'"

"West Branch." Michelle's tone was certain. "We'll leave tomorrow morning before daylight."

"We'll head out beyond Karthaus and get on the river," Roger added. "We'll find a secluded spot and set up camp."

"You'll need somebody to drive you out and then come home." George drummed his fingers on the table. "That way you won't have your vehicle parked along the river giving somebody a clue as to where you are."

"Absolutely!" Michelle flashed a smile at George. "So who can be our driver?"

"I'll do that," George volunteered.

"You have time?" Rick glanced up from his notes and caught George's eye.

"Not really. But this is more important. If Mrs. S. Q. Faulkner has to wait one more day for her mahogany bathroom, she may have some sort of emotional catastrophe or something—"

"*The* Mrs. S. Q. Faulkner?" Michelle raised her eyebrows.

"The one and only," George confirmed. "She's paid me so much money already, I shouldn't even be thinking about doing something for someone else. But her money can't buy everything. I'm your driver."

"Thanks!"

"We should park Roger's SUV at the iron bridge," Rick suggested. "That way the chief will find it there and assume that Roger helped Michelle escape by canoe on Thrush Creek. He'll be looking for you at the wrong place."

"Good idea!" George nodded at Rick. "We can take my pickup out to Karthaus."

"One canoe and one kayak for four people?" Rick questioned.

"That's no good!" Roger shook his head. "We'd have to put one adult and two children plus a whole bunch of gear in the canoe. That wouldn't be safe!"

"We need another canoe," Michelle glanced at the ceiling.

"Do the children have to go with us?" Roger glanced at Michelle. "We could find somebody to keep them till we get back. We could lie about who they really are."

"The children stay with me!" Michelle's tone left no room for argument.

George turned to Roger. "I saw a used canoe for sale along State Road, south of town."

"What shape is it in? Does it float?"

"I don't know. I can go check it out."

"Okay. I'll give you some cash. If it looks like it's usable, buy it."

"I can just write a check for it," George offered.

"Just a minute." Roger got up and hurried out to his car. He returned in a flash, with the duffel bag and set it down between Rick and George. "We've got plenty of cash to buy a canoe," he said as he zipped the bag open and removed the gun.

"Holy moly!" Rick peered into the bag.

"Jasper gave that to us." Michelle smiled.

"Gun and all!" Roger added.

"Wow!" George turned to Michelle. "How much is in there?"

"Don't know exactly." Michelle brushed her hair back. "He thought about twenty grand."

"That's hot money." Rick hesitated then continued, "We can't use that. We have to turn that over to the police."

"I think most of it is clean money," Michelle replied. "His brother Harold gave him a lot of money. And that didn't come from criminal activity."

"Jasper is a fugitive, running from the law." Rick shook his head slowly. "It's not legal for anybody to give him money or help him in any way. So all this money is hot!"

"Well, nobody knows how much is in there or how much is supposed to be in there," Michelle studied Rick's face. "We can take what we need."

"It's still hot money!" Rick declared.

"It's my money," Michelle said softly. "Jasper specifically gave it to me. I say we use what we need and keep track of how much we took. When things settle down, we'll turn over what's left. If they insist on having what we used, we'll pay it back." She reached down, picked up a pack of twenties and turned to George. "How much do you need for a used canoe?"

"I don't know." George shrugged.

"It probably won't be more than a couple hundred, unless it's something really sophisticated," Roger speculated.

Michelle peeled the paper band off the pack and counted it. "Fifty," she said. "That would be a thousand dollars. We'll start with that." She handed the whole stack of bills to George. "Just bring back what's left."

"Of course." George folded the wad over and put it in his pocket. He left, and the other three continued their planning.

"So how and when are you going to inform the authorities about Jasper?" Rick's eyes shifted between Roger and Michelle.

"I don't know," Roger replied as he tried to think of a plan. "If we call them on the phone, they can trace the call and know where we are. If it turns out that we're talking to the wrong person, that would be a bad thing."

"E-mail would be the same problem," Rick added.

"How about old-fashioned mail?" Michelle suggested. "I can write a letter telling who I am and everything I know about Jasper and Chief Theodore. We'll make one copy for the state police and one for the FBI. We'll drop them in a mailbox in another town on our way to the river tomorrow. By the time they get the letters, we'll be hiding out in the woods. By that time, the chief should be busy looking for me and trying to cover up any evidence of his involvement with Jasper. Maybe they can catch him red-handed."

"That sounds like a plan." Roger gave a nod of approval.

"So what other equipment do you need?" Rick drummed his pencil on the notepad.

"Well," Roger replied slowly as he did a quick mental inventory of his equipment. "We'll need a few more dry bags, PFDs for the kids, and we probably ought to get two short paddles. How about clothes, Michelle? Do you and the children need rain gear or anything?"

"Oh, I hadn't thought of that." Michelle pressed her hands to her temples. "Yes, we will need some things. Maybe some water shoes too."

"We'll need another tent too," Roger added. "I have a small one for myself. But we'll need to get a larger one for you and the children."

"So where and when do we get all these things?" Rick looked at Roger.

"We can swing by Lock Haven on our way to the river tomorrow. There's a couple outfitters up there. We should be able to find everything we need."

"Why don't you head east from here?" Rick suggested. "Drop the letters in a mailbox. Then turn north to Lock Haven, do your shopping, and then head west to Karthaus."

"Good suggestion! That's what we'll do." Roger gave a quick nod.

"What about food and water?" Rick asked.

"I have two large plastic containers for water," Roger smacked two fingers down on the table. "We'll fill them up here before we leave. I also have a water purification kit that we can use to replenish our supply when we need to. But I'll have to go shopping for food yet this evening."

"Roger, why don't you start working on shopping lists for today and tomorrow?" Michelle suggested. "And I'll start writing my letter to the police."

"You can use my computer." Roger pointed to his desk.

"I'll entertain the kids," Rick winked at Michelle.

"Tough job," Michelle quipped. "Earl is busy looking at pictures in the encyclopedia, and Abigail is sound asleep."

Eventually George pulled in the drive with a seventeen-foot Coleman canoe on top of his pickup. Rick and Roger circled the truck inspecting the boat from all angles. "It appears to be pretty good shape yet," Roger commented.

"That's what I thought." George scratched his head. "No life jackets and no paddles though. Just the boat—a hundred and fifty bucks."

"Not bad," Roger smiled. "It's just what we need."

Rick nudged George. "Roger is taking his car out to the iron bridge, and I'm bringing him back. We'll stop at the deli and pick up some cheesesteaks and burgers for dinner. Michelle will bring you up to speed on the rest of our plans."

After briefing George on their plans, Michelle handed him a copy of the letter she had typed.

> Dear Sirs:
>
> My name is Michelle Danklos, from Thrush Glen, PA. People believe that I drowned in a kayaking accident on June 20, 1987. However, I was abducted by an escaped convict who goes by the name Jasper (I don't know if that's his real name). He is approximately 50 years old, 6'3" and weighs about 215 lb. He has a tattoo of a sailboat on his right forearm. He grew up in Philadelphia, where he got involved in gangs. He spent a short time in the witness protection program, probably in the 1960s.
>
> He and I lived in a small cottage hidden in the woods along Thrush Creek. Go east from the concrete bridge on Lumber Mill Road. At the first bend, you will find an unpaved lane on your left. The lane soon becomes a footpath, which will lead you to the cottage.
>
> When I left, with my two children, Jasper was suffering from a rattlesnake bite. I do not know if it was fatal. If he

is still alive, he will shoot at intruders. He is armed with a 9 mm semiautomatic pistol. The place is also guarded by a vicious German shepherd named Ruger.

Jasper is being supplied with cash by his brother, Harold, who is a businessman in Philadelphia. Jasper is also being aided and protected by Sunset Township Police Chief, Theodore Miller. Jasper and another associate, who goes by Bobby, are blackmailing Chief Miller to get his cooperation. I understand that Chief Miller has been involved in other criminal activity, but I don't know anything about that. I also understand that Chief Miller has associates in high places who may also be involved in criminal activity.

I do not know how far this corruption extends or who I can trust. Therefore, I am going into hiding until these dangerous people are brought to justice.

Bobby is the leader of a crime ring from a major city. I think they may operate out of Harrisburg, but I don't remember what gave me that impression.

Jasper may have had some medical training or experience. At least he knows how to deliver babies.

I hope that's enough information for you to figure out who he is. I hope you can apprehend these criminals quickly. Until then, my life is in jeopardy.

Yours truly, Michelle Danklos

"That should get the response you need." George handed the letter back to Michelle. "I'll be praying for you."

"Thanks." Michelle paused for a second. "Tell me about Roger. He says he doesn't believe in God anymore."

"So he told you that already." George didn't sound surprised. "He likes to have a scientific explanation for everything. To him, that makes more sense than the theory of God. From the origins of the universe, to answered prayer, to whatever, he always comes up with an explanation that doesn't include God."

"So what kind of person has he become?"

"Oh, he's still a wonderful person." George sounded reassuring. "He doesn't drink, doesn't smoke, doesn't use drugs. He believes there are a lot of natural benefits that come from living by Christian principles."

"Well, it looks like he and I will be spending a lot of time together." Michelle studied George's face. "I was just wondering if he's still the same Roger I knew in high school."

"You and your children will be safe with him. Absolutely safe!"

"Thanks." Michelle smiled and let out a little sigh. *He said he doesn't drink or use drugs. He didn't mention porn. But if Roger had turned into some kind of playboy or other questionable character, George would have mentioned it.* She felt lucky to have a trustworthy friend like George, always sincere, always reliable.

It was 5:30 p.m. by the time Rick and Roger returned, and the children were already complaining of hunger. Their complaints quickly subsided as it became apparent that Rick and Roger had grossly overestimated how much a child could eat. After devouring a cheesesteak, Roger was off to the grocery store.

George and Rick placed Roger's canoe beside the Coleman, on top of the pickup while Michelle dealt with the leftover food. Then Rick started gathering Roger's camping gear, leaving the final packing for Roger. Michelle gathered a few more grocery bags and sorted and organized their clothes into smaller lots so that once they got the additional dry bags, she could just drop their bags of clothes into the large dry bags and still have some semblance of order.

"Have you checked out the sleeping quarters?" Rick asked Michelle.

"No, I haven't."

"We'll let you and the children have my room. Come, I'll show you." Rick gestured toward the stairs. "There's enough space that we can make a bed on the floor for one or both of the children. Or one of them could sleep in the bed with you. I'll sleep on a recliner in the library."

After a tour of the upstairs bedrooms and bathroom, Michelle asked, "May I give the children baths in the tub?"

"Of course!"

"They'll be fascinated by hot water coming right out of the faucet." Michelle seemed delighted with the idea. "We always had to heat our water on the kitchen stove."

"Where did you get your water?"

"Oh, we had plumbing, but no water heater."

"How do you pump water without electricity?"

"It was a gravity-fed system. Underground pipes brought water down from a natural spring farther up the mountainside. We had a kitchen sink, a toilet and a bathtub, all with fifty-eight-degree water."

"Sounds ingenious. But 'bathtub' and 'fifty-eight-degree water' don't belong in the same sentence." Rick shivered.

Michelle laughed. "Oh, I can tell you lots of stories. But that will have to wait. I do want to take a hot shower once again. I haven't had a shower for seven years."

"Absolutely! You must take a shower!" Rick stopped short, and he felt his face turning red. "I didn't mean that the way it sounded."

Michelle had another hearty laugh as they headed down the stairs.

By ten o'clock, the three men had all the food, clothes, and equipment loaded on George's pickup and covered with a tarp. The children had been bathed and were already sleeping. Michelle was relaxing on the recliner, in her pajamas, with her hair wrapped in a towel as the men came in from outside.

"Are you enjoying your freedom?" Roger asked.

George contemplated the question as Michelle smiled back at Roger.

"Freedom? I'm no freer than I was yesterday. I'm running for my life!"

"Sorry. That was a stupid question."

"No, it wasn't." Michelle seemed quite relaxed for a person in her situation. "Freedom can be an elusive thing. We can only be free when we accept our boundaries. I didn't spend the last seven years thinking about all places I couldn't go and the things I couldn't have. I just concentrated on enjoying the things I had. And in a way, I had freedom."

"So you're saying that we experience freedom when we accept boundaries?" Rick rubbed the back of his neck. "I'll have to think that one over a bit."

"Yeah. Take Jasper for example," Michelle appeared to be well prepared for this minilecture. "His life was actually easier when he was in prison. The government provided for all his needs, and he had people around to interact with. But he was miserable because he wouldn't accept the boundaries that were forced on him. After he escaped, he was still confined. He couldn't go out in public for fear of getting caught. There were lots of things he couldn't do, and there were things he had to do for his own survival. But he accepted all those boundaries, and he really enjoyed his freedom."

"I think she knows what she's talking about. I'll have to think it over while I'm going to sleep." George glanced at Roger. "What time do you want me to be here in the morning?"

"We want to be out of town before daylight," Michelle answered.

"How about we try to leave by four thirty?" Roger looked from Michelle to George.

"Okay. I'll be pulling in your driveway at four twenty," George started for the door. As he passed Michelle, he noticed a tear trickle down her cheek. "You okay?" he paused in his tracks.

Michelle looked up at him, smiled, and in a childish voice said, "I want my daddy." Then she broke the emotional tension with a compulsive little chuckle, and everyone laughed. George blinked back the tears as he remembered the struggles his own mother had gone through after his father walked out. He knew that many times she just longed for a shoulder to cry on. He understood how Michelle was feeling. He picked up a box of tissues and after taking one for himself, passed the box to Michelle, then walked quietly out the door.

16

Michelle climbed into bed as the two children slept in makeshift beds on the floor. She felt like a transient refugee, alone in her borrowed bed. It was the first time in years that she would be sleeping without Jasper by her side. She wondered how he was doing. Was he in pain? Was he suffering? Was he still breathing at all? She could hear the children breathing softly as they slept.

She heard the almost undetectable hum of the refrigerator downstairs and the sound of a car driving down the street, sounds she hadn't heard in seven years, sounds that once were so common that she never thought about them. Now these sounds brought back fond memories from her childhood.

She visualized the house along State Road, just a few miles from town, where she had lived with her parents and older sister. She remembered her dad picking her up and tossing her onto her bed, then tucking her in and kissing her good night. He was so strong and good-natured. She missed him. She missed the security she always felt when he was around. She remembered crying in her mother's arms when the family dog disappeared. Perky had always been a loyal companion. They had never found out what happened to him. Although her mother had never been fond of the dog, she grieved with her children over the loss of their pet and consoled them as only a mother can. Michelle's mind raced on to memories of lounging in her room at age twelve, discussing boys with her sister—the ones they liked, the ones they didn't, the ones they really liked, and why they liked them.

She cherished the memory of sitting in the grass on the edge of a hayfield on the hilltop that overlooked her neighborhood. It was there she would come to sit and dream about her future while gazing down on the tiny houses below. The world seemed so perfect from up there. The air was always fresh and clean. The noises of civilization were drowned out by the quiet whisper of the breeze blowing across the open field. She could see buildings as far away as the edge of town and majestic mountaintops beyond that. And if the air was just right, she might hear the faint chiming of distant church bells.

She dreamed of being married to a handsome man and living in a nice big house in the forest. It would be a place where her children (she would have at least three) could roam freely and enjoy nature. Being secluded in a little cottage, as she had been for seven years, wasn't at all what she had dreamed of. Her life was changing dramatically. Her future, and the children's, seemed so uncertain now. She wished she could go back once again to that favorite spot on the hilltop where everything seemed so positive and hopeful. Perhaps there she could see a bright new future for herself and the children. She would give a fortune to spend an hour on the edge of that hayfield gazing at the valley below, if only she could.

Her high school years had been very busy with school work, extracurricular activities, church, and social events. She had carried a heavy load of classes and tried hard to keep her grades up in all of them. She was on the yearbook staff and a member of the 4H club. She was active in her church youth group and had an ever-widening circle of friends.

On top of that, she had taken time for lots of canoeing and kayaking trips with her dad. Later she started inviting Roger along on those trips. She had lots of pleasant memories of whitewater trips with Roger and her dad. She had enjoyed it all tremendously. She loved everything she did, but she longed for a break, a little time to just sit back and do nothing. But she had never dreamed of years with no deadlines to meet, no bills to pay, no forms to sign, and no calls to return. She had never dreamed of a seven-year siesta.

She remembered the quietness of the little cottage along Thrush Creek. She remembered standing in the front room gazing out the window at the snow falling romantically through the pine trees and the only sound was the occasional crackling of the fire in the kitchen stove. She thought about the time spent with Jasper. Sometimes hours went by without either one saying a word as they quietly enjoyed the solitude of their life together. Other times they talked for hours. They shared their deepest thoughts and dreams. They had become soul mates. They talked about everything—everything except Jasper's true identity that is.

She remembered a warm summer night early in their life together, during the years she generally thought of as their honeymoon. It had been a hot humid day. In the forenoon, she had done what she often did on hot summer days when they didn't keep a fire in the kitchen stove, when heating water was not an option. She ran about six inches of fresh spring water into the bathtub and left it there to absorb warmth from the air during the day. By evening it had lost some of its chill, and she bathed in it to cool off and freshen up before going to bed.

The house was dark, except for the soft moonlight streaming through the windows. She was walking naked from the bathroom into the bedroom. As she passed the open bedroom window, the warm gentle breeze felt wonderful against her moist skin. She stopped and glanced out the window into the moonlit night. In contrast to the bright silver moon, the stars seemed dim against the midnight blue sky. The pine trees, the bushes, and the grass were all highlighted in silver and hundreds of fireflies were flashing their gold. A half dozen deer were grazing in the yard. Not more than ten yards from the window, a doe stood with her head high and silver-tipped ears forward. By her side, with white spots gleaming in the silver moonlight, her fawn nursed peacefully.

Michelle realized that the moonbeams playing on her own feminine form were creating a tantalizing sight for her mate, who was patiently waiting for her to come to bed. But the scene outside was so serene, so perfect, so natural, she just couldn't walk away. As she lingered, she heard Jasper getting out of bed.

In a moment he was behind her, looking over her shoulder. She still wondered if his eyes were focused on the scene outside or if they were turned downward. She remembered the feel of his hairy chest against her back and the gentleness of his touch as he slipped his arms around her. With her eyes closed and her lips puckered, she twisted to meet his lips. As he caressed her tenderly, her interest in nature quickly shifted from outside to inside.

The following spring, Earl was born, and life took on new meaning for both of them. With the arrival of a baby, they now had a purpose other than their own survival and their own well-being. They worked together to give the baby the best care possible in their primitive environment. Together they watched him grow and develop. They shared the joy watching him learn to crawl and then stand and take his first steps.

Then Abby came along, and again there was a renewed sense of purpose and responsibility. They both wanted the best for their children. They both knew, although they seldom discussed it, that someday they would have to expose the children to the real world. They couldn't go on hiding forever. And both knew that when that time came, life would change drastically for all four of them. They both knew that, but neither one had a plan as to how or when that would take place. The consequences were too unthinkable! Jasper always said he would rather die than go back to prison. But somehow, the children had to become part of society.

Now it was happening without any plan at all! How and where it would all end, nobody knew. But Michelle knew their lives would never be the same again. The forces were already in motion. It couldn't be stopped. They would just have to take one day at a time. She heard one of the children take a deep breath and let it out.

She wondered if Jasper was still breathing. Had she done the right thing? She had just walked out and left him there to die alone! How could she have done such a thing? She believed that a marriage was sacred and was for life. Now, she was actually running off with another man—her high school boyfriend, nonetheless! But she had no other choice. This was for the safety of her children. What else could she have done? She heard the refrigerator start running again. Her mind was running nonstop.

17

Roger glanced over his shoulder at Earl, who was leaning against the back of the driver's seat in George's pickup as they pulled out of the driveway. *I wish Michelle would make him sit down and fasten his seatbelt. He's got to get used to it sooner or later.* Earl seemed to be intrigued by the array of lighted numbers, letters, and symbols on the instrument panel. *That instrument panel must be as mystifying as his future. He understands very little of either.* But by the time they were several miles into the blackness of the countryside, he was leaning against his mother as his eyelids gradually closed. Abby was already sleeping in her mother's arms. Roger smiled as he tinkered with the CD player. *Those children obviously have no concept that they are running for their lives.* Neither child stirred as George stopped at a mailbox to drop Michelle's letters.

"Tell me more about Jasper's brother." George took a backward glance as he pulled away from the mailbox.

"His name is Harold," Michelle spoke softly. "He's a businessman in Philadelphia. He gives a lot of money to Jasper. That's about all I know."

"You said he likes to keep his hands clean." Roger looked back at Michelle.

"Yeah," Michelle agreed. "I don't think he's a criminal."

"Other than aiding a fugitive," Roger added.

"Do you know what kind of business he has?" George glanced in the rearview mirror.

"No, I don't."

"And you never met him?" George seemed to have a lot of questions. "You don't know what he looks like?"

"No. Why?"

"Is he older or younger than Jasper?"

"Older. I believe maybe ten years or so. So I guess he'd be about sixty. Why all these questions about Harold?"

"Well, I just think that he's somebody we need to be concerned about." George paused. "Obviously, he's a man with resources and connections to the underworld. He's got a good life and a reputation to protect. He doesn't want anybody to connect him to what was going on here at Thrush Creek. He could be as dangerous as Chief Miller. And we wouldn't recognize him if we met him face-to-face."

"I see what you mean." Michelle seemed to be replaying George's comments in her mind. "I just never thought of him as a dangerous person. But I guess he is. He sure has a lot to lose."

"And even more dangerous because we wouldn't recognize him," George added.

"So what do you suggest we do about him?" Michelle sounded concerned.

"I guess there's not much we can do," George responded thoughtfully. "God has brought you through so much already. I'm sure he'll continue to watch over you."

Roger folded his arms and leaned back against the headrest. He was no longer interested in where this conversation was going.

"I'm sure he will," Michelle's voice faded. "We just have to be vigilant."

The morning sun was lighting a clear blue sky by the time they stopped outside Lock Haven for the children's first McDonald's experience. "I'll take the children to a booth," Michelle said as

Roger opened the door. "You guys just go and order something for us."

"What do they like?" George turned to Michelle.

"It's no use giving them a choice. This is all completely foreign to them. Just get us some Egg McMuffins."

As George got in line to order, Roger noticed Earl prancing, so he volunteered to take him along to the men's room, never considering that this too was a completely new experience for the boy. When they returned, Earl excitedly skipped toward the booth and called out, "Mommy, there was a thing on the wall like a really big egg shell, and Roger peed in it!" Roger could feel his face turning red. He heard guests at surrounding tables snickering as Michelle instructed her son to keep his voice down.

The fast-food breakfast proved to be a hit with the kids, and soon they were all back in the truck reviewing the event. "Maybe we should reconsider our decision to take the children along into the outfitting stores," Roger suggested. "We don't want anything to happen that would attract undue attention."

"They go where I go," Michelle insisted. "I don't want to shelter them from this modern world any longer. Besides, we'll be buying clothes and PFDs and things to fit them. They need to be there."

"Well, they have to keep their voices down." Roger eyed Michelle sternly.

"They will," Michelle sounded confident.

The children were awed by the busy highways, overpasses, and wide variety of buildings as they made their way into Lock Haven. Their excitement was contagious, and Roger found himself pointing out all kinds of things he felt the children should notice. Before they got out of the truck at the first outfitter, Michelle instructed the children, "Stay right with me all the time. Don't touch anything. And keep your voices down so other people can't hear what you're saying."

The five filed into the store and meandered up and down the aisles stocked with all kinds of clothes and equipment. They found a red life jacket for Earl and a lavender-and-white one for Abigail. They picked up two large dry bags and two smaller ones, water shoes, two short canoe paddles, and a variety of other items. Roger grinned at the way the children followed their mother like ducklings, grabbing her hand and getting her to bend over every time they wanted to say something. These were not the kind of children he was used to. At the checkout, Roger pulled a wad of cash out of his pocket, counted off seven fifty-dollar bills, and handed them to the clerk. The clerk examined each one carefully, eyed Roger suspiciously, and then gave Roger his change. George and Roger stowed their purchases in the back of the pickup, and they were off to the next outfitter.

They were in the camping department looking at tents when Roger sensed that someone was watching him. He glanced around and noticed a gray-haired gentleman observing them from the next aisle. At the same time, Michelle brushed against Roger's arm and said softly, "We're being watched." They proceeded to select a family-sized tent and continued their shopping. Then they headed to the checkout, with the tent, rain gear, and miscellaneous other items in their cart. Roger noticed the gray-haired gentleman loitering near the exit. He tried to be a little more discreet in handling his wad of cash. As they stowed their things, the gray-haired man found his way to his car, a white Buick LeSabre.

"Who is that guy?" Roger studied Michelle's face.

"I don't know." Michelle seemed puzzled. "But he looks friendly. He smiled at me and the children."

"He sure was keeping his eye on us." George glanced at the Buick.

"Let's get out of here." Roger patted Earl on the rear as he opened the truck door for the children. "We're on our way to wild adventure on the West Branch of the Susquehanna!"

After pulling out onto the street, George glanced in the mirror. "He's following us." George sounded concerned. "The guy in the white Buick is following us."

"Maybe he just happened to be going the same way we are," Michelle reasoned.

"Maybe." But he didn't sound convinced; at every turn, the white Buick followed.

"Who could it be?" Roger turned to look out the back window. "Why is he following us?"

"I don't know," Michelle replied. "But I don't think he's anybody we need to worry about."

"Could it be Bobby?" Roger turned to Michelle with raised eyebrows.

"It's not Bobby!" Michelle shook her head.

"How do you know? You said you never met Bobby."

"This guy doesn't have the eyes of a criminal. This guy is a friendly, law-abiding old man."

"I wouldn't want to guess how old he is," George observed. "He has gray hair, but he appears to be in very good shape, physically."

"And he does look friendly," Roger admitted. "But looks can be deceiving. Do you think Chief Theodore has the eyes of a criminal?"

"Okay. You've got a point." Michelle still didn't sound very concerned.

Before getting onto Route 220, George deliberately made a wrong turn and headed away from the highway. The white Buick followed. Then George pulled into a parking lot, turned around, and headed back toward Route 220. The Buick followed the whole procedure. It followed them from Route 220 to Interstate 80. It followed them west on I80, up the exit ramp at Snow Shoe, and across the mountain roads to Karthaus.

George drove slowly across the bridge at Karthaus as Roger examined the river with wide eyes. "Wow, stupid me!" Roger suddenly realized something he'd overlooked. "I never thought about checking the water level! It's too late in the season to be canoeing this section of the river. Look at it! I've never seen it this low."

"I think it looks doable." Michelle sounded encouraging. "If we have to carry, we get out and carry. After all, we're not out here for the canoeing, we want to get away, remember? Low water means fewer people on the river. That's a good thing."

They drove on through the small town of Karthaus, turned left, and followed Route 879 past Frenchville. Then they made another left turn onto a narrow winding road that took them down to the river, then right onto a gravel road that followed the river a short distance to the Deer Creek canoe access area. The white Buick followed at a distance and pulled over into a small parking area on a knoll more than hundred feet away. There were no other vehicles and no other people anywhere in sight.

George and Roger got the canoes off the truck as the gentleman stood, leaning against the side of his car, with the warm sun beaming down on his gray hair. Michelle and Roger got busy filling their new dry bags with clothes and supplies while the children ran around exploring the area.

"Aren't you concerned about the kids wandering around with that guy standing over there watching us like a hawk?" Roger eyed Michelle.

"He doesn't frighten me at all." Michelle smiled.

"You act like you know something about him. What is it? Who do you think he is?"

"Well, I know you won't agree with this," Michelle paused and glanced at Roger. "But I'm thinking he might be a guardian angel."

"You're right," Roger shot back. "I don't agree with that. Don't be so naive!"

After the bags were filled and sealed, George opened a cooler of drinks and nutritious snacks they had brought along for this occasion. The children suddenly realized they were hungry and thirsty. While munching on snacks, Roger and Michelle started getting things packed into the canoes. "I think it will work best if you and Abby take my canoe," Roger suggested. "Earl and I can take the seventeen-footer."

"You're the captain," Michelle nodded. "Whatever you think best."

He studied the two canoes. "We'll try to put most of the weight in the seventeen-footer." They laid two large bags behind the bow seat in each canoe and stood one small bag upright in each bow to compensate for the weight difference between the child in the bow and the adult in the stern. Food containers, water jugs, and other equipment were stowed in the remaining space. Roger had his sixteen-foot canoe equipped with D-rings on the floor, so all the cargo could be roped firmly in place. The seventeen-footer was not equipped with D-rings, so Roger put a tether on each item and attached it to a thwart. If the boat capsized, things could fall out but stay connected to it.

"You got everything in there?" George seemed surprised.

"I think so." Roger did a quick mental review.

"And you've got the duffel bag with all the extra cash." Michelle flashed a smile at George.

"I'll keep it safe." George smiled back at her. "Do you want any more out of it before you shove off?"

"No. We still have about a thousand. That's much more than we need out here."

"If we're out here much more than a week," Roger added, "I'll have to walk to town and buy some more food. But other than that, we shouldn't need any money at all."

George and Roger carried the loaded canoes the sixty-foot distance down the steep slope to the water's edge as Michelle got the children into their PFDs. George gave hugs to everyone as they got into their boats, and when they were ready, he gave each boat a little shove. His heart was pounding, and it wasn't just from carrying the boats down the slope. He stood on a large rock that stuck out into the river and watched as Michelle and

Roger instructed the youngsters on how to use a canoe paddle. He checked his watch—12:08. He continued gazing down the river as they slowly began their journey into the wilderness and the gray-haired gentleman watched from above.

18

After the canoes had vanished from sight, George climbed slowly up the steep slope to his truck. The peaceful scene in his mind, of two canoes quietly heading into the freedom of the outdoor world, was quite a paradox to what he was feeling inside. Anytime now, this person called Bobby would be discovering that Michelle was missing. Then, as Jasper had put it, "all hell would break loose." As he stowed the cooler with the leftover snacks in the back seat, the gray-haired man got into his Buick. George drove out the gravel road and pulled onto the blacktop, with the white Buick trailing several hundred feet behind.

As he led the Buick across the winding mountain roads toward Snow Shoe, George wondered, *If this guy really is a guardian angel, why is he following me instead of Michelle and the children?* He had his doubts about Michelle's theory and felt that Roger was right in his assertion that Michelle was being naive by allowing her youngsters to roam so freely in his presence. Yet if this guy intended to do any harm, he had certainly passed up his best opportunity at Deer Creek. So if he meant no harm and he wasn't an angel, who was he? Someone who likes to keep his hands clean? Could it be that he somehow knew about the duffel bag hidden behind the driver's seat? *Maybe I need a guardian angel more than Michelle and the children do*, George thought as he merged onto Interstate 80 with the white Buick still in his mirror. George began wondering how long the man had been following them. Was he watching them before they noticed him in the store? Could he have followed them all the way from Thrush Glen?

As he had planned, George exited onto Route 150 and headed for State College. There he would visit a woodworking machinery dealer and get a quote on a radial-arm saw, just in case he needed an alibi for his trip. Somewhere on 150, between Bellefonte and State College, George realized that the man in the Buick was no longer tailing him.

Arriving home around three thirty, George immediately took the duffel bag into the house and hid it in the corner of a closet, with a blanket thrown over it. Then he went out to his shop to try to get some work done on the mahogany vanities he was building. As he passed through his office, he checked his answering machine—three messages from Mrs. Faulkner. Around five o'clock, he took a break and phoned Rick to report on the trip.

"Don't tell me any more," Rick responded after hearing that they had arrived safely. "I'm sure Chief Theodore will be around sooner or later, looking for Roger. I want to be able to honestly say that I don't know where he is. I'm not a very good liar."

"Okay. But I have to tell you to be on the lookout for a gray-haired man in a white Buick LeSabre."

"Why must I be on the lookout for a gray-haired man?"

"We don't know who he is. But he followed us from the outfitter to the river, and he followed me part way home. He didn't do or say anything to us. He just watched."

"So what am I supposed to do if I see a suspicious-looking gray-haired man in a white Buick LeSabre?"

"He's not suspicious-looking. He looks quite ordinary and very friendly."

"So what am I supposed to do if I see an ordinary gray-haired man in a white Buick?"

"I don't know. Just help us figure out who he is and why he's watching us."

"Okay. If I see him, I'll ask him."

"Sure, try the direct approach. Who knows, it might work."

"Hey, I'd like to get out of here and go for a bike ride before Chief Theodore comes around."

"Okay, see ya. Have a nice ride."

"See ya."

Rick was just getting his motorcycle out of the garage when a township police cruiser pulled in the driveway. The door opened, and Chief Theodore Miller strolled toward Rick. "Hi, Rick. How you doing?"

"Hi, Chief. I'm doing fine. I was just getting ready to take the Harley out for a spin."

"So I see. Well, it sure is a nice evening for a bike ride," Chief Miller responded pleasantly. "I don't want to hold you up. I just thought I'd drop in and see how Roger's doing. It seems like a long time since I talked with him." The chief did a pretty good job of covering his anxiety, but Rick sensed that something wasn't quite normal.

"Well," Rick paused as he rested the bike against the kickstand, "he's not here right now. I don't know when he'll be back."

"Oh. Where did he go?" The chief studied Rick's face.

"I don't know, sir." Rick glanced at the policeman's shoes. "He wasn't here when I came home from work. His canoe is gone. So he must have gone canoeing. He didn't ask me to pick him up. So I assume he probably took someone else along."

"Are you telling me your friend just went off on a canoeing expedition and didn't tell you where he was going?" The chief was looking straight into Rick's eyes. "I find that hard to believe."

"We don't always tell each other everything." Rick looked back at the chief. He could feel his face turning red as he continued, "We usually talk about our plans, but not always. It's not like we're a married couple."

"When did you last see him?"

"Well, I guess last evening." Rick tried to sound uncertain. "I didn't look in his room this morning. During the summer, I usually leave for work before he gets out of bed."

"You mind if we go inside and take a look around?" Chief Miller turned toward the house.

"No, sir, I don't mind," Rick answered, trying to be accommodating. "Is Roger in some kind of trouble?"

"Oh, no!" The chief followed Rick toward the house. "I just think it's mighty strange for him to go off canoeing and not say a word to you about it."

As Rick walked by the cruiser, he noticed Roger's walking stick lying on the back seat. He remembered that the stick had Roger's name on it. So he knew that Chief Miller knew that Roger had been to the cottage. He had to convince the chief that he knew nothing about this. More importantly, he had to conceal his knowledge of the chief's involvement.

The chief looked around carefully as they passed through the kitchen into the library. He quickly spied the video cassette lying on top of the VCR. "You guys like Winnie the Pooh?" he asked.

"Oh yeah! That's our favorite movie." Rick forced a laugh. "Actually, that's Roger's. I don't know why it's out here. When you live with a schoolteacher, you never know what's going to show up around the apartment."

"I think you've had children here."

"Children?" Rick tried to sound surprised. "Are you telling me that Roger is having children in the apartment while I'm away at work? Is that what this is all about?"

"You let me ask the questions," the chief replied, getting face-to-face. "If you care about your friend, tell me the truth. Where did he go?"

"I don't know!" Rick declared, staring straight into the chief's badge. "He's been talking about taking a trip to the Allagash

Wilderness in Maine. But he could never find enough people to go along."

"I'm going to find out where he went," the chief sat down at Roger's desk. "So you may as well just tell me."

"I think he's got some information on the Allagash in here," Rick opened the file drawer. He pulled out a folder and handed it to the chief.

The chief started leafing through the information. "That's not where he went!" the chief declared angrily. "His maps are still in here!" He flung the folder across the room.

"Well, sir, I was only trying to guess," Rick said sheepishly. "I told you I don't know."

The chief booted up Roger's computer and started rummaging through files. Rick hoped that Michelle had erased her letter to the FBI and state police. "Don't you need a search warrant for that?" Rick asked as he watched over the chief's shoulder.

"What's the password for his e-mail?" Chief Miller asked in return.

"I don't know, sir."

"You know it's against the law to lie to a police officer," the chief threatened him. "I could take this computer down to the station and have someone analyze everything on it. So you may as well just give me his password and save us both a lot of hassle."

"I don't know his password!" Rick declared with all honesty. "I told you, we're not a married couple. We don't share everything."

"You're withholding information from me!" the chief shouted. "Tell me where Roger is!"

"I don't know, sir." The words didn't come out quite as firmly as Rick intended. "Do you want me to call 911 and report that he's missing?"

"No!" the chief snapped. "I'm handling it! You don't need to call 911!"

"Well, I'm going to have to call somebody if you keep tearing my house apart."

"I'm sorry." The chief was obviously trying to sound sincere. But it wasn't working. "I get a little upset when I know that someone is not being honest with me."

"Sir, you haven't told me why you're all of a sudden so interested in Roger's whereabouts," Rick replied calmly. "This all started out as a friendly visit. Now it's turned into some kind of investigation. I suggest you leave and don't come back till you have a search warrant."

"I need to check his room yet." Chief Miller headed for the stairs. "You invited me in. I'm not leaving till I've finished my investigation. If you don't cooperate, you'll find yourself in a heap of trouble."

Rick followed the chief up the stairs to Roger's room. After the room was thoroughly ransacked, Rick asked, "Sir, do you see any camping gear?"

"No. Is this where he keeps it?"

"Yes, sir. Obviously, he went camping—canoe camping."

"Where?" the chief demanded.

"I don't know, sir," Rick insisted. "But the sooner you get out there and start tracking him, the sooner you'll find him."

"Okay," the chief agreed reluctantly, heading down the stairs. "But I'll be back. You haven't seen the last of me yet."

As the police cruiser pulled out of the drive, Rick was tempted to hop on his bike and follow to see where he headed next. But better judgment prevailed; he turned and pushed the bike into the garage. He was no longer in the mood for a bike ride anyway.

19

The crystal river reflected the broiling heat of the noon-day sun as Roger and Michelle picked their way between rocks and sandbars, always trying to find the best water. Roger planted his paddle on the river bottom and leaned on it, trying to force his boat forward across a bed of pebbles and small stones. "I guess we're stuck." He wiped the sweat from his face then stepped out into the shallow water. Grabbing the bowline, he towed the boat across the shallow with Earl still seated in the bow.

Michelle found a slightly deeper channel a bit to the right and scraped through without a problem. "Ahoy, Captain, how's the water over there?" she called with a smirk. A faint echo bounced off the hillside.

"We need more water than you do. We have more weight, plus this boat has a keel on the bottom and that one doesn't."

"Excuses, excuses," Michelle quipped. But it wasn't long till she was wading in the water, towing her boat across another shallow area. Roger studied her demeanor. *She seems to be having a good time in spite of everything.* They were in and out of their boats repeatedly as they slowly made their way down the canyon between tree-covered mountains. After about an hour, they stopped by a pebbled beach, had some snacks, and let the children spend some time playing in the shallow water.

Michelle took Abby's hand and waded out to the deeper water so Abby could get the feel of floating with a PFD. "See, it holds you up so you don't go under the water." She coaxed the little girl in deeper and deeper.

Earl didn't need any coaxing. When he saw what Abby was doing, he was right there to join the fun. "Look, Mom, I can swim," he said as he thrashed about with his arms.

"He's splashing me!" Abby reached for her mother.

The children seemed to be having a lot of fun with their mother, but Roger glanced at his watch and called out, "We better keep moving. We still have a long way to go."

Refreshed, they climbed back in their boats and pressed on. Earl was getting the knack of using a paddle and actually helped propel the canoe forward from time to time. But Abby's paddle seemed to create more drag than propulsion, and every now and then Michelle had to retrieve it from the river. She finally stowed the child's paddle and sounded just a little exasperated as she told Abby, "You don't need to paddle anymore. You can rest while I paddle."

"Maybe we should switch partners," Roger suggested. "Earl can paddle pretty well when he puts his mind to it. You might have to remind him every once in a while. But he's a good helper."

"Abby, you want to go in Roger's boat?"

The little girl agreed enthusiastically but insisted on keeping her paddle. As soon as Earl got settled on the front of Michelle's canoe, he started demonstrating his newly acquired paddling skills. But his arms soon tired, and he had to take a break. Michelle started teaching him the basics of reading the water. She showed him how to recognize the difference between shallow water and deep water by looking at the waves on the surface. She pointed out the location of underwater rocks that were not actually visible, but were only detectable by the turbulence they created. It was a bit much for a five-year-old to take in. But Earl was an eager learner, and soon he was offering his opinion on where the best water might be.

Abby seemed delighted to be canoeing with Roger and made a renewed effort to get her paddle going in the right direction. But she just couldn't seem to master it. Roger directed her attention to a number of colorful dragonflies that were darting about and occasionally hovering near the boat. He suggested that if she left her paddle rest with the handle sticking over the edge of the boat, a dragonfly might come and land on it. The suggestion worked, and soon she was sitting quietly, waiting for a dragonfly to land on her paddle.

Roger could see that the little girl was getting tired. He positioned a floatation cushion on top of the dry bags behind her so she could put her head down to rest. She curled up on the seat, with her head on the cushion, and soon she was sound asleep. Roger managed to get out and drag the boat across several shallow areas without waking her. After a short nap, she perked up and was ready to go again.

Eventually Michelle pointed to a small delta from a feeder stream. "Just ahead on river left," she shouted in Roger's direction. "That looks like a good place to get out and stretch. I think the kids need a break. And I could use one too."

"Okay," Roger called out as both canoes turned toward shore. As soon as they were out of their boats, the children seemed to have a renewed burst of energy. With snacks in hand, they collected colorful pebbles in the feeder stream.

Earl had quite a collection of pebbles laid out on a flat rock. But they began losing their sheen as the relentless, hot sun quickly dried them. "This one's still shiny," he picked up a dark amber-colored pebble nearly two inches long.

"Let me see that," Roger said as Earl held the pebble in the sunlight. "That one's different. The light is shining right through it." Roger took the pebble and held it to the sun, so Earl could see the glowing amber color on the shaded side of the stone.

"Is it gold?" Earl couldn't hide his excitement.

"No. It's not gold." Roger suddenly felt like a teacher again. "But I don't know what it is. It might be jasper."

Earl stared at Roger as if he had just said something that made no sense at all.

"Jasper is a gemstone," Roger explained. "It has the same name as your daddy."

"Can I take it home?"

"Sure. When we get home, we'll figure out what it is."

"Whatever it is, it seems to take a polish." Michelle commented as she brushed up beside Roger. "It's so smooth and shiny, almost as though someone already polished it. Is jasper found in this area?"

"I don't know." Roger handed the translucent pebble to Michelle. "It may be some other gemstone made up of quartz."

She examined it carefully, then handed it back to Earl. "Do you want to keep that in your pocket?"

As Earl slipped the pebble into his pocket, Roger glanced at his watch. "It's after three o'clock, and we haven't passed Rolling Stone yet. It usually takes only two hours to go from Deer Creek to Rolling Stone. So we're not making much headway."

"What's Rolling Stone?" Earl looked puzzled.

"It's just a place where a bridge crosses the river," Roger explained. "There's nothing else there, just a big bridge."

"Okay, children," Michelle ordered merrily. "Get in your boats!"

As they got underway, Michelle turned to Roger. "How far do you intend to go today?"

"After we get beyond Rolling Stone, we'll start looking for a good place to set up camp."

A little before four o'clock, they rounded a bend and viewed a long span of concrete high above the riverbed. "I'm a little surprised that I don't see a white Buick up there." Roger gazed at the bridge as they slowly made their way toward it.

"Just because we don't see him doesn't mean he's not up there somewhere," Michelle replied without really focusing on the bridge.

"That's true. But he didn't seem to be hiding the fact that he was watching us. I just wish I knew what the heck he was up to."

"There sure isn't much traffic on that bridge. I haven't seen one vehicle yet."

"That's normal. I hardly ever see anything crossing this bridge. It's kind of out here in the middle of nowhere. That's why I dread the thought that he, or anybody else, could be up there watching us and we wouldn't know it. That guy has been on my mind ever since we saw him in the store this morning."

Abby turned toward Roger. "God will take care of us."

"Good." Roger felt speechless. *You can't argue with a child about something like that.*

Earl was awestruck as they glided quietly past the tall concrete pillar supporting the bridge. As they paddled away from the bridge, the deep pool gradually became a shallow bar of pebbles and rocks. They bumped and scraped their way through without wading. But progress continued to be slow and difficult as they made their way downstream, occasionally dragging their boats across the shallows.

When they were well out of sight from the bridge, they began making frequent stops to explore grassy benches and hemlock groves that looked like they might provide a suitable campsite. But there always turned out to be something about the site that didn't quite suit Roger. He figured if they were going to be there for a while, they should have a really good campsite. So they would get back in their canoes and press on, looking for the perfect campsite. Finally, around five thirty, they found a grassy bench on river right that Roger deemed suitable.

"It's fine with me." Michelle sighed. "I'm ready to stop. It's been a long day for the children and for me."

Michelle and Roger started carrying dry bags up to the campsite. The children helped with some of the lighter items, like PFDs and paddles. When they had most of the weight out of the boats, Michelle and Roger each grasped an end of one canoe and carried it to the campsite, then returned for the other. Michelle relaxed and the children played while Roger set up the tents between two large hemlocks. The tents were far enough back on the bench that they were not visible from the river.

Finally Roger set up his camping stove, and by seven o'clock, he had a pot of beef stew ready. The children had already been begging for food, and Earl suggested that Roger should have brought his microwave along. The stew disappeared rapidly, along with bread, cookies, applesauce, and a variety of other items. Afterwards, Earl helped Roger wash the dishes while Abby went into the tent with Michelle and watched her spread the sleeping bags out on their pads.

It didn't take much coaxing to get the kids settled into their sleeping bags. Roger sat on a log, beside the tents, enjoying the quietness of the evening as Michelle tucked her children in. He could hear muffled voices coming from the tent as Michelle prayed with her youngsters.

Eventually, Michelle emerged from the tent and sat down beside Roger. "They're sound asleep already," she half-whispered.

"Sorry if I created some undue concern about the man in the white Buick." Roger watched Michelle out of the corner of his eye.

"Not a problem. Did you ever hear the term 'childlike faith'? They've got it. They're not afraid."

"Well, I'll try to watch what I say." Roger didn't want the children thinking that he was afraid.

"I'm really tired." Michelle took a deep breath and let it out. "I'm not used to working like that anymore."

"You're not? I thought you would have had a pretty tough life, these last seven years."

"Not really. Jasper didn't just call me his princess. He tried to treat me like one. He insisted on doing any chores that required physical exertion. The laundry was the toughest thing I did. And he often helped with that."

"Just how did you do laundry?"

"First we'd soak it in a bathtub of soapy water. Then we'd get down on our knees and agitate it a little bit by hand." Michelle's hands were going through the familiar motions. "We'd scrub any areas that were extra dirty, then drain the tub and rinse the clothes in fresh water, then wring the water out by hand, and hang them in the attic to dry."

"Jeepers-creepers, that sounds like quite a chore."

"We didn't wash our clothes any oftener than absolutely necessary," Michelle said with a chuckle. "And they didn't have to come out spotless."

"I'll do my best to treat you like a princess since that's what you're used to now." Roger grinned.

"Don't worry." Michelle bumped him with her shoulder. "I can still pull my own weight."

"Well, I don't expect we'll have many days like today. From here on, things should get a little easier."

"I hope so. I'm tired. I'm going to bed."

"Me too." Roger started putting his one arm around behind her to give her a good-night hug. But before his hand made any contact, she was on her feet and walking toward her tent. Roger sat there, stunned. Had she sensed the hug coming and deliberately avoided it? Or had she simply decided to go to bed without even thinking about a good-night hug?

20

A cardinal was singing, high in the hemlock tree and the melodious voice of a white-throated sparrow was ringing out from the mountainside as the morning light expanded around the sleepy campsite. Roger sat up in his sleeping bag and listened as the music continued. A blue jay started its raucous warning call as he crawled out of his tent and filled his lungs with the freshness of the morning. A half dozen other blue jays joined in the rowdy chorus as he gathered sticks and got a campfire started. He had a pot of coffee ready by the time Michelle emerged from her tent with smiling eyes and her hair in a single long braid. She stood up and stretched her sore muscles.

"Good morning. Can I get you some coffee?" Roger offered as he stepped toward Michelle, extending his arms.

"No, thanks." Michelle sidestepped the hug. "I quit drinking coffee. I'm used to a pace of life that doesn't require caffeine."

"What's wrong? You gave Rick and George each a big hug. But I get nothing. What's with that?"

"Those hugs didn't mean anything. I was just being polite. But between you and me, a hug is much more than a common courtesy. And I'm not ready to resume our relationship where we left off in high school. At this point, I don't even know what's become of my husband."

"I'm sorry. I wasn't being very sensitive," Roger said sincerely. Then with a grin he added, "I just wanted to be polite."

Michelle laughed and returned his smile. Roger helped himself to a cup of coffee then started getting ready to fry bacon and eggs. "You think the children will be up soon? Should I start cooking breakfast?"

"They're awake." Michelle glanced at her tent. "I suppose they'll be out here begging before it's ready." She was right. The children pranced around with empty plates in their hands while Roger broke eggs into a bowl. The aroma of the campfire and frying bacon permeated the fresh morning air, accentuating everyone's ravenous appetite. Platefuls of scrambled eggs and bacon disappeared like snowflakes on a sunny sidewalk.

After they were through eating, Roger brought a kettle of water from the river and placed over the fire. "I'm warming some water to wash up and shave. But I'll have more than I need for myself. If you need any warm water, just help yourself."

"I'm taking the children down to the river to brush their teeth." Michelle waved a toothbrush. "When we get back, I'll wash the dishes."

Abby did her best to help with the dishes while Earl and Roger combed the surrounding area for firewood.

About midmorning, Roger strapped on the revolver Jasper had given him. "Keep the children close to the camp. I'm going up along the river and to do a little target practice."

"Okay. If you must." Michelle didn't try to hide her adverse feelings.

"I must. I've never fired a revolver before. If this thing is going to be of any use to us, I have to be able to hit what I'm aiming at."

"I just don't like guns."

"Don't worry. I won't be shooting this direction," Roger added as he headed out. About fifty yards away, he found a dead tree trunk that had been broken off about six feet above the ground. It was about eighteen inches in diameter and partly rotten. It would be an ideal target. All he had to do was mark a bull's eye. He would be able to see where the bullets hit the tree and see how far from the bull's eye they were, assuming he could hit the tree. He picked an oval-shaped leaf from a small tree and found a sturdy twig. Then he poked the twig through the leaf and jammed it into a crack in the tree trunk.

He went back about a dozen paces, turned, and looked at his target. He cringed upon realizing that he had created a target the size of a man with a bull's eye the size of a man's heart. He took the revolver in one hand, cocked the hammer, aimed at the leaf, and squeezed the trigger. The blast jarred his wrist, and the bullet didn't even hit the tree. He cocked the hammer again and grasped his right wrist with his left hand. He aimed carefully and squeezed the trigger. The shot went a foot high and to the right. The third shot was a little closer, but still high. The forth went about a foot low, and the fifth just grazed the left edge of the tree. The final shot hit about two inches to the right of the leaf.

Then, with the empty gun, he practiced drawing, cocking the hammer, and aiming as quickly as possible. As he was practicing, a single-engine airplane came, flying up the river gorge. Roger watched as it made a half circle around the campsite and headed back down the river. He turned his attention back to his target. After considerable practice, it still seemed to take a long time to draw the gun from the holster, cock the hammer, and hold it steady on the target. Eventually, he reloaded the gun and took six more shots, starting each time with the gun in the holster. The results were worse than the first six. His hands were shaking, his heart was pounding, and his ears were ringing. *Enough practice for one day*, he thought as he reloaded the gun.

Roger felt like an old Western cowboy as he came swaggering into the camp, with his gun hanging at his hip. Michelle met him with raised eyebrows. "Did you see that airplane?"

"Yeah. Why?"

"What do you think they were doing?"

"Sightseeing, I suppose."

"You don't think it's unusual that they just came this far, circled our campsite, and went back?" Michelle scanned the flight pattern.

Roger shrugged. "Probably coincidence. To them, we were just a crazy family out here canoe camping."

"I don't know. To me it seemed like they were deliberately checking us out." Michelle seemed a little uneasy. "But I guess there's nothing we can do about it now. So why worry?"

After lunch, Roger busied himself creating more comfortable seating while Michelle watched the kids playing in the water. He placed a flat rock so it sloped toward a tree trunk, which leaned slightly away, forming a reclining chair. When he covered it with a sleeping pad, it became quite comfortable—comfortable enough that he dozed off before Michelle and the youngsters returned.

"Here, try this," Roger offered as he arose from his nap. "It's a special lounge chair for the princess."

"Not bad," Michelle leaned back against pad. "This is really comfortable."

"Soon I'll have us set up with all the comforts of home." Roger puffed up his chest.

"Not quite." Michelle grinned and shook her head. "Back in our little cottage, we at least had a toilet. Now I have to squat over a hole in the ground. And I guess I'm actually homeless. My life hasn't really improved, has it?"

"Don't blame me." Roger raised both hands. "It's not my fault we had to run off into the wilderness. I'm trying to make things as comfortable as I can."

"I'm not blaming you." Michelle smiled. "I appreciate everything you're doing for us. Really, I do." She could hear the children playing under the hemlocks as she and Roger continued their discussion.

"So tell me something." Roger sat down on the log, propped his elbows on his knees and turned his warm brown eyes toward her. "How did you get that hardened criminal to treat you like a princess?"

"Well, I just decided to be the kind of person that he would appreciate." Michelle gazed straight ahead. She couldn't look into Roger's eyes while thinking about Jasper. "Actually, that makes it sound way too simple. It wasn't that easy at first. When he locked me in the attic and went down to clean up his crime scene, I went ballistic. But when I settled down and got my head together, I had a little time to think. I didn't know what he was planning to do with me. I assumed he was planning to rape me or kill me, maybe both. Or maybe he had no real plan at all, but the outcome would still be the same. My life was in jeopardy." She felt her eyes filling with tears and the warmth of Roger's eyes gazing at her.

"I had already seen that he was capable of being kind," Michelle continued. "So I figured my best option was to try to be a great companion, a person he would not want to harm. When he came back into the house, I started thanking him for the way he was taking care of me and trying to make me comfortable. Then somehow, we got to talking about his past. He told me about growing up in Philadelphia. It was apparent that he was a lonely, lonely man. I realized that what he really needed was somebody to talk to. I kept listening for opportunities to compliment him or express appreciation."

"You were always good at that."

"He grew up in a rough neighborhood. As a teenager, he got involved in a street gang. He told me about a prominent gang member named Joey. Joey raped Jasper's younger sister, Darlene. She was only fifteen. After that, Joey was bragging about it to other gang members and bad-mouthing Darlene. He called her a bitch. Jasper said, 'I just couldn't take it anymore. So I shot him!' That was his first murder. After that, he left Philadelphia and headed west. He knew that if he hung around, some other gang member would retaliate. But they told the police who did the shooting, then he was running from the police and the gang."

Roger listened intently as Michelle continued. "He justified himself by using the story from the Bible about King David's son, Absalom. He said, 'Look what Absalom did when his half-brother raped his sister, Tamar.'"

"So he thinks if it's in the Bible, it must be okay." Roger sounded a bit cynical.

"I don't know." Michelle cocked her head. "What stands out to me in that story is that after the half-brother, whatever his name is—"

"Amnon."

"Yeah." *He still knows the Bible.* "After Amnon raped Tamar, he hated her intensely. I don't know if that's a normal reaction or not. But it seemed to be the same thing with Joey and Darlene. So anyway, I figured that if Jasper raped me, my chances of survival would go way down. On the other hand, if we developed a consensual relationship, or better yet, one based on love, my chances of survival would improve."

Roger swallowed hard.

"I still didn't know for sure why he had abducted me. But it didn't seem likely that he would do it just to have someone to talk to although that's what he really needed. I knew that sooner or later his libido would kick in, and he would want to satisfy his sex drive. How I responded would ultimately determine my fate."

Roger stared at the ground, still listening intently.

"So I decided to try to truly love him, in spite of who he was. That wasn't easy at first. I didn't want to be in love with anybody except you, Roger. And he was the one keeping me from you. But I decided to look for the good in him and try to love him the way Christ loves us, no strings attached. Who knows, maybe that's why God allowed it to happen. Maybe that's what I was there for, to love him."

"How could a loving God come up with a plan like that?" Roger raised his eyes to meet hers.

"That's a question we can't answer." Michelle paused. "I was in a difficult situation, and I had to make the best of it. So I chose to love him. Of course, when I started treating him kindly, he wanted to get intimate. That was difficult for me. But he was patient. He never forced me. Whenever he would kiss me, I would close my eyes and pretend that it was you, with a beard."

"That's disgusting!"

"That's how I got him to treat me like a princess."

After a short uncomfortable pause, Roger asked. "So did Jasper go to prison for shooting Joey?"

"No, I don't think so. The police did catch him. But he provided information on the gang and got into the witness protection program. But he couldn't stay out of trouble. He got involved in other criminal activity and wound up in prison anyway. That's just the kind of person he was at that time."

"So why do you keep referring to him as your husband?"

"Because as far as I'm concerned, we were married—by common law, that is. We never said any vows or anything like that."

"Well, you wouldn't have to look at it that way. I guess I just hate thinking that you're actually married to someone else."

"Either I was married or I was living promiscuously. Maybe you prefer to think of me as a slut, rather than a married woman, or possibly a widow."

"No, I'd never call you a slut! But I think you just like to tell yourself you were married so you can justify whatever it was that you thought was promiscuous."

"You're contradicting yourself," Michelle countered as she analyzed his comments. "You really do prefer to think of me as a slut! To you, that's more acceptable than the fact that I'm married."

"I'm sorry if that's what I implied. That's not what I meant. I really respect you, and I feel bad for everything you've had to go through."

"What I had to go through was not as bad as you think. There was a very tender and loving side to Jasper. We spent a lot of evenings snuggled up on the porch swing, watching the sunset and listening to the wood thrushes and katydids. We brought each other a lot of happiness."

"Yeah, but…I really don't want to hear about that."

Why doesn't he want to hear about my good times with Jasper? "I'm sorry. I wasn't trying to make you jealous," Michelle said tenderly as she started getting out of her princess lounge chair. "I need to go check on the kids."

That evening, after the children were tucked into their sleeping bags and the bright moon was shining down on the river, Michelle said to Roger, "You stay here. I'm going down to the river to take a bath."

He watched longingly as she walked toward the river, carrying her towel and bag of toiletries, till she disappeared from view. His eyes never left the spot till her form gradually came into view, walking up the moonlit trail toward him. "Ah, that felt good," Michelle said as she lay back in her lounge chair. "I don't think I've done that since Earl was born."

"Are you telling me that Jasper actually let you out of his sight so you could go skinny dipping?"

"Oh, no!" Michelle laughed. "We always went together."

"So you were just doing what you always do."

"What do you mean?"

"You were using your sex appeal to get what you wanted."

21

The next day, Michelle was wading in the river with the children, enjoying the midmorning sunshine while Roger, wearing his revolver, was cutting firewood with a small bow saw. They all stopped and looked to the sky when they heard the sound of a small airplane. A yellow-and-white single-engine plane came, flying up the gorge. It banked hard to the left, making a 360-degree circle around the campsite, and then continued up the river. "That's the same plane we saw yesterday," Michelle shouted as she and the children approached Roger.

"I guess you were right." Roger looked serious. "Somebody is checking up on us."

"That can't be good."

"I think it's time we get out of here." Roger gazed solemnly downstream. "Time to move on down the river."

"How about if we move up the river?" Michelle raised her eyebrows.

"What?"

"Up the river. Not far, just right over there," she pointed across the river, "to the last place we had looked at. There we'll be under a thick cover of deciduous trees. They won't be able to see us from the air."

"Good thinking! Nobody moves upriver. If they're looking for us, they'll be looking downriver."

They headed back to the camp and were just about to start packing when the plane came buzzing down the river. It turned to the right, then banked to the left as it arced around the campsite, then straightened out, and continued down the river.

Michelle started rolling up sleeping bags and camp mats as Roger started packing up pots, kettles, and dishes. When the tents were emptied, Roger dismantled them and folded them up. Food, clothes, and equipment all had to be repacked. They stowed a few miscellaneous items in the canoes and carried them to the water's edge. Then they carried the heavier packs down and loaded the canoes.

Finally, Michelle put PFDs on the children, and they got underway. They pointed their boats into the current at a slight angle and ferried straight across the river. Then they all got out and waded in the shallow water near the shore as Michelle and Roger took the bow lines and towed the boats upstream several hundred yards.

They heaved the boats up onto the steep brush-covered bank and started carrying their stuff on up the slope, across the railroad track, and into the forest. Earl was intrigued by the railroad as Roger tried to describe a freight train. "You just wait. If we're here a few days, we may see one," he told the youngster. After the boats were made light enough, they carried them up the bank and across the tracks to the new campsite.

After a brief, cold lunch, they started the process of setting up camp all over again—finding the best locations for the tents and putting them up, selecting a spot for the fire and building a ring of stones, and finding objects to sit on. The children enjoyed exploring the new area and started gathering dry sticks for a fire.

"Mommy, look what I found!" Earl called as he came running to Michelle with something in his hand.

"A morel mushroom! Where did you find it?" she examined the mushroom.

"Over there," he said, pointing. "There's a whole bunch of 'em."

"Let's find something to put them in," Michelle said as she started unpacking the cookware. "We can have mushrooms for dinner this evening." When they were through, they had a small kettle three-quarters full of mushrooms.

That evening, Roger cooked up a batch of beef stroganoff from packets of freeze-dried mixture while Michelle sautéed the morel mushrooms in a frying pan over the campfire.

"We shouldn't do this." Roger grinned at Michelle.

"Why not?"

"The smell of this meal will draw people in from a ten mile radius."

"Well then, we'd better eat it before they get here."

By the time the dishes were washed and dried, daylight was beginning to fade. The children seemed ready to settle down for the night in their new home. So Michelle tucked them in their sleeping bags and rejoined Roger at the campfire. "I miss my princess lounge chair," she said as she sat down on a flotation cushion supported by a rock.

"I'd make you another one, but I don't have a tree leaning the right direction."

"So we just make the best of what we have. That's all we can ever do."

"I'm amazed that your five-year-old knows about morel mushrooms."

"Sometimes Jasper would bring in a bunch of mushrooms and make them for us. He took Earl along hunting mushrooms a few times, so he knows what to look for."

"Did Jasper normally do the cooking?"

"We shared that. But whenever he brought in food from the wild, he prepared it from beginning to end. It was like a special treat for us."

"What other wild foods did you eat?"

"Fish, lots of fish. Sometimes turkey and venison, squirrel, wild raspberries. Once in a while we ate dandelion. But the kids didn't care much for that."

"Well, I guess I can't compete with Jasper on that. I've never been a hunter. But I'll do my best to take care of you and the children in whatever way I can."

"Thanks, Roger. You're so kind. I've often wished that things would have turned out differently—that we could have just continued the relationship we had in high school."

"Michelle, I think about that all the time. I've never found anyone else like you."

"You had other girlfriends?"

"Yeah. I had a few girls in college. But I never fell in love. It was just physical."

"You never seemed like that type."

"What type?"

"To just get physical. You and I had a great relationship. We really loved each other. But you never insisted on getting physically intimate. You were a real gentleman!"

"That's because your dad was always with us."

"Not always. We had our private moments."

"I haven't forgotten."

Michelle didn't reply as her mind went back to a time when she and Roger stood by Penns Creek, locked in a long embrace while her father walked into the woods to relieve himself. She could still feel Roger's lips pressing against hers, almost as if it had happened just moments ago. And this was still the same Roger. He hadn't changed that much. He was still a great guy, just as George had said. And she realized that she still really loved him.

She had to say something. *But is this the right time? Right now, we're forced into the situation we're in. Maybe it would be better to wait. But the longer I wait, the more difficult it will be.*

After a brief pause, Michelle took a deep breath. "I really appreciate everything you're doing for us, Roger." She leaned forward, resting her elbows on her knees and looked straight into Roger's eyes. "But let me be clear about one thing. I'm not going to get involved in a romantic relationship with someone who doesn't share my belief in God—not now, not later."

"But you got involved with that criminal. That was okay?"

"Jasper, at least, believed in God. He believed that God loved him and forgave his sins."

"Well, he was quite the upstanding citizen now, wasn't he?" Roger sounded very sarcastic.

"Granted," Michelle continued, "he never found freedom from his criminal lifestyle. And as I see it, the only way he could have been freed from that was to turn himself in and go back to prison. For him, that was unthinkable. But he believed in God."

"Well, I'm not going to just say I believe something I don't really believe, just to satisfy someone else. That would be dishonest. And it would only create problems farther down the road for both of us. I have to believe what seems to me to be the truth."

"I appreciate your honesty. And I agree that you can't just say you believe something if you don't really believe it. But you can choose to believe something you don't understand."

"And if I don't believe, I'm worse than him."

"That's not what I said! You know this isn't about being good or bad. It's about what you believe. And you can choose to believe."

Roger didn't reply. Michelle could see that something was gnawing at him. Did he feel that she was rejecting him? Was he feeling insulted because she had willingly made love to a convicted criminal?

"I don't get it," Roger said after a long pause. "I just don't see how you could truly love a guy like that."

"A guy like what? Roger, you don't even know him at all."

"I don't know all his criminal history, but I know he was a fugitive, I know he abducted you." His fists tightened. "Isn't that bad enough? He didn't deserve you!"

"Jasper also had a very tender and loving side," Michelle spoke softly, trying to control her aggravation. "He wasn't all bad."

"The fact is he was a criminal, an escaped convict. And as I see it, you've been aiding and abetting a criminal. A fugitive!"

"I had no choice!"

"Just yesterday, you were telling me all about the choice you made."

"I chose to love him! I didn't choose to be in that situation!"

"I know what you used to believe about abstinence and the sanctity of marriage. I can't see how you just threw all that out the window to be with this criminal."

"I didn't throw it out the window! I told you, he was my husband. And you're so jealous, you're not thinking straight."

"I *am* jealous. I admit it. But that doesn't justify your behavior. Some people are willing to suffer or even die, standing up for what they believe. But apparently you're not one of them. When the going gets tough, you take the easy way out."

"I don't think you care a thing about what would have happened to me. You'd rather see me get raped than see me give my affections to someone else. It's all about you, Roger, isn't it? You don't really care what happens to me. You only care about how it makes you feel!"

There was a long silence. The campfire had become a heap of glowing embers, and tree frogs were beginning to sing. An owl hooted in the distance as a chilly breeze whisked through the forest canopy.

Finally, Roger cleared his throat. "I'm sorry," he said sincerely. "I'm being a jerk. You're right. I *am* so jealous I'm not thinking straight. But I *do* care about you, Michelle. I really do."

"I'm sorry if I said anything that hurt you." Michelle wiped her eyes with the back of her hand.

"And," Roger continued, "you are right in deciding to not get romantically involved with someone who doesn't share your core religious beliefs. That's a wise resolution."

"Thanks," Michelle said softly. "And you know that resolution doesn't have to exclude you. It's up to you."

The glowing embers slowly faded to black. Finally Roger stood up and unbuckled his gun belt. "I'm going to bed."

Michelle sat staring into the darkness, thinking about Roger's stinging comments. She understood his jealousy, but his comments also revealed a deeper concern for his own natural desires than for her feelings. If that attitude continued, it could lead to serious conflicts. Just how far could she trust Roger? Was she in more danger now than when she was with Jasper? She remembered the good times she had with Jasper. She longed to feel his strong arms around her once again. In spite of his character flaws, she loved him dearly. She had spent the last seven years with a man approximately twice her age. Now she was with a younger man, steamed up with testosterone and burning with jealousy. And now, he too had taken to wearing a gun.

22

In the soft glow of the morning light, Michelle lay in her sleeping bag enjoying the cheerful singing of the birds while she watched her children sleeping. The peaceful sound of the birds was being interrupted by harsh crackling as Roger broke up sticks for a campfire. As she lay there listening to the conflicting sounds, she remembered George's words: "You and your children will be safe with him. Absolutely safe!" But she assumed George had not seen the situation from her perspective. She also remembered the jealousy and selfishness she had seen in Roger just the evening before. She couldn't rely on what someone else thought of Roger. She had to act on her own judgment.

Eventually, Michelle zipped her tent open and poked her head out. There Roger stood by the fire, sipping his coffee. He looked gorgeous, except for the gun hanging low on his thigh like an old-time Western gunslinger. She pulled on a pair of jeans and a tee shirt and went out to the campfire.

"The fire feels pretty good this morning, doesn't it?" Roger said, holding his hands over the fire.

Michelle nodded, staring at the fire.

She seems to have something on her mind. Roger eyed her as he rubbed his hands together.

She raised her eyes to his. "Roger, why do you wear that gun all the time?"

"It's for your protection."

"I'm not afraid. Are you?"

"No. But I need to be prepared for anything."

"Where's that brave man who came marching right up to our little cottage with nothing more than a stick in his hand?"

"You don't like me wearing a gun?"

"I don't want my son to grow up thinking that all men carry guns."

"I hadn't thought about that. He is at a very impressionable age, isn't he?"

"And I admire a man who has enough self-confidence that he doesn't need to rely on a gun."

"You're right. I don't need this," Roger said. He set his coffee cup down, pulled the gun out of the holster, ejected the six bullets, and pushed them into the empty slots in the belt. He unbuckled the belt and dropped the whole works in his tent.

When he turned around, he found himself face-to-face with Michelle. Before he knew what was happening, she had slipped her arms around him and was squeezing him passionately. She briefly put her head on his shoulder as he wrapped his arms around her. It felt so good to have her in his arms once again. But it was over much too quickly, and it left him wondering what it meant.

It was obvious that she really appreciated him getting rid of the gun. That he understood. But did the hug mean anything more than that? Or was she "just being polite?"

A bit before noon, the children were chasing each other around the camp when Roger detected the sound of small engines. He quieted the children, and then he and Michelle ventured out to where they could see across the river. Two four-wheelers were coming down the river along the far edge. Sometimes running on pebbled beaches and sometimes plowing through the water almost as deep as their wheels, they made their way down the river, past the tree Roger had used for a target, till they came to the beach just off the old campsite. They stopped, looked around briefly, then turned and drove right up to the grassy bench where Roger and Michelle and the children had been camping.

"Looks like they knew exactly where they were going." Michelle's eyes narrowed as the two men got off the four-wheelers and began strolling around the campsite.

"I gotta get my binoculars." Roger turned and hurried back to his tent. As he dug his binoculars out of his dry bag, he noticed the revolver lying on the tent floor and hesitated, but decided to leave it right there. On his way back to Michelle, he reminded the kids to stay there and be quiet.

Roger watched through the binoculars as the two men walked around their previous camp. "Tell me something, Michelle," he said. "Based on what you know about guardian angels, do you think a guardian angel would be over there checking out our old campsite?"

"Are you telling me that's our gray-haired friend over there?"

"Yeah. The man in the white Buick. It sure looks like him."

"Gee, I wonder who he is and why he's looking for us."

"Don't know. The other guy's wearing some kind of uniform—game warden, maybe. They both have side arms."

"They must have some connection to the people in the airplane. Nobody else would know where to look for us," Michelle speculated.

"They drove right in there like they'd seen the place before, with their own eyes. My guess is that at least one of them was in that plane," Roger added. They both watched as the two men walked over to where Roger had been shooting. The gray-haired man started picking up something from the ground while the other man walked back to the four-wheeler. "It looks like he's picking up my shell casings."

"That sounds like police work." Michelle's voice was almost jubilant. Roger watched as the other man returned with a machete and started hacking at the rotten tree trunk.

"Do you know if that gun was ever used in a crime?" Roger lowered the binoculars and turned toward Michelle.

"I know absolutely nothing about the history of Jasper's guns. But I'd say there's a pretty good chance that it was."

"I think he's trying to dig some slugs out of the tree trunk." Roger put the binoculars to his eyes again.

"Who would bother to do that other than police?" Michelle questioned.

"If they were working for Chief Theodore, they'd concentrate on looking for us rather than investigating the gun," Roger commented. "I'm sure the chief already knows as much about that gun as he cares to."

"The gray-haired man started tracking us before my letters were delivered to the state police and FBI. So he wouldn't be somebody responding to my letters."

"That leaves Jasper." Roger thought for a moment. "He's the only other person who knew we were headed to this area. He must have survived long enough to change his mind and send someone after us."

"He'd never do that!" Michelle declared. "Besides, that doesn't make any sense. If they were working for Jasper, they wouldn't be digging slugs out of a tree."

"Well then, maybe I wasn't the only person who had Jasper under surveillance. Someone who was watching him may have been tracking us from the very beginning. We just didn't notice him right away. And I'd still like to know how that rattlesnake ended up under the rock with Jasper's money."

"What do you think that has to do with this?"

"Somebody brought that snake into the area and put it there. And somebody has been following us. It could be the same person."

"If they're some sort of law enforcement and they're not connected to Chief Theodore, that's probably a good thing. They'd be on our side." Michelle sounded encouraging.

"But if they run tests on those slugs and find they came out of a gun that was used in a crime, they won't think that I'm on their side," Roger countered.

"Don't worry." Michelle smiled. "The police won't shoot an unarmed man."

"Okay, okay. I'm not wearing the gun anymore."

Eventually the two men mounted their four-wheelers and headed back up the river. "Do you think they accomplished their mission?" Roger asked. "Is that what they were after, to check out our campsite and gather slugs? Or do you think they were really looking for us?"

"I don't have a clue." Michelle turned toward their camp. "Let's go have some lunch."

"It feels like rain's coming," Roger observed as they headed back. "The air is really damp."

Michelle scanned the sky. "The sky is completely overcast too."

After lunch, Roger tied a rope between two trees. Then he put a tarp over it and stretched it out over the campfire and cooking area, with the one edge covering the entrance to Michelle's tent. By the time he was finished, a light rain had begun falling. The children seemed fascinated with the new set up and couldn't resist playing in the water that dripped off the edges of the tarp. Meanwhile, Roger was getting soaked as he worked at adjusting the height and slope of the tarp so that no pools would accumulate on it and so the runoff wouldn't go onto either tent.

"You could put on your rain gear," Michelle suggested.

"I'll dry off again. At least it's not as chilly as it was this morning."

The rain gradually increased through the rest of the afternoon and evening. The sound of the rain falling in the trees and on the tarp made everyone feel relaxed and lethargic. The dim light made it seem much later than it actually was. Going to bed early was as natural as bees making honey.

23

The steady rain continued through the night and into the morning, with occasional downpours. Roger had awakened repeatedly during the night and had gone back to sleep. Even after dawn, he lay in his sleeping bag, seeing no reason to get up, and drifted off to sleep again. Now he lay there, gazing at the top of his tent and feeling the hunger pangs in his stomach. Knowing the children would be hungry too, Roger crawled out of his sleeping bag and got dressed. He put on a raincoat and ventured out. Streams of water were coming down the mountainside everywhere. One of them was running right through the campsite, under the tarp he had stretched between the tents. His pile of firewood was still mostly dry. He heard voices inside Michelle's tent.

"Y'all keeping dry in there?" he asked.

"We're fine. How's it looking out there?" Michelle zipped the tent partway open and poked her head out.

"It's kind of wet. But I have dry firewood. I can build a fire and make pancakes."

"Yeah! Pancakes!" came the response from two little voices.

The foursome ate their breakfast sitting on the floor of Michelle's tent, since that was the driest place in the camp. Afterward, Roger set their dirty dishes out where the rain could rinse them. He would finish the job later.

The children began entertaining themselves inside the tent by harassing each other. So Michelle cuddled with Abby while Roger helped Earl sound out words from a book for young readers, which Roger had brought along for just such an occasion. "You really do quite well," Roger observed. "I bet your mom spends a lot of time teaching you."

"Too much," Earl replied.

Michelle and Roger glanced at each other and smiled. "I don't think he'll have any trouble keeping up with kids his age," Roger said.

"He's a smart boy." Michelle smiled proudly. But Earl was soon tired of reading, and they had to find another way to occupy their time. Michelle started singing, "When you walk through a storm, hold your head up high."

Abby joined in, "And don't be afraid of the dark. At the end of the storm is a golden sky and the sweet silver song of a lark…"

Before they were finished singing, Earl had started tossing his shiny pebble around, trying to make it land and stay on his sleeping bag. It wasn't a very challenging game. So Roger took off his belt and formed it into a small circle on the floor of the tent. Then he got the kids to compete at tossing the pebble into the circle from the opposite side of the tent. Before long, the score was ten to zero, but Abby didn't seem to mind. At Roger's request, Earl started throwing left-handed. Abby threw, sometimes with the right hand, sometimes with the left. It didn't seem to make any difference. The score was still lopsided. The little girl danced and giggled with delight when she finally got the pebble to land in the circle. That kept the kids entertained for close to an hour, before Abby started messing with Michelle's hair.

"You want to comb my hair?" Michelle pulled her braids out and shook her hair loose, handing a comb to Abby.

"Will my hair get as long as yours?" Abby asked as she pulled the comb through her mother's long blond hair.

"If we don't cut it, it will get long. But your hair is so curly it may not seem as long as mine."

Abby continued grooming her mother and admiring her hair as the rain continued drumming on the tent fly. "Where does wain come from?" she asked.

"It comes from the clouds." Roger suddenly felt like a teacher again. "Do you know what happens when the sun shines on something wet?"

"It gets dry," Earl answered.

"Where does the water go?" Roger turned to Earl.

"I don't know."

"When the sun shines on water, it evaporates," Roger explained. "That means it turns into something we can't see. It goes up into the sky. Then it turns into rain and falls down again."

"There must be a lot of water up there," Earl observed.

"More than you can imagine." Roger patted him on the knee and turned to Michelle. "Do you realize that one inch of rain on one square mile is more than seventy-two thousand tons of water?"

"God made the water!" Abby declared.

"That's right, honey. He did." But Michelle's attention was on Roger. "It's just unbelievable how much water can be floating around up there in the clouds."

"It's really neat the way the earth just keeps recycling water," Roger went on. "Only three percent of the water on earth is fresh water. But the supply is continually being replenished."

"And not just water, oxygen gets recycled too." Michelle appeared to be enjoying this discussion. Or had she just remembered how much he enjoyed nature trivia? Was she acting? "We use oxygen and combine it with carbon to make carbon dioxide. Plants use the carbon dioxide and release the oxygen for us to use."

Roger picked up her train of thought and completed it. "And the plants combine the carbon with water to make hydrocarbons. So the carbon is being recycled as well."

Abby had left her grooming job, and she and Earl were scrapping again, but Michelle ignored it. "And I don't see how people can believe that this whole system developed without a plan." Michelle looked at Roger. "To think that all our living and nonliving environment came about purely by chance just doesn't seem logical."

"Well, you need to study it with an open mind. There are lots of fossils that prove that things don't stay the same. They keep changing. Things are evolving even as we speak. No real scientist can just ignore the huge amount of evidence supporting evolution. A scientist has to look at all the evidence."

"Have you even looked at all the evidence just in your own experiences in the last couple weeks?" Michelle asked. "How do you explain all the unusual things that have happened to you?"

"Like what?"

"Like the dream you had that revealed to you that I was the one who built the pyramid. How do you explain that?"

"Mom," Earl whined, "make her get off my sleeping bag."

"Abby, sit on your own sleeping bag! And stop picking on your brother." Michelle turned her attention back to Roger.

Roger took Abby in his lap. "Dreams bring things to the surface that we have in our subconscious. I suppose I had it all figured out in my subconscious mind. But everyone was telling me not to allow myself to think that you might still be alive. So I was suppressing it. The dream just brought into my conscious thinking what I already knew."

"And what made that occur just hours before Jasper was bitten by the rattlesnake? If he wouldn't have been suffering from a snakebite, he would have shot you on the spot."

"If you knew he'd shoot me, why were you trying to lure me in there?"

"I wasn't trying to lure you in. In fact, I didn't really think about everything that might happen as a result of that pyramid I built. But I just had to communicate with you somehow. I kept seeing you on the creek, and I just had to let you know that I was still alive. I wasn't trying to get you into trouble with Jasper."

"Well, it worked out okay."

"But you didn't answer my question." Michelle fondled Abby's toes. "Do you think it was just coincidence that you had that dream just hours before Jasper was bitten?"

"Exactly! It was coincidence. Remember studying normal distribution? Remember that bell-shaped curve? Most things that happen fall in the middle of that curve. But there are those things that fall on the outer ends of the bell curve, things with a very low probability of happening. But they happen. It's normal."

"Wait a minute," Michelle interrupted. "That argument doesn't make any sense. I know it's been years since I studied that stuff. But wouldn't you have to have a set of statistics you could put on a graph to create that bell curve? I don't see how normal distribution has anything to do with what we're talking about. We're debating the probability that you would have that dream just before Jasper is bitten by a snake."

"Okay, forget the bell curve. What I'm trying to say is that unusual things do happen. They happen all the time. So in hindsight, you can always focus on something unusual about an event and say, 'Gee, that was odd. If that wouldn't have happened, things would have turned out differently. That must have been planned by God.'"

"So you're saying unusual things happen all the time, so they're not really unusual. The dream, the snakebite, the rose getting stuck in the eddy, the skunk escorting you past Ruger—that kind of stuff happens all the time. Is that what you really think?"

"No. I'm saying that just because something has a low probability of happening doesn't mean that it had to be planned."

"Is Ruger helping Daddy?" Abby asked.

"Honey, I'm talking with Roger right now." Michelle took a deep breath. "Okay, let's get back to the original question. What are the odds that you would have that dream on the very same morning that Jasper gets bitten by a rattlesnake?"

"Ah…I almost said 365 to 1. But that would be odds of hitting a particular calendar day. That wouldn't be right."

"Yeah, we're not limited to one year. So I don't know what that would be. But whatever it is, we have to multiply that by the probability that you would have the dream at all. What's that? A million to one maybe? So now we're at 365 million to one, or much more, maybe. Then we have to multiply that by the probability that Jasper would be bitten by a rattlesnake, which you say isn't native to the area. We're getting to some very slim odds."

"Right, slim odds indeed! But we both know it happened. So what?"

"You yourself have said several times that you think somebody planned for Jasper to get bitten by that snake. You look at that one event and you see a probability so low that you can't believe that it would have happened at random. Yet when you consider all the events together, you say they're just random events. That doesn't make sense. You can't have it both ways."

"Some person could have put that snake there, hoping it would bite him. But that doesn't mean that it's connected to all the other unusual events or that there's some sort of divine plan."

"Roger, sometimes I think you automatically block out any information that suggests that God exists."

"I don't think I block it out. But I don't have the preconceived notion that there *is* a God, so I don't interpret the information the same way you do."

"I just hope and pray that someday you see the light."

"I appreciate your concern. But I really don't think there's any reason for you to worry about me."

"Mommy," Earl butted in, "can I put on my raincoat and go outside?"

"Sure, honey," Michelle replied without thinking. "So, Roger, you think I misinterpret things to support my belief in God."

"I didn't say that."

"But you implied it."

"You can interpret things any way you want. I'm not trying to convince you to stop believing in God. I'm just explaining my beliefs because you keep pressing me."

"I do that," her voice dropped to a whisper, "because I care about you."

Roger paused then slid Abby off his lap. "I think Earl has a pretty good idea." He zipped the tent open and stuck his head out. The rain continued falling as Earl donned his raincoat and water shoes and ventured out to play in the streams of water cascading down the hillside. Roger roamed around the campsite, checking out the wet conditions. By late afternoon, the rain finally stopped and the sky began clearing. The evening sun was beginning to shine through the trees as Roger washed the dirty dishes that had accumulated during the day.

A gentle breeze whispered through the trees as water continued trickling off the hillside. Roger stopped abruptly. "Listen!" he cocked his head. "I hear a train coming. You kids want to see a train?" The two children took their mother in tow, and the four headed out to the railroad tracks. They stood by the tracks gazing down the railway at the bright light approaching. The purr of the diesels gradually became a thundering roar as four locomotives slowly took shape behind the blinding headlight. Abby stepped in front of Michelle and thrust her arms in the air. As Michelle picked her up, the little girl turned for another look at the massive objects coming closer and closer. At the sound of the air-horn, everyone instinctively took several steps backward. Earl watched with the eyes of an owl as a crew-man waved from the cab of the first locomotive. The adults waved back, but Earl stood, frozen, with his mouth open. One by one the giant diesels passed and thundered on up the grade as the endless string of freight cars rumbled on and on. Finally, the last car rolled by, and a hush fell over the wilderness camp.

"Well, kids, what did you think of the train?" Michelle looked at her children.

"I was scared," Abby said.

"I was too, a little bit," Earl confessed.

"You didn't even wave to the engineer," Roger teased.

"And the twain man saw us," Abby said innocently. Roger and Michelle glanced at each other, both realizing the mistake they had made.

"If you wanted to find somebody out here along the river, who would you ask to be on the lookout?" Michelle asked.

Roger nodded. "Ya know, I was just thinking it's about time we move down the river. I'd like to get a little closer to Karthaus anyway, so I can walk to town and call George. I'd like to find out what's been happening on the home front."

"Let's see." Michelle cocked her head. "What day is it?"

"Today's Saturday," Roger replied. "I might wait till Monday to call George. But we should make the move tomorrow. We'll have better water conditions than we had on Tuesday."

"Well maybe," Michelle seemed to be in deep thought. "The river is up a good bit already, and it'll probably keep coming up, depending on how widespread this storm was. It probably won't crest till tomorrow. By that time, we might have too much water."

"Let's plan on moving out first thing in the morning, if at all possible." Roger caught her eye. "We'll both take a good look at the river in the morning and make the final decision then."

"Before we start tearing the camp apart," Michelle added.

"Right," Roger agreed. "I trust your judgment, and I don't want to make this decision without your input."

24

Michelle loved the way the wet grass sparkled in the morning sun as she and Roger strolled down to the river. The air was pristine, and the sky a brilliant blue. The rocky riverbed had vanished beneath the smooth water that raced quietly along its winding course. "It's higher than it was last evening," Michelle observed.

"Yeah." Roger's eyes were focused on the water. "It's flatter than usual too. A lot of the rapids will be washed out."

"And some of them will be bigger than normal," Michelle added. "It won't look like this everywhere. There may be some new rapids at places that are usually just small riffles."

"True. The river can change so much with different water levels. I've never canoed it at this level. I don't really know what we'd be getting into."

"This would be great if we had our canoes filled up with airbags instead of loaded down with camping gear and if we didn't have any small children along."

"Yeah. That definitely increases the risks."

"Look at the shoreline." Michelle pointed. "All the gradually tapered beaches are gone. We go right from the steep bank into moving water. We've got bushes growing right on the water's edge. It may be hard to find a decent landing if we have to get off the water quickly."

"You're right. Bushes and tree branches can create strainers. Strainers are dangerous."

"So what do you think, Captain?"

"Hey, I'm not the captain." Roger's head spun toward Michelle. "We're going to make this decision together. But if this was a group of adults with the skills you and I have, I wouldn't hesitate. But I don't want to put your children at risk."

"The thing is, we're already at risk. Staying here is a risk. We have to move out, if at all possible. We don't know who is looking for us. But we know that now somebody knows where we are."

"I suppose by this time Chief Theodore is starting to feel the heat." Roger's eyes darted up and down the river. "I wouldn't want to meet up with him or anybody that's out to do a job for him. And I just don't know what that gray-haired guy is up to."

"Why did we ever go out to look at that stupid train?"

"I'm sorry. I was so eager to show your children their first train, I just wasn't thinking."

"It wasn't your fault, Roger. I wasn't thinking either. If you think you were eager, you can imagine how I feel. There's so much I want them to see."

"So we goofed once. Let's not follow it up with a second mistake. Do you think it's safe to move out?" Roger's eyes met hers.

"Well, it's certainly not as safe as I would like. We have to be really cautious, but I'm game to try it, if you don't think it's too crazy."

"No, I don't think it's crazy. We really can't tell which is riskier, staying or leaving. Who knows, the river may prove to be no problem at all." As they turned back toward camp, their hands accidentally bumped. Before Michelle realized what she had done, her hand fell into his, and their fingers interlocked just as naturally as they did back in high school. Immediately, she felt like she was being unfaithful to Jasper. But she couldn't let go. She squeezed his hand as they headed back to the camp to inform the children that they would be packing up and heading down the river.

Launching the loaded boats from the steep bank proved to be a bit delicate. They slid Michelle's boat in first and pulled it parallel to the bank. Roger got on his knees in the wet grass and held a firm grip on the gunnel as Michelle placed Abby in the bow seat, then took her position in the stern. As soon as she got underway, she came about and snuggled into a small eddy to wait for Roger and Earl.

Roger carefully slid his boat down the bank and into the water and braced it while Earl entered. Then he nimbly hopped into the stern, and they were underway. The water moved them along at a fast pace, and as they had hoped, most of the rapids had flattened out—but not all.

As they rounded a bend, Roger pointed downstream and exclaimed, "Leapin' lords! Look at that!"

Michelle gazed downriver at a series of large waves. "Wow! That would be fun if we had our boats equipped with airbags and weren't loaded down with gear."

"We've got plenty of room to stay to the right of it," Roger called back as he made a course correction. Michelle followed Roger, several canoe lengths back and a few feet to the left as they headed for the calmer water between the waves and the shore. Roger pointed at a spot in Michelle's path and shouted, "Hole!"

At first Michelle could hardly see anything in the location Roger had pointed at because the line of sight from her position went right over top of the hole. But she was quickly drawing closer, and now she could see that an underwater rock was forming a ledge. Water pouring over the ledge was creating a souse hole. The bow would glide easily over the hole, and the water was deep enough to carry her over the rock. But when the stern dropped over the ledge, the bow would pop up and the stern would be sucked under the water. She had to avoid the souse hole!

Michelle began back-paddling furiously. She was paddling on the right side. So the boat automatically started back-ferrying to the left as she slowed her approach to the hole. Her bow was within three feet of the hole, but she had ferried far enough left to clear it. One problem had been avoided, but another lay ahead!

The current was now drawing her diagonally into the first big wave. She had no time left to maneuver out of the swift current. She had to take the wave! But if the wave caught her boat at this angle, she would capsize for sure! She didn't want to put her three-year-old daughter into this kind of risky situation, but there was no time left to avoid it. She had to concentrate on controlling the canoe. She had to turn the boat—and quickly! Several powerful forward sweeps brought the bow around and headed her straight into the wave. But she hit it with too much force. The bow sliced into the wave. Michelle's heart sank! She knew what it was like in the bow of a canoe. She knew what Abby was facing. She could see it all through Abby's eyes.

As the bow sliced into the wave, buckets of chilly water splashed over the gunnels, wetting Abby from her face to her feet. Like a flash, the little girl dropped her paddle overboard, turned and started scrambling toward her mother. "Stay in your seat! Stay in your seat!" Her mother's order was quick and sharp. Abby sat back down, facing her mother. She had never heard her use that tone of voice. She had never seen such a look of concern on her face. She knew something was going terribly wrong. She froze in her seat as the second wave spilled over the bow, soaking her back side from her head to her heels. The screams came out of nowhere! She couldn't stop them!

"We're swamped!" Her mother shouted to Roger. They plowed into a third wave. Abby gripped the seat with both hands and stared wide-eyed at her mother who was kneeling in water up to midthigh and struggling to keep the boat upright. Abby felt the canoe roll to the side. She felt the seat drop away from under her. Suddenly water was everywhere! She felt her life jacket pushing up under her chin. The water was pushing her up and down. She had nothing to hold onto! She blinked the water out of her eyes and saw the canoe beside her, only a small part of it sticking out of the water. She stopped screaming for a second to spit water out of her mouth, but the screams kept coming. She saw her mother swimming toward her.

Roger's heart screamed along with the little girl. He knew what she was going through, but he had never experienced it at such a young age. He watched Michelle cradling Abby in her arms, trying to calm her down as they drifted through the final waves. Abby clung to her mother with a frenzied grip. Roger had already come about and was standing by to assist. "You all right?" he asked as he snatched a floating paddle from the river.

"Yeah, we're fine," Michelle gasped. "She's just frightened."

Roger wasn't sure that Abby would have agreed with that statement. "You want to put Abby in here? I'll grab your bowline and tow the boat to shore."

"Looks like we've got a good stretch of flat water ahead. We could do canoe over canoe," Michelle suggested.

Roger glanced down river as he thought about the rescue technique Max had taught them. But they had never practiced it with boats full of camping gear. "You're right." He looked back at Michelle. "That's a better idea." As Roger started maneuvering his canoe into position, Michelle convinced Abby to climb on her back.

Michelle rolled her canoe completely upside down while Roger positioned his canoe at a right angle to hers so that the one end of her boat pointed to the middle of the right side his boat, forming a large T. Michelle swam to the opposite end of her canoe. "You ready?" she called as she got into position.

"Not yet. I want to get some of the weight out of my boat." Roger picked up one of the dry bags of supplies, tossed it over the left side and let it float beside the boat, still tethered to the center thwart. He did the same with the second bag. "Now, Earl," he said gently, "I want you to turn around and face me. Get down on your knees, like I am. You can help me pull your mom's boat in. Okay? Ready?"

Earl nodded.

"Okay! We're ready!" Roger shouted.

With Abby on her back, Michelle pounced on her end of the upside-down canoe, pushing it as far down into the water as she could. Roger's end seesawed upward. Roger grabbed the end of Michelle's canoe and started carefully pulling it in on top of his boat. Earl heaved with all the strength in his little arms as they slid the upside-down canoe across the upright one. When it was halfway across and the two boats formed an X, they stopped, and Roger rolled Michelle's boat right side up. Then he quickly slid it back into the water and pulled it parallel to his.

He held onto the gunnel, stabilizing the boat, while Michelle boosted Abby into the bow. Abby got seated as Michelle swam back to just behind the center thwart, where there was open floor space inside the canoe. "I don't know if I can do this anymore." Michelle peered over the edge of the boat at her intended landing spot.

"Sure you can." Roger raised the edge he was holding, so that Michelle's edge would be a little closer to the waterline. He held it firmly as Michelle gripped the opposite edge of the canoe and pulled herself up till her hips were at the gunnel. Then she gave a strong kick and lunged forward, flipping herself over at the same time so that she landed on her butt in the bottom of the canoe with her feet dangling over the edge.

"Perfect!" Roger applauded. "You make it look easy." Earl seemed somewhat amused at his mother's athletic prowess while Abigail just sat in the bow looking bewildered. Roger hauled in the dry bags and stowed them in their places. Earl passed the paddles they had retrieved over to his mother, and they got underway again. The whole rescue took but a few minutes. Max would have been pleased.

Their clothes dried rapidly as they cruised along in the bright sunshine, looking for a suitable campsite. Before long, they stopped to check an area on river right. "It looks good enough for me," Michelle commented.

"It's not perfect." Roger glanced across the river. "But I don't want to go much farther or we'll lose the railroad."

"What do you mean?"

"From here I can cross the river and hike to town on the railroad. It's not far because the railroad takes a shortcut through a tunnel while the river makes a big loop around the mountain. If we go much farther, we won't have access to the railroad."

"Well then, I guess this is it." Michelle nodded. They started unloading the boats and carrying their stuff to the campsite under the trees. As they brought the last canoe under the cover of the trees, they heard the sound of a helicopter coming up the valley.

25

Hiding behind the cover of trees and bushes, Michelle put her arms around the two youngsters. She and Roger listened as a state police helicopter slowly made its way up the river, flying at low altitude. "What do you think that means?" she asked as the chopper disappeared around the bend.

"It means they're looking for us!" Roger looked at her as if he felt the answer was obvious.

"But why?" *Why doesn't he answer the real question?* "They must be responding to my letter. They must have talked to Rick and George. How else would they know where to look for us?"

"Well, I'm not ready to run out and wave to a helicopter just yet." Roger shook his head. "Rick and George aren't the only people who know we're out here. Jasper knew, although we don't know if he lived to tell anyone. And we have that gray-haired man that's been following us and the other guy on the four-wheeler, the train crew, and the people in the airplane. We don't know who any of those people are or what connections they might have."

"You're right. We best lay low till we know for sure that it's safe to come out."

"Tomorrow I'll hike to town and call George from a payphone. I'm eager to find out what's been happening at home."

"I am too," Michelle replied as they returned to setting up their camp. A few minutes later, the helicopter retraced its path down the river.

"The nice thing about those choppers is that you can hear them coming miles away," Roger said as they took cover. "They give you plenty of time to hide."

By midafternoon, they were comfortably settled in their new campsite. Michelle kept an eye on her children as Earl roamed around looking for mushrooms and gathering sticks for a fire. "I can't find any mushrooms," he complained as he handed Roger a handful of sticks.

"That's okay," Roger assured him. "We still have plenty of food. We'll just have dinner without mushrooms."

After dinner, Michelle washed the dishes while Roger gathered more firewood. As the evening sky turned red, they sat by the campfire while the children continued playing. "So, Roger," Michelle gazed into his warm brown eyes, "who do you turn to when your life is out of control, when everything seems to be going wrong and there's no one there to help you?"

"I don't know. I guess I never really thought about that. I guess I'd have to rely on my friends."

"When you're all alone," Michelle restated the question. "When there are no friends to help you, who do you turn to?"

"I don't know. I guess I'd have to find the strength within myself to face the situation."

"But when your own strength isn't enough, who do you turn to?"

"I don't know." Roger sounded just slightly annoyed.

"Haven't you ever felt totally helpless and alone?"

"Well, I guess I have," he replied slowly. She could see that he was remembering something, but he didn't say what. "But somehow, things always seem to work out eventually."

"Yeah, they always have, so far," Michelle added. "And who do you thank for that?"

"I know where you're going with this." Roger got to his feet and started examining the firewood he had gathered earlier. "There is no one to thank. There is no one to turn to. Our lives are filled with random events, and we just make the best of it. Is that what you want me to say?"

"No," Michelle answered softly. "It's what I expected you to say. But I just can't imagine living *my* life with that ideology. I think the last seven years might have turned out quite differently. If I wouldn't have been able to relax and trust in God's providence, I probably would have reacted in ways that would have put my life in jeopardy. I don't know if I would have survived."

"Well, I'm sure glad you found the strength to survive, no matter where you found it." Roger broke a stick over his knee and laid it on the fire. He watched as the stick slowly became engulfed in flames.

As darkness fell, Michelle called the children in and settled them down. The night was coming to life with a chorus of insects and frogs. The big, round moon was rising over the mountain as Roger crawled into his tent for the night. Michelle paused and gazed out the window of her tent at the rising moon. She longed to be in the arms of the man she loved—either one of them.

After breakfast, the next morning, Roger prepared for his hike to town while Michelle washed the dishes. "How long do you expect it to take?" She glanced at him.

"Probably less than two hours each way. But I'm not sure."

"And you have to go through the tunnel?"

"Yes."

"What if a train comes?"

"That's not very likely. How many days have we been out here? And we only saw one train."

"Is there a walkway through the tunnel?"

"No, just the tracks. It's a narrow tunnel. In fact, I remember looking at it and wondering how a modern locomotive could fit through."

"Isn't there some other way?"

"I'd have to hike over the mountain or follow the river around the mountain. I don't like either of those options. I'll just take my chances."

Michelle helped Roger carry his canoe down to the river. "Be careful," she said, giving him a quick little hug before he stepped into the boat. Roger ferried across the river, pulled his canoe up the bank, and hid it in the bushes. Then he climbed up to the railroad bed and headed east.

He approached the old stone arch tunnel entrance slowly, listening for the sound of a train. He turned on his flashlight as he entered the blackness of the tunnel. He walked slowly at first, thinking that if he heard a train coming, he could still make it back to the entrance. When he figured he had reached the point of no return, he started jogging. He watched his step carefully. The last thing he needed now was an overturned ankle. The tunnel was built on a sharp curve, so now neither entrance was visible.

He thought he heard the sound of diesel engines. He didn't stop to listen; he just picked up his pace. He was beginning to see light from the other entrance, but now the sound of the diesels was unmistakable. As he raced toward the entrance, he could see a headlight in the distance. He had to make it to the entrance before the locomotive! But it was hopeless. Even though the train was moving slowly upgrade, it was still going faster than he could run. "God, help me!" he muttered under his breath as he charged toward the light. The roar of the engines grew louder and louder as the headlight came closer and closer to the entrance. Roger wouldn't give up! He was getting close the entrance, but he couldn't get there in time! Suddenly the sound of the diesels died, and a blast of the air horn echoed through the tunnel. Due to the upgrade, the locomotive decelerated quickly as Roger shot through the narrow space between it and the stone wall.

The bright sun hanging just over the locomotive blinded Roger as he leaned against the stone abutment, panting. But he could see the silhouette of a crewman leaning over the railing shaking his finger. "Anybody else in there?" the crewman shouted angrily.

Roger shook his head. The crewman disappeared into the cab. The four locomotives simultaneously revved up their engines and thundered slowly into the tunnel. Gradually the train picked up momentum as Roger stood leaning against the abutment, still catching his breath.

From across the river, Michelle watched the train coming out the other end of the tunnel and wondered if Roger had made it through. Would he ever return? Was this man also to be taken away from her? If she was left alone, how would she get her children to safety? She thought about the questions she had drilled Roger with: "Who do you turn to?" She couldn't help but think about some worst-case scenarios. It was almost impossible not to worry. There was nothing she could do but wait and pray. It was sure to be a long day.

George shut down his bandsaw, walked into his office, and picked up the ringing phone. "Hello. George Lauger speaking."

"Hey, George, it's Roger."

"Roger! You okay?"

"Yep."

"Really?"

"Yeah. Why?"

"I've really been thinking about you this morning—just thinking you might be in some sort of trouble."

"Oh?"

"I know you don't believe in prayer, but about two hours ago, I just stopped working and spent a few minutes praying for you. Is everything okay?"

"Well, I was in a bit of a pinch."

"You were?"

"A freight train almost caught me in the Karthaus tunnel."

"What the heck were you doing in there?"

"Walking to town on the railroad track to call you."

"You got out okay?"

"I'll tell you all about it later. What's happening at your end?"

"How are Michelle and the kids doing?"

"They're all doing fine. What's been happening around home?"

"Oh, lots of stuff! Latest thing is Chief Theodore is dead."

"He's dead?"

"Yeah. They're saying he accidentally shot himself while cleaning his gun."

"Accidentally shot himself? He taught gun safety, for heaven's sake!"

"Well, they're still investigating. But that's the initial report. That just happened on Saturday. On Friday they found Jasper and carried his body out. The next day the chief accidentally shoots himself. How likely is that?"

"Yeah, right."

"Hey, the FBI would really like to talk with Michelle. We told 'em where you are. I think the state police were going to try to find you."

"Yeah. They flew a chopper up the river yesterday."

"They didn't see you?"

"We hid behind the trees."

"They say they can protect you better than you can protect yourselves."

"Any word on Jasper's brother or that Bobby character?"

"No. If the police know anything, they haven't told us."

"Remember that gray-haired man in the white Buick?"

"Yeah, I sure do. He followed me partway home."

"He did? He's been following us too."

"I saw a car like his driving real slow past my house, but I couldn't see the driver."

"One day a small plane circled, kind of low, over our campsite. So we moved across the river. The next day these two guys come down the river on four-wheelers and drove directly into our old campsite. One of them was that gray-haired guy. They acted like some sort of law enforcement, collecting shell casings and slugs from a stump I was shooting at."

"I haven't seen him with any of the police or detectives that are working the case from this end. I just don't know who he is or what he's up to."

"How's Rick doing?"

"He's doing fine. Chief Theodore gave him a thorough interrogation on Tuesday evening. Kind of tore your house apart. But Rick has things cleaned up and organized again."

"So he was looking for me?" Roger chuckled.

"Yeah. He found your car. We saw him running a four-wheeler up and down along the creek too."

"Well, at least he's out of the picture now."

"Yeah. The FBI wants me to tell you that it's safe to come home. They'll meet you wherever and escort you home. They'll arrange for all the protection you and Michelle need as long as necessary."

"I'm not committing to anything without discussing it with Michelle. We still need to be concerned about Jasper's brother and Bobby and that gray-haired man. We'll talk about it, and when we decide to come out, I'll give you a call. Until then, we'll just stay hunkered down."

"I agree, we need to let Michelle have her say in this."

"When you talk to the FBI, see if they know anything about that gray-haired man. I think it was probably him in the airplane."

"Okay."

"It was a yellow-and-white single-engine plane with a high wing. You know what I mean? The wing is above the windows. We saw him on Wednesday and again on Thursday. They ought to be able to track that down, especially if he filed a flight plan."

"A yellow-and-white, single-engine, high wing, on Wednesday and Thursday. Got that."

"Anything else that Michelle and I should know about?"

"I think we've covered it."

"Okay. I'll be in touch—sometime."

"Take care. See ya."

Roger replayed the conversation in his mind as he walked briskly down the road, turned onto the railroad tracks and headed back toward the tunnel.

26

As Michelle sat on a rock watching the children playing in the water, she kept glancing across the river, toward the railroad tracks, looking for any sign of a person on the tracks or moving through the bushes. Had Roger made it through the tunnel? Had he made it safely to town? *Why isn't he back? Will I ever see him again?* She shuddered to think that if Roger was killed, she wouldn't even see him in heaven. Deep in her heart, she yearned for him to return to his belief in God. If he didn't, they could have no future together. She would not be married to an unbeliever. "I have to find a way to convince him that God is real," she said under her breath.

She had started looking for Roger before one o'clock. Now it was after three. The air was dead, and the afternoon sun kept creeping ever so slowly toward the west. Time was moving at the speed of a glacier.

Finally, she saw the form of a man working his way from the tracks, through the bushes toward the river. He hoisted a canoe onto his shoulders and carried it the short distance to the river. Michelle stood eagerly by the water's edge as Roger ferried across. Then she waded in, grabbed the bow, and pulled him up on the shore.

As Roger stepped out of the boat, she threw her arms around him. "I was so worried about you when I saw that train coming out of the tunnel."

"That was a close one." Roger rubbed the back of his neck. "They actually stopped the train for me—or almost. I don't think it ever stopped moving completely."

"And I thought you'd be back around one, or shortly after that."

"Well, I didn't come back through the tunnel. I hiked over the mountain. That's why it took longer."

"I'm just glad you're back. What did you find out?"

He gently put his hands on her shoulders. "Your husband didn't survive the snakebite."

Michelle took a deep breath and let it out slowly. "I expected that," she sobbed as she laid her head on his shoulder. "But at least I didn't lose both of you."

"Do you want to talk to the children? Or you want some time alone or anything?"

"No. I've cried alone every night since we've been out here. I knew this was coming. I think I'll be okay now. It's not knowing for sure that's the hard part. You just keep wondering and hoping and thinking about the possibilities."

"I know. I remember. You just can't give up hoping."

"I guess you would know about that."

"And what about the children?"

"I'll talk with them when we say our prayers tonight."

"Is there anything I can do?"

"No, I guess not." Michelle returned to her seat on the rock. "Just tell me what else you got from George."

"Chief Theodore committed suicide."

"What!"

"Well, they're not calling it suicide. They say it was an accident. But I say it was either suicide or someone murdered him and made it look like an accident."

"Well, that's a good thing—for us, anyway."

"The FBI is really eager to talk with you. They say we should come home. They'll give us all the protection we need."

"So what did you tell him?"

"I said I had to discuss it with you."

"By the way, that yellow-and-white airplane was flying around again."

"I know. I saw him from the railroad track."

"He went upriver, then back down. We stayed out of sight, and they flew right by. I don't think they saw us."

"It seems kind of premature to be thinking about going home when someone is still obviously looking for us." Roger scanned the sky.

"Well, they might be on our side. I'm eager to go home anyway, even though I don't know where home is now." Michelle had long forgotten her childhood dream of a big house in the forest. Any place would be fine as long as she was surrounded by family and friends.

"I'm sure we can find a place for you that's better than what we have out here." Roger skipped a stone across the water. "The question is, will it be safe?"

"Safe or not, I'm ready to get back to civilization. We've got a law enforcement body we can trust on our side." Michelle paused as memories of old friends flashed through her mind. "If they're saying they'll protect us, I see no reason to wait."

"How do we know we can trust them?"

"I trust my instincts."

"And my instincts are different than yours."

"Roger, I've been detained for seven years. I want to go home!"

"Okay." Roger sighed. "Tomorrow morning we pack up and head down the river to Karthaus. I'll call George back and arrange a time and place to meet. And if I understood correctly, the police or FBI will meet us there and escort us home."

"I'm really eager to reconnect with old friends and family. There's so much that needs to be done. We have to find a place to live. We need to get Earl prepared to start school in the fall. The kids have never had any immunization shots or anything. They don't even have birth certificates. I'll need to get a driver's license again."

"And you've been presumed dead. I don't even know where you start with this stuff."

That evening, Roger sat alone in the dark as the campfire slowly died. He listened to crickets and frogs singing. From Michelle's tent, he heard voices talking and crying and laughing and praying. Then there was quietness, peaceful quietness. He wondered what it would be like for a couple who didn't share a religious belief, to try to comfort their children through a time of tragedy. He knew that Michelle was right in her decision to not get romantically involved with someone who didn't share her beliefs.

The next morning Roger was up at daylight. He rolled up his sleeping bag, took down his tent and started packing whatever was not needed for breakfast. By the time Michelle and the children got up, he had a fire going and a batch of pancake batter ready to go in the frying pan. "Pancakes again?" Earl complained. "I'm getting tired of pancakes." But you couldn't tell by the number he ate, that he was getting tired of them. After the breakfast dishes were washed and dried, they packed up everything and loaded the canoes.

By nine o'clock they were in their canoes and heading down the river. The water level had dropped a lot since Sunday, but not quite to the level it was before the rain. Conditions were actually pretty nice for casual canoeing. There was no big whitewater and at most places it was easy to find a channel with enough depth to get you through. They made their way through long, gentle riffles that ended in quiet pools till they came to the rapids above the confluence of Moshannon Creek. "This is known as Moshannon Falls," Roger announced. "But it's not really a falls."

Two pairs of trained eyes studied the water ahead as they worked their way slowly and carefully into the rapids, which consisted of a long boulder patch with rocks of all sizes creating ledges, riffles, and souse holes. Roger was enjoying the challenge as he chose his path between the hazards. Michelle followed, sometimes selecting a slightly different course. Roger glanced back at her. Her face showed both concern and delight. *She always did enjoy the challenges of choosing the best course and driving her canoe precisely where she chose.* It wasn't extremely difficult, but it required constant maneuvering and a vigilant eye for those rocks hidden just under the surface. Earl whooped and hollered each time they successfully negotiated a hazard, but Abby sat frozen, gripping the edge of her seat with both hands.

After they reached the pool at the bottom of the rapids, Earl stared downriver with wide eyes. "Look at that!" he pointed straight ahead at a section of really serious-looking whitewater. The sound of the water ahead was already drowning out the sound of the rapids behind them.

"Don't worry," Roger said calmly. "We're not going there. That's actually another stream called Moshannon Creek. It's flowing straight toward us. The river we're on makes a sharp turn to the left just ahead. But you can't see it yet." A few minutes later, they made the left turn and headed down the long, mostly straight section to Karthaus.

"When I call George, I think I'll see if they can meet us tomorrow afternoon at Keating," Roger said as they approached the canoe access area. "How does that sound?"

"That sounds good to me," Michelle replied. "That should give the police enough time to plan for an escort or whatever they want to do."

A little before noon, they pulled the canoes up onto the stony beach beside the boat ramp at Karthaus. Roger grabbed a strip of beef jerky and started walking to town while Michelle got out snacks for the children.

After George and Roger had discussed their plans and established a meeting place, George said, "Roger, do you remember a young lady named Kathy?"

"Oh shoot! I completely forgot about her!"

"I forgot to tell you, when you called yesterday, but she's been asking about you."

"I was supposed to go out with her on Friday."

"Yeah. She wasn't too happy about that. But Rick explained things to her."

"What did she say?"

"She was as surprised as everyone else to hear that Michelle is still alive. She didn't seem really overjoyed, though."

"Tell her I'm so sorry for missing our date!"

"Sure, we'll do that."

Thoughts of Kathy soon vanished from Roger's mind as he headed back to Michelle and the children, carrying a bag of ham-and-cheese sandwiches, caramel corn, and a bottle of Pepsi. The children came running when they saw him coming with the bag of fresh groceries. As he put the bag down and started passing out sandwiches to the eager hands, Roger glanced at Michelle and said, "We agreed to meet at Keating, tomorrow between two and three."

Michelle smiled. "Sounds good to me." She ate in silence, a far-away look in her eyes.

While munching on caramel corn, Roger turned toward Michelle with a grin. "Just leave it to George!"

"What are you talking about?" she asked with a puzzled look.

"All that stuff we were worrying about yesterday—finding you a place to live and everything. No need to worry. George is working on it."

"What?"

"He's planning to move in with his mother so you and the kids can live in his house."

"What?"

"It's perfect! Three bedrooms. You'll love it!"

"How could you ask him to do that?"

"I didn't say a word. He came up with this on his own."

"I don't know what to say." Michelle's eyes sparkled with tears.

"And he's already talked to his lawyer about some of your legal needs. He's talked with some of the ladies at church about helping you get settled in. Sounds like the whole community is coming together to help."

"When we're surrounded with people like that, it almost seems ridiculous to have police protection." Michelle brushed a tear from her cheek.

"Yeah, but we still need to take precautions. We still don't know who that gray-haired guy is or what he's up to. Harold and Bobby are still dangerous people."

"You're right. Didn't George find anything out about the gray-haired man?"

"He hasn't even had a chance to talk with the FBI since he and I talked yesterday. I guess he's making up for lost time with Mrs. Faulkner."

After lunch was finished, Roger sealed up the dry bags and got the canoes ready to go. "Everybody ready to head down the river again?" he called out.

"Yeah, I suppose we'd better not spend more time than necessary in a public place like this." Michelle glanced around the access area.

"It's kind of unusual to have this whole place all to ourselves," Roger added. "I guess we were just lucky."

"But we should get going."

"Yeah. We ought to get about a third of the way to Keating before we make camp so we don't have such a long day tomorrow. The kids will get tired of sitting in a canoe all day."

"They'll be all right." Michelle promised as she got Abby seated. "They're not used to being overstimulated by TV programs and video games."

"Is that what makes the difference?" Roger replied, pushing his boat into the water.

"Last one in is a rotten egg!" Earl called out as his mother prepared to launch her boat.

The two canoes pulled away from shore and turned downstream toward the old steel bridge. "One more day in the wild," Roger said, fixing his gaze downriver.

27

Roger gazed at the bright evening sun gilding the edges of dark cumulus clouds that hung over the horizon. He and his tired companions sat on makeshift chairs enjoying their dinner of beef stew and anticipating the next day's events. *This is our final campsite. Tomorrow we return to civilization, to a world still unfamiliar to the children and filled with uncertainties for Michelle—and me.* Abby interrupted the quietness. "Look, Mommy," she said, pointing into the brush.

A medium-sized black bear was ambling toward their camp. They watched quietly at first, enjoying the close encounter with wildlife. About twenty-five yards away, the bear raised on his hind legs, sniffing the air. "He smells our food," Roger observed as the bear returned to all four feet and continued strolling toward them.

"We don't really want him any closer." Michelle got to her feet.

Earl waved his arms, and shouted, "Go away, bear! We don't want you here!" Michelle started clanging a spoon against the kettle of stew. The bear stopped and looked at them for a moment, then continued slowly toward them.

"He's not afraid of us." Roger took a quick glance at Michelle.

"He's way too friendly for me!" Michelle added.

"Everybody, make lots of noise," Roger instructed as he walked to his tent, waving his arms and shouting. He ducked into his tent for a moment and emerged with the revolver. He pulled six bullets out of the belt. Dropping the belt on the ground, he loaded the gun and proceeded to the edge of the camp where he had a clear view of the bear.

"You're not going to kill it, are you?" Michelle suddenly sounded sympathetic.

"Not unless I have to. I just want to convince him to leave." As the bear stood broadside, sniffing at something on the ground, Roger aimed carefully at the ground in front of the bear and squeezed the trigger. Dirt splattered in the bear's face as the blast rang out. The bear bolted backward and took several bounding hops toward the underbrush. Then it stopped and looked back at the campers. Roger fired again, this time into the bushes behind the animal. The bear resumed his run for cover. As the bear disappeared into the underbrush, Roger fired the remaining four shots, sending bullets whistling through the bushes on both sides of the animal.

Roger returned, took another six bullets from the belt, reloaded the gun, and stuck it in the holster. "You mind if I keep this thing handy?" he asked as he wrapped the belt around his waist.

"No," Michelle replied. "Actually, I believe this is the first time in my life that I appreciate seeing a man with a gun. I don't like that bear, and I'm not convinced that he'll stay away."

"Yeah. I wouldn't be surprised if he comes back after things quiet down tonight. He knows there's food here, and he doesn't seem to have any fear of humans. I suspect someone's been feeding him."

"What are you going to do? You can't stay up all night watching out for him."

"No, I'll have to come up with a better plan than that." Roger scratched his head. "First of all, we need to gather up all our garbage and food scraps and make a pile some distance from the camp. Then we'll hope that he goes there before he starts tearing our camp apart. I'll see if I can rig up some kind of booby trap that makes noise to alert us if anything disturbs the garbage."

Earl watched with excited curiosity as Roger set up a network of strings surrounding the garbage. A tug on any string would pull a stick out of the fork in a tree branch. That would release Roger's Swiss Army knife, which was attached to a string. It would swing down and strike the edge of a kettle that was hanging from the tree branch.

As Roger tested his booby trap, Michelle and Abby came over to see the device that was making all the noise. "I've found yet another use for a Swiss Army knife," Roger said proudly. "You can use it for a bell clapper. See how this works. If any large animal tries to get to that garbage, he'll be sure to hit one of these strings." He pushed against one of them. The knife swung down and clanged against the kettle. "That should be enough to wake me up."

"Very clever." Michelle nodded and smiled.

"I'll keep the gun and flashlight handy all night," Roger promised. "If that bear comes back, I'll have a little surprise for him."

"Well, it looks like we won't have to lie awake worrying about a bear." Michelle turned back toward her tent. "Come on, children, let's get ready for bed. We've got a big day tomorrow."

The night was quiet and long. Roger awoke numerous times and lay in his tent listening to the stillness outside. Finally the morning light started filtering through his tent. He zipped it open and crawled out into the morning mist. Except for the heavy dew, everything looked just as it had the evening before. Roger got a campfire started, and before long, Michelle poked her head out. "No bear?" she asked softly.

"No bear," Roger confirmed. Soon the children were up and staring into the mist, looking for the bear. After a breakfast of instant oatmeal and hot chocolate, everyone got busy cleaning up, tearing down and packing.

The morning mist was still rising from the river as they headed out on their final leg. As the sun grew warmer, the mist quickly vanished into the clear morning air. A vee of ripples stretched out from the bow of Michelle's boat as she slipped ahead of Roger. "You'd better slow it down a little," Roger warned. "You're gonna wear yourself out by noontime."

"I know. I keep telling myself to slow down. But I just keep going faster."

"I know you're eager to get home. But if we get to Keating before Rick and George, that won't help us at all, will it?"

As they made their way downstream, the river grew a bit wider and shallower while the sun rose higher and grew hotter. They frequently ran into wide shallow areas where there was no way but to step out of the canoe and drag it across. Progress was slow, requiring frequent breaks for food and water or just to get out of the sun for a while. Roger couldn't help but notice Michelle's restlessness. As soon a food was distributed, she resealed the containers and put them back into the canoe, ready to get underway again. Each time they stopped to rest, she would pace about, eager to get back on the water.

It was close to three o'clock when they made a left turn and paddled up into the mouth of the Sinnemahoning Creek. Michelle's heart raced. On the delta between the river and the creek was a small grassy park where George and Rick stood waiting. As the canoes came to shore, Rick and George each grabbed a bow and pulled them up onto the grass.

As the four climbed out of the canoes, two uniformed state police troopers approached, accompanied by a man in civilian clothes. "These are your escorts," George gestured toward the troopers, "Trooper Lisa Brower and Trooper Lloyd Smith."

The plainclothesman stepped forward. "Hello. I'm Ivan Cox, special agent, FBI. How's it going?"

"We're glad to finally be here." Michelle sighed.

After a brief time of getting acquainted, Agent Cox said, "We'll take the four of you in that van over there. Your two friends here will load up your gear and catch up with us later. Our first stop will be your sister's place in Bellefonte."

"Your mother is there waiting for you," George added softly, leaning toward Michelle.

"Your sister is planning to put you up for the night," Agent Cox continued. "Then we'll head back to Thrush Glen sometime tomorrow. How does that sound?"

"Sounds great!" Michelle replied as she scooped up Abby and squeezed her, trying hard to control her emotions.

"We'll keep you away from the media as long as we can," Trooper Smith said. "But sooner or later you're going to have to deal with them."

"We've got some drinks and snacks in the van," Trooper Brower said as she patted Earl on the shoulder. "If anybody has any personal items you need to take along, you can get them now. Rick and George will meet us in Bellefonte with all the rest of your supplies."

"I guess I don't need my wallet, do I?" Roger glanced at the trooper.

"I wouldn't know what for. But if you want it, get it."

"I don't think I need anything," Michelle said, trying to think what she might need.

"You don't have a purse or anything?" The trooper raised her eyebrows.

"No," Michelle chuckled. "I've learned to survive without a purse."

Trooper Smith grinned. "You need to teach Trooper Brower how you do that."

Abby tugged on Michelle's hand. "Is Tooper Tower a mommy?"

Trooper Brower smiled as she fondled Abby's curls. "You may call me Lisa. And yes, I am a mommy. I have a little girl about the same age as you."

"I'll take the middle seat," Agent Cox said as he opened the sliding door. "That way it will be easier for me to talk with everybody. I want to get some information from you while we're driving."

Trooper Brower gave each of the children a box of juice and a small bag of animal crackers. Then she helped get them buckled into their child seats. Michelle climbed into the back seat, next to the children as the state troopers got situated in the front seat. Roger took the seat in front of Special Agent Cox.

"Everybody okay back there?" Trooper Brower asked as they got underway.

"This man you call Jasper," Agent Cox began, "he's the children's father, I assume?"

"That's right." Michelle nodded.

"And is everyone aware of what's happened?" Agent Cox studied her face.

"Yes, we know that he passed away." Michelle bit her lip. "I've told the children."

"Okay," Agent Cox continued. "His real name is Jason Keelson."

"Keelson?" Roger's head spun around. "I think that was the name of one of the previous property owners."

"Yes, it was," Agent Cox confirmed. "Your friends gave us all the information you collected. Jason is the son of Earl Keelson, who once owned the property where Jason was hiding."

"His father's name was Earl?" Michelle mused.

"That's right," Agent Cox nodded.

Michelle nudged her son and said, "You were named after your grandfather."

"Huh?" Earl replied with a puzzled look.

"Your daddy's daddy—his name was Earl. I guess that's why your daddy wanted to name you Earl," Michelle explained.

The boy looked pleased, but obviously more interested in the sights of the modern world passing outside his window.

"So," Roger said thoughtfully, "Jasper's father bought the land from Chief Theodore's grandmother."

"Were looking into that," Agent Cox replied. "We'd like to know what all went on between Chief Miller and the Keelsons. By the way, we have the bag of cash that Jason gave you. I'd love to let you keep it. But I can't do that. It's evidence. Our detectives are following that trail."

As they drove down Route 120, along the river, Special Agent Cox continued questioning them about Jason and his brother Harold, the chief, and the person known as Bobby. But most of the time, Michelle had to admit that she didn't know the answers.

Then the questioning turned to the gray-haired man. "We don't know who he is," Agent Cox admitted. "But to be honest, we haven't had time to look into that very much. We just know that he's not one of our people and he's not with the state police. But with the information you've given us, we should be able to track him down. We just have to find the time to work on it." Eventually they got off the interstate and followed Route 150 as it wound through the mountains beside Spring Creek.

"We're almost there," Trooper Smith called from the driver's seat as they entered the town of Bellefonte. "Time to wrap it up and get ready for a reunion."

Michelle admired the old Victorian buildings as they drove through the downtown area. Things hadn't changed much since the last time she had seen her sister's neighborhood. *But what about the people? Were they still as friendly as she remembered them?* As the van slowed to turn into the drive, she recognized her sister's house, a large Victorian house with arched-top windows. It was a two-story brick structure with wood corbels and heavy cornice moldings. All the wood trim was neatly painted in tan and burgundy. In the small but neatly manicured front lawn was a sign that read, "Mae King's Beauty Salon."

Trooper Brower turned in her seat and asked, "Did you know your sister owns a beauty salon?"

28

A young-looking, neatly dressed lady sat in an old stuffed armchair reading a magazine. Her hair was freshly colored and styled, and her makeup was done to perfection. She wouldn't have wanted anyone to guess that she was a fifty-year-old grandmother of four, two of whom she was about to meet for the very first time. She was looking at the magazine and turning the pages. But her mind was on the events that were unfolding and on the strange accounts she had heard regarding her missing daughter. It all seemed so unbelievable. At the sound of a vehicle turning in the drive, she put down the magazine and hurried to the door.

Mrs. Danklos and her oldest daughter's family gathered by the van as Michelle and the children climbed out. Tears rolled down her cheeks as she threw her arms around her missing daughter. Eventually Michelle squirmed free and introduced Abigail and Earl. Then, turning to the children, she said, "And this is your… grandmother. Or what would you like them to call you?"

"Mae's children call me Nana."

"Okay, children, this is Nana. And this is Aunt Mae," she added, turning to her sister with open arms. Nana gave Earl a quick hug, then scooped Abby up in her arms, hugging and kissing her and wondering why the little girl wasn't returning the affection.

After Nana put Abby down again, her son-in-law squatted down to the kids' level and said, "Hi, I'm Uncle Fred." Pointing to his children with a big smile, he added, "And these are your cousins, Rita and Tom."

"Earl, how old are you?" Aunt Mae asked, running the fingers of one hand through his hair while keeping her other arm around Michelle.

He put up five fingers. "Five."

"So you're just a little older than Tom," Mae commented. "He's almost five and Rita is six."

"It's my turn now," Fred said as he rose to his feet, extending his arms toward Michelle. "How are you doing? You're looking great."

Mae turned to her children. "Why don't you take Earl and Abigail inside and show them your rooms?" Earl hesitated, and Abby turned to her mother extending her arms upward.

"It's okay," Michelle assured them. "You can go inside and see their house. I'll be coming in too, pretty soon."

Nana watched the four children head indoors, but the adults seemed too busy talking to move from the spot.

Roger and Trooper Brower both blinked back tears as they stood by the van watching Michelle reunite with her family. To Roger, it felt a bit awkward to be standing with the police and observing, rather than participating. He didn't really belong with the police. But neither was he a family member, and he probably never would be. But the family didn't seem to realize that. They still thought of him as Michelle's boyfriend. They hadn't heard Michelle speaking of Jasper as her husband. They had no idea how much she loved the criminal who had abducted her. They hadn't heard Michelle declare that she would not be romantically involved with an atheist.

Roger knew that sooner or later there would be comments or questions regarding his relationship with Michelle. He wouldn't know what to say. He himself didn't know exactly where the relationship stood or where it was headed. Michelle's actions hadn't exactly conformed to her statement. He felt there was still hope for the relationship. But certainly, they would both need some time to sort out their feelings.

Eventually, Trooper Lloyd Smith interrupted the family chatter and informed Michelle that he and Special Agent Cox were returning to headquarters.

"I'll stay in touch." Agent Cox nodded to Michelle. "I need to set up a time for you to come down to headquarters and go over a lot of details. But that can wait a couple days."

"Trooper Brower will be with you the rest of the evening," Trooper Smith added. "And then we'll have troopers in patrol cars watching the house in shifts the rest of the night."

"Thank you so much." Michelle glanced from one officer to another. "I really appreciate everything you're doing."

"Everyone, come on in the house and make yourselves comfortable," Mae called out as the van backed out the drive. But moving the group was a slow process. It appeared that no one wanted to move first, for fear of missing out on part of the conversation. As the group migrated into the living room, Mae and her mother started setting out food and drinks. Somehow, the children in the upstairs rooms figured out what was happening in the kitchen. By the time Mae invited the adults to come help themselves, the four kids were already orbiting the smorgasbord on the kitchen table.

About that time, George and Rick arrived with the canoes and camping gear. Mrs. Danklos ushered them right in and directed them to the food line. After chatting with the other two guys, Roger went to Trooper Brower and asked, "Am I staying here for the night or am I going back to Thrush Glen?"

"I understand they have a place for you to sleep here. But if you would rather go on home, that's okay. You just won't have any police protection."

"We have plenty of space here," Mae confirmed. "We eventually want to turn this place into a bed and breakfast."

"I think Michelle and the children need the police protection more than I do." Roger looked back at the trooper.

"And they are the ones I am charged with protecting. As long as you stay with us, you'll have that protection too. But if you want to leave, you're free to do that."

"Okay then. I appreciate the offer, but I'm going home with Rick and George."

The guys showed their appreciation for the food the best way they knew how—by eating as much of it as they could. Then they went out to the truck and brought in the bags containing Michelle's and the children's clothing, sleeping bags, and personal items. When that was done, they said their good-byes and headed for home.

"Mae, could I get you to give me a haircut?" Michelle brushed her long hair back.

"Of course!" Mae replied enthusiastically, "My time is all yours. How about a complete makeover?"

"What?"

"You probably don't even know what the latest styles are, do you?"

"I'm sure I don't."

Mrs. Danklos started reading a story to the grandchildren as Mae offered to take Michelle to the salon for a makeover. Trooper Brower followed them into the salon.

"So where's Daddy?" Michelle asked as soon as they were away from their mother. "Roger told me they're divorced."

"Yeah, they're divorced. I don't know where he is."

"You don't keep in touch with him?"

"Can't! He just moves around from place to place and never tells us where he's going."

"Roger said he thought he was in California."

"He was, for a while. But he doesn't seem to be there anymore."

"I can't believe he would just take off and not tell you where he is."

"If he knew that you were still alive, I'm sure things would be different."

"What do you mean?"

"Well, you always were Daddy's little girl."

"And you were Momma's big girl. You never had any time to spend with Daddy."

"I would have had time." Mae rolled her eyes. "But I didn't enjoy risking my life trying to ride a tippy canoe down some wild river."

"You missed out on a lot of good times. Daddy and I had so much fun together."

"If you only knew how much Mom worried when the two of you were off on you whitewater adventures…"

"Actually, we never did anything very dangerous. She just worries about everything. I always felt perfectly safe with Daddy. He really knew what he was doing. He taught me so much about safety."

"When you disappeared, she blamed it all on Daddy."

"Oh." Michelle paused, trying to picture the conflict in her mind. "And they didn't have a good relationship to begin with. No wonder they got divorced."

"Mom! What did you do to your hair?" Earl exclaimed as the three ladies returned from the salon.

"I asked Aunt Mae to cut my hair and color it." Michelle grinned at her son. "Do you like it?"

"Nope," Earl answered without hesitation. "You don't look like my mom."

"Oh, Earl!" Lisa patted him on the shoulder. "Don't say that! Your mom is pretty."

Michelle just laughed and said, "I taught him to be honest."

"The kids will get used to it," Mae promised.

"It's about time for me to be going," Trooper Brower said. "But don't worry. Somebody will be watching the house from a patrol car all night."

"I'm not worried," Michelle assured her.

"And I'll be here at eight in the morning to take you shopping," the trooper promised.

"Okay, kids," Mae called out. "It's time to get ready for bed." The announcement didn't generate the negative response that Mae had predicted. The children seemed eager to share their bedrooms with their cousins. In no time, they had their pajamas on and their teeth brushed. Of course, actually quieting down and going to sleep took a little longer—much longer, in fact.

Michelle tossed and turned on her air mattress in an unfinished guest bedroom. It was much more comfortable than what she was used to. That wasn't the problem. She was wide awake, reminiscing. Memories of her dad raced through her mind. She thought about his love of adventure, his cautious assessment of the risks, and his reliable decisions. She thought about the numerous times she and Roger had accompanied him on whitewater excursions. She remembered the good times with her sister, playing with dolls and talking about boys. She remembered her mother reading books to them—Nancy Drew, Tom Sawyer, and lots of others. Now, it all seemed so long ago. Her life had turned into an adventure of its own. She longed to return to those simpler times, to just curl up in her father's arms and know that everything is okay.

She wondered when she would see her father again. How could she find him? Somehow, she would find a way. As soon as things got settled down, as soon as she was finished telling and retelling her story to the police and friends and family, as soon as she could do as she pleased, she would find her daddy.

29

Thursday morning was a blur of activity in the King household. Michelle hadn't experienced this kind of hustle and bustle in seven years. It was kind of fun once again, except everyone had to wait their turn to use one of the two bathrooms. "We need more bathrooms before we can turn this into a bed and breakfast," Mae reminded her husband.

"I know that." He winked at Michelle as he slipped a CD into the player. If anyone wasn't awake, they soon would be.

Nana was helping Abby get dressed as Mae set out a variety of breakfast foods. "Just grab what you want whenever you're ready," she called out from the kitchen. "I'm not going to try to get everyone to the table at once."

At three minutes to eight, Trooper Brower pulled in the drive with the van. "You girls just go," Fred called over his shoulder as he dropped a bagel into the toaster. "Nana and I have everything under control here."

As Michelle and her sister exited, they met Lisa Brower, dressed in a casual outfit, walking toward them. "Good morning." Lisa smiled. "Did everyone find a place to sleep?"

"Oh yeah," Mae replied with a chuckle. "But now I'm ready to get out of there for a little while. It's feeding time at the zoo in there."

"My sister's not a very good animal trainer," Michelle quipped. "She just puts the food out and lets the animals fight over it."

"Survival of the fittest." Mae laughed as she glanced up at the bright morning sky.

"Now I might not look like a state police trooper," Lisa turned to head back to the van, "but don't worry. I am on duty, and I've got my gun in my purse."

"That's fine," Michelle tried not to sound sarcastic. "It seems I'm always surrounded by people with guns."

"Now, Michelle, you don't need to worry about paying for anything." Mae glanced at her sister. "We'll put it all on my credit card. And there's a whole bunch of people who want to help pay the bill."

"Oh, so I won't need this." Michelle pulled a wad of cash out of her pocket and waved it at Mae.

The trooper immediately shielded her eyes with her hand. "I didn't see that! And I don't want to know where you got it."

"Oh!" Michelle felt her face turn red as she quickly stuffed the cash back in her pocket.

"You keep that out of sight." Lisa grinned slightly as she eyed Michelle. "Put everything on Mae's card, like she said. You can spend that cash sometime when I'm not around."

"Thanks," Michelle said sheepishly as they climbed into the van.

As they strolled through the mall, Michelle kept glancing around and behind her. Something didn't seem right. Her children weren't there.

"You missing somebody?" Lisa glanced at Michelle.

"Yeah. I keep looking for the kids. I guess this is the first time I've ever been away from them."

"They'll be all right," Mae assured her.

"I know. It just seems strange." *But they'll miss me just as much as I miss them. What if Abby starts crying and nobody can console her?* Michelle couldn't seem to get her mind focused on shopping. Eager to get back as soon as possible, she quickly tried on whatever Mae suggested. If Mae thought it looked good, she agreed to take it. In little more than an hour, they were headed back to the van with several new outfits.

"I think we probably broke a record," Mae quipped. "We'll have to do this again sometime when you can relax and enjoy it."

Thursday morning had also been a blur of activity at George's house. Roger wandered from room to room checking out the new decor. In little more than half a day, the house had been transformed from a bachelor pad into a cozy home for a mother and two children.

Michelle's friends, Joanne and Sheryl, and four other ladies responsible for the transformation, sat in the family room chatting and awaiting the arrival of the new occupants. Roger strolled into the kitchen where several men in work clothes were helping George dispose of his last few cans of beer. One of them raised his can. "You're too late. This is the last one."

"That's okay." Roger chuckled. "I'm not old enough for that."

At about one thirty, Trooper Lloyd Smith parked his patrol car along the street in front of the house. George met him at the door. "You got everything under control here?" The trooper glanced about the group.

"I think so." George nodded.

"You're personally acquainted with everyone here?"

"Yes, sir." George invited him in and introduced everyone.

"And you haven't seen anything of that gray-haired man in the white Buick?" Trooper Smith questioned.

"No, sir," George replied.

"Good. Trooper Brower and Special Agent Cox are on their way with Michelle and the children. They should be here in less than half an hour. If you see any strangers hanging around, you let me know." As they waited, George gave Trooper Smith a tour of the house and his workshop. Roger considered going along out to the shop but felt more inclined to just stay in the house and wait for Michelle.

Finally the van turned in the drive and pulled around to the back door. As the crew of volunteers made their way into the back yard, Trooper Brower walked around the van and opened the sliding door. Special Agent Cox stepped out first, followed by a professional-looking young lady in heels and a belted tunic dress that complimented her elegant figure. Then Earl and Abby popped out. They stopped and looked up at the lady, as if she were their mother.

"Holy cow! That's Michelle!" Roger exclaimed. He was used to seeing her in khaki shorts and water shoes with a long blond braid down her back. Now here she was, looking just as beautiful as she did in high school, only more mature and sophisticated. As Roger and Michelle stepped toward each other with open arms, the group of ladies moved in. It was one polite little hug for Roger, then greetings of all kinds from the group of old friends. Roger and George stepped back and watched as Michelle reunited with friends she hadn't seen since high school.

George seemed antsy, like he thought he should be doing something other than watching. As Roger listened to the ladies chattering, George opened the back of the van and gathered up all the luggage, most of it still in dry bags from the canoe trip. With several shopping bags in one hand, a dry bag in the other, and another dry bag slung over his shoulder, George started toward the house.

Well, there goes the landlord acting like a bellhop. Roger nudged his way through the group of ladies and proffered his arm to Michelle. "Let me show you to your new home."

Michelle smiled through her tears and grasped his arm. Earl and Abigail followed as Roger led them onto the back porch and into the sparkling kitchen. George proceeded up the open staircase with his load, brushing against the freshly polished oak banister. He disappeared into master bedroom as Roger escorted Michelle into the family room with the group of volunteers following. Several ladies showed Abby and Earl to their rooms while the others urged Michelle in all directions to see the things they had provided.

As they returned to the family room, Michelle released Roger's arm and grasped George by the arm. "How can I ever thank you? You didn't have to do this. It's too much."

"It's no big deal," George replied modestly. "The house is bigger than what I need right now. My mom still had my room just like it was when I lived there. She's just two doors down, so I still have easy access to my workshop. This is such a practical solution. To do anything else would have been ridiculous."

"I can't tell you how much this means to me." She squeezed his arm and kissed him on the cheek.

Trooper Brower poked her head into the family room and asked, "Michelle and Roger, could you join us on the back porch for a minute?"

They followed Lisa to the back porch where Agent Cox was waiting. "Trooper Smith and I are leaving," he said. "But first I want to bring you and Roger up to date on the latest developments."

"Okay." Michelle grasped Roger's arm again.

"This morning," Agent Cox continued, "Jason Keelson's brother Harold was found dead. They found him floating in his swimming pool at his home in Philadelphia. Initially, it looks like an accident. But of course, we're doing an autopsy and continuing to investigate."

"What are the odds?" Roger shook his head. "First of all, Jasper gets bitten by a snake that's not normally found in this area. Next, Chief Theodore, who taught gun safety, accidentally shoots himself. Now Jasper's brother accidentally drowns in his own pool. I can't believe these are all accidents. Somebody is trying to get rid of everyone who knew what was going on in that cottage."

"We're looking very carefully at all those deaths," Agent Cox sounded convincing.

"We don't want you to worry." Trooper Brower put her hand on Michelle's shoulder. "We'll have someone here around the clock as long as necessary."

"Have you found out anything about that gray-haired man?" Michelle looked at Agent Cox.

"No. Actually we've been more focused on figuring out who Bobby is. We seem to be making some progress on that one. We've identified a person of interest, but we haven't been able to make a definite connection yet."

"Do you have him in custody?" Roger asked.

"No," Agent Cox paused. "He's dead."

Earl burst through the door and yelled, "Mommy, come! Abby fell down the steps!" Michelle rushed inside to find Joanne holding Abby in her arms.

"I don't think she's hurt bad," Joanne said as she passed the crying child to her mother. "She just tumbled down the last few steps." The crying soon subsided, and Abby was ready to continue exploring their new home.

Not long after Agent Ivan Cox and Trooper Lloyd Smith left, Mae and Fred arrived with their youngsters and Nana. "Looks like you're all settled in already," Mae observed.

"Well, I haven't unpacked our clothes yet," Michelle replied. "But everything else was done before I got here."

As Michelle showed them around the house, two more ladies showed up with a big kettle of homemade chicken corn soup and lots of other goodies. Rick dropped in as soon as he got off work.

"You gonna take the kids to see fireworks?" Fred asked as he sat down next to Michelle with a bowl of soup in his hand.

"Fireworks? I hadn't thought about that. I guess the Fourth of July is coming up soon, isn't it?

"It's tomorrow." Fred cocked his head, watching Michelle out of the corner of his eye.

"Tomorrow? Really?" Michelle seemed surprised. "Yeah, I hope we can see some somewhere. Of course, the kids have never experienced anything like that."

"There's a small show down here at the park tomorrow night," Rick chimed in. "They shoot 'em off from the other side of Thrush Creek. It's not a big show like you would see in State College or Harrisburg. But it's kind of nice."

"That's good." Michelle sounded pleased. "I wouldn't want to it to be too big for the first time. They might be scared out of their wits."

"The smaller the crowd, the better," Trooper Brower advised. "I suppose this will be a small hometown crowd with a lot of people you know. I won't deprive you of that. And the local media is being very cooperative. But you have to keep thinking about security."

After dinner, the volunteers gradually began leaving. Mae and her family headed back to Bellefonte. As the three guys relaxed in the family room, Roger relayed the information from Agent Cox about Jasper's brother.

"So do they still think these are all freak accidents?" Rick's eyebrows furrowed.

"He just said they're taking a careful look at all of them," Roger explained. "I'm sure they'll find something. Obviously, somebody must be behind all this. I'd just like to know who."

George caught Michelle's eye. "It's kind of scary, isn't it? All these deaths…"

"Not really." Michelle smiled back at him. "Right now I'm so overwhelmed by everyone's generosity and God's providence. I don't think I could feel scared if I wanted to."

Life and Death

30

Trooper Lisa Brower paced back and forth, keeping a close eye on the groups of spectators accumulating in the park. She paid particular attention to gray-haired men, although there weren't many who fit the description of being in prime physical condition. Roving vendors were selling cotton candy and cold drinks. The elementary school band was playing patriotic music while friends and neighbors greeted each other. The trooper never strayed far from Michelle and her children. Rick, Nana, Fred, and Mae sat on lawn chairs, chatting as the pink sky gradually faded to midnight blue. In front of them, several blankets were spread out on the grass. Roger, Michelle, George, and the four children relaxed on the blankets, watching for the first rocket to blast into the sky. "If you see that gray-haired gentleman or anybody suspicious, you let me know right away," Lisa had told them earlier. "You know who your friends are. I don't." It concerned Trooper Brower that she didn't know exactly what this gray-haired gentleman looked like and that no one knew who Bobby was or what he looked like. But what concerned her most was that Michelle seemed almost oblivious to the danger she was in.

Michelle was having a great time. Most of the time, she was on her feet, greeting people and chatting with old friends. "Where's George?" she asked as she returned to the blanket beside Roger.

"He went to but soft pretzels for everybody." Roger leaned against her.

"Well, hi there, Roger," a female voice called out as a group of young ladies approached. "It looks like you haven't fallen off the edge of the earth after all."

"No, I'm still alive and doing fine," Roger quipped as he got to his feet.

"I can see that." The speaker shot a stern glance at Michelle.

"I'm so sorry about missing our date." Roger strolled along beside her for a moment. "I didn't mean to. It's just that some things came up that were out of my control. I had no choice."

"I have a phone," she replied with a tinge of bitterness. "You could call me—if you wanted to."

"I will," Roger promised. He stopped, and the ladies kept walking. "I'll call you."

"Who was that?" Michelle asked as Roger got seated again.

"Kathy Keller. She teaches third grade at our school," Roger explained. "She and I went out a few times."

"Oh. That explains it."

"I'm such a jerk. It seems I'm always needing to apologize to somebody for one thing or another."

"You're not a jerk. You just care enough to say you're sorry. That's one of the things I admire about you. A lot of guys are too proud to do that."

"I don't think she sees it that way."

"I don't think she likes me." She bumped her shoulder into Roger's. "If looks could kill, I'd be dead."

"She's not dangerous." Roger chuckled. Then in a more serious tone, he added, "There's someone else you need to be more concerned about. We just don't know who it is."

Kaboom! A red streak soared into the night sky. *Bang!* Michelle felt the impact of the blast against her chest as the dazzling white starburst lit up the park. Abby scurried into her mother's arms. Earl froze on the spot. But the obvious delight of his cousins eventually convinced him that this was actually fun. However, Abby remained skeptical, cuddling against her mother with her hands over her ears.

“Roger, you said you thought my dad was in California,” Michelle said as they gazed at the sky. “Where did you get that information?”

“From your sister.”

“So I guess you don’t know any more than she does.”

“No. Why?”

“Oh, I’m just trying to find somebody who knows where he is.”

“Mom, have you heard anything from Daddy recently?” Mae looked at her mother.

“No, not a word.”

“You don’t know where he is, then?” Michelle asked.

“Last I heard was that place in California. I have no idea where he is now.”

“Somehow, I’m going to find him,” Michelle declared, staring at the sky.

“Good luck,” Mae retorted.

Michelle smiled as she looked at her daughter’s face. Although she kept her hands clamped over her ears, Abby’s eyes said she was enjoying the show. But right up through the grand finale, she insisted on the security of her mother’s arms.

On Saturday morning, Roger called Kathy and apologized again for breaking their date without contacting her. He tried to explain the reason for his quick disappearance.

“I think when you saw Michelle again, you simply forgot all about me,” Kathy argued.

“Well, to be perfectly honest, I have to admit that there’s some truth in that,” Roger paced as he spoke. “But our lives were in danger—and still are. We had to get away quickly and quietly. We had a lot of planning and preparation to do, and only one evening to do it. I didn't have time to think about anyone or anything else."

"I understand." Kathy sounded like she was maintaining her opinion. "Rick explained it all to me last week. He told me how the police chief interrogated him and tore your house apart."

"And I thought Michelle was dead." Roger turned on his heel. "You can imagine what a shock it was to see her alive!"

"Is Rick there?"

"No. He's at church rehearsing for tomorrow with the band."

"When he gets back, remind him that he promised to give me a ride on his motorcycle sometime."

"He did?"

"Yeah, and today is a perfect day. The weather is great, and I have no plans for the afternoon."

"Okay, I'll remind him," Roger promised. "He should be back in a half hour or so. I'll tell him to call you."

Roger was sitting on the porch reading *Canoe Magazine* when Rick returned. "Did you promise somebody a ride on your bike?" Roger glanced up from the magazine.

Rick shook his head with a puzzled look. "I don't know what you're talking about."

"Kathy said you promised to take her for a ride."

Rick shook his head again. "We did talk about biking. But I didn't know I promised a ride or anything else."

"Well, you're supposed to call her. It's a beautiful day, and she has nothing to do."

"What? She's your girlfriend. I'm not trying to cut in."

"Don't worry about it. She's just jealous of Michelle."

"So now she's trying to use me to make you jealous?" Rick cocked his head.

"Yeah, maybe," Roger chuckled. "Go ahead. Take her for a ride. Spend all afternoon with her, for all I care. I don't need her breathing down my neck while I try to figure out where I stand with Michelle."

"Well, it is a great day to go riding," Rick remarked as he headed inside. After a brief phone call and a change of clothes, he roared away on his bike. Roger didn't see him again until late that evening.

"It must have been quite a ride," Roger commented as Rick came into the library.

"Yeah, we had a really nice time." Rick sank into the easy chair. "We took a relaxing ride through the mountains. We stopped at a nice restaurant, then we rode up to Slate Point Vista and watched the sunset."

"The vista on a Saturday evening? What was that like?"

"There wasn't anything wild going on. There were two parked cars there. I can only imagine what was going on inside. Of course, we were standing outside, in front of everyone. So we weren't doing anything inappropriate—a little cuddling and kissing, that's all."

"Just trying to make me jealous, aye?"

"Well, you wanted me to get her off your back."

"Yeah, keep doing it. I'm not jealous. As long as Michelle's in the picture, I'm not really interested in anyone else."

Michelle stood quietly at the back of the sanctuary as the worship band finished warming up. It had been more than seven years since she had attended a Sunday morning worship service. And this was the first ever for her children, who stood one on each side, holding her hands. She led them down the aisle and slipped into the pew next to George. Lisa Brower followed behind and took the seat by the aisle.

After the opening song, the worship leader welcomed everyone, including the news reporters, and announced that after the service there would be a fellowship meal as a welcome-home celebration for Michelle and her family. Everyone was invited to stay and enjoy the food and fellowship.

This was the first time the children had ever seen a band performing, and they really enjoyed the worship singing, especially when the band led an old hymn they had often heard their mother singing. The kids sang along enthusiastically: "When peace like a river attendeth my way, when sorrows like sea billows roll; whatever my lot…" Maybe the lyrics meant nothing to the children. But Michelle got too choked up to continue singing as she thought about the peace that had sustained her through seven dark years of uncertainty.

On Monday, as Roger was finishing his lunch, there was a knock on the door. He opened the door to find Ivan Cox and another gentleman. They both flipped their badges and identified themselves as FBI agents. "We need to talk with you," Special Agent Cox said.

"Come on in," Roger replied.

Agent Cox laid a photograph on the kitchen table and asked, "Is that you?"

Roger stared at an aerial photo of himself aiming his revolver at the rotten tree trunk.

"It's a rhetorical question." Agent Cox looked at Roger. "We know it's you. Where did you get the gun?"

"Jasper gave it to me."

"Jasper. You mean Jason Keelson?"

"Yeah. He gave it to me while Michelle was packing up their stuff."

"Why haven't you told us about it?"

"Uh. Well, uh…"

"You didn't think that gun would be an important piece of evidence?" Agent Cox spoke in an even tone.

"Do you have a permit to have a handgun?" his partner added.

"No, sir." Roger was beginning to feel like an outlaw.

"We could charge you with a number of things." Agent Cox remained pokerfaced. "But that's not what we're here for. We just need to confiscate the weapon."

"Can you show us where it is?" his partner added.

Roger led them to his room, opened the closet, and pointed to the top shelf.

"Did the holster and belt come from Jason too?"

"Yes, sir."

"We'll just take the whole works, just like that," the agent said as he slipped it into a plastic bag.

"And this is the gun you used to shoot at that stump?" Agent Cox studied Roger's face.

"Yes, sir."

"Then this is the link we've been looking for." Cox turned to his partner. "This gun tells us who Bobby is."

"You figured out who Bobby is?" Roger wanted more information.

"You got anything important to do in the next couple hours?" Agent Cox asked as they started down the stairs.

"Nothing that can't wait."

"We'd like you to come down to the station. There are some things we want to go over with you and Michelle. Trooper Brower will come by and pick you up in a few minutes."

The two agents left, and twenty minutes later Trooper Lisa Brower pulled in with the van. Michelle was sitting in the front passenger's seat. Earl and Abby were in the next seat.

"What's up?" Roger asked as he climbed into the seat behind the children.

Michelle shrugged. "I don't know. We're supposed to meet someone."

"I don't know a whole lot," Lisa added. "But it's nothing to worry about."

When they arrived at the police station, Trooper Lloyd Smith led them down the hall to a meeting room. "I believe you've seen this guy before," he said as he ushered them in. On opposite sides of a conference table sat Special Agent Ivan Cox and the gray-haired gentleman.

The gray-haired man smiled as he rose to his feet. "Hello. I'm Dan Phillips. Sorry, if I frightened you the first time we met."

Michelle smiled back. "We never knew what to make of you."

"I'm a retired state trooper. And now I'm a self-employed private investigator."

"Have seats." Agent Cox gestured toward the chairs. "Make yourselves comfortable."

"For a while I thought you might be a guardian angel," Michelle admitted as they got seated.

Dan chuckled. "Well, I guess that's exactly what I was trying to be. When I saw the group of you in that store, I knew something was wrong. At first I thought that you and the children might be hostages. But your behavior didn't seem quite consistent with that theory and the guys didn't look like criminals. But something just wasn't right. So I followed you."

She was right about him all along, Roger mused. "And that was you in the airplane?"

"Yeah. When I saw you with that gun, I figured I'd better keep an eye on you till I figure out what you're up to. But then you disappeared."

Michelle and Roger both laughed. "We moved across the river and upstream," Roger said with a smirk.

"Upstream? No wonder I couldn't find you."

"They went upstream, just like your golf ball." Cox quipped, grinning at Phillips.

"Don't forget," Phillips chuckled, "I still won, just like usual."

"It was Michelle's idea to move upstream," Roger continued. "I have to give her the credit for that one."

"I must have gone right by you on the four-wheeler then." Mr. Phillips glanced at Roger.

"Right. We watched you digging my slugs out of that tree trunk."

"And that's what we're here to talk about," Agent Cox added. "We didn't bring you down here just to meet Dan, although I'm sure you're relieved to know that he is nobody you have to worry about. Those slugs he retrieved prove that your gun was used in several crimes, crimes committed by a Jack Roberts, also known as Bobby. He was the kingpin of a small ring specializing in burglary and trafficking stolen goods between Harrisburg and Philadelphia. He'd also do an arson job once in a while."

"Is that the guy you told us was dead?" Roger asked.

"Correct," Agent Cox nodded. "Wednesday night he was filling his car with gas when something caused the gas to ignite. He died at the scene."

"One more." Roger glanced at Michelle.

"Some of the men who operated with him in the past are already serving time in prison," Cox continued. "There's probably more who we haven't apprehended yet. But we don't think they pose a particular threat to you since they weren't directly connected to Jason Keelson. Neither of you have any knowledge of who those people are or what crimes they've committed. So you're no threat to them. Since Bobby died accidentally, his friends have no reason to retaliate against anyone. So we believe this threat has been eliminated."

"I'm glad to hear that," Michelle responded with lack of emotion.

"Now, concerning Chief Theodore Miller," Agent Cox turned to Michelle, "you were right. He did have friends in high places. But we haven't found any evidence that any of those friends knew about his ties to the underworld. And as far as we know, those underworld ties were limited to Jason and Bobby. So there doesn't seem to be anyone connected to Chief Miller who would continue to be a threat to you."

"Looks like my job is being eliminated," Trooper Brower quipped.

"Well, we've got lots of other work for you," Agent Cox paused and shuffled his papers. "Since Jason's brother, Harold, also died accidentally, there's no reason for anyone to retaliate for him. His associates are cooperating with us. We don't believe there's anyone on his end who would try to harm you."

"Any questions on that?" Trooper Smith asked.

"So are you all finished with your investigation already?" Roger looked at Agent Cox.

"Far from it." Agent Cox cleared his throat. "We're continuing to examine a lot of evidence and follow up on a lot of leads. But right now we're just reassessing the dangers to you and your friends."

"Michelle, what do you think about all that?" Trooper Smith studied Michelle's face. "Do you feel you still need Trooper Brower by your side?"

"No." Michelle glanced at her children. "I'm not scared."

"And you, Roger?" Smith asked.

"Don't you guys think all these accidental deaths are just a little suspicious?" Roger couldn't cover the indignation in his voice.

"We've been looking at that," Agent Cox replied evenly. "And we'll continue to look at everything very carefully. But so far, we haven't found any evidence of foul play in any of these cases. And we haven't found anything to connect them to each other."

"What do you mean?" Roger demanded. "The connection is obvious! All these men had a firsthand knowledge of Jasper's whereabouts and activities. Michelle and her children are the only surviving persons who had that knowledge. And you say there's no danger? I tell you, there's still someone else out there—someone we know nothing about!"

"We understand your concern," Agent Cox raised his voice ever so slightly. "And this investigation is far from over. Michelle, how do you feel about Roger's concerns? Do you feel you need continued protection?"

"Look," Michelle began thoughtfully, "I really appreciate everything the police have done for us the past few days. But when I think about my whole experience, it wasn't the police who protected me the last seven years. It wasn't the police who brought me through two deliveries without the help of a doctor. It wasn't the police who protected my children so they never needed any medical attention. I know where to put my faith, and I don't need somebody walking beside me with a gun."

Roger rolled his eyes. *She's so naïve.*

"That was very well said." Lisa leaned over and gave Michelle a squeeze.

"Then as far as I'm concerned," Agent Cox said, turning to Trooper Smith, "we can discontinue that service."

"Michelle, are you okay with that?" Trooper Smith eyed her judiciously.

Michelle nodded.

"When we're all through here then, Trooper Brower will drive you to your homes and drop you off," Smith said. "But don't hesitate to call if you feel you need us for any reason."

"I can't believe this!" Roger blurted out. "You promised protection for as long as we need it! Now you're pulling out already?"

"I think we all just agreed that it's no longer necessary," Trooper Smith reiterated.

"I didn't agree. And I don't agree!"

"As I said, just call us any time for any reason, and we'll be there."

"You're all making a big mistake!" Roger shook his head.

As they prepared to leave, Dan Phillips turned to Michelle. "Is there anything I can do for you, Michelle? As I said before, I'm a private investigator. But the truth is, I have very little work. I have lots of time on my hands. I'm also a licensed pilot. I have my own plane. If there's anything I can do to help you out, it won't cost you a thing."

Michelle thought for only a moment before asking, "Do you think you could help me find my dad?"

31

That Thursday, about noon, Roger dropped in to chat with George. The door to his workshop was open, but when Roger popped his head in, he found the lights were turned off, and everything was quiet. From the back door of the house, Michelle called out, "He's in here. Come on in." Roger started toward the house. It really wasn't George he had come to see anyway.

"Have you had lunch?" Michelle asked as Roger entered the kitchen and breathed in the barbecue aroma. George and the children were seated at the table with plates full of meatballs in barbecue sauce, glazed carrots, and buttered noodles.

"I had a sandwich," Roger replied.

"Pull up a chair," Michelle instructed as she put another plate on the table. "We need help getting rid of all this food. My refrigerator is full of leftovers, and the ladies keep bringing more meals."

"She makes me come in for lunch every day," George said as Roger got seated. "I'm gonna get fat if she keeps this up."

"Well, you ought to have something for the use of your house." Michelle flashed a smile at George.

"You don't owe me anything." George smiled back at her. "This just gives me a chance to pay you back for everything you've done for me. If it weren't for you, I'd probably be a lonely eccentric nerd.

You know what I'm referring to. You were kind to me during a time when I needed it most."

Roger remembered the sixteenth birthday party she had thrown for George. Apparently George realized that event had been a turning point in his life. *She has always been my girlfriend, but she and George have developed a genuine friendship, unencumbered by romance. I suppose he would do anything for her.*

"How's the search for your dad going?" Roger intentionally changed the subject.

"I'm not sure." Michelle cocked her head. "Mr. Phillips spent some time with Mae, trying to get everything she knows. He's heading up to New York to talk with Mom on Saturday. He says he needs to get to know the person he's looking for."

"I'm not sure you should be giving him a lot of personal information."

"Why not?" Michelle's eyes narrowed.

"I just don't trust him." Roger paused. "Something just doesn't make sense. Those guys are golfing buddies—him and Cox. Did you catch that in our meeting on Monday?"

"Yeah. So what?"

"We gave Cox a good description of Phillips and his car and airplane. And he said he had no idea who this gray-haired man was. They golf together regularly, and it took them this long to figure out that they were working on the same case. Either these guys are idiots or they're not telling us the whole story. And I don't think they're idiots."

"You were suspicious of Bobby Billmant too," Michelle reminded him. "And now we know that the Bobby in this case wasn't Bobby Billmant after all."

"Now there's an idiot!" Roger grinned, shaking his head.

"I hear he's seeing a counselor," George interjected.

"He needs it," Roger quipped. "I hope it does him some good."

"Well, Roger," Michelle seemed to be looking for a new topic, "you got anything new on your theory about all the freak accidents?"

"No." Roger gazed into her eyes. "And I just hope I don't wake up some morning to find that you're the latest victim."

"I think you worry too much," Michelle said with a smile.

"I worry because I care about you." Roger felt a slight quiver in his voice. "And it just doesn't seem logical that all four of those guys would die in separate freak accidents. Somebody has to be behind all this."

"Tell me how somebody could have arranged any one of those accidents without leaving a trace of evidence for the police."

"I don't know," Roger admitted. "I'm not a criminal or a detective. I can't answer that question. I'm just looking at the probability of having four freak accidents."

"So," Michelle went on, "you're choosing to believe that somebody planned this, even though you don't understand how it could have been done. This proves what I was trying to tell you last week: you *can* choose to believe something you don't understand."

"Last week we were arguing about the existence of God. On that issue I have a theory that makes more sense than the theory of God. So I choose to believe that theory. But in this case, the theory that somebody planned four homicides makes more sense than four freak accidents. So I believe that."

"Okay." Michelle smiled agreeably. "You might be right. Somebody planned and carried out these four events. But I'm not afraid because I believe that the one who did it is the same one who has been protecting me for the last seven years. Of course, you can't believe that because you have a theory that makes more sense than the theory of God."

"You just wait and see," Roger replied. *She's so naive.* "They say the investigation is far from over. When it's over, you'll see that I was right. Sooner or later we'll have the evidence that those deaths were not accidents after all."

"We'll see." Michelle turned to George. "George, what do you think?"

So now she values George's opinions are more than mine? Roger clenched his jaw.

"Well, Michelle," George began thoughtfully, "you and I both know that God is in control of everything. We know we can trust Him. Yet we still have this dilemma that bad things happen to good people. I don't know why, but we know it's true. So we need to take some precautions for our own safety. Roger could be right. There could be another person that we don't know about yet, a person who is trying to get rid of anyone who might implicate him."

"I guess it could be," Michelle shrugged. "But I really doubt it."

"Well, Roger is right about one thing. The odds are very low for having four freak accidents involving four individuals who are all connected to this case—very low. In fact, I'm kind of concerned because it seems to me that the FBI is too eager to write these off as accidents. It makes me wonder if someone involved in the investigation is covering something up."

"You think I should have kept the police protection?"

"No, I'm not saying that. I don't think you should live your life in fear. If you don't feel like you need a police escort, then that's okay. But you just need to stay alert and cautious. Even though we trust God, we still need to take a good bit of the responsibility for our own safety and well-being."

"Where are you going, Earl?" Michelle asked as her son left the table.

"I'll be back," Earl replied as he hurried into the living room and up the stairs. Soon he was back with a wooden checkerboard in his hands. "See what I made," he said proudly, handing the board to Roger. The board was made up of small squares of maple and walnut, neatly glued together in a checkered pattern and trimmed with a cherry molding around the perimeter.

"Wow! You made this all by yourself?" Roger commented, glancing at George.

"George helped me," Earl admitted. "Next we're gonna make some bird houses."

"You really did an excellent job." Roger handed the board back. "Do you know how to play checkers?"

"Yeah, my dad taught me. You wanna play?"

"Maybe, after I'm finished eating."

"You need to finish your meal too," Michelle reminded Earl.

After lunch was over, George headed back to his workshop, and Roger sat down with Earl to play checkers. The end of each game was followed by a challenge for another match. "Who's winning?" Michelle eventually asked.

"I won five, and he won three," Earl replied with a big smile.

"Well, I'm out of practice. I usually play chess," Roger quipped, winking at Michelle. It wasn't the game that was important to Roger. It was just being in the house with Michelle and the children. After noticing how much time George was spending with them, he just didn't want to leave.

Conveniently, he remembered that he had volunteered to tutor Earl. So he brought up the subject with Michelle. "Could we start with just a couple times a week?" Michelle asked.

"Sure. I could come like Mondays, Wednesdays, and Fridays and spend about an hour with him. If his attention span isn't that long, we can cut it short or play checkers. As he gets accustomed to it, we can increase the time."

"Okay, we'll plan on that." Michelle gave a quick nod.

On Sunday, Michelle and the kids rode to church with George. After church, Rick joined them, and they headed to Betsy's Ice Cream Parlor for lunch. "Rick, your worship band really sounds great," Michelle said as George pulled onto the street.

"Thanks." Rick smiled back at her.

"And you do a super job on the guitar."

"It's not *my* band. But I enjoy play with them."

"If you need anyone else, I'd be glad to help."

"I'm sure they'd be glad to have you. Let's see, you play the flute, don't you?"

"That was a long time ago. I don't know what's become of my flute. I suppose my mom sold it while I was away. But I like to sing. I can always play the tambourine if I need an instrument."

"We can always use another good vocalist. Why don't you come to practice on Saturday morning?"

"Can you pick me up?"

"Of course."

"Isn't it a beautiful morning?" Joanne commented as Michelle opened the door for her friend.

"Actually, I haven't even been out of the house yet this morning." Michelle glanced at the blue sky. "Come on in. I'll be ready in a minute."

Joanne stepped into the kitchen where the children were eating their breakfast. "Aren't the kids coming along?"

"George is going to keep an eye on them for me. He said he's got some paperwork he can bring in and work in here till I get back."

"Boy, it must be great to have a guy like that around," Joanne remarked. "So where do you want to go for breakfast?"

"You're the driver. It's up to you. I'm not particular, especially when I'm living off everyone else's charity."

Momentarily, George strolled in from his shop, carrying several folders and a pocket calculator. "It's so nice of you to do this." Joanne flashed a smile at George as he plopped his things on the table. "You probably have lots of other work you could be doing."

"Well, I gotta do my paperwork sometime. A Tuesday morning is as good as any other time."

"We shouldn't be gone very long," Michelle surmised as she kissed the children goodbye.

"Take all the time you want." George glanced at Michelle. "You need this. Every once in a while you need to get away from everything and just enjoy some time with an old friend."

"Who are you calling old?" Joanne snapped back, pretending to be angry.

"I didn't mean it that way. You ladies have a nice breakfast now."

"We will," they assured him as they slipped out the door.

"That George is somethin' else." Joanne sounded spellbound as they strolled toward the car.

"I can never repay him for everything he's doing for us," Michelle remarked.

"I'm sure he doesn't expect to be repaid. He just likes to do things for people."

"I know."

As they drove to the restaurant, their conversation shifted from George to Roger. "So why aren't you going out with him?" Joanne asked.

"Well, I'm not ready to start going out with anybody just yet. And Roger doesn't believe in God anymore."

"I know. I guess that could be a problem. But he's still a great guy."

"Yeah, I still like him. I just wish he'd change his beliefs."

"Maybe someday, something will happen to him that will turn him around."

"There have already been so many things that should have made him stop and think. He just refuses to see the hand of God in anything. The day he hiked in to our cottage, would you believe, a wild skunk actually came out of the woods in broad daylight and went in front him to protect him from Jasper's guard dog? He just sees that as a coincidence—a very convenient coincidence."

"It still took a lot of courage on his part."

"Yeah, that's one of the things I admire about him."

"So what was it like, living with that Jasper character?"

"Not as bad as everybody thinks. He was very kind and gentle most of the time."

"Really?"

"And," Michelle smiled, "he was actually a very good lover."

"You miss him?"

"Yeah, of course I miss him." A tear momentarily clouded her vision. "But life is so different now. I'm surrounded with so many friends. I hardly have time to think about the past." Time flew by as the two chatted about everything from high school memories and what became of their classmates, to the latest fashions and TV shows.

That Friday, after tutoring Earl, Roger turned to Michelle. "Would you and the kids like to go along to the mall tomorrow morning? We could pick up some arts-and-crafts supplies for the kids and spend a leisurely morning shopping for whatever interests you. They've got a lot of stuff on sale. We can get lunch there or go to a restaurant and be home whenever."

"Sorry. I'd like to," Michelle paused to consider Roger's motives, "but I'm going with Rick to worship band practice tomorrow morning. Although if you want to take the kids to the mall, that would be great. Otherwise, they'll just go over to George's mom till I get back."

"Okay. We can do it that way." His disappointment was obvious.

"I'll give each of them twenty dollars from the money Jasper gave us. You can help them buy a gift from their dad."

"Okay. It's too bad you can't come along," Roger continued coldly. "But if you'd rather be with Rick than me, then I'll just watch the kids for you."

"Roger," Michelle said firmly. "You know that's not what this is about. I like being with you and I appreciate everything you're doing for us. I really like you as a friend. But just in case you forgot, I am not going to be going out with someone who does not share my belief in God. I haven't changed my mind on that."

32

Rick lay in his recliner watching the evening news and trying to relax after a busy Monday at the bank. He heard a vehicle pull in the drive and assumed it was Roger returning from his tutoring session with Earl. A minute later, George walked in.

"Hey, George, what's up?" Rick said as he sat up and straightened the recliner.

"I just need somebody to tell me I'm crazy," George replied as he strolled into the library and sat down in the other easy chair.

"Okay. You're crazy," Rick quipped. "What you got on your mind?"

"I know it sounds outrageous. But I'm thinking about buying that chunk of land along Thrush Creek, where the cottage is."

"The whole thing?"

"Well, originally I was just thinking of a small piece where I could build a house someday. So I called Mrs. Stoner at her home in Philadelphia to see if she would be interested in selling part of it. At first she didn't seem very interested. But when she realized that I was someone from the local community, she started asking questions. When she found out that I'm the guy that's providing a house for Michelle and her children, all of a sudden she wanted to sell me the whole thing. Said she'd take whatever I can afford. She's not concerned about the money."

"Wow! You'd better jump on that before she changes her mind."

"I don't want to steal it from the old lady. Who knows, maybe she's senile or something. I don't want to take advantage of an old person."

"How big is this piece of land?"

"She wasn't sure. She thinks it's over a thousand acres."

"All woodland?"

"Yeah. I know it has a lot of valuable timber—lots of mature cherry and oak trees and I don't know what all. If someone manages it right, they could sell timber for years to come and still be left with a healthy forest. There's road frontage and river frontage that could be sold off for building lots. I could give her a fair price and still make tons of money."

"Okay, what's stopping you?"

"I don't have that kind of money to invest. I'm still paying off the mortgage on my house and shop. The bank would think I'm crazy if I came in and asked for a loan to buy a thousand acres."

"Well, I'm not the loan officer," Rick replied. "But I know you're in good standing with the bank. Your business is doing well, and you're paying off your debt at a good pace. If the bank agrees that this is a good investment, who knows? I think you ought to at least find out how much you'd need."

"I guess I'll keep working at it." George rubbed the back of his neck. "It's just kind of scary to think of borrowing that much money."

That night, as George lay in his bed, he pictured a beautiful log house with a large stone fireplace and cathedral ceiling in the family room, and a front porch overlooking Thrush Creek. Where would he be in ten or twenty years? Would he have a wife and children to share his dream home with? What if he fell in love with someone who didn't want a house in the forest?

He thought about the risks. What if the bank loaned him the money but he wasn't able to pay the taxes and interest? He would lose everything, and the bank would get the property at a bargain price. This would be a much greater risk for him than for the bank. But the payoff could be fantastic! He could have a beautiful home in an ideal location and make lots of money in the process.

His mind went back to the dream he had more than a month prior. The words of Dr. King reverberated in his ears: "Keep serving others and you will be greatly rewarded." Was this to be his reward for letting Michelle use his house? He also remembered the warning: "It's an elusive reward. The moment you start seeking the reward, you start losing it." What would be his inner motive for borrowing such a huge sum of money? *Selfishness?*

Just as he was beginning to doze off, he was jolted awake by the sound of a woman screaming. He pulled on his jeans, grabbed a flashlight, and ran outside. As he started across the neighbor's backyard, toward Michelle's house, he was blinded by a spotlight from the neighbor's window. "George! What's going on?" the neighbor yelled as he swept the spotlight across the yard.

"I don't know!" George replied resuming his barefooted trot toward Michelle's place. He shined his flashlight in all directions but saw nothing. Running up onto the porch, he banged on the door and yelled, "Michelle, are you all right?" Inside, he could see her in her nightgown, talking on the phone. Although her gown covered her meagerly from shoulders to midthigh, her alluring charm permeated the dimly lit kitchen.

After she placed the receiver down, she came and unlocked the door. "What's going on?" she asked as she opened the door. "I'm on the line with nine-one-one."

"Was that you screaming?" He remained focused on her well-being, barely noticing her scant attire.

"No! I couldn't tell where it came from. They're sending the police."

"Good! I was afraid someone was attacking you or something. I'll keep looking." George turned and stepped over to the edge of the porch as Michelle returned to the phone. As George swept his flashlight across the driveway and around his workshop, the neighbor arrived with his spotlight and hunting rifle.

These houses were on the very edge of town. Their back lawns were bordered by woodland, and it was there that the slope of the mountain increased dramatically. The two men walked to the back of the lawn, shining their lights behind the shop and up into the forest. Long eerie shadows swayed with the movement of the lights as they checked around the neighboring buildings and lawns. Nothing seemed unusual, other than the number of dogs barking. The one neighbor's beagle seemed especially focused on the woodland behind the houses. They swept their lights through the forest over and over but saw nothing unusual.

Outside lights were on at every house, and one by one, neighbors emerged to join the search. Eventually the township police cruiser came up the street sweeping its spotlight around each building. The officer pulled into Michelle's drive and got out of the car. Before he could go to the door, neighbors began converging around him describing what they had heard. Michelle came out, fully dressed now, and joined in describing the horrific screams she had heard.

"Is anyone missing?" the policeman asked.

The neighbors had already been checking on each other, and a quick review revealed that everyone was accounted for and no one had screamed. Another neighbor from the fourth house on the other side of Michelle's, who everyone called Bronco, joined the group and confirmed that the screams did not come from his place.

"It may have been a bobcat," the officer suggested. "Or maybe…there have been several unconfirmed reports of a cougar in the area. Of course, the Game Commission says there are no cougars in Pennsylvania."

"And most of us don't believe that," Bronco, who was an avid hunter and wildlife expert, responded. "I know one thing—those screams didn't come from a woman. Think about it." He turned to George. "You thought it sounded like it was right outside your house. It sounded the same to me. How far apart are our houses?"

"Oh, I'd say six hundred feet, at least."

"At least! You know any woman who can scream that loud?"

"No."

"It had to be a big cat! Probably a cougar. The only problem I have with that theory is that this isn't the normal mating season for cougars or for bobcats."

"I thought they mate any old time," the officer replied.

"Well, it's possible," Bronco agreed, "but rare."

"That's what it had to be," the officer concluded as he opened his car door. "I'll report this to the Game Commission, and they can investigate farther if they want to." After the policeman left, the group gradually dispersed, and one by one the houses went dark.

Rick got off his bike and hung his helmet over the handlebar. He pushed the bike into the garage where Roger was putting registration stickers on his canoe.

"Anything new around the community?" Roger asked.

"Not that I noticed." Rick sounded distracted. "I just had to go air out my brain a little. It's been a rough week so far, and we still have another day to go. They brought this guy into the bank to analyze everything we do. Every form we fill out, everything we enter into the computer—everything we do, he has to know why we do it."

"Oh, one of those experts."

"I guess it's necessary, though. In a lot of cases, it turns out we really don't know why we're doing things. We're just following standard operating procedure. As needs change, we add new procedures to supplement the old ones. But we don't stop to rethink all the old procedures. After a while, everything gets bogged down in red tape."

"Our school administration office needs to do something like that. They've got this outdated computer program. The computer is supposed to help you, right? In some cases they actually do extra work, just to satisfy the computer. I'm sure it started out as an efficient system. But it has evolved into an inefficient web that nobody seems to understand completely."

"Evolution! That's a good analogy," Rick whipped around to face Roger. "When things evolve, they get worse, not better."

"They don't always get worse."

"Think about that," Rick reasoned. "In an office environment, where we have intelligent human beings at work, organization and efficiency deteriorate as procedures evolve. But out in nature, where things happen at random, you think things evolve into a higher degree of order and sophistication. That doesn't make sense to me."

"Well, you're not looking at it correctly." Roger paused as he formulated his argument. "In the process of evolution, not all species survive. Those that don't adapt to the changing environment become extinct. If your bank didn't adapt, it too would become extinct and your inefficient procedures would die with it. Some other more efficient bank would take your place and its efficient procedures would replace your inefficient ones. So in the long run, evolution would result in an improvement."

"But the new bank would have used intelligent planning to come up with those efficient procedures. Without planning, everything goes downhill."

"It's a hypothetical situation. So we don't really know how those procedures evolved."

"I guess I'll never convince you that this marvelous world we see around us required intelligent planning," Rick concluded as they headed toward the house.

"So what else is new?" Roger quipped.

"Michelle got a job. But you probably know that already."

"No, I didn't know that. Where's she working?"

"She'll be starting at Sunset Hardware in about two weeks, is what she told me at band practice. That is, if she can find someone to take care of the kids."

"Did she get her driver's license yet?"

"She's working on it."

"You got any more plans with Kathy?" Roger tried to sound nonchalant.

"Nope. I haven't seen her since the other Saturday when you told me to take her for a bike ride."

"Okay. I just thought maybe that would have started something."

"No. I don't think she's really interested in me. She was just using me to try to make you jealous." Rick cocked his head. "Is it starting to work?"

"No. But now I know where I stand with Michelle."

"Where do you stand with her?"

"She likes me as a friend, just a friend. She's never going to go out with me. She doesn't want to get involved romantically with someone who doesn't believe in God."

"So what are you going to do about that?"

"I guess I'll see if I can patch things up with Kathy."

"That's not your only alternative, you know."

"Yeah, I hear ya." Roger was well aware of the other alternative.

"I'm sure Michelle will be disappointed with that response."

If I truly love her, I have to be honest about my true beliefs. "I believe what I believe. I'm not going to lie about it."

33

"How was your first day at work?" Sheryl asked as Michelle stepped through the doorway.

"Interesting," Michelle replied with a sigh. "It seems so different from anything I've done in the last seven years. But I'll get used to it. How were the kids?"

"Great. They get along so well with my kids. It's no problem at all."

"I'll pay you as soon as I get my first paycheck."

"I told you not to worry about that till you get your feet on the ground. This is what friends are for. Actually, I should be paying your children for entertaining my kids while I do my housework."

"Just don't let them hear you say that or they'll be expecting it. George pays them for doing little things every once in a while. They don't understand that most people don't do that."

"It must be nice having George close by so much of the time."

"It is. He's a great guy. He's always finding ways to be helpful. You don't even have to ask him."

"He's changed."

"Haven't we all?"

"By the way," Sheryl turned toward Michelle, "did you see that last article in the paper about you?"

"No. I quit reading that stuff."

"They're playing you up to be some sexy naive little country girl. With all the lunatics in our society, I'm afraid that's just going to attract the attention of the wrong person."

"Well, I'm not a little girl, and I'm not naive."

"I know. But the lunatics don't know that. And you and your kids, living there in that house all alone...Michelle, I worry about you."

"Don't worry. I have good neighbors who look out for me." Michelle thought about her neighbor, her landlord, her friend. "George, in particular."

"I think Joanne would like to go out with him." Sheryl grinned. "She's always fussing about what a wonderful person he is. But I don't think he's interested in dating."

"Maybe he's just waiting for the right one to come along." Michelle knew that George had hopes of having a family of his own someday. And she knew he would be an excellent husband to whoever the lucky lady turned out to be.

"Who's waiting for the right one?" Earl asked, walking into the room.

"Never mind," Michelle replied. "Go get your sister. Tell her it's time to go home."

Roger sat at his desk gazing at maps and reviewing his information on the Allagash Wilderness Waterway. A hot July had turned to a humid August, and most of his favorite whitewater runs were no longer navigable. Someday he would explore the Allagash, but not this year. The new school year was only a month away now. So far, the summer had proven to be one that he would never forget, the canoe camping, the time spent with Michelle, and the perplexing mysteries that started it all. One mystery still dogged his mind. Who was responsible for the deaths of Chief Theodore, Jasper, Harold, and Bobby? Absorbed in thought, he didn't hear George's pickup pulling into the drive.

"You home?" George shouted as he opened the back door.

"In here," Roger answered from the library.

"You still making plans to go to Maine?" George asked, noticing what Roger had on his desk.

"Just dreaming."

After chatting about a variety of issues, Roger asked, "Anything new on your dream of buying that property?"

"I'm having an appraiser look at it. I want to know what it's worth. Not only that, I want Mrs. Stoner to know what it's worth too. She probably has no idea."

"So what made you start thinking about buying it in the first place?"

"Well, I've always dreamed of having a little place in the country to build a house and raise a family. But I don't need a thousand acres for that. Somehow that little dream turned into a dream of making a lot of money."

"It's always good to dream, I guess."

"So how are things going with you and Kathy?"

"Fine. We've gone out a couple times in the last two weeks. I think she's forgiven me for taking off with Michelle without a word."

"So you enjoy being with her, I take it?"

"Yeah, she's fun. We have a good time together."

"Good. I'm glad to hear that." George hesitated and cleared his throat. "How would you feel if I asked Michelle out?"

"What?" Roger stammered. It wasn't the first time he had thought about the relationship between George and Michelle. His mind immediately flashed back to the more-than-polite hug she had given George on the afternoon of her rescue and the jealous feelings that had welled up within him. He suppressed his feelings and answered honestly and evasively, "You don't need my permission for that."

"It's not permission I'm asking for," George came back, looking straight into Roger's face. "I want to know how you'd feel. I guess what I'm saying is, I value our friendship and I don't want to do anything that might jeopardize it."

Roger could feel his ears turning red as he glanced down at the floor, trying to convince himself that he was no longer in love with Michelle. "To be honest, I'll probably be a little jealous of anybody she goes out with. But I have no right to feel that way. I have no right to hold her back. I just have to deal with it, and I won't let it interfere with our friendship." Roger knew he had said the right thing, but he wasn't sure it was completely true.

"Of course, I haven't said anything to Michelle yet." George leaned back in his chair. "I don't know how long I should wait. She really hasn't had very much time to grieve for Jasper."

"I don't think she really needed much time to grieve for him." Roger frowned. "It's not like they were a normal married couple."

George raised his eyebrows. "I wouldn't assume that."

A few days later, during lunch, Abby accidentally called George "Daddy." As they all laughed, George noticed that everyone seemed to sympathize with her mistake. There was a common feeling there. After the meal was over and the children returned to playing in the other room, George asked Michelle, "How are the children coping with the loss of their father?"

"Pretty well." Michelle paused. "They miss him, of course. But their lives have changed so much. They don't have time to just sit around and think about the way things were. I think they're adapting pretty well."

"And you?" George gazed deep into the pools that were forming in her blue eyes.

"I miss him. Some people seem to think I shouldn't. But I do. They think of me as a released hostage rather than a widow. They don't think about the fact that for seven years, he was my only companion, the only other adult in my life. He was the only person I could talk to until the children came along. For seven years he and I did everything together. He's the only man I ever slept with in all my life. And they think I should just forget him."

"It's not that easy, is it?"

Michelle shook her head and wiped her eyes.

"You just go ahead and grieve as much and as long as you need." George hesitated, not sure that he should continue. "But when you're finished grieving and you're ready to start going out socially, you let me know. I'll be waiting."

Michelle's eyes sparkled through the tears as she smiled back at George. "I was hoping you'd feel that way," she said softly.

"You were?"

"I don't know how long it will take for me to be ready for that. I don't even know *how* I'll know that I'm ready."

"You just take your time. I'm not trying to push you."

Roger glanced at the red sun hanging just over the mountains to the west as he and Kathy came out from the Olive Garden, carrying Styrofoam boxes of leftover dinner entrées. *Red at night—canoeists delight.* As they headed up the highway toward Thrush Glen, he decided to broach a more serious topic. "You don't seem to mind the fact that I don't believe that there's a God."

"Well, I wish you did," Kathy replied without emotion.

"Isn't that important to you?"

"Yeah, kind of."

"But you go out with me anyway."

"Roger, I love you no matter what you believe. Why are you making a big deal out of this?"

"I don't know. It's just that Michelle refused to go out with me because I don't believe the same thing she does. And that seems to make sense, if your faith is important to you."

"Here's what concerns me more! You're judging me based on how I compare to your previous girlfriend. I'm not Michelle! Okay?"

"I'm sorry. I didn't mean it that way."

"Are you going to go through the rest of your life feeling sorry for yourself because you can't have Michelle?"

"No. But how am I supposed to get her out of my system without talking about it?"

"Okay, I'm sorry. I've never been through what you're going through. I guess I have a hard time understanding what it's like."

The next morning, Roger strolled into the kitchen to find Rick finishing his breakfast. "What are you up to so early on a Saturday morning?" Roger asked.

"I'm going to the auction," Rick replied.

"What auction?"

"Chief Theodore's widow. She's getting rid of a bunch of their stuff."

"Is she moving?"

"Yeah. Somewhere around Lancaster."

"So what are you looking to buy?"

"There's an old Martin guitar on the sale bill. I'd love to have that, if it doesn't go too high."

"Old Martin guitars always go too high, don't they?"

"Yeah. Maybe I can get lucky," Rick replied as he headed out the door.

By midafternoon he was back, carrying a cardboard box stuffed with miscellaneous books and papers.

"No guitar?" Roger glanced at Rick.

"No guitar. Somebody else needed it much more than I did."

"So what you got there?"

"I don't know what all's in here," Rick replied as he set the odd collection on the table. "I bought it for the music." He started leafing through one of the spiral bound songbooks. "There's a lot of good old southern gospel in here."

Roger dug through the music and came up with another book, a journal. "Good Lumber Company," he read out loud as he opened it. "It looks like a ledger from the lumber company. Let's see, Mr. Good's daughter was the chief's grandmother. So Mr. Good was his great-grandfather."

Rick put down his songbook, found another journal, and started leafing through it. "It looks like he was a meticulous record keeper. He's got all kinds of information in here—kind of a cross between a diary and a business ledger."

"Yeah. He's got the date, number of board feet, species, price, everything. George will love this. He'll spend all day studying these old ledgers."

"A lot of good information there, I guess, if you're interested in lumber anyway," Rick commented as he pulled a smaller booklet out of the box and opened it. The writing inside was appeared to be that of a child's. Rick started reading aloud, "Charles Comiske–St. Louis Browns, 1887. Buck Ewing–New York Giants, 1889." He flipped several pages. "What is this? A list of baseball cards?" he continued reading, "James Ryan–Chicago Whitestockings, 1888. Joseph Mulvey–Philadelphia Quakers, 1887. Sam Berkley–Pittsburgh Alleghenys, 1887."

"That's what it says on the cover," Roger pointed out. "Sammy Good's Baseball Cards."

Rick flipped the book over. "Sure enough. I didn't even notice the cover. So he collected baseball cards. I wonder what he did with them."

"That collection would be worth a fortune today." Roger knew what Rick was thinking.

"Tell me about it." Rick started rummaging through the rest of the stuff in the box. "I wonder if any of them are in here."

"You hear these stories of someone buying a box of junk and finding something really valuable." Roger watched Rick's expression.

"Yeah. When's it going to be my turn?" Rick questioned, his fingers scraping the bottom of the box. "It doesn't look like I got lucky this time."

"How much did you pay for that box?"

"A dollar."

"Wow! You'll be able to sell those journals to George for two dollars. You'll double your money and have your music for free."

"Yeah, I'm in the big times now."

34

Michelle felt the heat radiating from the cars that were broiling in the noonday sun outside the little church along Thrush Creek. She felt the sun beating down on her shoulders as she and the children climbed into the back seat of George's pickup. "Can we go to Betsy's?" Earl asked as George got behind the wheel.

Rick hurried across the parking lot and hopped in the passenger's side. "Where're we going?" he asked.

"Sounds like the kids want to go to Betsy's Ice Cream Parlor," George replied.

"Yeah, ice cream!" Abby sang out cheerfully.

"Well, you have to eat something else first." Michelle knew what a battle that would be.

Rick glanced over his shoulder and the children. "We all need ice cream on a day like this, don't we?

"Yeah, ice cream!" the two sang out together.

"I just love that old building with its creaky wooden floors," George sounded enchanted. "And the player piano and everything. The place has a charm, all its own."

"And it's air-conditioned," Michelle added. "I can't believe how quickly I've become addicted to air-conditioning."

"How did you ever survive seven years without it?" Rick glanced at her.

"Well, it never got this hot out there in that cement-block building under the pine trees. It really wasn't too bad."

During lunch Rick told George about the box of ledgers and other stuff he bought at the auction. "Sounds interesting," George responded with a twinkle in his eye. "When do I get to see it?"

"Anytime," Rick replied. "You can all come right over. I have no big plans for the afternoon." So from the ice cream parlor, they headed to Rick and Roger's place.

Roger had spent the morning studying a number of books and articles he had collected about Venus flytraps and other carnivorous plants. He wanted to know the origin of this unique species. *How did it evolve?* He soon realized the he was not the first to raise this question. But he could not find a definite answer. Some scientists speculated that the Venus flytrap evolved from other carnivorous plants that had sticky leaves. But that didn't explain how the plant developed the ability to sense an insect on its leaves and the ability to snap the leaves together quickly. Both those features had to work together and work properly before they could be of any benefit to the plant. Even if the plant already had the ability to digest insects, it seemed unlikely that the other two features would have evolved simultaneously through the process of natural selection.

He learned that the trigger hairs were so sophisticated that they could tell the difference between food and random debris that might fall on the leaves. He also learned that the leaves could snap shut in less than one third of a second. Improvements, he figured, could have evolved by natural selection once the plant had achieved the ability to catch *some* insects. But to go from sticky leaves to a successful snap trap would have been one giant leap for plant kind. If it evolved in small steps, it would have had to gain some benefit with each step.

The more he learned about the plant, the more intrigued he became. *What was it*, he wondered, *that Charles Darwin found so fascinating about these plants? Was it just their amazing complexity or was it that they suggested something contrary to his theory?*

Michelle lost control of the kids as soon as they walked into Roger's place. They rushed into the library to join Roger while the other three gathered around the kitchen table to examine Rick's box of junk. George got absorbed in the ledgers while Rick reviewed the baseball card collection, commenting on the value of various cards. Michelle found the songbooks more interesting.

"Man, I'd love to buy lumber for these prices," George mused as he closed one journal and picked up another. As he flipped the pages, an envelope fell out on the table. "What's this?" he asked as he picked up the envelope and held it up for Rick to see. The envelope was sealed and printed on the back were the words "Treasure Hunt."

"Treasure hunt?" Rick read aloud as he took the envelope from George's hand. "I have no idea what this is."

Roger was already on his feet, heading for the kitchen. "Bring me a letter opener," Rick called across the room. Roger grabbed a letter opener from his desk and brought it to Rick. Rick slit the envelope and pulled out a piece of paper.

He unfolded the paper and started reading aloud:

> Hear ye, young men, pay attention and a treasure you may find. No, not one treasure, but two. One treasure lies at the end of the search. But the treasure of knowledge you will find along the way.
>
> Whether you intend to become a ship's captain or a carpenter, an engineer or surveyor, you must study a problem from every angle. Now heed my instruction, and further directions you will find buried in a sealed container, three feet underground. Go to the gate at the head of the

> mill race. Turn away from the creek and set your course straight in line with the breast of the dam. Go one yard for each United States president."

"It sounds like Mr. Good set up a treasure hunt for some group of young men," George glanced around the group.

"It seems like it was supposed to be something educational," Roger added. "He said something about the knowledge you find along the way."

"The envelope was still sealed," Michelle observed. "Does that mean that no one ever searched for the treasure?"

"Maybe it's still out there." Rick turned to George. "That would be on the land you're thinking about buying."

"I noticed that," George replied. "At least that's where the directions are. Who knows where he buried the treasure?"

"Well, he wouldn't have buried it on someone else's property," Michelle reasoned.

"And who knows what he buried?" George spread his hands, palms up. "This isn't the loot from some pirate ship. This was just some kind of educational game. It's not likely to be a valuable treasure."

"Whatever it is, it's worth more today than when he buried it," Rick countered. "We could at least go out there and see if we can find the directions. It doesn't sound like that would be too difficult."

"Before we can dig for the directions," Roger pointed out, "we'll have to dig for the remains of the gate to the mill race. I don't know where that was, but that's our starting point."

"Let me remind you," George sounded like a statesman, "I haven't bought the place yet. Anything that's out there belongs to Eva Stoner."

"Is there any date on that paper?" Michelle asked.

Rick checked both sides of the paper, "No. No date."

"Which journal did it come out of?" she asked.

"This one," George lifted the book off the table.

"What year is it?"

"Nineteen twenty-six. Why?"

"Number of US presidents," Michelle replied. "We need to know when he set up that treasure hunt. Of course, just because it's in that journal doesn't mean that's when he did it."

George turned to Rick. "Make a note of that. Let's go through this whole box very carefully before we rush out and start digging holes. After all, we have no deadline and no competition. Let's take our time."

"What are these rocks on your bookshelf?" Earl asked, walking into the kitchen with a piece of stone in his hand.

"Those are my fossils," Roger explained. "They're stones that have an imprint of something that lived a long, long time ago. Here, let me see which one you've got."

Earl handed the stone to Roger.

"See this," Roger said, pointing at the fossil. "This is a trilobite. This little creature lived in the water a long time ago. The crabs and crayfish we have today came from trilobites."

"Is it alive?" Earl looked puzzled.

"Oh no. It was alive more than two hundred million years ago. After it died, it got buried in the mud. Then the mud and the trilobite turned to stone. So now when we break open the stone, we can see what the trilobite looked like."

Abby wedged her way between Roger and Earl to take a look at the fossil. "Did God make the twibe-o-lites?" she asked.

"What do you think?" Roger looked at the little girl.

"God made everything."

"Well then, there you have it." Roger glanced at Michelle. "I guess I should be letting you explain this your way."

"You're doing okay," Michelle affirmed. "I don't have a problem with your explanation. Just because it's more than six thousand years old doesn't mean that God couldn't have made it. We don't know how much time transpired between the first two verses of Genesis."

"What do you mean by that?" Roger seemed eager for an argument.

"The first verse says that God created the heavens and the earth," Michelle explained. "The second verse says that it was without form. There could have been billions of years in between there with all kinds of living things, which were then destroyed before God created life as we know it."

Roger pointed to the fossil. "This definitely has form, doesn't it? If this is something that existed before verse two, then the Bible is not accurate in saying that the earth was without form."

"I think you're both being too technical," George interjected. "Genesis was never meant to be a scientific explanation of how or when God created the earth. It simply tells us that he did it and explains it in a way that even a child can understand."

Michelle nudged the boy. "Earl, go put the fossil back where you found it."

"This thing's older than Mom," Earl muttered as he headed for the library.

Roger chuckled at Earl's comment, but it appeared to trigger a memory. "Let's see, Michelle, you have a birthday coming up, don't you?"

"Yes. You remembered."

"When is it?" Rick asked.

"Friday." George flashed a smile at Michelle. "We should take you out for dinner on Friday evening."

Michelle smiled approvingly.

"Friday evening doesn't suit me." Rick threw up his hands. "But the rest of you can go anyway."

"Roger, why don't you see if it suits Kathy? We can make it a foursome," George suggested. "I'll see if my mom can watch the children."

Michelle wasn't sure if George was considering this a date or not. But she was sure that she was eagerly looking forward to it.

On Wednesday evening, Michelle was washing the dinner dishes and Earl was drying them when the phone rang. Michelle wiped her hands on the tea towel and hurried to the ringing phone. "Hello."

"Hello. Michelle?"

"Yes."

"This is Dan Phillips. How are you doing?" After a bit of small talk, Dan said, "I haven't made an awful lot of progress in the search for your dad. But I'd like to bring you up to date on what I've learned so far."

"Okay." She was eager to hear anything, even if it wasn't much.

"Could I come by on Saturday?"

"Not right in the morning. But after about ten o'clock."

"Okay. I was also wondering, have your children ever had a ride in an airplane?"

"No, they haven't."

"Well, if you and your children would like, I'll take you all up for a little ride on Saturday afternoon. That will give us a chance to talk and the kids will enjoy the ride."

"Thanks!" This was just the kind of opportunity she wanted to provide for her children. She tried to imagine how they would respond to this modern adventure. "I'm sure the children would like that."

"Can I pick you up around one o'clock? Our flying time will only be about ten or fifteen minutes. But we'll have about a half hour to the airstrip. Then I have to get the plane out of the hangar and do my preflight checks. I'll probably have you back home by three."

"Great! Yeah, one o'clock would be fine. We'll be looking forward to it."

35

Amid the Friday evening bustle and noise of the restaurant, George slipped into the booth beside Michelle as the foursome finally got seated. But none of the four seemed to mind the noise or the slow service or the waitress, who was more assertive than friendly. George listened raptly as Michelle and Roger, who were seated across from each other, entertained their partners with stories from their canoe-camping experiences—meals cooked over a campfire, the awesome mushrooms, Michelle and Abby capsizing, hiding from the helicopter and four-wheelers, Roger racing the train to the tunnel entrance, chasing the bear, and on and on. Each story was told in great detail, and George suspected a bit of embellishment.

Kathy glanced across the table at George and rolled her eyes. He could tell she was feeling left out.

George just smiled and turned his attention to Michelle. He was glad that Michelle and Roger were still on good terms, and he wasn't going to let Kathy's jealous attitude invade his feelings.

"Mr. Phillips called me the other evening." Michelle turned her eyes to George.

"Any news about your dad?" George raised his eyebrows.

"He said he hasn't made much progress. He's coming over tomorrow to talk more. Then he's taking the kids and me up for an airplane ride."

"What?" Roger exclaimed softly. "With all these freak accidents, or supposed freak accidents, happening to people who were connected to Jasper, you're going for an airplane ride with someone we hardly know?"

"Well, I guess I know him better than you do," Michelle retorted.

"I don't think either one of us knows him that well," Roger argued. "And if he hasn't made that much progress, couldn't he just give you an update over the phone?"

"Yeah, that does sound like it could be some kind of ploy to get you and the kids alone," George observed.

"You don't trust him either?" Michelle turned to face George.

"Well, I haven't actually met him like you guys have. The only time I saw him was when he was following us. I've never even talked with him. But it seems to me that if he would be putting as much effort into finding your dad as he put into tracking you guys out there on the Susquehanna, he would have found your dad already. It doesn't seem like it should be that hard. Your dad isn't hiding from anybody. He's not on the run. He just stopped corresponding with his family. So why hasn't he found him already? It makes me wonder if he's really doing what he said hc would do. If not, what's he up to?"

"Good point," Roger agreed. "His whole offer to help could have been a tactic to stay in contact with Michelle."

"You guys are way too suspicious." Michelle shook her head. "I'm not a gullible teenager anymore. I know how to evaluate people. This guy is a kind old man who wants to do something nice for my kids. We all know that if he intended to do any harm, he passed up the perfect opportunity at Deer Creek."

"What time is he coming?" George drummed his fingers on the table as he thought about his schedule for the next day.

"About one o'clock."

"You mind if I just happen to be there? I'd like to chat with him a little before you leave. And if I'm not comfortable with the situation, I'll get in my pickup and follow you just the way he followed us."

"Would it make any difference if I minded?" Michelle looked him in the eye.

"I don't think so." He winked at her.

"Okay then, be there. I appreciate your concern. Really, I do. Just don't embarrass me."

"I won't embarrass you. I'm not going to interrogate him. I just want to chat with him a little."

The next day, George sat at the kitchen table as Michelle cleared away the lunch leftovers and dirty dishes. He watched the children running circles around the kitchen with their arms spread out like the wings of an airplane. Amid the commotion, Roger dropped in. "You mind if I hang around till your pilot shows up?" he asked.

"Would it make a difference if I did?" Michelle grinned.

"Hey, if you don't want me here, I'll leave." Roger sounded sincere.

"No. Stay." Michelle gestured toward the table. "Let him see that my friends are always by my side. And maybe you'll see for yourself that there is no reason for your concern."

"I hope that's what we see," George said as he pushed a chair out from the table with his foot. "Roger, have a seat before you get run over by an airplane."

"I don't have to ask if the kids are excited about this," Roger observed.

Before long, the white Buick pulled in the drive. Dan Phillips and his wife got out and came to the door. "Hi, Michelle. This is my wife, June," Dan said as Michelle opened the door.

"Hi. Come on in and meet my friends," Michelle said as she ushered them in. After introductions and pleasantries, she suggested, "Why don't you have seats and tell us what you found out about my dad?"

As they got seated, Mr. Phillips pulled a piece of paper out of his shirt pocket and pushed it across the table to Michelle. "Here's an address and phone number. That's where he's supposed to be living now. I've been calling and calling. No one answers the phone. There's no answering machine. It just rings and rings."

"Mendota, California," Michelle said, staring at the piece of paper.

"That's correct. Mendota is about fifty or sixty miles from his previous address. It's a small town in the farming country east of San Jose."

"And you think this is where he is?" Michelle glanced at Mr. Phillips.

"It's the address on his California driver's license. If he's moved again, he hasn't informed the state yet. The phone number is still in service, so I believe he's still living there. I just wish someone would answer the phone so I can be sure I'm on the right track."

"So what do we do next?" Michelle asked.

"Well, June and I are planning to fly to California, rent a car, and do some vacationing in the area. While we're there, we'll drive to his address and check it out. If he's not there, we can talk to neighbors and try to find someone who knows where he is."

"Well, it sounds to me like you're making progress."

"Now, this isn't going to happen right away," Phillips continued. "I have another case I need to wrap up first, and I'd like to be home for the holidays. So we probably won't head for California before January. In the meantime, we can both keep calling that number and see if anyone answers."

"Thanks. I don't know how I can ever thank you enough for all you're doing."

"Are you flying your own plane to California?" George studied Phillips's face.

"No. For that distance, it's more practical to use a commercial airline. It gets pretty tiring sitting in that little cockpit for that many hours. Plus, you have to make a lot of fuel stops."

"As a private investigator, how do you see the deaths of Jasper and his brother and Bobby and Chief Miller?" Roger seemed eager to get his question in. "Do you agree that they were all freak accidents?"

"Well, I haven't investigated those cases myself. But I know Ivan Cox personally, and I trust him to do a thorough investigation and come to the right conclusion."

"You agree with him then?" George raised an eyebrow.

"That's not what I said. Last I heard, the investigation wasn't over. And, Roger, you certainly have a logical question."

"Here, look at this." Roger pulled a sheet of paper out of his pocket and unfolded it. The paper was filled with handwritten statistics and calculations. "Those four men died in a span of eleven days. In the United States, we have about seven deaths per year from snakebites." Roger led them through his calculations, concluding that the probability of dying from a snakebite during a specific eleven-day period is one in 1.3 billion.

"Okay, I follow you." Phillips nodded and waited for Roger to continue.

"There are about six hundred deaths per year from accidents with guns." Roger went over his calculations step by step, concluding that the odds of dying from an accidental shooting during an eleven-day period are one in 14.4 million. "And that's for the average person," he added. "I haven't done anything to account for the fact that Chief Theodore was an expert on gun safety."

"I agree with you." Phillips looked from the paper to Roger. "The odds for Chief Miller would have been a lot slimmer. But that gives us a number to look at anyway."

Avg. number of snake bites in U.S. – 7 per yr.
7 ÷ 365 days x 11 days = 0.2 bites in 11 days
U.S. Popolation 260 million ÷ 0.2 = 1.3 billion
Probability – 1 in 1.3 billion

Deaths from accidents w/ gons in U.S. 600 per yr.
600 ÷ 365 days x 11 days = 18 deaths in 11 days
260 million ÷ 18 = 14.4 million
Probability – 1 in 14.4 million

Drownings in U.S. 9 per day
Assuming 10% to be adults in pools = .9 per day
.9 x 11 days = 9.9 drownings in 11 days
260 million ÷ 9.9 = 26.3 million
Probability – 1 in 26.3 million

Deaths from gas pump fires in US. 2 Per yr.
2 ÷ 365 days x 11 days = .06 deaths in 11 days
260 million ÷ .06 = 4.3 billion
Probability – 1 in 4.3 Billion

1,300,000,000
x 14,400,000
x 26,300,000
x 4,300,000,000

2.1×10^{33}

"There are about nine deaths from drowning per day in the US," Roger went on. "Most swimming pool drownings are children. But I couldn't find any statistics specifically for adults. So I just assumed ten percent of the nine to be adults drowning in pools. And that's probably high."

"Okay, that's a reasonable estimate," Phillips agreed. "Adults in swimming pools certainly isn't more than that. And the majority of those would involve foul play. But go on. I didn't mean to interrupt."

"So we see that the probability of Harold drowning in his pool during that eleven-day period is one in 26.3 million."

Phillips nodded agreeably.

"And finally, the gas pump fire. On the average, there are two deaths per year due to gas pump fires. And going through the same mathematical process, we can determine that the probability of dying in a gas pump fire during an eleven-day period is one in 4.3 billion."

"You've got some really long odds there," Phillips acknowledged. "And if you want to know the probability of all four of those happening in the same eleven days, just multiply those four numbers together."

"Exactly!" Roger pointed to the bottom line of his calculations. "That's what I did. The probability that all four of those happened as freak accidents during an eleven-day period is one in two times ten to the thirty-third power."

"Wow!" Mr. Phillips shook his head. "Two times ten to the thirty-third, that's a two with thirty-three zeros behind it! That's a big number! It does seem pretty obvious that those were not all accidents."

"That's what I'm trying to prove!" Roger slapped his knee.

"Well, I assure you, Agent Cox won't quit till he's satisfied that he's got it right."

"Mom, when are we going to the airplane?" Earl whined.

"Soon. Just be patient," Michelle hushed her son.

"You do a lot of flying?" George asked.

"I'd like to do more," Phillips replied with a twinkle in his eye.

"He flies every chance he gets," June added. "He's always looking for an excuse to go somewhere in his plane."

"The kids have been really looking forward to this." Michelle patted Earl on the shoulder. "Haven't you, son?"

"Well, I guess we should get going then." Phillips smiled and glanced around the group.

"It's been a pleasure meeting you, gentlemen," June said politely. "It was nice of you to come and stand by your friend. Dan forgot to tell Michelle that I would be coming along. You must have been worried, honey," she added turning toward Michelle, "making arrangements to go flying with a man you hardly know."

"I think I've gotten to know him well enough," Michelle replied as they got to their feet. "I wasn't worried."

"Good." June patted her husband on the arm. "He wouldn't hurt a gnat."

"I don't have any more room in the plane, but you guys are welcome to follow us out to the airstrip and see us off," Mr. Phillips offered.

"You want to go?" George glanced at Roger as they both remained seated.

"It's up to you," Roger replied.

"I've got work to do." George rose from his chair. "I should mow the lawn yet this afternoon. But thanks for the invitation."

As Michelle pulled the door shut behind the group, Roger and George headed for the office in George's workshop. Roger glanced at George as they entered the office. "So you figure he's all right, huh?"

"I think Michelle was right, he's a kind old man who wants to do something nice for her and the kids." George sat down at his desk.

"Yeah, she's a pretty good judge of character."

"That she is," George quipped. "Pretty and a good judge of character."

"Is *that* what I said?" Roger chuckled.

"That's the way I heard it."

"Well, maybe that's a better way to put it."

"And she still has a lot of feelings for you, Roger." George leaned back in his chair.

"You think so?"

"I know so! And you still have a lot of feelings for her too, don't you?"

"Does it show?"

"Last evening at dinner, the two of you couldn't keep your eyes off each other."

"We were sitting straight across from each other. What were we supposed to do, sit with our heads turned sideways?"

"It's obvious. The two of you are made for each other." George wasn't giving up on his relationship with Michelle. But neither did he want to be romantically involved with a woman who was in love with another man. "Roger, if you would just return to the beliefs you were raised with, she'd forget about me so fast your head would spin."

Roger thought for a few moments and then replied, "You don't understand. I can't just say I believe something if I don't really believe it. And I don't really believe that stuff anymore."

George considered what to say next. Arguing with Roger would only make him dig his heels in deeper. Eventually, the silence became too awkward. "So, what are you up to this afternoon?"

"Not much," Roger replied, staring at the wall behind George. "How long has that motto been hanging there?" George glanced over his shoulder at the blue glass motto with neatly painted white lettering:

> "I know the plans I have for you," declares the Lord, "plans to prosper you and not to harm you, plans to give you hope and a future."

"Oh that." George looked back at Roger. "I made that about two months ago. It's been hanging there ever since."

"I never noticed it before."

"I decided to make it in response to a dream I had. Back around the beginning of June, I dreamt that I met Dr. Martin Luther King. He told me that there are a lot of good things in store for me. I don't know whether the dream means anything or not. But I believe the Bible. And that's a verse right out of the Bible."

"I know it is." Roger seemed perplexed. "This is really weird though. I woke up this morning with that verse running through my mind. I couldn't figure out why I was thinking about a Bible verse. I haven't read the Bible in years. But now I guess it makes sense. I'm sure I saw that motto hanging there a million times, and it was in my subconscious, even though I didn't consciously notice it. So it just somehow surfaced as I was waking up this morning."

"Roger, I think God is trying to speak to you, and you're not listening."

Roger remained silent. George could see that he was in serious thought and felt it was best not to interfere with the process.

"You think about that," George added. "I have to go mow the lawn."

As George went out and started mowing, Roger sat, staring at the motto. Did it mean anything at all? Or was it just the words of an ancient prophet who believed in a god that never existed? Was there any reason to expect something good to happen? Was there any way he could believe this religious stuff? Michelle was right, of course. He could choose to believe something he didn't understand. But could he truly believe something that contradicted what he did understand? Was it simply a matter of choice?

He had been to church many times. He knew what it was like, and it didn't appeal to him. He could never pretend to be something that he wasn't. He had to be true to himself.

He got up, walked to his car, and headed home with questions swirling through his mind. *Is it simply a matter of choice? Can I truly believe?*

36

George came out of his workshop, wiping sweat from his face as Earl and Abby hopped out of the white Buick. The kids ran to meet him, both talking excitedly. "Did you see us?" Earl asked.

"We saw you mowing the grass!" Abby pranced with excitement.

"We flew right over the house!" Earl added. "Didn't you see us?"

"I saw an airplane." George patted him on the shoulder. "I thought it was probably you."

The youngsters continued their enthusiastic reporting as George strolled over to the Buick. Mr. Phillips rolled his window down as Michelle climbed out of the back seat. "Do you think the children had a good time?" George asked, winking at Michelle.

"I don't know." Michelle gave the children a stern glance. "I haven't heard either one say thank you."

Two little voices responded with, "Thank you, Mr. Phillips."

"You're welcome," Phillips replied with a smile. "That was one of the most enjoyable trips I've ever given to anyone."

"We sure appreciate it," Michelle added.

"George," Mr. Phillips paused and looked him in the face, "next time I see Agent Cox, I'll try to get some answers for you folks. You guys have a legitimate question, and it deserves a complete and honest answer."

"Thanks. Roger will be glad to hear that. He worries a lot of about Michelle's safety."

"Here's my card." Phillips handed a business card to George. "I'd appreciate if someone would send me a copy of Roger's probability calculations. I'd like to show that to Cox."

After the Phillips left, George spent the next hour listening to children's descriptions of their flight and being amazed at how much Earl had learned from Mr. Phillips.

The next day, as the little group headed for their Sunday lunch at Betsy's, Rick asked, "What in the world did you say to Roger yesterday?"

"Who, me?" George questioned as he mentally replayed the conversation.

"Yeah, you. He was really quiet when he came home yesterday. He was really thinking about something. You could see it on his face, but he wouldn't say much. He just said, 'George got me thinking about some stuff.' That's all I could get out of him."

"I was just trying to get him to believe in God again. I told him that I think God is trying to talk to him and he's not listening."

"Well, you got him thinking, that's for sure," Rick observed. "I never know how much I should say to him. The more I try to convince him, the more he resists."

"You can't push him into anything," Michelle added. "You have to give him time to think things through and make his own decisions."

"That's what I did. I told him to think about it. Then I went out and mowed the lawn, and he sat there staring at the wall."

George couldn't help but notice that Michelle strolled along closely beside him as they walked into the ice cream parlor. Earl found an empty booth and scooted in, expecting his mother and Abby to slip in beside him, as usual. Instead, Michelle nudged Abby into the opposite side of the booth and slid in beside her, leaving enough room on the end for a third person. George had no problem figuring out where he was to sit.

After everyone had finished their sandwiches and they were waiting for desserts to arrive, Michelle cocked her head to face George. "I'd like some advice. This morning Pastor John asked me if I would speak about my experience some Sunday morning. I don't know if I want to do that."

"Why not?"

"It's too personal. I don't want to talk publicly about the private things that went on between me and my husband."

"Why do you think you'd have to talk about that aspect of it?"

"Well, that's what everyone seems to be interested in. People have a lot of warped opinions of what was happening to me the last seven years. I'd like to dispel the rumors, but I'm not comfortable talking about it in public. And I haven't become an expert on how women should respond if they're attacked. I can't give advice on stuff like that. What worked with Jasper may not work with someone else. He was a rather unique person. My experience with him doesn't make me an authority on the subject."

"There's lots of other stuff you could speak about." George put his hand on hers. "You could shock everybody by telling them how much God loved a criminal named Jasper." Michelle's eyes met George's, and a smile slowly spread from her eyes to her lips as she considered his suggestion. "And," George continued, "I remember you telling us about freedom, how accepting boundaries brings freedom. I bet you could preach a sermon on that. You could teach us an awful lot about contentment and relying on God."

"You might be right." Michelle was obviously thinking it over.

"Depending on how you handle those topics, you might even dispel some of the rumors without addressing them directly." George squeezed her hand.

"I think you should do it," Rick prodded.

"I'll have to think about it some more." Michelle's attention was being diverted to the sundaes the waitress was placing on the table.

"George, you got anything new on your efforts to buy that land?" Rick glanced up from his sundae.

"No. I have to call Mrs. Stoner and talk some more. But I haven't got around to it."

"Don't let that dream die." Rick's spoonful paused in midair. "She did say she'd sell it for whatever you can afford, didn't she?"

"Yeah, something like that," George said as he recalled Mrs. Stoner's words in his mind.

Later that afternoon, after Rick had gone home, George and Michelle stood by the kitchen door chatting while the children played in the next room. "Do you want to know what else I told Roger yesterday?" George asked.

"What?"

"I told him that you still have a lot of feelings for him. And if he became a believer, you'd forget all about me."

Michelle looked deep into George's eyes. "Well," she said slowly, "you're right about the first part. I do have some fond feelings for him. But I disagree with you on the second part. Roger and I make a good whitewater team. But beyond that, I don't know.

"You see, in a canoe, the person in the stern has the most control. But the person in the bow has the best view of what lies ahead. So you really have to be able to understand each other and work together. When I was in the bow, Roger could read my paddle strokes and body language and know exactly what I wanted to do without me saying a word. He'd follow my lead, and things usually went real smooth. It's really great when two people can work together with that kind of unity."

"You two make a good team," George affirmed, though he hated to admit it.

"But I don't think he and I would have that kind of unity in facing the rest of life's problems, especially now that he has a completely different view of things. I just don't think we could work together that well. But one thing I'm sure of, George," she shook her head, "I couldn't forget you just like that."

George exhaled a sigh of relief. He wasn't sure what to say or do next. All he could think about was taking her in his arms and pressing his lips against hers. But that didn't seem appropriate. She was still a recent widow, grieving for her husband. "It's nice to hear that," he said. "I guess I ought to be going." She reached out and gave him a quick hug before he slipped out the door.

George finished his breakfast alone on Monday morning. He had too much on his agenda for the day, and he wanted to get an early start. He was running a bit ahead of his normal schedule, but it was unusual for his mother to not be up by this time. Before heading over to his shop, he walked down the hall and called out, "I'm leaving for work, Mom."

There was no reply.

"You okay, Mom?" he called even louder from outside her door.

Still no reply.

He knocked on the door and opened it slowly, calling out, "Mom! You all right?"

Mrs. Lauger was lying in bed with her hands folded across her abdomen. Her eyes were closed and her mouth partly open. "Mom," George said, shaking the mattress with his knee as he touched her hands. Her hands were cold, and her face was pale. He touched her face. It was just as cold as her hands. George stood frozen for a few long moments, unable to believe the obvious.

His mother had gone to bed early the evening before, saying she was feeling a bit under the weather. But other than that, she had been in good health. His eyes filled with tears as the reality of the situation sank in. His heart pounded as he slowly picked up the phone and dialed 911.

The children were still sleeping as Michelle came into the kitchen to start getting breakfast ready. Glancing out the back window, she noticed a red reflection flashing against the side of George's shop. She stepped outside and looked toward Mrs. Lauger's house. An ambulance was parked in the drive, with the lights flashing. Michelle ran across the backyard of the house in between, across the driveway, and right into the Lauger's house.

George was standing in the family room talking with a paramedic. "What's going on?" Michelle asked, approaching George with open arms.

"Mom died," George said and burst out crying as they threw their arms around each other. The next twenty minutes were just a blur—waiting for the coroner and watching them wheel the body out to the ambulance and turn off the flashing lights.

Michelle realized that George's schedule had gone from difficult to impossible—contacting relatives, making funeral plans, trying to take care of business commitments, and playing host to well-wishers. There just wasn't enough time to do it all. Michelle took care of all his meals, cleaned the house, and kept after the laundry. *If that happened to me, I'd at least have a sister to help me. He has nobody.* She knew that George and his mother had a very close relationship, much closer than she had ever been with her mother. *He must be devastated.* On Tuesday, she baked George's favorite cookies, snickerdoodles.

Arriving home late that evening, George found a small wicker basket, full of snickerdoodles, sitting on the kitchen table. A note attached to the handle read, "Take two of these, and call me in the morning." The cookies were wrapped in packs of two, with a strip of white paper around the two cookies, then clear cellophane around the whole pack. George snatched a pack from the basket and unraveled the cellophane. On the inner surface of the white paper, he found Michelle's handwriting. He straightened the paper and read it while munching the cookie.

Shared Grief
Share with me the tears you're hiding.
You needn't smile or say a word.
Just let me come quietly to your side.
I know the need for solitude,
And you need not cry alone

—I. Rhoda Thistu

The next evening, he opened a pack to find the Psalm 23 neatly written on the inside of the white paper. Each evening, before going to bed, George opened another pack of cookies to find a poem, a verse from a hymn, or something from the Bible. He straightened the papers and stacked them neatly back in the basket. The evening after the funeral, he found a verse from an old hymn.

Till He Come
When the weary ones we love
Enter on their rest above,
When their words of love and cheer
Fall no longer on our ear,
Hush, be every murmur dumb;
It is only "Till He come."

—Edward H. Bickersteth

George looked forward to what he would find in the cookie wrapper each evening, and he was becoming even more fond of snickerdoodles. The supply lasted through the following week. In the last pack, he found a poem with no author's name, just the initials, MD.

Stronger Bonds

Death cuts like a saw, ripping the wood,
tearing each fiber,
Separating what has always been together,
Leaving raw edges and broken fibers.
But when the saw is done, the craftsman begins his work.
From the pieces that remain
He selects those with beauty, character, and strength.
He matches piece to piece
And joins them with bonds stronger than the wood itself.
When the shaping and polishing are completed,
A thing of beauty has been created.

George read it over and over, thinking about how his mother's passing had strengthened his relationships with so many people. He had reconnected with his cousin, whom he hadn't seen in years. He'd even seen a new side of Bobby Billmant. A few days after his mother's death, Bobby had called and volunteered to mow the lawn. And he had done an excellent job, the edges and walks were neatly trimmed. Now he was planning to come and do it again. Bobby wasn't totally weird.

George looked out the window toward Michelle's house. A light was still on. He felt closer to her now than ever before. He had to thank her for the poem and for everything else she was doing. He walked over and knocked on the back door.

Michelle flipped on the outside light to see who was there, then quickly opened the door and invited him in. "I just wanted to thank you for the poem," he said, "and for everything else…" Before he knew what was happening, they had their arms around each other. His forehead touched hers as he bent to gaze into her eyes. She was blinking back tears. So was he. She tilted her head back slowly, and their lips grew closer and closer until he could feel hers touching his. Finally, they were joined firmly in a moment that neither wanted to end.

37

Roger gazed at the mountainsides blazing with fall color under a crystal blue sky. He felt the warm sun on his arms and face. It was just enough to take the edge off the chilly breeze. *It doesn't get any better than this!* Recent rain had replenished Thrush Creek just enough to make it navigable by kayak. Although Roger had promised himself he would never again go out on the river alone, he just couldn't resist. It felt great to once again spend a relaxing Sunday morning on the water, letting his thoughts flow as freely as the river. After church was over, Rick would shuttle him back to his SUV at the iron bridge. But first they would join George and Michelle and the kids for lunch.

Roger hadn't seen much of Michelle since Earl started school and was no longer being tutored. Michelle had gone out with George a number of times, and it sounded like that relationship was going fine, although that thought didn't give Roger a particularly good feeling. But he was seeing much more of Kathy, now that they were both back to teaching and occasionally getting together on weekends. Still, it seemed he spent as much time thinking about Michelle as he did Kathy.

This was the morning that Michelle would be speaking in church. She had invited him several times, but he had heard as much about her relationship with Jasper as he cared to. She had said that wasn't what she would talk about, but still he looked for an excuse not to go. The idea of spending a morning sitting in a church pew just didn't appeal to him. The improved water level and beautiful weather was adequate reason.

As he gazed at the colorful mountainside reflected in a quiet pool of water, he wondered what would become of George's dream of owning it. He wished the best for George, but he hated the thought of cutting down trees and building houses. *And somewhere along that mountainside, there may be a buried treasure of some sort.*

Roger glided into the shore just above the remains of the old dam. He stepped out of his boat and surveyed the area where the dam breast ran into the bank. The whole area was covered with sand and silt that had built up over the years. It was impossible to tell how far the dam breast ran underground or where the opening to the mill race once had been. But it appeared that digging up the past would not be too large a task for several men with shovels. The area just downriver from where he supposed the underground dam breast to be was heavily overgrown with bushes and small trees. A few of the largest trees may have been fifty to sixty years old. Some of the area was a bit low and marshy and may have been the location of the race, which once channeled water to the mill.

As he explored the area, he could almost hear a gunshot echoing through his memories, reminding him of the last time he had ventured into this area. Although he knew that danger was past, it still gave him an eerie feeling. He remembered the macho feeling of having a gun hanging at his hip. He thought about the challenge of holding the gun steady and squeezing the trigger and the satisfaction of seeing the bullet hit close to the bull's eye. He decided he would pay a visit to Sunset Hardware and take a look at their guns.

Satisfied with what he had learned about the topography of the area, Roger climbed back into his boat. He paddled out to the middle of the creek, turned downstream, went through the old dam, and rode the waves one more time. His thoughts drifted from one thing to another as he casually made his way down the creek.

Earl, Abby, and Rick were standing by the shore as Roger approached the little church. "Mr. Koralsen," Earl said as Roger pulled his kayak up onto the grass, "Sometime I'd like to go canoeing again."

"Good. I'm glad to hear that. I guess we'll have to talk to your mother about that."

"Why do you call him Mista Ko-alsen?" Abby asked.

"That's his name," Earl shrugged. "In school, that's what everybody calls him."

"I'll bet it was kind of chilly out there this morning, wasn't it?" Rick stuck his hands in his pockets as they headed toward the parking lot.

"Not too bad." Roger looked up at the sky. "Fresh air and beautiful scenery, what more could you ask for?"

"You missed a really interesting talk this morning," Rick sounded enthralled. As they neared the building, George and Michelle came out and joined them. "I was just telling Roger that he missed a really interesting talk," Rick continued. "You did an excellent job on that, Michelle."

"That's what everybody has been telling her," George added.

"And you all missed a very beautiful morning on Thrush Creek." Roger glanced back at the creek and opposing hillside.

"There will be lots of other beautiful days to enjoy the outdoors," Rick argued.

"On the other hand," George replied, "I'll bet this won't be the last opportunity to hear Michelle's speech either." Putting his arm around Michelle, he added, "You're gonna get invitations to speak in lots of other churches—bigger churches—and other events."

"We'll see. Maybe I can pick up a little extra income through it. That would be nice."

Roger climbed in the car with Rick while Michelle and the children got seated in the pickup with George, and they all headed out to Joe's Deli & Grill. Upon entering the restaurant, Rick and the kids claimed a large corner booth while Roger, George, and Michelle ordered. After bringing the food to the table, Michelle and George slid in next to each other, and Roger slipped in on the opposite side. During lunch George and Michelle teased each other with coded comments and banter that nobody else seemed to understand.

She's still doing it. Roger's eyes roved over Michelle's lovely form. *She's still using her sex appeal to manipulate the men around her. Only now it's George.*

"So, George," Roger interrupted the flirtatious teasing, "have you talked with Mrs. Stoner recently?"

"Yeah, I've been pretty busy, but I did call her and talk a little more."

"Of course you did." Michelle eyed George with a mischievous twinkle. "She's your other girlfriend now."

"She got the estimate from the appraisers." George poked Michelle with his elbow. "You're just jealous. She's more like a mother than a girlfriend."

"Two million, you said, right?" Roger questioned.

George nodded. "She didn't seem really surprised by that. I thought that might blow her away. But I guess she knows what's going on."

"Did you make her an offer?"

"Not yet. But I did ask permission to dig around the dam breast to try to find the gate to the mill race."

"What did she say?"

"She said that would be okay. And then she said, 'You know, they say there's buried treasure on that land.'"

"She knows about it?" Rick was suddenly interested in their conversation.

"Yeah, but she said it's not worth much. It's just," George paused for dramatic effect, "a collection of baseball cards and a few dollars' worth of coins."

"The baseball cards!" Rick exclaimed. "They're worth a fortune!"

"But they could have gotten moldy and rotted away to nothing by this time." George always had to look at the practical side of things.

"I was looking over that area this morning," Roger said. "If the three of us go out there with shovels, it won't take long to uncover the top of that dam breast and find our starting point."

"Okay." George glanced at the other two guys. "Maybe some Saturday, if the weather stays nice. If not, maybe it'll have to wait till spring."

After lunch, George and Michelle and the kids headed home while Rick and Roger headed to the iron bridge. While the children played in their rooms, Michelle called the California phone number that Dan Phillips had given her. The phone just rang and rang, like it always did. She had tried calling on all kinds of odd hours on every day of the week, but never an answer. *How can someone live somewhere and never be there to answer the phone?* she wondered as she hung up the receiver.

With the river gurgling in the background, Roger opened the door of his Explorer and climbed in while Rick turned his car around and headed home. As Roger drove casually along the mountain roads, he thought about their meal together. He couldn't get over the way Michelle had ignored him. Although he had never been as intimate with Michelle as he was with Kathy, he still spent more time thinking about Michelle. He understood her convictions about chastity, and he respected that. In fact, it made her all the more desirable. Like a mountain climber gazing across the valley at a peak higher than the one he's standing on, he longed for the opportunity to go there.

He wondered what went on between Michelle and George when the two were alone. How intimate had they become? He was annoyed by the thought that George might be enjoying privileges that he had only dreamed of. *George? The guy who wouldn't even look at a* Playboy *magazine? Ha-ha!* He had no reason to believe that was actually the case. In fact, he knew Michelle well enough to know that she was serious about her convictions. He tried to get thoughts of Michelle and George out of his head, but his suspicious heart just wouldn't let it go.

He wondered when her romantic interest in George really began. He remembered that even back in high school, she showed a special interest in him. She gave him public recognition for his talents and did things to boost his self-image. He thought about the sixteenth birthday party she planned for George. Did she have eyes for George then already? That was a long time ago, and it really didn't matter. But still, he couldn't stand the thought that his high school sweetheart may have actually had a crush on someone else.

He remembered the afternoon when he helped Michelle escape from the little cottage. He couldn't forget how she reacted when George walked into the room. He could still see her running to him and hugging him passionately. She claimed she was just being polite, but to Roger, it appeared to be much more than that. He couldn't get the scene out of his mind. *What is it about George that she prefers him rather than me?*

Visions of Michelle and George sitting at the table having a good time together kept annoying him as he loaded his kayak in the churchyard and then drove home. After stowing his boat in the garage, he went into the house and began reviewing lesson plans just to give his mind something else to think about.

On Tuesday, Michelle was working an evening shift at the hardware store while George watched the children. As she strolled through the store, she came across Roger standing in front of the gun display case, holding a blue steel revolver in his hand as he chatted with one of the other sales clerks.

"Roger!" she stopped in her tracks. "What are you doing here?"

"What does it look like I'm doing?"

"I never expected to see you looking at guns."

"I kind of liked that gun Jasper gave me."

"What happened to that brave man who insisted he never needed a gun?"

"Michelle, I'm trying to sell this man a gun," the sales clerk said. "What are you trying to do?"

"Okay. I'll go back to the housewares department, where I belong."

At home, while Earl was playing in his bedroom, Abby came to George with a *Winnie-the-Pooh* book. "Can you wead this to me?" she asked. They sat on the couch and read the book. After the book was finished, Abby looked up at George and said, "Earl said you're gonna marry our mommy and then you'll be our daddy."

"He did?" George responded with a chuckle. "Whatever gave him that idea?"

"I don't know."

"Did he tell your mother that?"

"I don't think so."

"Well, Earl doesn't know what he's talking about. Your mother and I would have to talk about that first. But one thing is for sure," George said as he put his arm around the little girl, "I would love to have you for a daughter."

She just smiled and snuggled her head against his chest.

38

Michelle stood over the heat register with the warmth from the furnace rising over her as she listened to the cold wind howling though the bare maple tree outside her window. An early snow squall was whitening the edges of the driveway. She leaned back against George as he slipped his arms around her waist. They watched the snowflakes flying as she silently contemplated the news they were about to share with others. George brushed his lips against her ear and asked softly, "So, who do we tell?"

"Well, we have to tell my mom and my sister first."

"Of course. But what about our friends?"

"They'll all find out sooner or later."

"Yeah. I was thinking mainly of Roger. I just don't know how hard this is going to hit him."

"I really don't want to face him." Michelle stared out the window.

"Well, neither do I. But he is a special friend to both of us. If we don't say anything to him and he finds out through the grapevine, he may feel insulted—like we don't want him around."

"Did you think how awkward it would be to go directly to my old boyfriend with news like this?"

"Yeah. And I'm sure he'll feel hurt, somehow. I know he's still fond of you, even though he's been going out with Kathy for months."

"You can tell him sometime. I don't want to be there."

"If we don't give him the opportunity to air his feelings, he'll go on harboring whatever anger or jealousy he's feeling. And our friendship with him will slowly die—or maybe not so slowly. But I don't want that to happen. We both value his friendship."

"I don't know what I would say."

"Maybe when the time is right, the right words will come." George kissed her on the cheek. "I'm not going to force you into an awkward situation. I'll let you decide whether or not you should be there when I talk to him."

On the day before Thanksgiving, as Roger was driving home from school, he decided to drop in to chat with George. *And if Michelle happens to be there, so much the better*. He strolled into the shop where George was working on a set of kitchen cabinets. As the two chatted, they meandered into the office and sat down. George seemed to have something on his mind. It seemed like he wanted to say something, but he wasn't coming out with it. Eventually, Michelle came out and joined them.

"Hi, Roger," Michelle said as she crossed the room and took the seat opposite from him. As she sat down, she caught George's eye and half-whispered, "Did you tell him?"

"Not yet."

Roger glanced from one to the other, wondering who was going to tell him what.

"We have something to tell you," Michelle began.

"We haven't told hardly anybody yet," George continued. "But since you're a close friend to both of us, we didn't want you to hear this through the grapevine."

Roger's mind shot ahead to what he anticipated was coming. He glanced at Michelle's hand to see if she was wearing a diamond. But she was sitting hunched over with both hands tucked between her knees.

Michelle's eyes dropped to the floor as she said softly, "I'm pregnant."

"What!" Roger flew out of his chair. He stood there with his mouth open, not knowing what to say next. He took two strides toward Michelle, and suddenly the words came without consideration. "You wouldn't even go out with me because I don't share your religious beliefs. But you hop right into bed with him! What kind of religious belief is that?" George was already on his feet by Michelle's side as if he was about to defend her. Roger's fists tightened. *He'd better not open his mouth.*

"That's not what it's about, Roger," Michelle said softly. "We both know it was wrong."

Roger bent forward and shouted in Michelle's face, "Then why did you do it?" He turned quickly and started toward the door. Stopping abruptly, he turned back toward Michelle and added sarcastically, "Oh, I understand. You were just being polite." Then he stomped out the door. As he exited, he muttered, "You can both go to hell, see if I care."

George and Michelle remained speechless and still as Roger slammed his car door and revved up the engine. His tires screeched as he pulled out of the drive and sped away.

"If he doesn't care, then why is he so upset?" George said slowly as he put his hand on Michelle's shoulder. He expected that she would stand up so he could give her a hug. Instead she pulled away from him.

"I just want to be alone," she said as she got up and slowly walked out of the office and into the house. George stood alone, staring out the window. Eventually he walked into his shop and finished up a few odds and ends. Then he turned off the lights and ventured into the house.

Abby met him in the kitchen. "Why is Mommy crying?"

"Where is she?"

"Up in her room."

"Oh, Roger said something that wasn't very nice," George explained. He went up the stairs and paused outside Michelle's room. "You okay?" he asked, knocking on the door.

Michelle opened the door slowly, stepped out and slipped her arms around George. "I'm sorry," she said with a squeeze. "I just needed a little time to myself."

"It's okay. I understand," George said as he wrapped his arms around her and gently massaged her shoulders. "Should I go get us a pizza for dinner?"

"I can make something," Michelle replied.

"No. Pizza!" both kids yelled from the bottom of the stairs.

After the pizza, a TV program, a few games, a bedtime story, a snack, and another story, the kids were finally settled in bed. George and Michelle sat on the couch, quietly discussing their situation. "Mom agrees with you," Michelle sounded sad. "We shouldn't just rush off and get married."

"It's not that I don't want to," George explained. "I think we just need to give it some time and make sure that it's the right thing."

"We've both had significant losses to deal with. I guess we're both trying to fill the voids we're left with." She put her hand on his thigh. "Maybe we should get some counseling."

"That wouldn't be a bad idea."

"And maybe we should do that before we start telling a lot of people what our plans are."

"Married or not, I plan to take my responsibility as a father. I'll give you all the support you need, financially and every other way."

"I wasn't worried about that. And the ladies at church have been so helpful. They always seem to be looking for things they can do for me."

"I don't know if we can count on that to continue. Who knows how they'll react when they find out you're pregnant. They may ostracize us. Some religious people can be really cruel at times."

"Now you're sounding like Roger." Michelle gave him a soft punch on the biceps. "But I can't argue with you. I know it's true."

"Why don't I set up a meeting with Pastor John?"

"Why don't you?"

"Okay, I will."

The next day, George drove Michelle and the children to Bellefonte to have Thanksgiving dinner with her family. Nana came down from New York so the whole family could be together. Mae roasted a turkey and set out a delicious meal. Everyone was having a great time. But at times George noticed that Michelle seemed distracted and lonely. He knew she was missing her father. He knew how much she wanted her children to finally meet their grandfather. He wondered if she would locate him in time to welcome the new little one into the world.

"Have you told everyone about the pregnancy?" Nana half whispered to Michelle after the children had left the table.

"It's no longer a secret, Mom. We can talk about it."

"You embarrass me and make me happy at the same time."

"We know we did wrong, Mom. We're dealing with it."

"Do you feel like you're really safe over there in Thrush Glen?" Mae asked as she started clearing the leftovers from the table.

"Safe as I would be anywhere else." Michelle shrugged. "Why?"

"Oh, I just worry about you sometimes. Have there been any more so-called freak accidents involving any one you know?"

"No. And it's no use worrying about it." Michelle sounded sure of herself.

"You're so feisty. I should have turned you into a redhead instead of a brunette."

"I'm starting to go blond again."

"In more ways than one."

"How about a game of canasta?" Fred waved a deck of cards at the sisters.

"I haven't played that in years," Michelle replied with obvious delight in her eyes.

"You and me can take on the guys," Mae suggested.

"You'll have to give me a refresher course." George scratched his head. "I don't think I remember how to play it."

"I'll coach you," Nana offered. They got seated as Fred dealt the first hand. It seemed the sisters could read each other's minds as they laid out their melds, always knowing what to hold and what to discard. Hand after hand the sisters racked up points while the guys complained about the cards they were drawing.

"Maybe this wasn't such a good idea after all," Fred conceded as the ladies reached the winning score of five thousand points. After more games and more food, George was ready to head home, and Michelle somehow seemed to understand. They finally tore the children away from their cousins and headed back to Thrush Glen.

As they were driving, George brought up a subject that was never far from his mind. "I've been doing some research on Mr. Good."

"Mr. Good from the lumber company?" Michelle questioned.

"Yeah. I'm trying to figure out when he may have set up that treasure hunt. The baseball cards in his collection were from the late eighteen hundreds. The earlier ones were entered in a child's handwriting. The later ones, from like the 1890s, the handwriting is more mature. But the handwriting on the clues for the treasure hunt is much neater. So I'm guessing that quite a few years passed in between there."

"That's a smart way to look at it."

"He died in 1933," George continued. "So I'm guessing it was probably sometime between about 1910 and 1933."

"So which presidents were serving during those years?"

"Taft was president in 1910. He was the twenty-seventh. And Franklin Roosevelt became president in 1933. He was the thirty-second."

"So somewhere between twenty-seven yards and thirty-two yards," Michelle observed.

"Yeah. We might have to dig a fifteen-foot trench just to find the directions."

"Well, it's like you said before," Michelle concluded as George pulled into the driveway. "There's no rush."

As the children headed into the house, Michelle kissed George good night. He headed across the moonlit lawn toward his empty house. For much of his life, it had been just him and his mother living there. But now his house had become a dark and lonely place. He needed a family. He had observed lots of families, but he had never before experienced family like he had today. This was a family he could be part of.

39

"You've got to come look at this!" Michelle shouted over the noise of the table saw. George shut down the saw, and she continued, "I was working at the sink when I heard something. I looked around, and there was a little round hole in the window of the back door."

"How big a hole?" George raised his eyebrows. Apparently he understood her concern.

"About as big as my finger." She turned and followed George to the house.

George took one look at the hole. "That's a bullet hole! Did you see anybody?"

"No. I didn't hear a gunshot either."

"It could have been just a stray bullet. I hope nobody was aiming for you."

"You never know." Michelle bit her lip. She had already considered both possibilities. "Either way, it's kind of scary."

"We've never gotten a good explanation of those four freak accidents." George put his arm around her shoulder. "I hate to think there might still be somebody out there who wants to get rid of you."

"I guess I've learned to live with that possibility. I seldom even think about that anymore."

"Well, think about it."

"I am. We need to call the police."

While waiting for the police, George checked around the room and found another hole in the wall opposite the door. "I suppose that was the same bullet," he said, glancing back at the door. The police checked the scene thoroughly, took pictures, and asked all kinds of questions.

After checking the alignment of the two holes, the one officer turned to Michelle. "You said you didn't hear a gunshot, right?"

"That's right," Michelle nodded.

"Well," he continued, "either this shot was fired from the roof of George's shop, which you would have heard, or it's a stray bullet from way up the mountain somewhere. Being that this is the first day of buck season, I think we can conclude that it's a stray bullet."

"I suppose that's a logical assumption," Michelle agreed. "But I'd like you to report this to Special Agent Cox of the FBI."

"I'll let him know. But we'll probably never know who fired the shot."

Roger stood in front of the refrigerator studying Rick's stash of cold beer. It wasn't much of a stash—hardly enough to get a good buzz. *Why am I even thinking about this?* He closed the refrigerator and walked into the library, picked up the remote, and flipped from channel to channel, looking for something that would catch his interest. Although he hadn't yet started his Christmas shopping, he had no desire to go out and compete with all the other shoppers on this Saturday morning. He leafed through a magazine, but nothing aroused his interest enough to keep him reading. He didn't really feel like doing anything. His mind kept coming back to his last conversation with George and Michelle.

Why did I react so horribly? He analyzed and reanalyzed his harsh response. He had made himself look immature and stupid. How could he redeem his image? How did George and Michelle feel toward him now? He could just let the situation go and see what happens to their relationship with him, or he could make a phone call and try to patch things up. He didn't want to do that. But he felt he had to. Finally he went to the phone and dialed George's number.

"Hello."

"Hello, George. It's Roger."

"Hey, Roger. What's up?"

"Not much. What's up with you?"

"Not much."

"Well, ah…I just wanted to apologize for what I said to you and Michelle."

"Well, maybe we should have handled it a different way," George replied. "We knew it would be awkward. But we thought we ought to be upfront with you."

"Ah…I guess I kind of made an ass of myself. It just kind of hit me the wrong way."

"I can understand that."

"See, when Michelle's religious beliefs trumped her relationship with me, I could accept that. That seemed to make sense. But then when you trumped her religious convictions, all of a sudden, I'm the lowest card on the table. That kind of hurt."

"Roger, you *are* a card, but not a low card." Roger chuckled as George continued. "And I didn't trump her religious beliefs. Her beliefs haven't changed at all. We just screwed up."

"Well, I feel really bad about the way I reacted."

"Hey, man, don't worry about it."

"Okay. Well, tell Michelle I apologize for everything I said."

"I think she deserves to hear that directly from you."

"What?"

"We came directly to you, didn't we, even though that was really difficult for her? I think that took a lot of backbone on her part. And she deserves the same respect we gave you."

"Okay, I'll call her."

After George got off the phone with Roger, he started thinking about another call that he needed to make. He hated to do it, but sooner or later, it had to be done. He picked up the phone and dialed Eva Stoner.

"Hello."

"Hello, Mrs. Stoner. This is George Lauger calling."

"Oh. Hi, George. How are you?"

"I'm fine. How are you doing?"

"Pretty good, for an old woman. Did you find what you wanted to dig up out there on my land?"

"No, actually we haven't done any digging yet. That will have to wait, for now. I called to tell you that I can't buy the land."

"Oh. The bank won't give you the money?"

"No. It's not that. They would loan me some anyway. But maybe not enough to give you a fair price."

"That's okay. The price isn't important."

"Here's the problem. I have other responsibilities now. I can't invest any money in land right now."

"What sort of responsibilities?"

"Well, I told you I was going out with Michelle, didn't I?"

"Yes. How are things going between the two of you?"

"I'll let you be the judge of that. Uh…" George hesitated. "We're going to have a baby."

"Oh! Congratulations! Or…ah…did I miss something?"

"No, we're not married."

"Well, that happens a lot these days. I wish you the best."

"Thank you."

"Are you planning to marry her?"

"We're going to get some counseling before we make that decision."

"Well, good for you. I think you'll make a fine father."

"You do?"

"Sure. You care about others."

"Thanks for your encouragement."

"You're welcome."

"Well, I just wanted to let you know that I can't buy the land."

"I understand your situation. And I think you're doing the right thing. But if you want to go out there and dig, you go right ahead. Anything you find is yours."

"Eva, if those baseball cards are in good condition, they could be worth a fortune."

"And I can't think of anyone who deserves it more than you do."

"Well, thank you."

"Just keep me informed. And I would like to come to the wedding."

Eva's encouraging words echoed in George's ears over the next several days. He appreciated her offer to let him dig for the treasure. But even more, he appreciated the way she accepted the turn of events and encouraged him in his new responsibilities. And if there was to be a wedding, he would remember to invite her.

As Christmas approached, it seemed to Michelle that time accelerated exponentially with extra work hours, Christmas shopping, counseling sessions, and doctor visits. The week before Christmas, she and George returned from a counseling session with some somber advice. After Michelle got the children settled in bed, she and George started wrapping Christmas presents.

"It sounds like Pastor John agrees with what you said a couple weeks ago," George commented as he rolled a layer of wrapping paper across the table. "We've been using each other to fill the voids from our previous losses."

"But I wasn't suggesting that we should break up."

"I know. But I understand what he's saying. We should test our relationship, cool off the romance, and see how we feel toward each other then."

"He may be right. But it won't be easy to do." She hated to even think what it would be like. "You're here every day working in your shop, and when you're not there, you're right next door. You take care of maintenance on the house, you help out with the kids, and you provide transportation whenever we need it. How can we avoid seeing each other?"

"You're right. It won't be easy. We'll have to get some other people to step in and help with some of the things I've been doing."

"Well, we don't have to get anybody to watch the kids on Saturday mornings while I'm at band practice."

"Why not?"

"They asked me not to sing with the band anymore. Somebody thinks I'm not a good role model for the young people."

"Oh for heaven's sake! That didn't come from Pastor John, did it?"

"I don't think so. But I'm not sure who's behind it."

"And I suppose those speaking engagements we were hoping for probably won't come your way either."

"Yeah, right. Who would want a pregnant, unmarried mother of two speaking in their church?"

"Don't go beating yourself up. We know God has forgiven us, even if others haven't."

"I know," Michelle agreed. At least George could always come up with something positive. "But I don't know how I would be able to get along without you."

"Well, it's not like we can't see each other at all. We just have to avoid spending any time together alone."

"You'll have to start eating your meals alone at your house. The kids will miss you too."

"Are you willing to give it a try for a little while?" George paused and caught her eye.

"After Christmas," Michelle replied.

"After New Year," George said with a wink.

"Okay. After New Year." Michelle gave a quick nod.

On Christmas morning, George showed up before the children were out of bed.

"What? The kids are sleeping in on Christmas morning?" George sounded surprised.

"They've never seen what this is all about." Michelle tried to imagine what the day would be like for the youngsters.

"They know they're getting presents," George mused. "But they never seemed real excited about it."

"I think that's about to change. They know this is a big deal for most kids. But the reality hasn't sunk in yet."

"So how did you celebrate Christmas before?"

"Well, Jasper would bring in some evergreen branches, and we would use them to decorate the cottage."

"No tree?"

"No. We didn't have anything to decorate a tree anyway. I would tell the children the story of Jesus's birth. Presents were limited to what we could make or do for each other."

"Sounds simple, but really nice, in a way." George cocked his head. "Maybe that's the way we should all do it."

"Are you kids coming down to open your presents?" Michelle called up the stairs. The question was answered by two pair of feet hitting the floor. As the children came down the stairs in their pajamas, George started pulling presents out from under the tree. By the time the presents were all opened and the children had eaten breakfast and gotten dressed, it was time to start getting ready to go to Aunt Mae's for Christmas dinner.

Like usual, dinner at Mae's house involved a large home-cooked meal at noon, with leftovers and other snacks all afternoon. After the main meal was over, everyone moved into the living room to exchange presents. After the presents came the games. The adults started a game of canasta while the boys played computer games and the girls played with their new dolls. Michelle watched her mother moving from room to room, checking on all the activities. She knew her mother really relished the company of her grandchildren. *But how would Daddy interact with them?*

The children's normal bedtime was approaching by the time George loaded their presents in the car and Michelle got the children to put on their coats to head home. As they drove back to Thrush Glen, Michelle couldn't help but wonder what the day would have been like if her dad had been there.

40

"You ready to hit the slopes?" Roger asked as George walked in the back door.

"You bet!" George couldn't remember when he felt this eager for a day with the guys.

"Six inches of fresh powder overnight." Rick tossed the newspaper onto the kitchen table.

"Sounds great!" George felt his stomach rumble. "You guys are planning to stop for breakfast, aren't you?"

"Sure thing." Roger slipped into his parka.

"Good! 'Cause if you're not, I'm in trouble."

"Can't head out for a day of skiing without a big farmer's breakfast," Rick commented as they headed for Roger's Explorer, which was warming up in the driveway.

George admired the scenery as they rolled along quietly on snow-covered country roads winding through the pristine mountains toward the interstate. He thought about the tract of land along Thrush Creek. "So, George, how are you coming with the purchase of that woodland?" Roger glanced at him in the rearview mirror.

He must have read my mind. "Oh, I called Mrs. Stoner and told her I can't buy it."

"You did what?" Rick turned in his seat.

"Well, I have other responsibilities now," George explained. "I can't risk losing everything I've got on some investment that may not work out. What if I couldn't make the payments? I'd lose everything."

"I think you're passing up a chance to strike it rich." Rick shook his head.

"My business can provide enough for me to support a family," George argued. "And if I want to expand, I could hire a craftsman or two to build the things I design. I could triple my output without investing any more in my facilities."

"But if you buy the land," Roger countered, "you may be able to provide for your family in a way most of us only dream of."

"If I can be satisfied with what I have, I'll have plenty." George's words came out with a little more emphasis than he intended. "If I'm not satisfied, I could lose it all."

"So did you and Michelle set a wedding date yet?" Rick asked.

"Nope. We're giving it some time."

"What d' ya mean?" Rick glanced over his shoulder. "You've already given it some time."

"Yeah, I thought that would be a no-brainer," Roger added.

"We're kind of, like, breaking up for a while," George explained. "We're gonna stop seeing each other and see how we feel about marriage in a couple months."

"Wow! That won't be easy," Rick observed. "You're there all the time."

"Not all the time. I don't sleep there."

"Oh yeah?" Rick and Roger grinned at each other.

"Well, just once," George admitted. "But you're right, it won't be easy. We gotta get some help lined up to do some of the things I've been doing. She needs somebody to watch Earl after school till she gets home from work."

"Abby still goes to the babysitter, doesn't she?" Roger sounded interested.

"Yeah. Sheryl is her babysitter."

"I could bring Earl along home from school, pick up Abby at Sheryl's place, and stay with them till Michelle gets home," Roger suggested.

Rick glanced at George and raised his eyebrows.

"I'll tell her you volunteered." George didn't know how Michelle would respond to that idea. "It's up to her. She can call you and work out the details. It's no use I get involved. After New Year, I won't be seeing her anymore."

Throughout the day, as George rode the ski lift or waited in line, his mind kept returning to Roger's offer. *What is he up to? He has Kathy. But will he ever give up on Michelle?*

On New Year's Eve, George and Michelle invited Roger and Kathy for an evening of Monopoly and pizza. Of course, there was a lot more to eat than just pizza. Michelle had set out a whole buffet of hors d'oeuvres, leftover Christmas cookies, a fruit tray, and lots of caffeinated beverages. She perused the layout one more time as she invited her guests to help themselves. She watched Roger as he followed Kathy to the food bar. "So, Roger, George tells me you volunteered to watch the children after school." She noticed Kathy look up from the plate she was filling.

"Yeah." Roger glanced at Kathy then at Michelle. "I could bring Earl home from school and pick up Abby and watch them till you get home from work."

"Oops! I missed my plate!" Kathy stooped over to pick a chunk of pineapple off the floor.

"That would be a big help," Michelle watched Kathy out of the corner of her eye. "Can you start on Monday?"

"Sure." Roger sounded delighted.

"Okay, thanks. I'll tell Sheryl to expect you."

"Somebody needs to fill me in." Kathy's eyes narrowed. "George, are you going somewhere or something?"

"Oh." George chuckled. "Didn't Roger tell you?"

"Tell me what?"

"Well, Michelle and I decided to try divorce first. And if we don't like that, then maybe we'll get married."

"Oh?" Kathy responded with a puzzled look. She studied for a moment then her face cleared. "Oh!"

Michelle tried to hide her smirk as it became obvious that Kathy understood Roger's motives. "So you're like splitting up for a while?" Kathy glanced at George.

"Yeah," George replied. "Most people get married first, then split up. But we don't do things in the normal order."

"So I've heard," Kathy quipped.

Michelle had promised the children that if they could stay awake and be good, they could stay up till midnight and watch the ball drop in Times Square. As the Monopoly game wore on, the children watched video after video till both were sound asleep on the couch. As the countdown approached midnight, Michelle woke the children. They watched with total lack of enthusiasm while the crystal ball descended and the crowd cheered the arrival of year 1995. Michelle carried Abby upstairs, with Earl trudging behind, while Roger and Kathy got ready to leave.

Finally, Michelle and George stood alone by the back door in a long tearful embrace. The party was over. The new year was beginning with the cold and dark of January, like it always does. But this new year seemed extra cold and extra dark. After multiple good-bye kisses, she watched George step out into the cold and walk across the snow-covered lawn to his dark empty house.

During the following week, Michelle got settled into the new routine. It was working pretty well, but she knew that sooner or later this arrangement with Roger would have its challenges. The first one had just presented itself. She stared out the kitchen window as she slowly washed the dishes, trying to decide what to do. When the last piece was dried and put away, she went to the phone and called her sister.

"Have your children ever been to the Pennsylvania Farm Show?" she asked.

"Yeah, once, a couple years ago," Mae replied

"Are you going this year?"

"We haven't talked about it. Why?"

"Well, Roger has been talking to the kids, and he's got them all excited about going to the farm show. And, of course, he's volunteering to take us, me included. I don't really want to spend that much time with him. But I don't want to disappoint the kids either."

"I get it. You need somebody to make you a better offer."

"Right!" She knew Mae would understand.

"And it would be more fun for the kids to see it along with their cousins," Mae continued.

"That's what I was thinking."

"I'm sure we can work something out. Do you want to go too? Or do you just want us to take the kids?"

"I hardly have time to go. I don't want to take off work more than I have to."

"Okay. Let me talk to Fred, and I'll call you back with the details."

Roger seemed a little disappointed when Michelle told him about their plans. But he didn't argue. This plan was obviously more practical and better for everyone—everyone except him, that is.

A few days later, when Michelle got home from work, Roger presented her with a small box, the type that jewelry comes in. "I just realized that I still have something of yours," he said. As she took the box, she felt like she was about to be pulled into his arms. Her arm brushed against his as she slowly opened the box. There was the souvenir key ring from Washington, DC, with her name on the back. And next to it lay her necklace with their engraved initials.

"Thank you," she said while thinking to herself, *What do I do with that? I don't want to wear it anymore.*

Each afternoon, as George worked in his shop, he found himself glancing out the window, watching for Michelle to come home. And when she did, he counted the minutes till Roger left. What troubled him was the fact that the time was gradually increasing. *What could they possibly be doing in there for eight minutes and thirty-five seconds?* But he couldn't go in and see. That was off limits for him. He would just have to wait and see how they felt in two or three months—if he could wait that long.

Late one evening, Michelle's phone rang. She picked up the receiver and said, "Hello."

A familiar male voice said, "Hello, Michelle?"

"Daddy!" She could hardly believe her ears.

"How you doing, kiddo?"

"Fine. Daddy, where are you?" Her heart raced.

"I'm in California. I just met your friend, Dan Phillips."

"He found you!" Her eyes flooded with tears. "Are you all right?"

"Yeah, I'm fine. I work on a cruise ship. I'm not here very much."

"A cruise ship? When can you come home?"

"As soon as I can catch a plane."

"I can't wait for you to meet my children. I have two, a boy and a girl."

"Yeah. Dan was telling me about your experience. We all thought you drowned."

"I know. Everybody thought that. What do you do on the cruise ship?"

"I work at the outfitters desk. I'll tell you all about it when I get there. Can you meet me at the airport? I'll try to get a flight into Harrisburg."

"Sure! Just let me know when to be there."

"I'll call you back as soon as I can book a flight. Oh! It's late there, isn't it?"

"Don't worry about that! Just call me any time!"

"Okay, I'll talk to you soon."

"Oh, and, Daddy…" She wasn't ready to end the conversation already. "I have another one on the way!"

"What! A baby?"

"Yeah!"

"Dan didn't tell me that!"

"Oh, I guess he doesn't know. It's not until June."

"Wow! I can't wait to see you."

"Me too."

"I'll call you back as soon as I can."

"Okay, see ya."

"Bye."

"Bye-bye." She hugged the receiver before she hung it back on the cradle.

41

With a cup of coffee in hand, George flipped the light switch and took a deep breath as he started toward his workbench. The acrid smell of oak lumber and the mildly sweet smell of cherry wood blended with the coffee to create a unique aroma. This was his own little universe, a place where his creative ideas took shape, where rough lumber was transformed into works of art. He set his coffee on the workbench and looked over the partially assembled china cabinet sitting on the floor in front of him. As he started removing the pipe clamps he had put on the evening before, he heard the front door close. He looked up to see Michelle coming through the office, into the shop.

Her face was beaming with excitement. "George, guess what! My dad called last evening!"

"Wow, what a surprise! Where's he at?"

"California. He's flying in this afternoon! I'm meeting him at the Harrisburg airport at five fifty."

"Great! That's wonderful! Do you need anything? Do you want to use my pick up?"

"No. I'll take my car. It has plenty of room. But he might need a place to stay for a couple of days."

"Well, I've got an empty room."

"That's what I was thinking. I don't know if he booked a hotel or anything. Maybe he won't need it. But this would be nice. He'd be right next door."

"How long is he staying?"

"I'm not sure. A week, maybe."

"It's no problem. He can stay with me. You taking the kids along to the airport?"

"You bet! They've never seen a big airport."

"Are you calling Harrisburg a big airport?"

"Well, for them it will be. And I can't wait for them to meet him!"

"It will be nice to have someone to share my house with for a few days. It gets lonely over there."

Their eyes met and locked. "I know what you mean," she said softly.

George could hardly keep from throwing his arms around her. He picked up his coffee and took a sip. "You let me know if you need anything else."

"I will," she replied as she turned to leave. It seemed really awkward to let her walk away without at least a little hug. George sipped his coffee as he watched Michelle walk to the door and head for the house.

The children looked around with wide eyes as Michelle led them past the ticket counters, up a flight of stairs, and out the concourse. Earl wanted to stop at every window and look out at the planes and trains of luggage wagons and fuel trucks moving around. They were a bit early, so they made frequent stops to enjoy the activity outside. Michelle kept checking her watch and urging them on. A few minutes after they arrived at their gate, the plane rolled up. Earl stood by the window watching as the plane rolled closer and closer. He backed away several steps and turned with wide eyes looking for a place to run, thinking that the plane was about to crash right through the glass. But after it stopped right on its mark, he cautiously stepped back up to the window to see what was to happen next.

With the children at her side, Michelle watched anxiously as a line of passengers emerged from the doorway. "There he is!" she said, stooping down to Abby and pointing at an athletically built man with graying hair and a thick mustache. He was well tanned, with wrinkles around the corners of his jovial blue eyes. "That's your grandpa—the one wearing blue jeans and a white polo shirt." Michelle started waving to get his attention. Abby did the same.

Recognizing his daughter, he broke out of line and hurried over to them. He dropped his carry-on bag and threw his arms around Michelle, picking her right off her feet like a little girl.

"These are my children," Michelle said as her dad set her back on her feet. "This is Abigail, she's three. And Earl is almost six."

"So these are my grandchildren," her dad said with a smile. He bent over with his hands on his knees. "It's so nice to finally meet you. I think we'll have a lot of fun together." Michelle was sure they would.

"Can we call you Grandpa?" Earl asked.

"Yeah. 'Grandpa.' That would be fine. Most other people call me Max. And your mother calls me Daddy. But I like being called Grandpa."

As they waited by the luggage conveyor, Max leaned over and quietly asked, "Now these two children, they're to that guy that abducted you, right?"

"Yeah. Jasper is their father."

"And the one on the way is...Roger's?"

"Oh no, Daddy. We have a lot to talk about. Do you remember George Lauger?"

"George Lauger?" he repeated thoughtfully. "Quiet kid. You did a birthday party for him."

"Yeah. That's the one. He owns the house I'm living in."

"He owns your house? When you put it that way it sounds like he's not your husband."

"No, not yet. We might get married. I hope we do. But we're still trying to decide."

"Well, I'm eager to get to know George a little better."

"You will. Did you book a hotel or anything?"

"No. I figured I'd work something out after I got here."

"Good! George has an extra room in his house."

"His house? This guy owns two houses?"

"Yeah."

"Why haven't you married him already?"

"Daddy! I'd never marry a man for money! If I learned anything in the last seven years, it's that money isn't important."

"So what is important?"

"Being with the people you love. Doing all you can for those you care about."

"Okay. Can't argue with that. So how does a young fellow like George acquire two houses?"

"He bought the house I'm living in. And he's still paying for it. He inherited his mother's house. She died of a heart attack in August. He's not a rich man. But I really like him."

"And he has a room for me?"

"Yeah. I've already checked it out with him. He'd be glad to have you stay there while you're in town."

"And where is his house?"

"You remember where the Laugers lived on Oak Street, don't you?"

"Oh. Yeah."

"And my place is just two doors away."

"Oh. That's perfect then."

Finally the luggage arrived, and they headed out to the parking lot. The children tagged along quietly as Michelle and her dad continued drilling each other with questions. Time flew by as Michelle wound her way through the concrete jungle of overpasses and intersecting interstates and headed west on Route 322.

"You feel safe living in Thrush Glen?" Max asked.

"Of course."

"Dan Phillips told me that someone is killing off everyone who knew anything about that guy you were living with."

"His name is Jasper, Daddy. He was a nice man with a horrible past. And we weren't just living together. As far as I'm concerned, he was my husband."

"Okay, but that wasn't my point. I'm asking if you're safe in Thrush Glen, with everything that's going on there."

"I don't worry about it."

"You could come to California. There's lots of opportunity out there."

"Everybody here has been so good to me. This is home. I couldn't think of leaving."

"You're not afraid of this guy that's killing people?"

"We're not even sure that there is such a person. And I'm not going to live my life in fear of the unknown. I'm not running away from whatever or whoever caused those deaths."

"I'm not sure if you're being brave or naive."

Michelle chuckled. "Mae says I'm just being blond."

"She always was jealous of your hair."

"Well, if you stay for a while, you can form your own opinion as to whether I'm acting like a dumb blond or a brave brunette. But I'm not going to California with you."

"Okay. It was just a thought."

The kids were sleeping by the time they reached Thrush Glen. But when they got out of the car to run into the house, the cold mountain air seemed to give them a renewed burst of energy. They couldn't seem to stop running once they got inside the house. They ran from room to room, turning on lights and then giving their grandpa a very quick tour of the house. He barely had time to look inside one room before they were leading him to the next.

"You children want a snack before you go to bed?" Michelle asked as soon as they calmed down a little.

"Already?" Earl complained.

"Yes. Tomorrow is a school day. You've got to get to bed. And your grandpa has had a long trip. He's probably tired."

"Well, it's only five thirty by my time." Max glanced at his watch.

Michelle set out a platter of Rice Krispie treats and a bowl of grapes.

"Rice Krispie treats!" Max eyed the platter. "I think I'll have to have one of those too."

"That's why I made them." Michelle smiled. As the children enjoyed the snack with their grandpa, Michelle phoned George and asked him to come over. After helping himself to a Rice Krispie treat and a handful of grapes, George sat down and started getting acquainted with Max. Then he helped him carry his luggage across the frozen lawn and showed him to his room.

As George lay in his bed that night, he kept visualizing the glow on Michelle's face. He knew this reunion meant a lot to her. He wondered what it must be like to have that kind of relationship with a father. He hadn't seen his own father since the day he walked out on him and his mother when George was only twelve years old. And he had no desire to reconnect with him now. From his observations over the years, it seemed that having a close relationship with one's father was rare indeed. But he vowed to himself that he would be a dependable, loving father to the baby Michelle was carrying.

42

Michelle was busy getting breakfast ready for the children when her dad rapped on the window of the back door. "Come in," she yelled. "Have you had breakfast already?" she asked, as he opened the door.

"Yeah, I had breakfast with George. Great guy! He was just showing me around his shop. Man, he makes some nice stuff."

"I know. You're not telling me anything new," Michelle replied nonchalantly. But inside, she was elated with the impression George was making on her dad. "Did you sleep well?"

"Yeah. It took a little while to go to sleep. I'm still on California time, I guess."

"Hey, if you'd like to have my car today, you just have to ride along this morning then come back and pick me up at work at five o'clock."

"I don't think I need to go anywhere."

"I thought maybe you'd just want to drive around town and see some old friends." Michelle remembered what it was like to reconnect with old friends. She hoped to make her dad's visit as nostalgic as possible. "Earl, finish your cereal and go brush your teeth! The bus will be here before you know it."

"Well, that would be kind of nice, if you don't mind me using your car," Max seemed mildly enthused with the idea. "There's a lot of people I haven't seen for a while."

After Earl got on the school bus, Michelle got Abby ready to go to the sitter.

As they drove to the babysitter, Max was getting his first look at the town in daylight. "Well, that hasn't changed," he commented as they passed the old general store. "This town is like a step back in time."

"And most folks around here seem to like it that way," Michelle added. She knew her dad had always loved this quaint little community. In her peripheral vision, she could see her dad's head oscillating from side to side as they drove from the sitter up Main Street to Sunset Hardware. He didn't say much, but she knew he was taking it all in. "Don't forget to pick me up at five," she said as she handed him her keys.

"Hi, Grandpa!" the two youngsters called as Max woke up from his nap on the couch.

"Hi, Max." Roger walked into the room behind the children. "I could hardly believe it when the kids told me their grandpa was at their house. It's good to see you again."

"Hey, you too, Roger. How you doing?"

"I'm doing fine. I suppose Michelle told you, I bring the kids home and stay with them till she gets here."

"Yeah, she did. But you won't have to stay today. I can watch them."

"That's okay. I can stay." Roger seemed eager to stay. "I have something I want to give to Michelle anyway."

"Oh, what d'you got there?"

"I was in the bookstore and saw this." Roger handed a book to Max. "I thought Michelle would like it."

"*Keystone Canoeing*." Max glanced at the cover.

"Yeah, it's a guide to all the canoeable waters in Pennsylvania," Roger explained.

"She'll love this," Max commented as he leafed through the book. "Lots of river maps and descriptions, distance, time, difficulty. Looks like a great book."

"It is a great book."

"Well, you better watch out." Max eyed Roger. "You keep giving her gifts like this and you'll end up stealing her heart away from George."

"We wouldn't want that to happen now, would we?" Roger quipped with a slight grin.

"You can just leave the book here, and I'll see that she gets it. I'm going to take the kids and pick her up at work and then take them out for supper."

"Okay then." Roger sounded a little disappointed. "I guess there's no reason for me to stay."

As they drove toward the hardware store, Max asked, "What's your mommy's favorite restaurant?"

"She likes the ice cream parlor," Earl replied.

"Yeah! Ice cream," Abby agreed.

"Betsy's Ice Cream Parlor?"

"Yeah!"

"You eat ice cream in this cold weather?"

"You can get a hot fudge sundae," Abby replied in all seriousness.

Michelle smiled as her dad recounted his conversation with Abby. She understood the children had their hearts set on ice cream, so she agreed that Betsy's was her favorite restaurant. *After all, that place will bring back a few pleasant memories for Daddy.*

"It still looks the same," Max commented as they approached the front door of the ice cream parlor. He took a deep breath as he entered. Michelle was sure the smell of the old wooden building would bring back a flood of memories. During their meal, Max told several stories of things he remembered from when Michelle and Mae were growing up. Michelle could see that the atmosphere of the old building and the sound of the nickelodeon piano were having an effect on her father.

When they arrived home, Michelle picked up the book that was lying on the kitchen table and started leafing through it. "Daddy, where did you get this?"

"Oh, it wasn't me," he replied. "Your boyfriend dropped that off for you."

"Well, how nice. That was very thoughtful of him, especially since he doesn't even have an interest in canoeing."

Max chuckled. "Not that boyfriend. The other one."

"Roger?"

"How many other ones do you have?"

"Bless his heart." Michelle paused as her mind flashed back to some of the great times she'd had canoeing with Roger. "He just doesn't give up."

"I can see why you want to take your time with this decision," Max observed. "You've got two very well-qualified young bachelors to choose from."

"It's not that. In fact, it wasn't even my idea to break it off with George. Our marriage counselor suggested it, and George thought it was good advice. So we agreed to give it some time."

"It probably is good advice. You don't want to end up married to one person and wishing you were married to the other."

"Well, we're not rushing into it," Michelle confirmed. "We're taking our time to make sure it's the right thing for us."

After her dad went over to George's place for the night, Michelle reviewed the conversation in her mind. She wondered if her dad had a preference between Roger and George. But regardless whether he did or not, it wasn't his decision to make. It was hers. And her heart and mind couldn't agree.

Saturday was cold. Michelle glanced at the gray sky as she got the children into the car. *It looks like it could start snowing any*

minute. She and her dad climbed into the front seats and headed for Bellefonte to visit Mae and her family. The children had a great time together, like always. But the atmosphere among the adults seemed a little more like the weather outside.

Polite greetings and a bit of small talk were followed by an awkward silence. Michelle tried to get an interesting conversation started about her dad's job on the cruise ship. But no one showed any real interest, and Max was smart enough to not make a big story out of something his listeners weren't interested in hearing. After a few long hours, Michelle decided they better head home before it starts snowing and the roads get bad.

On Sunday she convinced her dad to go along to church, although he admitted he hadn't been to a church service in a long time. "I guess it would be good for me to go once again," he said without enthusiasm.

"You'll see a lot of people you haven't seen for years."

"That's what I'm afraid of. I don't know what they all think of me by now."

"It doesn't matter what they think," Michelle declared.

"You're right. It doesn't matter."

That afternoon, Max went along with George to Roger and Rick's place to watch football with the guys.

Roger gave Max a grin. "Now we don't want to hear any stories from the good old days when you played football without helmets."

George turned to Max. "You played football without a helmet? That explains a few things."

Max smiled. "It's so nice to be among friends."

At halftime, everyone wandered into the kitchen looking for refreshments. "So how's the job market around here?" Max asked as he popped open a can of beer.

"Pretty good," Rick replied. "People who want to work can find something to do. It may not be the greatest job in the world or the highest pay, but people can find jobs."

"You thinking about staying?" George sounded pleased with the idea.

"This is still home. I'm thinking I might move back."

"My dad's looking for a truck driver," Roger offered.

"I don't have my Pennsylvania CDL anymore."

"Well, you can get that again. You know how to drive a truck."

"I suppose I could."

"My dad has nice trucks too, easier to handle than that dump truck you used to drive."

Max knew Roger was trying to get a reaction. "That wasn't a bad truck," he replied with a twinkle in his eye. "It just took a real man to drive it."

"He doesn't have any of those old double-stick Macks where you had to use both hands to shift gears." Roger grinned and waited.

"I haven't seen one of those in a long time. You young guys wouldn't even know how to drive a truck like that."

"Trucks have changed. Some of these new trucks have more gauges and gadgets than you old-timers ever dreamed of."

"I'm sure I could get used to that." Max paused and thought about what it would be like to drive a nice new eighteen-wheeler. "Maybe I'll have to talk to your dad before I head back to California."

As Max told Michelle what he was thinking, he could see the excitement building in her face. "Let's check with George and see if you can move in with him permanently," she suggested enthusiastically.

"We've already worked that out." Max grinned. "He just has to figure out how much he's going to charge me."

On Monday, Max visited Koralsen's Trucking Company and talked with Roger's dad. He wasn't promised a job. But he came away knowing that he had a good opportunity to pursue as soon as he got his CDL.

"I just need a week or two to wrap things up out there," he said to Michelle on Wednesday morning as they prepared to leave for the airport. "Then I'll load my stuff in my pickup and head across the country."

"Can you get all your stuff in a pickup truck?" she asked.

"I don't have any furniture," he replied. "Just my golf clubs, guns, and fishing rods. My kayak can go on the roof. Oh, and a couple boxes of clothes and a computer and my tools. It will easily fit in my truck."

"So you'll be back in two or three weeks?"

"Yeah, three weeks, tops. I'll keep in touch with you."

"It will be great to have you home again, Daddy. Really great!" Her voice broke with emotion. "And you'll be here when my baby comes. And you can walk me down the aisle at my wedding."

On Thursday evening, when Michelle got home from work, she found Roger and Abby sitting on the sofa, looking at a book. "I discovered I had something else of yours," Roger said as he raised the book so Michelle could see the cover.

"My high school yearbook!" Michelle exclaimed.

"I saw your picture," Abby said proudly as Michelle sat down beside Roger.

Roger turned the page slowly, with Michelle leaning on one arm and Abby on the other. "Oh. There's Patty Potter," Michelle commented. "I wonder what ever happened to her."

"Married a farm boy and moved up to the Finger Lakes," Roger replied, turning another page. "And there's Burpy. I don't know what's become of him."

"I hope he found a better nickname," Michelle quipped with a chuckle.

Michelle hardly noticed when Abby got off the sofa and headed to her room. She and Roger continued leafing through the book and reminiscing. With their heads so close together that she could feel the warmth radiating from Roger's face, they reviewed the autographs and pictures.

"There's that picture of George in shop class," Michelle commented. "I remember sneaking up on him with my camera and waiting and waiting for him to raise his head so I could see his face. He was so intent on his work. He had no clue that I was there."

"That's not how he tells it."

"What do you mean?"

"He says he didn't see you. But he could feel you watching him."

"Really?"

"Michelle, you have so much charisma, so much karma, or whatever it is. People can just sense your presence. It's like one magnet attracting another. You can feel it."

"Well, you've got quite the magnetic personality yourself."

"Michelle, when I was kayaking, and you were watching me from behind those louvers, I could feel it. I could sense that you were watching me. That's why I was never completely convinced that you were dead."

"So how do you explain that *scientifically*?"

"I don't know. I just know that you are really special."

"Thanks, Roger. I'm flattered, especially considering that those comments are coming from the most popular schoolteacher in Sunset Township." Even though her mind had decided that George was the one for her, her heart still longed for Roger.

"When are we going to eat?" Earl asked as he came down the stairs.

"Soon. I'll get you something in a little while."

"Mom, why is your face all red?"

43

One breath of the chilly mountain air was enough to put the vitality in Michelle's steps as she sprinted from the car to her back door. It had been a slow Monday at the hardware store. All day she had looked forward to her evening with the children. And to be honest, she also looked forward to the few minutes she would spend with Roger. She pulled off her coat as she walked into the cozy atmosphere of her family room. There was Roger on the floor playing Chutes and Ladders with the children. She gave each of the children a hug and sat down to read her mail.

When the game was over, Roger came to Michelle carrying a bag with something large and flat inside. "I was going through some old pictures, and I found this. So I had it enlarged and I got George to mat it and frame it for you." He pulled the picture out of the bag and handed it to her.

It was a photo of her at age seventeen, standing along a river with her dad, scouting a section of whitewater that could be seen in the background. Both were wearing floatation vests and helmets, and each had a canoe paddle in hand. Their expressions were serious but delightful as they gazed at the impressive rapids.

"Thanks, that's really neat." A smile spread across Michelle's face as she studied the picture. "Where was it taken?"

"I'm not sure. I think it was on the Lehigh River."

"I love the expression on my dad's face. He looks so perceptive," she said as she started going around the room, holding the picture up in various locations. "I have to find the right spot for it."

"We went to so many places with your dad. It's hard to remember which pictures are from where."

"We did have a lot of great trips together, didn't we?" Michelle's pulse quickened as highlights of those trips flashed through her mind.

"I have lots of fond memories. Lots." Roger was gazing at her with his warm brown eyes.

"Well, thanks so much," Michelle said after she seemed to settle on a spot for the picture. "I really appreciate it."

"You got any plans for Sunday?" Roger asked as he prepared to leave.

"Just going to church. Why?"

"Well, it's Valentine's Day, you know."

"I know." *What does that have to do with us?* She couldn't look into his eyes.

"So if I come to church on Sunday, can we go out for lunch afterward? Kids included, of course."

Michelle knew that Roger understood how much she wanted him to come to church. She knew she was being manipulated. *But what would it hurt to have lunch with him?* "What makes you want to come to church?"

"Well, I never said there's anything wrong with going to church." He shrugged. "You can get some good input there, even if you don't believe everything."

"Okay." Michelle flashed a smile at him. "You come to church, and we'll go out for lunch."

Later that evening, she paced back and forth by the phone. What would George say? She had to be upfront with him. She didn't want to do anything behind his back. Maybe she should just call it off with Roger. Finally, she picked up the phone and punched George's number. "George, I just had to talk to you," she said softly.

"Why, what's up?"

"Roger is coming to church on Sunday."

"This Sunday?"

"Yeah. But he's only coming so he can take me out for lunch."

"Oh. Now it makes sense. He wants to take you out for Valentine's Day."

"I really don't want to be with him, George. The only reason I agreed to do it is so he'll come to church." She knew that wasn't quite true.

"Well, that's one way to get the rascal to church, I guess. Is it just you and him?"

"No. The children are going with us."

"That's good."

"Are you okay with this, George?"

George hesitated and cleared his throat. "Michelle, I trust you. If you say you're only doing it so he'll come to church, I believe you. You have to know what's in your heart. After all, the reason we decided to go through this time of separation was so that we could get a better understanding of what we really want."

He didn't actually say he was okay with it. "Don't worry, George. You're still the one I really want. I miss you so much."

"I miss you too, Michelle."

Around midmorning on Saturday, Michelle's doorbell rang. At the door was a delivery man with a cute little bouquet of fresh flowers. As Michelle set the flowers on the table, Abby asked, "Where did you get those, Mommy?"

"They're from your grandpa," Michelle replied. "He sent them to us for Valentine's Day. He says he'll see us soon."

"Is he coming today?"

"No. It'll probably be about a week yet."

In less than an hour, a second delivery man arrived with a dozen red roses. "Wow! This is too much!" Michelle said admiring the roses. She took hold of the card, turned it over, and read silently, "Darling, save your heart for me. Love, George." The last line of "Save Your Heart for Me" started running through her head. Although she couldn't remember the rest of the lyrics, the song just wouldn't stop. She finally forced the song out of her head by singing "The Rose" while running the vacuum cleaner.

After finishing her cleaning, Michelle sat on the couch and gazed at the picture Roger had given her. She thought about the good times she'd had canoeing with Roger and her dad. She cherished the memories of those rare, private moments when she and Roger were alone. Roger was even more handsome now than he was then. And to her dismay, she realized she was really looking forward to their lunch tomorrow.

George noticed all the men in the pews turn their heads as Michelle walked down the aisle in a skimpy red dress and ushered her children into a pew several benches in front of him. *Why is she wearing that dress? I know, it's Valentine's Day. But she has other red dresses. Why this one? Is she trying to look like a sexy little teenager? Or is she trying to impress Roger?*

The worship service had just begun when he glanced over his shoulder and saw Roger standing at the back of the sanctuary looking over the congregation. Heads turned as he walked down the aisle and slipped into the pew beside Michelle. George hid his emotions as he glanced down at the empty space beside him. Although Roger sat attentively and had no interaction with Michelle, George couldn't help being distracted by the situation.

He noticed every turn of Michelle's head as the pastor spoke on and on about the difference between love and libido. Libido, according to Pastor John, was a natural desire for self-preservation and therefore was self-serving. Love, on the other hand, was from

God and therefore was focused on serving others. Despite the distraction, George was catching some of the sermon. He asked himself, *Who needs to hear this more, Roger or me?*

Due to Valentine's Day, the cozy little restaurant was busier than a normal Sunday. Their usual rustic decor was accented with hearts and roses while romantic love songs were playing over the intercom. "We should have gone to Betsy's," Earl said as they stood in the lobby, waiting for a table.

"There would be a waiting line there too," Michelle assured him. "Every place is busy today."

During the meal, Earl whispered something to Roger, who was seated next to him in the booth. Roger whispered something back.

"What are they talking about?" Abby asked.

"I don't know," Michelle replied. "I guess it's a secret." The guys just grinned and kept shoveling food into their mouths.

As they were getting back in the car to head home, Roger got a small box from somewhere and handed it to Earl. Earl quickly stuck it in his coat pocket and climbed into the back seat.

"You have your car at the church, I suppose?" Roger questioned as they got underway.

"No. We rode to church with George this morning. So you'll just have to drop us off at home."

"Oh. I thought you two were avoiding each other."

"We are, to some extent."

All the way home, Abby kept asking Earl, "What do you have?"

And he kept answering, "It's none of your business."

"Are you coming to church again next week?" Michelle asked as Roger pulled into the driveway. Part of her hoped he would say yes and part hoped for no.

"I don't know. I haven't made any plans yet." After parking the car, Roger got out and opened the back hatch. He reached in and brought out a large box of assorted chocolates and handed them to Michelle.

"Roger," she said with a sigh, "this is too much."

"No, no," he replied. "Just take it. It's for you and the kids."

She took the box and shook her head. "You're wasting your time, Roger. I'm not going to get romantically involved with you." But she knew she already was. As Roger got back into his car, she followed the children into the house and sat the box of chocolates on the table.

"I have something for you too, Mommy," Earl said as he pulled the box out of his coat pocket and handed it to her. "You remember that shiny pebble I found along the river when we were canoeing?"

"You're giving me your pebble?" she asked suspiciously, as she opened the box.

"No. We had somebody make something out of it."

"I see!" she said as she lifted out a pair of earrings. Each one had a dangling oval-shaped disc made from the amber-colored gemstone.

"Thank you! And is it actually jasper?" she glanced at her son.

"I don't know." Earl shrugged. "I guess it is."

"So who made the earrings?"

"Somebody that Roger knows."

"And you paid him, I suppose?"

"Paid him? It was my pebble. Why would I pay him?"

"You're right. It was your pebble. Thank you so much."

Later that afternoon, as Michelle sat in the family room trying to read, she couldn't stay focused on her book. Her mind kept going back to Roger. Would he ever stop pursuing her? What should she do about him? She couldn't return the chocolates. The children had heard him say that the chocolates were for them too. She couldn't return the earrings; they were from her son, although she knew Roger was behind it. She had told him that he was wasting his time. But was that enough to get him to stop? *Do I really want him to stop? Will he show up at church again next Sunday, expecting to go out for lunch? But he's a great guy, and a wonderful friend*, she thought to herself. *And if he keeps coming to church, he might eventually change his mind about some things.*

On Thursday, when Michelle came home from work, a silver pickup with a cap on the back was parked in the drive. Earl met her at the door and announced, "Guess what! Grandpa's here!"

"I told you he would be here today, didn't I?" Michelle said as she walked toward the family room where her dad and Roger were playing checkers on Earl's checkerboard.

"I can beat both of 'em," Earl bragged as Max got up to hug his daughter.

"Did you have a good trip?" Michelle asked.

"Yeah. But I'm tired."

"You still got stuff to unload?"

"No. All my stuff's over at George's place."

"What are you hungry for?"

"Just about anything," Max replied as he sat down and turned his attention to the checker game.

When the game ended, Roger left and Michelle started setting the table. "Daddy, next week, could you start getting the kids and watching them after school?"

"Sure, I'd love to." He sounded delighted. "Of course, sooner or later I'll get a job. But till then."

"Thanks. You just got to help me stay away from Roger. He and I are getting just a little too friendly."

"Oh? What do you mean by that?"

"The more I'm around him, the more I want to return to the old times. But those old times are never going to come back, Daddy. He's changed. He and I have no future."

"And what about George?"

"George and I are much more compatible. I know that in my head. But I just have to get Roger out of my heart."

44

Roger looked up from the newspaper to see George approaching the back door. *I wonder what he's up to so early on a Saturday morning.*

"What are you guys doing inside on a nice morning like this?" George asked as he walked into kitchen.

"I just don't get moving as early you do," Rick set his coffee mug down. "What are you up to?"

"Man, I got cabin fever." George glanced out the window. "Thc birds are singing. The flowers are pushing up through the ground. And I just want to get out and do something outside."

"Like what?" Roger asked. He had been feeling the same way.

"Well, I thought it would be a great day to take a couple shovels and go out there to Thrush Creek and hike down to the dam. I'd like to see if we can figure out where that gate to the mill race used to be."

"Good idea!" Rick said, tossing the business section of the newspaper on the table. "Can you wait till I get back from band practice?"

"Sure. By then, it'll be a little warmer anyway," George replied.

"Count me in." Roger got to his feet.

While Rick was at band practice, the other two searched the garage for a shovel that was last seen standing in the one corner. When they found it under the workbench, they put it with the shovel and digging iron that George already had in the back of his pickup. Then they went into the house and filled a small cooler with sandwiches, snacks, and drinks.

By ten thirty, the three were heading into the woods just above the concrete bridge.

"Look at that oak tree!" George said, tapping the shovel handle against a large tree trunk. "That's red oak. That thing's well over three feet in diameter. And look how tall and straight it is. Man, you could get a lot of nice lumber out of a tree like that."

"And it's not like that's the only one." Rick stopped and turned 360 degrees. "There's lots of 'em. Look at the trunk on that one!"

"That's a wild cherry," George added. "Not quite as big as the oak, but worth a lot more."

"I see why you say there's a lot of timber ready to be harvested out here," Roger commented. But he wasn't so eager to see that happen.

"Yeah, some of these trees need to be taken out to let more sunlight in and promote growth on the forest floor," George continued. "That'll create a better habitat for wild life and create a nice extra income for somebody. And I wish it were me."

"Well, it still could be you," Rick reminded him. "How many times did Mrs. Stoner tell you the price isn't important? She'll sell it for whatever you can give."

"I don't want to take advantage of the old lady." George shook his head. "And besides, I have other responsibilities now. I don't want to risk losing what I've got and not be able to provide for the baby."

"If you would have stayed in your own bed, you wouldn't have that problem," Roger quipped.

"Yeah, I know." George hung his head. "One mistake can affect the rest of your life. Now we just have to make the best of the situation." All along the one-mile hike, George kept pointing out trees that were valuable and ready to be harvested. And Rick kept reminding him that it could still be his.

"Maybe if we find this treasure, you can put that toward the purchase of the land," Rick suggested.

"I'm not counting on that till we actually have it." George seemed to be picking up his pace. "There's a good chance those baseball cards didn't survive this long underground. And if they did, and if we find them, I'm not claiming the whole thing for myself. We each get a share of it."

After briefly surveying the area around the remains of the old dam, Rick and George started digging off the sand and silt that covered the concrete. Roger stood by the edge of the creek, watching the water flow and longing to be gliding across the water in his kayak. A few minutes later, he was offering to dig while someone else rested. They dug a shallow trench, exposing the top edge of the dam breast. After uncovering a little more than ten feet of the dam breast, the concrete ended. "This might be our water gate." Roger stopped digging and unzipped his jacket.

"It is getting warm, isn't it?" George said as he did the same. "Let's keep digging and see what we find."

Before long they had exposed a rectangular opening, thirty inches wide by two feet deep, in the concrete dam breast. The gate itself, which probably had been made of wood, was completely gone.

"There's no doubt that this is the spot we were looking for." Rick gazed at the opening. "But do we measure from this side or that side or the middle?"

"I don't know. I guess we'll have to figure that out before we come back the next time. George dropped his shovel and picked up the cooler. "But right now, I'm ready for my sandwich." Roger felt the same. He and Rick followed George over the edge of the creek and sat down on the dam breast.

"Man, I'm glad you suggested this," Rick said as he opened a can of Pepsi. "It's a perfect day for this."

"It's beginning to sound like spring," Roger observed. He listened as woodpeckers drummed and songbirds offered their mating calls while staking out their territories. The remaining patches of melting snow contributed to the sounds of water trickling into the swollen creek while a hawk soared silently down the valley. The three lunched quietly in the warmth of the afternoon sun as they enjoyed the sounds of spring. They left their imaginations bask in the thought of buried treasure.

Later that evening, after George had filled Max in on the day's events, Max asked, "Would you and your buddies be interested in an early spring canoe trip?"

"Isn't the water awfully cold?" George tried to imagine what it would feel like to get dunked in that river at this time of year while the snow is still melting.

"Sure. But this is when you have the best water conditions." Max seemed undaunted. "You just have to dress for it."

"I don't know. I've never done very much canoeing."

"We can go over to Pine Creek. Lots of novices canoe the Pine. I'm sure I can get Roger to go along, but it would be much better with the four of us."

"I've heard stories about Pine Creek. I don't think that's for me."

"Don't worry about what you've heard. Ansonia to Blackwell is not a difficult section of water. The only reason it has such a bad reputation is because it attracts so many beginners who don't know how to handle a canoe. But if you're in the boat with me, you'll have nothing to worry about."

"Well, let's check with Rick and Roger. If they agree to go, I'll go too."

The next afternoon, the four got together to plan their canoe trip.

"Dress in layers," Max advised. "Wear wool and polypropylene and things that don't absorb much water. Stay away from cotton.

Cotton absorbs water like a sponge and stays wet forever. I'll be wearing polypropylene long johns and undershirt along with a heavy woolen shirt. I have a pair of slacks made of an acrylic that's not very absorbent. I have a fleece-lined nylon jacket. I'll have neoprene boots and gloves. And on top of all that, I'll have my rain gear. Even if it's not raining, I'll wear that to protect me from the spray. And it helps to seal out the cold wind too."

"Of course, rain gear doesn't keep you dry if you fall in the water," Roger added.

"That's right," Max agreed. "If I go in the drink, I'll be just as wet as anybody else. It's always a shock when that cold water hits your skin. But with the stuff I'm wearing underneath, I'll soon warm up again. And of course, I'll have spare clothes in my dry bag. Everybody needs to bring a complete set of spare clothes."

"I'll be wearing my dry suit on top of my other clothes." Roger glanced from Rick to George. "It's kind of like rain gear, except it seals completely. So I'll stay dry, even if I get dumped out of my boat."

"Where do you recommend shopping for that kind of stuff?" George asked. He was sure he didn't want to get dunked in cold water.

"I can take you to a number of good outfitters," Roger replied. "Or if you want to rent a neoprene wet suit, I can show you where to do that. It really doesn't cost much to rent a wet suit for the weekend."

Somehow, a neoprene wet suit sounded good to George. "I think that's what I'll do," he decided.

"I've got plenty of warm clothes for cycle riding," Rick surmised. "I don't think I need to rent anything."

"And one other thing," Max concluded, "absolutely no alcohol! At least until we get off the water. As you guys know, even though alcohol makes you feel warmer, it's doing just the opposite. It's cooling you off and making you more susceptible to hypothermia."

The week rolled by quickly as the guys continued planning, gathering supplies, and packing.

George felt the warm sun in his face as he breathed the crisp morning air while the four prepared to set out from Ansonia. He noticed the look of concern on Max's face as he eyed Rick. "Blue jeans? Is that what you're wearing?"

"Yeah, I'll be fine," Rick said confidently. "I've got long johns on too."

"Your jeans are cotton," Max said sternly. "If you get wet, you're gonna be cold."

"I've got spare clothes in Roger's dry bag," Rick assured him.

"Well, it looks like it's gonna be a nice day," Max reasoned. "Maybe you'll be all right."

"It looks like the weather man miscalculated a little bit," Roger observed.

"I hope he miscalculated," George added. "That sun feels pretty good. I hope it keeps shining."

George was awestruck by the beautiful view as they entered the gorge, commonly referred to as the Pennsylvania Grand Canyon. Steep tree-covered mountainsides bordered the creek on both sides. "At least it's not too crowded today," Max observed. "In a week or two, this creek will be full of boats and rafts."

The water level was elevated by melting snow and was carrying them along at a good pace. It seemed to take no time at all to cover the first mile and a half. "Wow! Is this the Owassee already?" Max shouted over to Roger as they approached a slight bend to the right.

"I believe it is," Roger shouted back.

"What's the Owassee?" George asked.

"It's a class two rapids," Max replied nonchalantly. "We'll go down a straight section of fast water here. That will take us into a sharp left turn, also known as the devil's elbow."

"I've heard of that." Suddenly George wasn't sure this trip was a good idea.

"We just have to keep to the left," Max said with confidence. "What most novices do is follow the main current on the right. Then they even paddle forward, so they're moving even faster than the water. They get to the corner, and they can't make the turn. The current takes them right into a couple of big rocks. When they see they're going to hit the rock, they lean away from it, which is exactly the opposite of what they should do. Then they capsize and their canoe gets wrapped around the rock."

"What do you want me to do?" George asked.

"Just stop paddling," Max replied. "We'll just take it slow. When we get down there, I might call for you to draw left, so you can be ready for that."

"How do I draw left?" George asked.

"Oh! You're not familiar with a draw stroke?"

"No."

"Okay, just don't do anything. Let me handle it."

George glanced over his shoulder to see Max backpaddling a few strokes as they approached the turn. Then with a strong forward sweep, he turned the canoe into the channel to the left of the rocks. "I've seen a lot of canoes wrapped around those two rocks," he said as they slipped by with ease. After splashing through the trailing waves, they both glanced back to see Roger and Rick following at a safe distance, apparently having no problem.

"I hope that sun keeps shining," Rick said after they made it through the waves. "That water's cold."

"Did you get wet?" Roger already knew the answer.

"I got splashed pretty good."

"That's why you ought to have your rain gear on."

"I didn't get that wet. I'll be all right." Before Rick's clothes had time to dry completely, a bank of clouds was moving across the sky. By the time they stopped to eat their lunch, the sun had disappeared and a strong cold wind was blowing upstream. After a quick lunch, Roger asked, "Rick, you want your rain gear? I can easily get it out before we shove off."

"No, I'm okay," Rick replied.

Roger knew he should have pushed the issue a little harder. But he didn't.

"I think we're making pretty good time," Max observed. "Hopefully we'll be off the water before the weather gets much worse."

As they pushed on toward Blackwell, the temperature kept dropping and occasional snow flurries and drizzle pelted their faces. Roger was paddling hard, trying to keep up with Max and George, but it seemed Rick's paddle strokes were getting weaker. "You okay?" Roger shouted against the wind.

"Yeah, I'm just cold," came a weak response.

"Paddle hard, man! Keep your blood flowing! We should soon be there!"

Rick didn't respond. Or if he did, Roger couldn't hear it. Rick's paddle strokes kept getting weaker, and occasionally his blade caught the water on the return stroke, sending up a splash, which the wind brought right back over him. He was getting wetter and weaker by the minute as the effects of hypothermia were becoming more and more evident. Roger knew it was time to act. "We gotta get you into dry clothes now!" he said as he pulled a whistle out of his vest pocket. He blew three long blasts on the whistle. Max looked back, and Roger waved his paddle toward the left shore.

Roger started turning left. About forty-five degrees into the turn, the bow bumped on a rock, jarring and tilting the boat. Roger threw his weight onto his left knee, but Rick flopped helplessly over onto the right gunnel. The right edge of the canoe dipped under the surface, sending both men into the frigid water.

Roger quickly got to his feet in swift water that was a little above his knees, and grabbed hold of the swamped canoe. Rick finally staggered to his feet about thirty yards downstream in water that was about the same depth. "Just get to shore!" Roger shouted. "I got the boat!" With that, he turned and started lugging the canoe toward shore. As he pulled the canoe up onto the bank he looked back at Rick. He was still standing in the same spot with a dazed look on his face. "Man, you gotta get to shore!" Roger shouted, dropping the canoe partially on the bank and partially submerged. As Roger started back into the fast-moving water, Rick's legs buckled, and he slowly collapsed into the water.

45

Max and George had already come about and were paddling hard against the swift current as Rick floated helplessly toward them. "Get ready to grab him!" Max yelled as he guided the canoe into Rick's path. George was hunched over on his knees, reaching over the gunnel with his right arm as they approached. "Grab him! Grab him!" Max shouted. George got a firm grip on Rick's life vest and pulled him up against the side of the canoe as Max started ferrying toward shore. "Just hold him like that!" Max ordered.

"Hang in there, Rick!" George shouted to the unresponsive deadweight.

Roger came charging through the knee-deep torrent, grabbed the bowline, and started towing them toward the shore. As soon as the bow hit the shore, Roger grabbed Rick by the armpits, dragging him up on the shore to a flat area covered with long dry grass and dead weeds. "Rick! Talk to me!" Roger shouted as he gently laid Rick on the ground. "George, get my dry bag!"

Max pulled his canoe well up onto the shore then hurried to assist Roger, while George sprinted almost a hundred yards up along the river to Roger's canoe. He unleashed the dry bag, slipped his arms through the shoulder straps and jogged back to where Max and Roger were busy removing Rick's wet clothes. "I've got a wool blanket in there," Roger said. "Get it out here!"

"Are you going to do the honors or should I?" Max glanced at Roger.

"I will."

"Okay then, why don't you start getting undressed? By the time you get out of that dry suit, I'll have the rest of his clothes off."

George came with the blanket as Max stripped off the last piece of Rick's underwear.

"Let's get that blanket around him! Here, tuck it up underneath him!" Max said as he rolled Rick on his side. George spread out the blanket behind Rick and tucked the one edge along the length of his body. Max pulled the rest of the blanket toward Rick, scrunching approximately half of it into a narrow pile against Rick's back. Then he rolled Rick onto the blanket, grabbing the edge and pulling it through underneath Rick.

As Max wrapped the blanket around Rick, an idea hit George. "We should have put the life jackets under him for padding."

"Good idea!" Max gave a quick nod. "That'll help insulate him from the cold ground. Get all the life vests and spread them out flat." They quickly arranged the life vests into a layer beside Rick. Then they each took hold of one edge of the blanket and gently lifted Rick onto the pad.

By that time, Roger had stripped himself completely naked. He quickly lay down on the blanket beside Rick and wrapped his arms around him. "God, he's cold!" Roger said as he pulled Rick's shivering body tight against himself. "Wake up, Rick! Talk to me!"

Max wrapped the blanket snugly around the two, and then pressed his fingers against Rick's neck, checking his pulse. As Max got up and started toward his canoe, George and asked quietly, "He's just trying to warm him up, right?"

"That's right," Max replied with a slight grin. "There's nothing else going on here. We just want to have as much skin-to-skin contact as possible. We need to transfer heat from one body to the other as quickly as we can."

"I never heard of anything like this before," George marveled that the other two seemed to know exactly what to do without any discussion.

"It's a recommended treatment for hypothermia." Max gestured toward the bow of his canoe. "Let's bring our canoe up here and put it behind them to break the wind." After they carried their canoe up to where the other two men were, Max suggested, "Why don't you start gathering some wood for a fire. I'll finish this." After removing his dry bag and everything else from the canoe, Max rolled the boat over and slid it close behind Roger, partially covering the two on the ground.

"That helps," Roger said with a slight shiver. "It felt like that wind was coming right through this blanket."

"We'll get a fire going here in a minute," Max surveyed the area quickly.

"Not too close," Roger replied. "Too much heat too quickly can cause problems. The main thing we need to do is get his body core warmed up."

Max opened his dry bag and pulled out a plastic container of emergency supplies. "I've got matches and fire starters in here." He handed the box to George as he began selecting the proper place to build a fire. He picked a spot about four feet from Rick, and soon they had a small fire blazing. George kept gathering sticks, breaking them over his knee, and placing them on the fire.

"Come on, Rick! It's time to wake up," Roger said loudly for what seemed the hundredth time.

"What's goin' on?" Rick replied in a slurred, shivering voice.

"Hang in there, buddy! You're gonna be all right." Roger sounded ecstatic.

"Stay awake! Don't let yourself go to sleep!" Max instructed as he squatted down, pressing his fingers against Rick's neck. "Your pulse is getting better. You're coming around. Just hang on and stay with us!"

"We've got a good fire going now," George said. "I can make some coffee. That should help get him going again."

"No, no!" Roger replied. "Don't give him any caffeine. That would stimulate his circulation and cause too much cold blood to come back to the core too quickly. That could cause a heart attack! We gotta let this happen at its own pace."

"You could make some plain hot water though." Max nodded to George. "That would be good to give him when he's ready to sit up and drink something."

"We've got instant coffee for those of us who need it," Roger added. "And I'll be needing it myself pretty soon." After putting a pot of water over the fire, George hiked back to Roger's canoe. He hoisted it over his head and lowered the carrying yoke onto his shoulders, then headed back to the campfire.

Gradually Rick became more and more alert as Roger continued to engage him in conversation, which at first was rather incoherent. "Max, can you slide this canoe back a little so I can get out of here?" Roger asked. "It's time for me to get something hot to drink. Or next thing I'll be the one that needs help."

"Jeepers! You're naked!" Rick observed as Roger got to his feet. "What the heck's going on?" He suddenly seemed to realize that he too was lacking clothes.

"Nothing weird," Roger assured him as he pulled on his long johns, which George had hung by the fire. "I was just trying to get you warmed up again." By the time Roger had finished dressing, George had a cup of instant coffee ready for him. As Roger drank his coffee, Rick rolled over to face the fire.

"Looks like you're doing all right there," Max commented as he slid the canoe up close to Rick. "But I'd like you to stay lying down for a while yet. Your body's blood pressure controls may be all out of whack. If you try to sit up, you might pass out." The cold wind continued blowing as the three huddled around the fire, each holding a piece of Rick's spare clothing to the fire to warm them. As Rick lay on the blanket, Max and Roger helped him slip into his long johns, jeans, and socks.

"Do you want to try to sit up so we can get your shirt on?" Roger asked.

"Slowly," Max advised. "If you feel lightheaded, just lie down again."

"I feel okay," Rick said after he got himself upright.

"Your coordination seems to be getting better," Roger observed as they got his shirt around him. With shaking hands, Rick started fumbling with his buttons. Roger watched for a few seconds then added, "But it's not that good yet. You'd better let me do that." Meanwhile, George and Max repositioned the canoe, more on its side, to create a taller windbreak.

"Can I have a cup of coffee?" Rick asked as the others came back to the fire.

"Not coffee." Roger glanced at Rick. "We can give you hot water. That will help warm up your core temperature."

George poured about a half a cup of water and handed it to Rick. His hands shook as he brought it to his mouth and began sipping the hot water.

"Your body was shutting itself down," Roger explained as Rick continued sipping. "When our core temperature gets too low, our bodies do an amazing thing. They start shutting down circulation to the extremities. It seems the body knows that frostbite isn't as bad as heart failure. So it allows the limbs to get cold while it tries to protect the vital organs. The heart rate slows, and the blood pressure drops."

"Animals do much the same thing when they go into hibernation," Max added. "But they're able to reverse the process and power up again without any problem."

"We usually need a little help getting powered up again," Roger went on. "But the process of shutting down helps the body to cling to life as long as possible."

"So you're saying this all happens for a reason," Rick eyed Roger.

"That's right," Roger agreed. "The reason is to keep you alive."

"That is really amazing," Rick said with a twinkle in his eye. "I have a friend who says that there's no reason for anything. Nothing has any purpose. This is just the way we happened to evolve through a random process."

"I see you're feeling much better," Roger replied flatly. "There's a lot of hot air coming out of your mouth again."

After more hot water and a Snickers bar, Rick was on his feet again, huddling around the fire with the other three, as they rotated themselves, trying to keep both sides warm. Max started talking about getting to Blackwell. "We can't be far at all from Blackwell," he said. "George and Rick could walk the rest of the way on the railroad track. We've got enough daylight left for that. And that way, we'll eliminate the risk of having Rick dunked a second time."

"The railroad is being converted into a bike trail," Roger commented. "It should be easy walking."

"That's better yet," Max agreed. "Roger and I can solo the boats down to Blackwell. By the time you get there, we'll have the boats loaded, we'll have the truck warmed up, and we should be waiting at the railroad crossing."

George and Rick each took another Snickers bar and headed for the railroad bed as Max and Roger started throwing everything into their dry bags. As they turned and started down the railroad bed, George look back to see a cloud of steam rising as Roger poured a baler of water onto the fire.

Rick seemed to be functioning pretty normally again as the two walked along briskly. The wind didn't seem to buffet them quite as badly as it had out on the open water. As they walked, George reviewed the whole episode in his mind. It had been quite an adventure, and despite the near tragedy, he wanted to learn more about canoeing.

Eventually, he looked down the trail and spied Roger hiking toward them. Within minutes, they were all back in the warm cab of the truck.

"Now," Max said, "we just have to find a nice warm restaurant with a payphone so I can call Michelle and tell her not to worry."

"She's not one that worries very much," George glanced at Max.

"No, she isn't. But she knows just how long this trip should have taken."

46

Michelle studied George's demeanor as the four tired men unloaded their gear. "You'll probably never want to go canoeing again," Michelle said as she caught his eye.

"Just the opposite." He flashed a smile back at her. "I've learned so much on this trip, and now I realize how much more there is to learn."

"Daddy really knows how to make it interesting, doesn't he?"

"Yeah. He's got my interest. But I'd like to wait for warmer weather."

"You're a smart man." Michelle smiled as she thought about getting George involved in her favorite sport.

"Your dad was showing me all kinds of paddle strokes: the J-stroke, the C-stroke, sweeps, and draws."

"And I suppose he taught you the proper technique for the basic forward stroke?"

"Yeah, keep the shaft vertical, feather the blade on the return stroke. It's amazing how much easier it is when you use the proper technique."

"It sounds like you're off to a good start."

"If I'm gonna do something, I like to know how to do it right."

"I'd love to help teach you more, but I don't think I'll be doing any canoeing this summer." Michelle rubbed her rounded belly.

"The baby still doing fine?" George raised his eyebrows.

"Yeah, she's been really active lately."

"She? You know what it is?"

"No. I don't know why I said that. It could be a boy. I don't know."

"I can hardly wait for June." George sounded genuinely eager.

"Well, you just have to wait." Michelle tried to hide her own eagerness. "I don't go early."

George felt the warmth of the morning sun on his face as he breathed in fresh spring air. Everything had distinct feeling of springtime. "You guys ready to dig for buried treasure?" he asked as Rick and Roger came out onto the porch.

"I'm ready to dig for the directions," Rick quipped.

"Okay, get technical," George shot back with a grin.

"You figured out where we need to dig?" Roger asked.

"Well, that's still pretty much of a guess." George scratched his head. "The envelope with the information was stuck in the ledger for 1926. That's right in the middle of the range that I figured it could be. So I say we start with that."

"Okay," Roger agreed. "In 1926, Calvin Coolidge was president. He was the thirtieth. So we go thirty yards."

"Thirty yards from what?" Rick threw up his hands. "We don't know if we measure from the middle of the gate or one edge or the other."

"The directions say, 'Go *to* the gate at the head of the mill race,'" George reasoned. "It doesn't say to cross over the race or go to the middle of it. I assume that means you go to the nearest edge."

"That's good enough for me." Rick shrugged. "There's only one way to know for sure."

"That's right," Roger agreed as they headed for George's pickup. "The sooner we start digging, the sooner we find out if we're right."

"Of course, we could be off by at least two presidents in either direction," George remarked as he climbed into the driver's seat. "So we could end up digging a twelve- to fifteen-foot trench before we find it." As they drove, they speculated on how long it would take to dig a fifteen-foot-long trench, three feet deep, by hand.

With an ax, a digging iron, two shovels, a fifty-foot tape measure, and a small cooler, they made their way through the budding forest. "Too bad we didn't have weather like this last Saturday," Roger said exactly what George was thinking.

"Yeah, I feel lucky to be alive." Rick let out a sigh.

"You had me scared." Roger stared straight ahead. "For a while, I thought my premonition was coming true."

"What you talkin' about?" Rick cocked his head.

"Oh, for some time I've just had this feeling the something bad is about to happen to one of us."

"That's called women's intuition. Apparently you're getting in touch with your feminine side." Rick grinned as he glanced at Roger out of the corner of his eye.

"We men can sense things like that too." Roger remained serious. "We just don't pay as much attention to our feelings as women do. We ignore our feelings. So women get credited with having a sixth sense."

"So you think you had some anticipation of what was to happen last week?" Rick questioned.

"That may not have been it." Roger shook his head. "That turned out all right in the end. And it's crazy, but I still get that feeling."

"And do you think that your worrisome feeling is an indication that something is actually about to happen?" George wondered how seriously Roger was taking this.

"Well, it could be." Roger sounded serious. "Didn't you ever hear of someone having a premonition about something?"

"Sure," George replied. "But then again, I believe in a God who knows the future. So for me, it all makes sense. But if there's no God, then where does someone get a sense of a future event?"

"Oh, there are lots of things we know about the future," Roger argued. "Some of it is in our conscious mind and some in the subconscious. You never know what all is going on in the subconscious."

George mulled over Roger's assertion. "Yeah, I agree. We can predict the weather. we can determine the paths of the planets. we can predict market trends. The more we know about something, the more we can predict how it will behave. But those are all different from getting a premonition concerning something that you know nothing about."

"Well, maybe it doesn't mean anything at all," Roger conceded. "Maybe it means I've been spending too much time thinking about those four freak accidents."

"You still don't believe they were accidents, do you?" Rick glanced at Roger.

"No way!"

"Those four deaths occurred in less than two weeks." George thought back over the months. "And that was eight months ago. Has anything happened since that? Do we have any reason to believe that kind of danger continues?"

"Your mother?"

"That was a heart attack. I wouldn't put that in the same category as those freak accidents."

"A bullet through Michelle's kitchen door, doesn't that count?" Roger shot a stern glance at George.

"Well, that was a stray bullet from a hunter." George shook his head as they stopped at their previous dig.

"You can't prove that." Roger argued. "Am I the only one who is concerned about Michelle's safety? Don't you guys care about her and the kids?"

"Of course we do!" George shot back, dropping his tools on the ground. "She's carrying my baby! You think I don't care about her?"

"You don't seem very concerned," Roger remarked snidely.

"And your feelings go beyond concern. You're still hot for her. How does Kathy feel about that?"

"That's none of your business! But she understands."

"Well, I'm not the one having a premonition that something bad is about to happen to somebody." George tried to keep the emotion out of his voice. "On the contrary, I keep being reminded of the dream I had where Dr. King told me that good things are in store for me."

"I guess that means we're going to find this treasure," Roger speculated glibly as he took the ax and turned his back on the other two. He started hacking at the heavy undergrowth that closed in the edge of the forest, clearing a line of sight from the dam breast into the woods. After he got through to where the larger trees were, there was little that needed to be cut away.

Rick and George measured off ninety feet from the edge of the gate and double-checked to be sure they were still in line with the dam breast. "This is the spot," George said. "Let's dig!"

A chipmunk perched on a nearby rock scolding as Rick and Roger started digging. George used the digging iron to pry stones out of their way. "He buried it three feet deep," Roger said as he pushed the shovel into the ground. "But how much soil has eroded since then?"

"Or how much soil has eroded from farther up the mountain and been deposited here?" Rick added. "It could be more than three feet deep."

"I don't see any signs that either is happening." George scanned the area. "We just have to dig till we find it." Their hole got more and more elongated as they dug deeper and deeper.

"We don't know what kind of container or how big a thing we're looking for, do we?" Rick remarked.

"No. But I think we'll know it when we see it," George speculated.

Eventually Rick's shovel struck something that sounded different. He scraped a little more dirt away and announced, "It looks like we've got something here." They quickly shoveled more dirt away to reveal what appeared to be the lid of a five-gallon bucket. They kept shoveling around it till they had exposed enough of the bucket to pull it out of the ground.

It was a metal bucket with a lid that had metal tabs, which were bent down around the lip on the top edge of the bucket. The entire bucket and lid were heavily coated with some kind of tar, presumably to seal it or protect it from rust. "It's really heavy," George observed. "I hope it's not full of water."

"What can we use to open it?" Rick smacked his pants pockets.

"We need something to pry those tabs up." George glanced over their supply of tools. "I should have brought a screwdriver."

Roger reached in his pocket and pulled out a Swiss Army knife. "This should work," he said as he started trying to get the blade under one of the tar coated tabs. It took some time, but one by one, he pried the tabs loose. Finally they pulled the cover off to reveal a bucket full of dry sand.

George dug his fingers into the sand. "Ah! There's something in here," he said with delight. He grasped the object and lifted an antique canning jar out of the sand. It was a one-quart jar with a glass lid that was held in place by a wire latch. Inside was a rolled up piece of paper. "Well, at least the jar is worth a few bucks," he said as he raised the latch, lifted off the lid and tilted the jar toward Rick.

Rick pulled the paper out, unrolled it, and read:

> This is point A. To find point B, go west by south the distance from home plate straight across the pitcher's mound to second base. From point B, go southeast by east a distance equal to the height of the world's tallest building.

> There you will find the treasure, in a sealed container, three feet underground.
>
> Note: All directions are from true north, not magnetic north.

"This guy likes to make it interesting," George remarked.

"What direction is west by south?" Rick's eyes narrowed.

"Could it be another way of saying southwest?" Roger looked puzzled.

"He also says southeast by east, so I don't think it's that," Rick argued.

"We'll need to do some research," George replied. "I love it."

"And we need to find out what the tallest building was during the Coolidge administration," Roger added.

"We'd better remeasure to the exact spot we found the bucket," George gazed at their elongated hole, "just to be sure it was Coolidge."

"We can do that after we eat," Rick replied. "All this exercise is making me hungry!" There was no argument on that suggestion.

"If he protected those baseball cards as well as he protected these directions, they should be in good shape," George speculated as they strolled toward the dam breast with their lunch box in hand.

"You'd certainly think that he would have." Rick smiled broadly. "His records would seem to imply that he valued his collection."

"And don't forget, there's also supposed to be a bunch of coins in there." Roger's face beamed with excitement. "Rare old coins can be worth a lot too."

"I think I know where I can borrow a transit," George said as he thought about a friend who did surveying.

"We've got to get our dimensions first." Rick glanced at the other two. "Anybody know the distance from home plate to second base?"

"No, but we all know the distance from base to base." Roger sounded like a teacher again. "So we just use the Pythagorean theorem to get the diagonal. That should be easy enough."

"And if you can't do the math, you could always go to a baseball diamond and measure it," Rick added.

"This all sounds a little too simple." George did a mental review of the directions. "Somehow, I think we're going to run into something we're not expecting."

47

George leaned back in his office chair with his hands folded behind his head, wondering what it was Michelle had come to see him about.

"George," she said, leaning forward and laying her arm on the edge of the desk, "When my dad starts his job, could you keep an eye on Earl after school again?"

"Sure, I'd be glad to," he replied calmly. Inside, he was dancing. "Do you want me to pick him up at school?"

"Oh, no. I'll have him start riding the bus again, and I'll get Abby at the sitter on my way home from work."

"Well, that's no problem at all then. We'll get right back into our old routine."

"Thanks. I just don't want to give Roger another excuse to be stopping by every afternoon."

Hallelujah! George gazed earnestly into her eyes. "Does that mean you've made up your mind?"

"About us?"

"Yeah."

Michelle nodded slowly. "My *mind* has been made up for a long time. But Roger keeps tugging at my heartstrings."

"You and he have a lot of good memories."

"We do. But that's all in the past, and I want to keep it there. A future with Roger would be altogether different from those memories."

"Michelle," George said as he leaned forward, propping his arm on the desk and keeping his eyes fixed on hers, "I think we've tried this separation thing long enough."

"Oh, I agree wholeheartedly! And not just because it's inconvenient. I really miss our time together. Three months is long enough for me to know how I feel."

"Me too," George agreed. "Do you think we should see what Pastor John thinks?"

"We're adults," Michelle flashed a grin. "We don't need his permission."

"So you want to go out Friday evening?"

"Sure."

"You're not even going to ask where we're going or what we're doing?"

"No questions asked. Surprise me!"

"Oh. Now I have to come up with something really good," George remarked with a grin.

"Anything will be fine," Michelle said as she got to her feet and leaned across the desk with her lips puckered. George rose slightly from his seat and stretched toward her. As their lips met, the phone on George's desk began ringing. He reached for the phone on the fourth ring as Michelle quickly said, "See ya Friday, if not before."

George's evenings were busy the rest of the week. When he wasn't thinking about what to do for a surprise date, he was researching the world's tallest buildings and looking for information on compass directions. Even while doing his research, the date was always somewhere in his mind. Michelle had said that anything would be fine, but he wanted this date to be special, something she would never forget. But the date was only a few days away now. Where could they go on such short notice? It had to be a place that would mean a lot to her, somewhere they had never been to together.

Michelle lay in her bed anticipating their date the next evening. She loved George, but she still had to let go of Roger. She'd thought she already had, but now she wasn't sure. *The hard part is letting go of that vivacious little teenage girl who was so crazy about him. I need to let go of those teenage dreams and little girl fantasies. I need to accept the fact that my life hasn't turned out the way I dreamed. I'm a grown woman now, with children of my own. I need to let go of using my youthful charm to manipulate people.* She turned over and buried her face in her pillow. *I have a lot to let go of before I can honestly say yes to George.*

On Friday morning, before leaving for work, Michelle poked her head into George's shop and asked, "Can you tell me how I should dress tonight?"

"Casual," came the reply. "Dress to be outside till dark."

"Okay. See ya this evening," Michelle said as she turned and walked toward her car, wondering what to expect.

That evening, George loaded a few things in the back of his truck and drove next door to pick up Michelle. They turned up Main Street and headed out of town into the efflorescent countryside. Following the winding mountain road, they rolled along between pastures and plowed fields and through small patches of woodland.

"I actually had some expert advice on this," George said as he slowed down and turned into a farm lane, directly across the road from the ranch house, which was Michelle's childhood home.

"We're going to visit my old neighbors?" she speculated out loud.

"No. But I got permission to drive on some of their field lanes." George watched her out of the corner of his eye. "My expert tells me that you have a favorite spot on top of this hill. And being seven months pregnant, I didn't think you'd want to hike up on foot, like you used to."

"Oh, how neat!" Her enthusiasm was obvious. "I haven't been up there since I was like twelve or thirteen."

"You'll have to tell me which way to go now," George said as he puttered along between the barn and the implement shed.

"Turn right at the T. And you might want to put it in four-wheel drive. It gets pretty steep at places." They skirted around the edge of a hay field, then up a steep grade through a small orchard. They continued climbing, with a hedge of raspberries on one side and a wheat field on the other. The lane finally leveled out between hayfields on the rounded hilltop. "You can stop right up there on the top," she beamed with delight. "You'll be amazed at the view!"

George parked the truck on the lane, stepped out, and looked back in awe at the valley they had come from. Michelle came around the truck and snuggled up beside him, pointing out all the landmarks that could be seen as far away as the edge of Thrush Glen. "Mae and I used to pack sandwiches and snacks in a bag. Then we'd come up here and sit on the ground and eat while we talked about things that little girls talk about. After we were finished eating, Mae would go home, and I would just sit here for another hour or so, enjoying the view and dreaming about my future."

"Well, you won't have to sit on the ground this evening," George opened the tailgate. He got out two folding lawn chairs and set them up behind the truck. Then he unloaded a small charcoal grill and ice chest. As the charcoal heated up, he handed Michelle two books, one of poetry and one of cartoons. "Take your pick," he said.

Soon he had shish kebabs of steak cubes, shrimp, and other tidbits sizzling over the charcoal. They talked, ate, and shared poetry and cartoons as the sun sank lower and lower. "So this is where you came to dream about your future." George clasped her hand in his.

"Yeah, but I never dreamed of this. This was a wonderful idea, George."

"Well, as I said, I had some expert advice. But tell me what sort of things *did* you dream about?"

"Oh, let's see. I remember dreaming about being married to a handsome man and having a big beautiful house in the forest."

"A log house?"

"It could be log. That would certainly be more cozy than cement block. I had it all laid out in my head. But I don't remember thinking about what it would be made of."

"My dream is to have a nice log house in the woods overlooking Thrush Creek. But now I don't know if that will ever happen."

"Don't give up on your dreams, George."

"What else did you dream of?"

"Oh, I don't remember. They were just fantasies. I certainly never dreamed of spending seven years living in a little cottage with no electricity and no phone. I never dreamed of having two children to an escaped convict. A lot of things I wouldn't have chosen. But looking back, I wouldn't change them if I could."

"You certainly have a good attitude about the whole ordeal."

"It always feels good to realize that you've had a positive influence on someone else's life. I suppose Jasper changed more during our time together than in all his years in prison."

"Do you have any lingering fears? Like, do you ever think there might still be someone wanting to get rid of you?"

"Not really. I know those four deaths remain a mystery. But I refuse to worry about it."

"And do you ever feel like I don't care because I don't keep questioning your safety?"

"No! Of course not. You don't have to be like Roger!"

"Good. He was trying to make me feel like I don't really care about you."

"Well, I know you care. And what he thinks doesn't matter."

The sun gradually turned to a red ball of fire and sank behind the mountain. As soon as the last of the sun disappeared, George started packing things away. "Your dad promised me, if I don't have you home right after dark, he'll come looking for us."

"And you took him seriously?"

George shrugged and chuckled. "I guess I shouldn't have."

"We should watch the stars come out," Michelle suggested. "And I'd like to hear more about your dreams for the future." After putting the grill and ice chest on the truck, George sat down again, and they continued their discussion till the sky was full of twinkling lights.

Finally they folded up their chairs and climbed into the truck. As George turned the truck around, the headlights swept across the hayfield, exposing at least a dozen pairs of eyes. "I didn't know we were being watched," Michelle remarked as they headed down into the dark valley.

"My mom told me to always remember that I'm being watched," George paused as he thought about his mother's advice. "But I didn't think she was talking about deer."

The next day, George dropped in to chat with Rick and Roger. "Well, I found out what west by south means," Roger said eagerly.

"Okay. What did you find out?" George glanced at Roger.

"The old mariner's compasses had thirty-two points. West by south would be a point halfway between west and west-southwest."

"That's exactly what I came up with."

"Of course, modern navigators just use the number of degrees from north," Roger added.

"Or to put it in surveyor's terminology," George explained, "it would be south seventy-eight degrees and forty-five minutes west. But I haven't even tried to figure out the distance from home plate to second base."

"A hundred twenty-seven feet and three inches," Rick and Roger said almost simultaneously.

"Okay," George replied. *It seems like we're all together so far.*

"That gets us to point B." Rick glanced at George. "Did you find anything on the tallest building?"

"Woolworth Building in New York. Built in 1913, it was the world's tallest building until 1930. That takes us all the way through the years of President Coolidge."

"How tall?" Rick raised his eyebrows.

"Seven hundred ninety-two feet."

"Okay," Roger concluded. "All we have to do is measure it off and dig."

"I'll check with my buddy and see when we can borrow his transit," George offered.

"Measure it off and dig." Rick cocked his head. "That *sounds* easy enough."

48

"Okay, I promised you folks some answers." Dan Phillips glanced around the group that had assembled in Michelle's family room. "Sometimes it takes a while, but I do keep my word. You guys were concerned that those four deaths may have been homicides planned to look like accidents." He paused as Michelle placed a bowl of pretzels and a tray of cheese on the coffee table. "Or maybe you're no longer worried about that?"

"I'd like to hear what you found." Roger wasn't about to let him off without a good explanation.

"I'm not worried," Michelle said as she got seated. "But I am curious."

"Okay, let's start with the case of Jason Keelson," Phillips continued. "As far as I can tell, Roger was right. Rattlesnakes are not known to be native to the area where this snake bite occurred. However, they could easily survive in that environment. And living things do move around from one territory to another. Sometimes it's due to a natural disaster like a flood or sometimes they hitch a ride on something man is moving from place to place. But it happens.

"Of course, the snake could have been deliberately put there, as Roger has suggested. However, that would be a very unlikely way to plan a murder, since the person would have no way of being sure that the snake stays in the location and bites the intended victim. The odds of someone successfully carrying out a homicide by that means seem even more unlikely than it being a natural accident."

"I don't believe it was an accident." George snatched another pretzel from the bowl. "I think the snake bit him intentionally."

Phillips laughed heartily. "That joke's older than you are. Any other comments or questions on the Jason Keelson case?"

"That's not a very definitive answer." Roger wasn't amused. "But I'm more interested in what you found on Chief Miller."

"Okay, let's look at his case next." Phillips shuffled his notes. "It appears the chief was sitting down at the kitchen table to start cleaning his pistol when the gun somehow fell on the floor and discharged. We know that the gun was at the floor when it went off because of the powder residue on his shoes and on the floor. The bullet grazed the side of his left knee and entered under his chin."

"So it wasn't suicide after all." George furrowed his brow.

"But," Roger wasn't satisfied, "couldn't someone have murdered him and set it up to look like an accident?"

"Not a chance," Phillips continued. "If someone were to set up that scene, I don't know how they would hold the gun on the floor and aim it accurately at the vital area. They wouldn't have been able to get their eye behind the gun. And if they would have attempted that, they would have been in position to get a good swift kick from the chief's size 12 shoe. There were no signs of a struggle on the chief's body or in the room. All the evidence seems to indicate that this was in fact an accident."

Roger frowned, contemplating what he had just heard.

"Roger, you like to calculate probabilities." Dan Phillips grinned. "Figure out what the probability is for that gun to hit the floor at just the right angle to discharge and hit a vital area. I know the odds are against it, but that's what happened."

"Okay, I won't argue with you," Roger conceded.

"Now as for Harold Keelson, records show that he had just had his pool filled earlier that day. The water was cold, about fifty-nine degrees. He had been drinking heavily before he went into the pool. Roger, you're a whitewater enthusiast. You probably know all about the dangers of cold water and alcohol."

"That combination can be deadly," Roger replied.

"So you're familiar with hypothermia."

"More familiar than I care to be." Roger remembered his episode with Rick.

"With the amount of alcohol he had in his blood," Phillips continued, "he probably felt nice and warm while the cool water was sucking the heat right out of him. He lost control of his limbs and was unable to get himself out of the pool. He drowned in less than three feet of water.

"None of the evidence at the scene suggests any foul play. The home security system shows no one entering or leaving the home during the period of time that this occurred. We have to conclude that this was an alcohol-related accident, nothing more."

"People just don't realize how dangerous alcohol can be," Michelle commented, shaking her head.

"That leaves Bobby," George remarked, glancing at Phillips.

"Right. Jack Roberts, the guy you call Bobby, died in a gas pump fire. The whole incident was captured on security video. There was no one else at the scene. Ignition appears to have come from a spark of static electricity. There was no foul play. This was a freak accident."

"But I showed you the probability that all these are accidents," Roger argued. *Two times ten to the thirty-third power.* "It's like almost impossible!"

"I know," Phillips agreed. "And that has Agent Cox beating his head against the wall. He's a lot like you, Roger. Everything has to have a logical explanation. This seems impossible, and yet it has to be true. They were all accidents!"

"So how do *you* explain that?" Roger asked.

"Well," Phillips replied, "I only know of one who can control the behavior of a rattlesnake and cause a gun to hit the floor at just the right angle."

"I don't buy that theory!" Roger blurted out. He knew exactly where Phillips was going with that argument.

"Then come up with your own explanation," Phillips challenged, giving Roger a pokerfaced glance.

"Would anybody like more tea or lemonade?" Michelle seemed to be trying to defuse the situation.

"I have another question," Roger continued. "You and Cox are friends. You golf together regularly. How come it took you almost three weeks to figure out that you were working on the same case? We gave Cox descriptions of you, your plane, and your car. And he didn't realize we were describing his buddy? I find that hard to believe."

"That's a good question, and it gives you reason to believe we're not being honest with you," Phillips admitted. "We are friends, and we do golf together, but not on a regular basis. We might go two to four times each summer. And when we do, we don't usually talk business. We golf for the fun of it. But I don't know why it took Agent Cox so long to realize that you were describing me. In his defense, I had just bought the Buick, and he probably wasn't aware of that. As far as he knew, I was driving a blue Lincoln."

"That's a good enough explanation for me." Michelle got to her feet.

"Thanks for the inside information," George said as Mr. Phillips rose to leave. "It's nice to know a little more about those cases. We just never had any details before."

"I think Agent Cox was being rather tightlipped about it because he can't come up with an explanation to satisfy himself. 'Act of God' isn't part of his vocabulary," Phillips commented.

"Thanks so much," Michelle said as she walked to the door with Dan Phillips.

"You're welcome. And if you have any other questions or concerns, don't hesitate to call me."

George turned to Roger. "You got any plans for Saturday, May the second?"

"May the second? That's in two weeks," Roger did a mental review of his calendar. "I think I'm free."

"I got my buddy's transit lined up for that day."

"Okay! So we'll finally go dig up that treasure!"

"Tell Rick to keep that day open."

"He's been keeping his Saturdays open just for this."

Max had just returned from a few days on the road. He backed the eighteen-wheeler into the driveway beside George's house. Earl came running over and said, "Grandpa, Mom said you're supposed to come over for supper."

"Okay, tell her I'm hungry," he replied. "I just want to take my stuff in the house and wash up. Then I'll be right over."

George came in from his shop. Max thought about how quickly his daughter and George had fallen back into the routine of having their meals together. Michelle was putting the last few items on the table as the men and children were gathering around and getting seated. Michelle turned to her dad and asked, "And to drink, would you like water or this?" In her left hand she held up a bottle of Coke, grasping it in such a way that he couldn't help but notice the sparkling diamond on her finger.

"Oh, what's this on your finger?" he exclaimed, taking the bottle in one hand and grasping her hand with the other. "Congratulations!"

"We just got engaged this past Sunday," she beamed.

"So do you have a wedding date set?"

"Not yet. We're going to wait till after the baby comes."

"Probably sometime in August or September," George added.

"Then you haven't made any wedding plans yet," Max surmised.

"No. Why?" Michelle sounded very interested.

"Oh, a long time ago I came up with some unique ideas that I'd like to run by you and see what you think. But it's your wedding. If you don't like my ideas, that's okay."

"So what are your ideas?"

Max pictured it in his mind. He didn't have a presentation ready. He needed a good presentation. "We can talk about it some other time. It's been a long time since I've given it any thought."

On Saturday morning, Roger paced back and forth as he waited. He had a small cooler packed with lunch for the three. George was expecting to arrive with the transit about the time Rick would get home from band practice. Time ticked by slowly until the other two arrived, and they were on their way.

"I'm eager to see what we find," Roger said as George parked by the concrete bridge.

"Yeah, and then to see how much it's worth," Rick added.

"We can't carry everything at once," George said as they got out of the truck. "Let's just take thc transit and tape measure and the ax to clear a line of sight. After we find our spot, we can come back and get the digging tools."

"And the lunch?" Roger asked.

"Leave it here for now. We can eat here when we come back for the other tools."

"Sounds like a plan," Rick said as he picked up the ax.

Even though he was enthused about digging for buried treasure, George couldn't help noticing the value of the standing timber as they hiked through the woods. But he kept his thoughts to himself while the other two speculated on the value of the baseball cards and coins.

They set up the transit over the spot where they had found the bucket. "South seventy-eight degrees and forty-five minutes west," George said, peering through the transit. "We don't even need to clear a new path. It's the same path we cleared last time."

"Remember," Roger gazed down the path toward the dam, "those directions are from true north."

"Yeah," George replied. "I've already adjusted for the declination. And, gentlemen, we have a problem."

"What's that?" Rick asked.

"I don't even have to measure." George stepped back from the transit. "We came this way ninety feet. Now we're going back a hundred and twenty-seven. That puts us right in the middle of Thrush Creek!"

"What the crap!" Roger appeared to be running the numbers through his head. "That'll be right out in the deepest, swiftest part. How can we shoot from there?"

"Here, take a look." George extended a hand toward the transit.

Roger peered through the device. "It looks like point B is right behind where the dam used to be, in the middle of the creek."

"Why would he use a point like that?" Rick looked puzzled.

"Maybe he just wanted to give his students, or whoever they were, another problem to solve," George speculated.

"They would have had to figure out how to build some kind of stationary platform to set a tripod on in the middle of the creek." Rick scratched his head.

"That would have been right in the hydraulic behind the dam," Roger argued. "That would have been crazy to send a bunch of inexperienced young guys out there to try to do anything. Those hydraulics are really dangerous."

"There's no hydraulic there now," Rick pointed out.

"No. Just a deep swift current." Roger shook his head.

"Well, I'm not going to have time to build an island," George said. "Michelle is due next month. And after that we're getting married."

"You are?" Rick exclaimed, slapping George on the back. "Congratulations!"

"Congratulations," Roger said in a more somber tone.

"If neither of you two have a brilliant solution," George glanced at the other two, "I guess we may as well carry our things back to the truck, eat our lunch, and go home."

49

"George, what do you think I should do with this?" Michelle asked, holding up an urn that looked like a cheap imitation of something from ancient India.

"What is it?" George asked with a puzzled look.

"It's Jasper's ashes."

"Well, that's completely up to you. What would *you* like to do with it?"

"Maybe this sounds silly. I know it's not really him in here. But I don't think he would like being confined to such a small space. He wanted to be free."

"That's not silly. People do all kinds of things to carry out the wishes of the deceased."

"I don't really know what his wishes were. But I don't think he would want to be kept in here. And I don't think he would want a grave marker telling everyone where he is. I think he would prefer to be free and not have anyone know where he is, to become part of the natural environment. He would want his ashes to go into the soil and be absorbed by the plants."

"Okay. Why don't we take them out and spread them in the woods somewhere?"

"Where would be a good place?" Michelle asked as she tried to think of the ideal spot.

"That's up to you." George looked at her and smiled. "Sunday is supposed to be a beautiful day. We could go up to Slate Point Vista in the afternoon and throw the ashes out from the point and let them settle into the forest below."

"That's a great idea! Jasper would love that."

"Do we want to invite anyone to go along? Do you want to have any kind of ceremony?"

"No ceremony. He wouldn't want that. We could take a few friends along, but none of them actually knew him. Except Roger, that is. He met him once."

"Okay, we'll invite Roger."

"Do you think Kathy would want to go along?"

"She might. I think they're getting along a little better now that we're making wedding plans."

"Roger and Kathy, that'll be enough. Jasper wouldn't want a big group."

A warm breeze blew through the open window as George drove slowly up the narrow mountain road toward the vista. The children seemed eager for whatever was going to happen. Although Michelle had explained exactly what they were planning to do, it seemed they still weren't quite sure what to expect, but they were eager anyway.

Roger and Kathy were already standing by the railing, enjoying the view as George pulled into the parking space. As soon as the truck stopped, the kids were out and running to Roger and Kathy.

"Be careful!" Michelle called. "There's a big cliff on the other side of that railing!" Both children stopped short of the fence and took a quick step backward as they stared through the railing with wide eyes, suddenly realizing how high up they were.

As the adults leaned on the rails chatting about the scenery, the children gradually moved closer to the fence to gaze down at the valley far below. Before long, Earl was sticking his head through between the rails to get a better view of a vulture that was soaring below them. "Don't do that, son," Michelle scolded. "You can see well enough from this side."

"Let's see, the wind is coming this way." George felt a breeze blowing across his face. "We should go over to that corner to spread the ashes. We don't want the wind to blow the dust back in our faces." The group moved to the corner and watched quietly as Michelle held the urn firmly by the pedestal. She removed the lid and flung the ashes out into the air.

"Free at last!" she said as a small cloud of dust slowly drifted down over the valley and disappeared.

George turned to Roger and said, "Our disappearing fisherman has disappeared forever."

"Well, not forever," Michelle interjected. "He will reappear someday."

"Okay, I stand corrected," George conceded. "I wasn't thinking in those terms. He disappeared until the resurrection. Is that better?"

"Much better." Michelle glanced skyward. "I imagine he's up there smiling down on us right now."

George nodded. "He could be."

"People can put him down and call him a criminal and a murderer," Michelle continued, "but I know he's up in heaven, celebrating with the Savior who forgave all those evil deeds."

"It's amazing," Roger shook his head, "that despite all the scientific knowledge we have today, people still believe stuff like that."

"Oh, Roger!" Kathy retorted. "Do you have to argue about everything?"

"I wasn't arguing. I was just making an observation," Roger argued.

"That's okay." Michelle smiled at Kathy. "He makes us think about what we really believe. That's a good thing. But, Roger, I wish you wouldn't say things that might stifle my children's hope of seeing their father again someday."

"Stifle their hope?" Roger sounded slightly irritated. "You just threw his ashes to the wind! You don't think that's going to stifle their hope? Then you want to jump on me about something I said!"

"The children understand that his spirit was not in those ashes. They know that he is in heaven, and I don't like it when you try to make that belief sound ridiculous."

"If you want to brainwash them into believing what you believe, don't expect the scientific community or the educational system to help you with that. What are you going to do when they get old enough to think for themselves? Send them to a monastery where they're isolated from modern science? Move back into your little cottage in the woods where they have no contact with the world?"

"Roger, that's enough!" Kathy said sharply.

As the group lingered by the fence, a bee buzzed around Abby's face. She took several quick steps backward, toward the railing. Just before backing into the fence, she tripped and fell backward. Instinctively, she doubled over to land on her butt. Being doubled over, she tumbled through the fence, between the middle rail and the bottom rail, which was just inches off the ground. Michelle screamed as the little girl tumbled and slid down a short steep slope and came to a stop on a ledge about seven feet below the overlook. Beyond the ledge was a vertical drop of several hundred feet.

Before George could think what to do, Roger was over the fence and sliding down to where Abby had stopped. He picked her up and quickly hoisted her over his head. George reached through railing, grasping Abby by the arms and pulling her to safety. He quickly turned and passed the stunned child to her mother.

As Abby sobbed and clung to Michelle, Roger struggled to climb the short distance to the railing. The slope was covered with broken pieces and chips of slate. The more he struggled, the more the slate gave way under him as he slipped closer and closer to precipice. Before anyone had time to assist him, his feet had slipped over the edge. He grasped desperately with his hands, but everything he grabbed onto gave way. "God! Help me!" he cried out as he disappeared over the edge, amid a small avalanche of slate chips. Kathy let out a scream as the rest stood, frozen in shock and disbelief.

With Abby still clinging, Michelle threw an arm around Kathy. George spun around toward his truck. "Come on! We gotta go call 911!" The five piled into George's pickup, and they were off to find a phone.

After the phone call, they returned with haste to the gated access road that led to the base of the cliff. Time seemed to stand still as they waited for the ambulance and rescue team to arrive. "There's no way he could have survived," Kathy sobbed.

"Don't give up hope yet." George tried to sound encouraging. "If he landed on a slope where could roll or slide to a stop without hitting something solid…"

"Miracles can happen," Michelle added.

Eventually a few firefighters and a policeman arrived and unlocked the gate to the unpaved access road. Several four-wheel drive vehicles and the ambulance slowly made their way up the trail. Friends and spectators were forbidden beyond the gate. Finally the coroner arrived, got out of his car, and climbed into a waiting four-wheel-drive pickup, which immediately headed up the trail.

As the group waited by the trailhead, Abby pointed into the woods and said, "Look! A baby deer!" About sixty feet off the trail a tiny fawn was getting to his feet. The group, including the policeman and firefighter, watched in awe as the white-spotted little fellow stood on his wobbly legs, looking this way and that. His mother could not be seen anywhere.

"It looks like he's just learning to walk," George observed as the fawn took a few unsteady steps and stopped. After a brief pause, he continued walking slowly away from them, eventually disappearing into the underbrush.

Despite the slight diversion, it seemed like hours until the policeman relayed a radio message from the rescue team. It was the message they feared they would eventually hear. Their friend's heroic action had cost him his life.

There was nothing more to do. The somber group climbed into George's pickup and headed back to town. After dropping the ladies and children at Michelle's place, George went to visit Rick. The township police cruiser was just leaving as George arrived. "The police told you what happened, I suppose?" George said, glancing at the floor.

"It's unbelievable," Rick replied.

George shared his eye witness account, and the two sat, staring at the walls, not knowing what to say next. "Remember," Rick said, blinking back tears, "he told us he had a premonition that something bad was going to happen to one of us."

"That's right, he did. And he still had enough guts to go over that railing."

"I think God was trying to warn him."

"If it's any consolation, he did call out 'God! Help me!' just as he went over the edge."

"He said that all the time. He didn't mean anything by it. It was just an expression."

"I know. But this time it sounded like he really meant it."

"Well, you never know, do you?"

"Earlier, he had been arguing with Michelle about life after death. He came down pretty hard on her. But I don't think it was because of anything she said. I think deep inside, he always heard a little voice telling him, 'Roger, you're wrong.' And I think that's why he kept trying to prove himself right."

"Maybe he had time to change his mind while he was falling," Rick wiped his eyes.

"It probably would have taken a good five seconds to fall that far," George surmised.

"When you think you're going to die, an awful lot can go through your mind in five seconds."

Days passed slowly as a shocked community came together to support the friends and family of one of their most beloved schoolteachers. Friends and acquaintances from near and far stood in long lines, chatting and encouraging each other as they waited to file past the casket and pay their final respects.

At the funeral, the story of how Roger saved Abby's life was referred to over and over. Max told the story of how Roger saved Rick from hypothermia. And the way he told it, it seemed that Roger was responsible for the entire rescue. School administrators and parents praised him for his work in the classroom. Michelle spoke at length about how he bravely marched up to their little cottage to confront Jasper, armed with nothing more than a walking stick, and how he helped her and the children escape into the wilderness.

Despite all the stories of heroism, some even laced with humor, an overwhelming sadness saturated the atmosphere. No one suggested that Roger was now in a better place. Nobody said he was receiving an eternal reward for a life well lived. Pastor John had a short sermon emphasizing the eternal consequences of putting one's faith in Jesus or not doing so. No one expressed any expectation of seeing Roger again. It was a sad good-bye—hopelessly sad.

50

George and Michelle were busy stuffing envelopes with wedding invitations when they heard the deep-throated purr of a Caterpillar diesel engine and the sound air brakes. Michelle breathed a sigh of relief. "Sounds like Daddy's back."

"I suppose he'll be over for something to eat in a little while," George said as the rig backed toward George's driveway.

"We're just having soup this evening, if that's okay." Michelle glanced at George. She just didn't feel up to doing anything more than that.

"That's fine with me." George seemed preoccupied. "We do have an invitation here for Eva Stoner, don't we?"

"Yes, I distinctly remember putting her name and address on an envelope."

"I'm eager to meet the old lady. So far we've only talked by phone."

"She won't know anyone, will she?"

"I guess she won't. But she said she would like to come."

"Is she originally from this area?"

"I don't know. She seems to have an interest in our community."

Before long, Max was at the door.

"Hi, Grandpa!" Abby called as she ran to meet him. He picked her up with a hug and walked over to the table to see what Michelle and George were doing.

"How are the wedding plans coming?" he brushed Michelle's cheek with the back of his hand.

"Great! Everyone involved loves your idea."

"Good. I'm looking forward to it myself," Max said with a smile.

"Is that an original idea?" George asked. "Or has someone done it before?"

"I don't know. Someone may have done it before. But I don't know of anybody." Max shrugged.

"So it's original." George gave a quick nod.

"You hungry?" Michelle glanced at her father.

"Yep. Haven't eaten since breakfast."

"I'll get something ready shortly." Michelle shifted in her seat.

"No. You just stay sitting and tell me what to do." Her father studied her for a second. "I can cook. How are you feeling?" He seemed to already know how she was feeling.

"Like I'm just about to have a baby." She grinned at him.

Max heated the soup, with Abby's assistance, while George packed the invitations in a box and set the table. After the meal, Max persuaded Earl to help him with the dishes so Michelle could relax. As soon as the dishes were put away, Max headed home to catch up on his sleep. George entertained the children till their bedtime.

After tucking the children into bed, George kissed Michelle good night. "Don't hesitate to call me." He gazed into her eyes. "I'll be ready to go at a moment's notice."

Max looked up from the newspaper as Abby came down the stairs in her pajamas. "Where's Mommy?" she asked.

"George took her to the hospital last night." He took a sip of coffee and watched for the little girl's reaction.

"Did she have the baby?"

"I don't know. I'm still waiting for George to call."

"I hope it's a girl," Abby said as she climbed into his lap.

Eventually Earl came down the steps, rubbing his eyes. "Where's Mom?"

"She's having a baby!" Abby replied enthusiastically. "And I hope it's a girl."

"One girl is enough," Earl said grumpily.

"You kids want some breakfast?" Max asked.

"Sure, Grandpa," Abby responded. "I'll help you."

"Okay. What do you want?"

"Lucky Charms!" both answered.

"Oh. That's a pretty tough order," he replied with a grin. "I'll need your help with that." He proceeded to look for things in all the wrong places. Giggling constantly, Abby instructed him on where to find the cereal bowls, spoons, milk, and cereal. While they were eating, the phone rang.

Max picked up the phone. "Hello."

"Hello, Grandpa. It's a boy—seven pounds and fourteen ounces."

"Great! Seven pounds, fourteen ounces. Everybody doing fine?"

"Yeah. He's healthy. Michelle's doing fine."

"And what did you name him?"

"Roger Maxwell."

"Roger? Not George?"

"No. It's Roger. We both agreed on that. I suggested it. But she was thinking the same thing before I even said anything."

"That's a good name. He was a good man."

"Sounds like we all agree on that. You can bring the kids in to visit later this morning."

"As soon as they finish their breakfast and get dressed, we'll head over there."

"Okay. See ya later."

Max turned to the children as he hung up the phone. "It's a boy. Is that okay?"

"Yeah. That was my second choice, anyway." Abby sounded delighted.

"They named him Roger?" Earl questioned.

"Yeah. Roger Maxwell," Max said with a smile. "And his birthday is June thirteen. I gotta remember that."

"When is June thirteen?" Abby asked.

"It's today," Max looked at her.

"Today? He was born on his birthday?"

"Yeah, how about that?" Max replied with a chuckle.

"Silly girl," Earl said shaking his head.

"Okay. Let's go get you kids dressed." Max hustled them toward the stairs. "Then I'll take you to the hospital to see him."

Although the hospital stay seemed long to Michelle, to Max it seemed like no time at all before his daughter and grandson were home and baby Roger was sleeping comfortably in the cradle George had made for the occasion. Nana came down from New York, and Mae and her family came to visit for an afternoon. Everyone was trying to help. But to Max, it seemed each one was also making life a little more complicated for his daughter. Then, gradually, things got back to normal—or at least as normal as could be expected with a newborn in the house and wedding plans in the works.

"What are you thinking?" Michelle asked one evening as George sat on the sofa staring into space while baby Roger slept in his arms.

"Oh, I'm just trying to figure out how to build a solid base to set up a transit in the middle of Thrush Creek," he replied softly as he glanced down at his son.

"When are you ever going to have time to do that?"

"I don't know. Probably not for a long time. But I gotta get it done before anything happens to Mrs. Stoner or she sells the land to somebody else or something like that."

"I wouldn't lose any sleep over that."

"But I can't help thinking about it. It's a problem to be solved, and I just have to figure out how to solve it. I can't help myself."

"Well, Mr. Good's directions did say that you have to think about a problem from every angle, didn't they? So I guess you're following the directions—thinking about it from every angle."

"Every angle! That's it, Michelle!" George exclaimed as the infant jumped and started crying. "Oh, I'm sorry." He tried to soothe the baby. "I didn't mean to scare you. Go back to sleep." But baby Roger kept right on squirming and crying. Finally George handed the baby back to his mother, saying, "I think he wants something I don't have."

"Yeah, I suppose he's probably hungry again." Michelle cradled the infant in her arms and began nursing him. "Now what was it that got you so excited about every angle?"

"That's the solution." George tried to control his enthusiasm. "There's got to be a way to figure out the heading directly from point A to the treasure without actually going to point B. We just have to use that information to figure out the angles."

"George, you're a genius."

"Not really. Now I'm going to have to brush up on my geometry. I don't have a clue how to figure that out."

"I'm sure you'll figure it out sooner or later. You always seem to find a way. That's one of the things I admire so much about you."

"I wish Roger were here. He would have known how to do that. I really miss him."

"So do I," Michelle admitted. "But on the other hand, I am so glad that things never worked between him and me."

"So am I."

"I do really pity Kathy, though."

"Me too." George's mind was still working on the treasure hunt. "I wonder where I could pick up a textbook on geometry or trig."

"We have a lot of other priorities right now, George."

"I know. I have to admit, finding the treasure doesn't seem very important compared to getting married. But I can't seem to stop trying to solve it. It's like a puzzle. Once you start, you can't stop till you complete it."

"So if you want to get that off your mind, just think about what things will be like after we're married," Michelle suggested. "I love to think about that. All my childhood hopes and dreams could still come true—with you by my side."

"Yeah." George noticed the glow in Michelle's eyes. Her face radiated pure happiness as she sat in the soft light, cuddling their infant son. "And my childhood hopes and dreams are coming true as well," he added softly. "The treasure sitting right here in front of me is worth a million times more than anything buried out there in the woods."

51

"It's beautiful!" Michelle said as she stood next to her father, admiring his latest purchase. "I love it! It'll be perfect."

"That's an impressive piece of woodworking." George glanced at Michelle and her father. They both beamed with delight. "I'm always amazed at how they make them things, but I've never been tempted to try making one myself."

Max smiled broadly, obviously pleased, not only with his purchase, but more with his daughter's reaction to it. "Yeah, I like it too." He put his arm around Michelle and gave a little squeeze. "I think it's just what we need."

"Very nice!" George commented as he rubbed his hand gently over the smooth side of the cedar strip canoe lying in his lawn. "I love the way the glossy finish highlights the natural blend of the light and dark colors in the wood. You have the redness of the cedar hull along with the white ash thwarts and gunnels. It's gorgeous!"

"It's got the cane seats too," Max pointed out. "They're lightweight and really quite comfortable. And I got myself a nice wooden paddle to go with it."

"Have you water-tested it?" Michelle asked.

Max nodded. "A little bit. It has good initial stability. The final stability is nothing to brag about. But it'll be an excellent flat-water boat."

"What do you mean by initial stability and final stability?" George tried to picture the boat floating on the water.

"Initial stability is the boat's tendency to stay level on the water." Max extended his hand in a horizontal position. "Final stability is how far the boat can tilt before it capsizes."

"Oh, that's interesting. I never realized there are two kinds of stability. I've got so much to learn about canoes."

"Think about chairs, George." Michelle seemed eager to explain. "Initial stability is like a four-legged kitchen chair. It sets flat on the floor and doesn't rock easily. But you know what happens when you sit on that chair and rock back on two legs. You reach a point where all of a sudden the chair flips over backwards. It has very poor final stability. Compare that to a rocking chair. You wouldn't stand on a rocking chair to change a light bulb, because it has no initial stability. But you can sit on it and rock back as far as you want. The farther back you go the more the chair wants to return to an upright position. The rocking chair has excellent final stability."

"That's a good illustration." Max seemed impressed with his daughter's explanation. "Each different hull design has a unique combination of initial and final stability. And of course, that affects how maneuverable they are."

"Well," George quipped, "as long as I'm not the one maneuvering it, everything should be fine."

"Now you just have to find a good place to keep it so it doesn't get all weather-beaten," Michelle advised as Abby came running across the lawn.

"Little Roger woke up!" Abby called out as she approached.

"I'll be right over!" Michelle turned and headed back to her house. Max went into the garage to clear a space for the canoe, and George returned to his office to work on the project that had been bugging him for the past several weeks.

He had found small blocks of time here and there to work at it. But finding quality time to really delve into the project was next to impossible. Michelle had bought him a scientific calculator, and he was educating himself on using the trig functions. On a note pad he had drawn a right triangle and written:

Sin = Opposite leg / Hypotenuse

Cos = Adjacent leg / Hypotenuse

Tan = Opposite leg / Adjacent leg

On his drawing board, he had a sketch of the area around the broken dam, with an angled line running west by south from point A to point B. Another line went from point B, southeast by east to the treasure. Horizontal and vertical gridlines created two right triangles.

One by one, he had figured out the angles from Mr. Good's directions and used the trig functions to determine the length of the legs of the triangles. Now all that was left was to figure out the angle and distance from point A directly to the treasure. But he was running out of time. Before he could spend any more time on this, he had a deck to build.

"You all ready for tomorrow?" Rick asked as he strolled into George's office.

"I think so," George replied, turning away from the drawing board to face Rick. "Max and I have already put in the underground electric line. So we'll have power for the power tools. We've got the posts set. So in the morning we can start putting up the joists. Then we'll be ready to lay the decking and put up the railing. If we get a few volunteers, it should all come together pretty fast."

"So what's the deal? Is the church paying for this or are you donating it or what?"

"Max and I are splitting the cost of the materials. We're counting on volunteers to help put it together."

"And it's down by the creek, right?"

"Yeah. The back row of posts is in the water and the front row is on the bank. You'll go up two steps from the ground onto the deck. So they'll be able to use it as a stage for outdoor concerts and stuff like that—and weddings, of course."

"So the audience will be seated on the lawn."

"Right. The lawn has the perfect slope. It's level enough that people can sit comfortably on chairs and sloped just enough to give the folks in the back a little better view. So we don't have to build the stage up very high. We'll set up a bunch of chairs for the wedding, and everybody should be able to see just fine."

"September the fifth is gonna be here before you know it. You think we'll get it all done tomorrow?"

"I don't know. It gets a small floating dock attached. If we don't get that part done tomorrow, I don't know when I'll have time to finish it. The lights and receptacles can be wired up later, as long as they're working by September fifth, that is."

"Getting married shouldn't be that much work."

"Tell me about it! Rick, I've got so much work I don't know which way to turn. I've got two big projects that people want finished before the holidays. I thought I had plenty of time, but now my calendar is getting all filled up with other stuff."

"Well, I'll be out to help right after band practice."

"I bet it'll be hot this afternoon," Max remarked as he and George prepared to unload a radial arm saw from George's pickup.

George observed how the morning mist hovered over the creek and how the dew-coated grass sparkled in the August sunshine. "I hope we get a bunch of volunteers out here before it gets too hot. If we don't have to work late in the afternoon, that would be fine with me."

One by one, volunteers showed up with hammers and power drivers, and the stillness of the morning gave way to the clamor of a construction site. The guys laying the decking joked about putting in a trap door at the spot the groom would be standing. The guys building the steps claimed they had a nail point protruding at just the right spot to snag the bride's train. George took the ribbing in stride, threatening to dock their pay if things were not done to his satisfaction.

A workman with a well-stocked tool belt turned to Max and asked, "Are you all ready for your next career?"

Max looked puzzled. "What's that?"

"Wedding planner. I hear you're quite the wedding planner now."

Max chuckled. "If I'd plan any more weddings, they'd all turn our exactly like this one."

"I haven't yet heard what these wonderful plans are."

"You'll just have to wait and see."

Another worker joined the conversation. "Yeah, we come out here and volunteer our time. You'd think they could at least pay us with a little inside information."

"I was going to do that." George grinned. "But your pay is being docked, remember?"

Just before lunch, Pastor John arrived to check out the project. "I didn't realize it would be this big," he commented as he observed their progress. "Man, we'll be able to do all kinds of things out here."

Michelle and her friends, Joanne and Sheryl, arrived at noon with a large crock pot of beef barbecue, rolls, potato salad, drinks, and a variety of finger food. The half dozen sunburned workers gathered under the shade of a large old maple tree as Pastor John asked a blessing on the food and the project.

"It looks like it's really coming along." Michelle gazed at the deck. "I'm just trying to visualize what it will look like on our wedding day. You don't have much to do anymore."

"There's a lot of little things yet." George stood beside her, gazing at the deck.

"You'll have to be careful when you go up the steps," Rick said with a smirk. "There's a nail sticking out there that's likely to catch your train."

"That's okay," Michelle quipped. "I'm just wearing blue jeans anyway."

By midafternoon, the volunteers started finding reasons why they had to leave. But the project was basically completed. By the time George started packing up his things, the floating dock was already attached, the lights and receptacles were mounted and just needed to be connected.

By the end of the next week, George had finished up the remaining details on the deck. As he sat at his drawing board late one evening, Michelle poked her head into his office and said, "Good night, honey. I'm going to bed. I'll see in the morning."

"I got it!" George announced enthusiastically. "I know where the treasure is, and I know how to get there."

"Great!" Michelle responded. "I knew you'd figure it out."

"Well, at least I think I know where it is."

"You're not so sure after all?"

"Maybe I'm being a little too presumptuous, thinking that I could teach myself trigonometry and solve this correctly on the first try. But I think I've got it. Now I just have to get out there and dig to prove it."

"Now when are you going to find time to do that?"

"Not till after the wedding, for sure," George replied. "But as soon as I can, I'd like to get out there and dig it up before Mrs. Stoner decides to sell the land to somebody else."

52

Saturday, September 5, broke clear and sunny. The dew had already evaporated from the grass as two ushers set up chairs in neat rows facing the new deck. White ribbons and bows decorated the railing behind a row of four large potted ferns. A pair of wild geese glided quietly across the water, hardly disturbing the mirrorlike surface. A sound technician was busy setting up and testing equipment. Soon a florist showed up to finish the decorations while a photographer strolled about with a camera in his hand and a light meter dangling from a cord around his neck.

Members of the bridal party came by to look things over, before they disappeared into the church to get dressed for the occasion while musicians did their final sound checks. Finally, the guests began arriving, some dressed in their finest and some dressed for a more informal event. Several mallards swimming near the shore entertained the guests while soft music drifted from the large speaker boxes.

A long white limousine pulled up to the edge of the lawn. The driver got out and opened the back door, and a well-dressed elderly lady stepped out. She walked with a fancy cane, which she didn't seem to really need. The usher proffered his arm. "Eva Stoner, friend of the groom," she said as she grasped his arm. The usher escorted her down the aisle to the seat traditionally reserved for the groom's mother.

Eventually Mrs. Danklos was escorted to her seat. The recorded music stopped, and the keyboard player took his place as the pastor and three men walked onto the stage and took their positions. Rick and the other groomsman stood next to George, but they left a vacant space between George and Rick for the honorary best man, Roger Koralsen.

The keyboard played as the bridesmaids and maid of honor, in their royal blue satin, promenaded slowly down the grassy aisle, each carrying a single red rose. Stepping up onto the wooden deck, they took their places and turned toward the audience. Then Earl came escorting Abby with her basket of flowers. Guests smiled, and cameras flashed as the two dilly-dallied down the aisle, Earl handsomely decked out in a tuxedo to match the groomsmen and Abby in a pretty blue satin dress of a lighter shade that blended beautifully with the bridesmaids. They took their places, and the music stopped.

The keyboard player craned his neck, looking toward the back of the audience. The audience watched for Mrs. Danklos to get to her feet. She glanced over her shoulder but remained seated. George glanced about nervously. The groomsmen looked at each other and shrugged their shoulders, obviously pretending that nobody knew what happened to the bride. George smiled and nodded to Mrs. Danklos, and she rose to her feet as the musician started playing "Here Comes the Bride."

The audience rose to their feet and turned toward the back as George stepped down and escorted his soon-to-be mother-in-law up onto the deck. He leaned down to her and pointed up the creek to where a beautiful wooden canoe was emerging from the bank. In the bow sat the bride, wearing her flowing white gown and veil. She sat facing her father, who was wearing a long-sleeved white shirt and black bow tie. Over that, he wore a pristine blue life vest, which matched the color of Abby's dress.

The audience, seeing nothing behind them, soon realized the bride was coming from another direction. The photographer had come up onto the deck, and the whole bridal party was lined up along the railing watching as Max paddled slowly and smoothly, hardly causing a ripple. Guests were getting out of their seats and coming to the water's edge for a better view of the approaching bride. As the boat slowly came closer, cameras clicked and ladies commented on Michelle's lovely gown and exquisite hairdo. The middle of the canoe was filled with flowers, cascading down from tall spikes of gladiolus at the center to green leafy vines dangling over the gunnels. And everything was perfectly reflected in the placid water.

Max approached the dock in a wide semicircle, giving guests and photographers a view from every angle as the keyboard played a medley of songs including anything from "Row, Row, Row Your Boat" to "Moon River," "Sloop John B.," and "Proud Mary." Finally, Max eased up to the dock from the downstream direction. The two groomsmen steadied the boat as Max stepped out and offered his hand to his daughter. She took his hand and, lifting her dress with the other hand, she gingerly stepped up onto the dock, exposing her bare feet for only a moment.

As the bridal party resumed their positions, Pastor John asked the audience to be seated. Then Max escorted his daughter up the ramp from the floating dock, onto the deck, where she grasped George's arm. Then the ceremony got underway.

After the music, the vows, the rings, and everything else, Mr. and Mrs. George Lauger joined hands and hiked briskly to the back of the audience, followed by the two children. An usher came forward to escort the maid of honor and the rest of the bridal party followed. Ushers escorted the bride's mother to the back and then Mrs. Stoner.

"It was a lovely wedding," Mrs. Stoner said as she greeted George with a hug. "I wish you many years of happiness."

"It's so nice to finally meet you," George replied. "I'm so glad you could come."

"I wouldn't have missed it for the world. This is such a wonderful community, and I haven't been out here for years."

"Did you grow up around here?" Michelle extended her arms.

"No, I grew up in South Carolina. But when my husband was still living, we used to come out here to our summer cottage several times each year. The people around here are so friendly."

"Well, I hope you're having a wonderful time here today." George patted the back of her hand.

"Oh, I am! And these must be the children that were born in my cottage," she said as bent down to Abby and Earl.

"They're the ones." Michelle smiled broadly.

"You're really pretty," Mrs. Stoner said looking straight into Abby's eyes. She patted Earl on the shoulder and added, "And you're a handsome young man." She straightened up and turned to Michelle. "I feel so sorry for everything you had to go through. My lovely little cottage probably seems like a place of horror to you."

"Oh, no," Michelle replied. "That was our home, and it served us quite well. And it's really a beautiful location."

"It is a lovely spot. And I wish you the best," she added as she gave Michelle another hug and then moved on.

As the guests mingled, amateur photographers as well as the professional were having a great time taking pictures of folks dressed up in their finest, posing in unique settings. Photos were being taken on the deck, in front of the deck, along the bank, or even in the canoe. Little by little, the group migrated into the fellowship hall where the caterer was making the final preparations.

After a long drawn-out meal, interspersed with traditional rituals and open mic comments and stories, the couple made their way from table to table to chat with their guests. Finally, as guests were beginning to leave, the bridal couple stood in front of a table full of wedding presents that had been opened and put on display.

There were all kinds of useful household items: towels, blankets, cookware, lamps, and chinaware. They picked up miscellaneous items that caught their attention and checked them over briefly, making comments about how or where they would be used. George picked up a thin flat box made of white cardboard. The card attached was signed by Eva Stoner. As he opened the box, his eyes popped wide open, and his jaw dropped. "Look at this!" he exclaimed in a whisper as he tilted the box so Michelle could see the deed lying inside.

A note card stuck to the front of the deed read, "It's all yours. Just contact my attorney to finalize the transaction." The attorney's business card was pasted below.

"Is it the whole thing?" Michelle asked, as George picked up the deed and started scanning through the legal description of the tract of land.

"I believe so," he replied, continuing to scan the lengthy details. "Yes! One thousand one hundred ninety-two acres!"

"Unbelievable!" Michelle remarked, squeezing her husband's hand. "Now I guess you can stop worrying about her selling it to someone else."

"No more worries," George agreed, returning the squeeze.

The tired couple relaxed in the pool at the mountain resort. It had been a long, wonderful day. Both had been up early, making final preparations for the wedding. Now that was over and they finally had time to relax and enjoy each other. With one arm around Michelle's waist and the other hand grasping hers, George swayed to the slow music running through his head. Together, they swirled round and round as if ballroom dancing in slow motion—in swimming trunks and a bikini.

Not only was the water refreshing, but being in water almost to her shoulders made Michelle feel light on her feet. All day she had felt like she was walking on air. But her feet knew that wasn't actually the case. Now, with her toes just touching the bottom of the pool, she swirled effortlessly in the arms of her husband. She laid her head on his shoulder and whispered, "I think I'm ready to go to bed."

He slipped both arms around her and pressed his lips against hers for a moment, then replied, "me too."

With renewed energy, the couple climbed out of the pool, grabbed their towels and dried themselves—somewhat. Clasping hands, they breezed down the corridor, around the corner, down another hallway and disappeared into their suite. The door closed for a moment then reopened a few inches. A hand came out and hung the "Do Not Disturb" sign on the door handle. The door quickly closed again.

53

George sat on the sofa holding little Roger. While he enjoyed cuddling his infant son, his mind was working on the buried treasure. He heard Michelle come down the stairs after tucking the other two children into bed. "I can't believe that this Saturday we'll be married three weeks already," she commented as she snuggled up beside him.

"Three glorious weeks." He leaned hard against her.

"Glorious!" she agreed with a smile.

"I promise you, someday I'll take you on a real honeymoon." George returned her smile.

"Three days was fine. We had a wonderful time. And I wouldn't have wanted to be away from the baby any longer."

"I've got my work pretty well caught up now." George swayed back and forth with the baby. "This Saturday is supposed to be nice. I think I'll see if it suits Rick to go out and dig for buried treasure."

"There's no reason to rush to do that, now that we own the land." Michelle didn't seem enthused about the idea.

"I know. But it's going to be a nice day to be out in the woods."

"Some nice day we should take the kids and just go for a leisurely walk out there and see if we can find a good location for our dream home." Michelle stroked the baby's dark curls.

"Well, I already made arrangements to get the transit on Saturday."

"Oh. You did that without even discussing it with me?"

"Well, I didn't realize you were concerned about that."

"I just think it would be nice to wait till the kids are old enough to help."

"We can take Earl along."

"Sure. But he won't be able to actually help you very much. In a few years, he'll be able to comprehend some of the math. He'd understand what you're doing with that transit. It would mean so much more to him in a few years. Right now he doesn't even comprehend the value of an old baseball card."

"It'll be quite a few years before he can understand trigonometry. I don't want to wait that long."

"I can't believe that treasure is more important to you than the children."

"No! It's not that the *treasure* is that important. I just have to prove to myself that my figures are right. It would be like taking a test and waiting ten years to find out how you did. That would be ridiculous!"

"Well, if you think you have to do it, go ahead." Michelle obviously had not changed her mind. "But I still think it would be nice to wait till the kids are a little older."

Why is she all of a sudden opposed to this?

Michelle cherished the scene. Saturday morning's golden sunlight streaked through the back door as Rick and George sat in the kitchen with George's diagram and work papers spread out on the table.

"It looks like you're becoming quite a mathematician," Rick commented, gazing at the diagram.

"He's been working really hard at that," Michelle added proudly as she stacked the breakfast dishes in the sink.

"Well, you helped me." George glanced over his shoulder at Michelle. "I don't know if I ever would have figured out how to use these trig functions without your help."

"I just got you started. You did the rest." She couldn't help but admire him. "But it is really fascinating though, I have to admit."

"See, first we figure out how far it is from point A to point B, going due west then due south." George directed Rick's attention to the points on the drawing. "Mr. Good gave us the distance directly from point A to point B as the distance from home to second base. That's 127.28 feet. The heading is west by south. That's eleven and a quarter degrees south of due west." He went on to explain how he calculated that point B is 124.83 feet west and 24.83 feet south from point A.

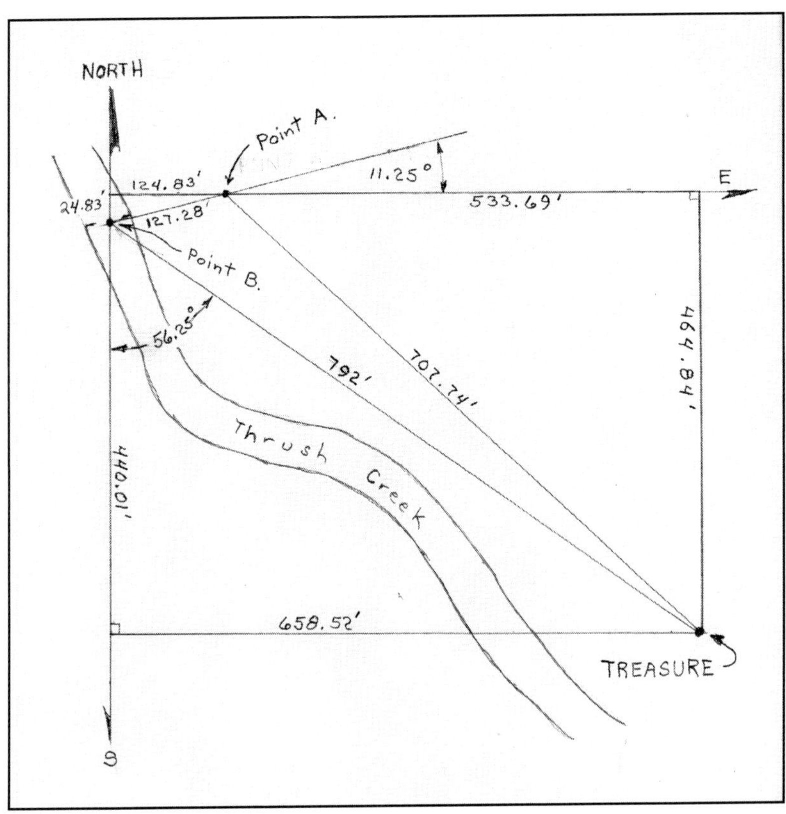

"Okay, I follow you," Rick responded.

Earl listened with a baffled look on his face. What his new daddy was doing with numbers must have seemed like science fiction to him. Michelle was sure he didn't understand it in the least. But still it appeared to intrigue him. She wondered what he would be doing with numbers in a few years.

"Now we do the same thing from point B to the treasure," George continued.

Point A to Point B

Cos 11.25° X 127.28' = 124.83 Due West

Sin 11.25° X 127.28' = 24.83 Due South

Point B to treasure

Cos 56.25° X 792' = 440.01' Due South

Sin 56.25° X 792' = 658.52' Due East

Point A to Treasure

	658.52' East		24.83' South
−	124.83' West	+	440.01' South
	533.69' East		464.84' South

$$\sqrt{533.69^2 + 464.84^2} = 707.74'$$

Arc Tan (464.84 ÷ 533.69) = 41.06°

From point A, go South 41.06° East, 707.74 feet to the treasure.

"But you use the distance of the world's tallest building," Rick added.

"Right. It's 792 feet. And our direction is southeast by east. So that would be fifty-six and a quarter degrees from due south." He went on, explaining his calculations and how he combined the dimensions from the two previous triangles to form a third triangle. He explained how the solution of the third triangle gave him the heading and distance from point A directly to the treasure. "So we see," George concluded, "that from point A, we go south 41.06 degrees east a distance of 707.74 feet, and there we find the treasure."

"Great!" Rick replied. "You've got our heading and the distance. What else do we need?"

"I just wanted to see if you can find anything wrong with my figures."

"Hey, I could study those figures all day, and I couldn't tell you if you made a mistake. It sounds logical to me. I'm ready to get going."

"I've got the transit and the shovels in the truck. I guess we're ready to go. Come on, Earl, we're gonna go dig for buried treasure."

Earl picked up the small cooler with the lunch Michelle had packed as she kissed George good-bye. "Don't you want your papers?" she asked.

"I've got the two numbers we need in my pocket." He patted his shirt pocket.

After the men left, Michelle sat down at the table. Joanne was coming by in about an hour to take her and the two younger children shopping for the day. As she sat at the table, she looked over the neat drawing George had prepared. The more she looked at it, the more it intrigued her. As she started reviewing his notes and dimensions, she began to understand why George was so captivated by it. She began punching numbers into the calculator and checking the results. She studied carefully as she repeated the calculations over and over. Finally, she folded the drawing over and slipped all of George's notes inside. Then she took a pen and wrote a note on the back of the drawing.

As the guys climbed out of his pickup, George looked around at the goldenrod blooming along the edges of the lane. He breathed the crisp mountain air as he looked up at a few trees that were beginning to show some early fall color. "This is going to be a great day," he commented. "I can feel it."

"I've got a paper bag in my pocket just in case we find some mushrooms," Earl said as they headed into the woods with the transit.

"Oh, so you came prepared." George glanced at Rick with raised eyebrows.

"Yeah. Mom likes mushrooms."

"Roger told me you like to find mushrooms." Rick glanced down at the boy. "It's too bad he isn't here for this."

"Yeah. He liked mushrooms too." Earl picked up an acorn and gave it a throw.

"I meant he would have enjoyed helping us find the treasure." Rick gave Earl a pat on the shoulder.

"He was a great guy," George agreed. "He was always fun to be with, even if I didn't agree with him on a lot of stuff."

"He calculated the probability of those four freak accidents." Rick shook his head. "And he came up with odds so low that he figured there had to be a plan or a conspiracy. Yet he had no problem believing that life began spontaneously, with no plan at all."

"It seems to me that the probability of life beginning spontaneously would be much lower than the probability of four freak accidents." George shifted the transit to his other shoulder. "But, of course, I haven't actually done the math on that."

"Well, a lot of scientists have. And they come up with some pretty big numbers."

"Bigger than ten to the thirty-third power?"

"Oh my, yes! They say one of the first steps toward the beginning of life would have been for a number of amino acids to come together to form a simple self-replicating peptide."

"A peptide?"

"Yeah. That's not a living organism. It's just the first step toward life. And the probability of the simplest peptide forming at random is one in ten to the fortieth power."

"Ten to the fortieth," George mused. "That number would have seven more zeros than the number Roger came up with for the freak accidents."

"Right. So we can say that the probability of a simple peptide forming is ten million times less than the probability of those four accidents."

"And yet," George shook his head, "he believed that someone must have planned the accidents, but not the beginning of life."

"Go figure." Rick chuckled.

"He was so thoroughly convinced that everything evolved without God or any supernatural power. It would be harder for me to believe that than it is to put my faith in God."

"He spent a lot of time researching the evolution of Venus flytraps." Rick cocked his head. "He would never say why. I don't think he ever found what he was looking for."

"Or maybe, what he found didn't fit his theory," George suggested.

Earl followed along quietly as they approached point A, where they had dug up the directions more than five months earlier. He watched with curiosity as George set up the transit. Then he accompanied Rick as they cleared a line of sight while George directed them from the transit. The trees formed a tight canopy overhead, and there was little growth at the forest floor, so clearing a line of sight was fairly easy. Earl held the end of the tape as Rick measured off a distance, sticking a spike into the ground and spraying a fluorescent orange circle around it. Then Earl held the tape on the spike as Rick measured off the next distance. Eventually they had measured off 707 feet and 9 inches. Rick motioned for George to come.

"Is that the spot?" George asked in disbelief as Rick pointed to a fluorescent orange dot in the middle of a large outcropping of solid rock.

"That's it."

"How did he ever dig a hole here?

"There's no place in a ten-foot radius where he could have possibly dug a hole three feet deep."

"I can't believe it."

"Seventy years ago, maybe there was soil here, and it eroded away," Rick suggested.

George scanned the area and shook his head. The rock layer slanted into the hillside, and at a distance of about ten feet from the dot, the rock became covered with soil. A few feet beyond that stood a large oak tree. "That tree over there must be at least a hundred and fifty years old," he argued. "There's no exposed roots—no signs of erosion."

"What about magnetic north? Did you forget to adjust for the…uh…"

"Declination? No, I adjusted for that."

"I don't know then. Do we want to double check our measurements?"

"Yeah, we must have measured wrong," George concluded. Rick and George remeasured while Earl watched. They came within two inches of the first spot.

"Well then, I must have made a mistake in my calculations," George admitted. "I was so concerned about proving myself right, and I proved myself wrong."

"Your figures looked good to me. But I'm no expert on trig."

"We're close to a place where we often find a lot of mushrooms." Earl didn't seem at all disappointed at not finding the treasure.

"Mushrooms!" George said with a chuckle. "Well maybe we can bring something home for your mother after all. Show us where the mushrooms are."

Earl headed off to the northeast as George and Rick followed a few paces behind. "Michelle was right," George said quietly to Rick. "I should have waited till he was older. He's more interested in mushrooms than baseball cards."

"Well, it looks like you'll have another chance to do that," Rick replied.

"Earl, wait!" George called after walking about a hundred feet. "Come back here. Look at this area! Wouldn't this be a beautiful spot to build a house?"

"I guess," Earl shrugged his shoulders.

"It's more level," Rick observed. "It wouldn't take so much excavating."

"That's what I was thinking." George scanned the area. "And that outcropping of rock creates a bit of a window in the forest. I wouldn't have to cut down a lot of trees to get a good view of Thrush Creek and have a nice front lawn. It looks like there would be a good layer of bedrock for a foundation. We could have a daylight basement with a big porch above looking out over the valley."

"It sounds like you got it all figured out." Rick didn't sounded interested in any more details.

"The mushrooms are just up here a little farther," Earl said as he turned to continue on.

"Okay," George replied. "Let's see if we can find some mushrooms." After leading them another hundred feet, Earl spotted a mushroom.

"There ain't very many here right now," Earl said as they searched the area, occasionally finding one or two. "Sometimes there's a whole bunch of 'em."

"Well, we have enough," George replied as they headed back. "Your mother will really like this." When they came to the level area, George stopped again to view the site from a different angle and imagine how a house would best fit.

"We should mark this spot to show Mom sometime," Earl suggested.

"Right." George took the can of spray paint from the tool pouch Rick was wearing. He sprayed a small heart onto an eighteen-inch flat rock and said, "This is where my heart is. Someday this will be our home."

"Now you just have to remember where that rock is." Rick surveyed the landscape.

"Well, it's just a little over a hundred feet northeast of the point we marked out there on the big rock," George replied.

"I'd say it's less than a hundred feet," Rick argued.

"I bet it's more."

"We'll measure it. Loser buys pizza."

"Okay," George agreed.

They stretched out the tape measure—ninety-seven feet and four inches. "Okay. I was wrong again." George admitted. "I owe you pizza."

"I'd like to have it right now," Rick quipped as they gathered their equipment and headed back to the truck. "I'm hungry!"

"I can't wait to go over my calculations and see if I can figure out where I made a mistake," George said, picking up the pace.

"Maybe you should get someone else to look over your figures. Oftentimes another person can spot a mistake sooner than the person who did the calculations."

"Anybody who can show me my mistake will be my greatest hero."

"It's probably something really simple, something so obvious you just keep overlooking it."

"Okay. When we get back, you show me what I'm overlooking, and I'll put you up on a pedestal right beside Einstein and—"

"I didn't say I could do that." Rick cut him off.

"And Batman," Earl added.

"Yeah. On a pedestal with Einstein and Batman." George laughed.

After finishing off a late lunch, they loaded up and headed home with their treasure, a dozen mushrooms.

"I don't get it," George said as they rolled along toward town. "I don't understand why Michelle made such a big deal out of this. It's like she thinks my heart is all wrapped up in finding this treasure—like I don't care about her and the kids. I've told her before, she's my treasure. That's where my heart is—with her and the kids."

Rick felt compelled to give some kind of intellectual comment. But all he could come up with was, "Well, I guess you won't always see eye to eye on everything."

The men arrived home before Michelle. As they walked into the kitchen, George picked up the note Michelle had left on the back of his drawing. "That lovin' rascal!" he said, still studying the note. "She knows I made a mistake! She's not sayin' what it is, but she knows!" He handed the note to Rick. "Here, read this."

Rick took the paper.

> *Sorry, guys. Too bad you didn't find the treasure. We all make mistakes. Let's hope the kids excel in math. But until then, think about this. Jesus said, "Where your treasure is, there your heart will be also." So according to my logic, if you want to find your treasure, look where your heart is.*
>
> *Michelle*

Epilogue

Michelle watched three-year-old Roger Maxwell pitter-patter across the hardwood floor in his bare feet and sit down on the flagstone hearth of the large fireplace as she and George gave Eva Stoner a tour of their new log house. The old lady leaned on her cane and tilted her head back as her eye followed the stonework up to the peak of the cathedral ceiling. "And you built this yourself?" She sounded impressed. Michelle was delighted.

"Well, not completely," George replied modestly. "I hired a mason to do the stonework."

"Local stone?"

"Yep. Every one of them came right from this property."

"And the logs?"

"Not the logs. It's ironic. I've been selling a lot of timber and using the money to buy other timber for the house. But what we have growing here is a lot of cherry and oak. That stuff's too valuable to make logs for a house."

"Well, it sure is beautiful. You have a lovely home here."

They meandered out onto the porch and gazed at the secluded valley with Thrush Creek flowing quietly toward them. Earl and Abby, now nine and seven, were kicking a soccer ball around the front lawn while a wood thrush called out from the surrounding forest. "Your children seem right at home out here, don't they?" Eva remarked, turning to Michelle.

"They are right at home," Michelle agreed. "Out here is where they were born, if you recall."

"I remember. Are they doing okay?"

"They're doing fine."

"And what about the cottage?" Eva glanced at George.

"We're going to restore it," George replied. "It needs a little work. But structurally, it's as solid as a rock."

"I have a lot of pleasant memories from that cottage." Eva leaned on the porch rail, gazing into the distance.

"And I do too." Michelle put her hand on Eva's arm.

"We're not going to change it much," George continued. "We just want to bring it back to its original beauty and charm. We're not going to install electricity."

"We just want it to be a cozy little hideaway, with indoor plumbing, a wood stove, and kerosene lamps," Michelle added. "It'll be another place we can have overnight guests in addition to the room you're staying in."

"A cozy little hideaway, that's just how I remember it." Eva sounded pleased. "I'm so glad you invited me to come and see what you're doing with this place."

"And we're glad you could come and spend a couple days with us," Michelle replied as they strolled back into the living room. Eva stopped again and gazed at the massive stone fireplace. Her attention seemed to be fixed on one stone in particular. In the center of the structure, six feet from the floor, was an uncut stone. All the others were dressed and cut by the mason to fit neatly into the structure. But this eighteen-inch flat stone still had its naturally weathered surface exposed and had fluorescent orange heart spray-painted on it.

They all settled into comfortable chairs as George told the story of how he had come upon the location for the house while searching for the buried treasure, and why he had spray-painted the heart on the stone. He also told about Michelle's very prophetic statement, "Look where your heart is."

"Of course, when I wrote that," Michelle added, "I had no idea he was going to paint a heart on a rock out here in the woods. And I wasn't actually referring to the buried treasure."

"And you had no trouble finding the treasure?" Eva grinned.

"Oh, I had plenty of trouble," George responded. "But thanks to my wife, who is obviously much smarter than I am, we eventually figured it out. We, of course, dug that up before we built the house."

"And I understand that the baseball cards were worth a lot of money after all."

"Yes, they were. Of course, I split that with my friend, Rick. He's the one who found the directions in a box of stuff he bought at an auction. He used his half to buy my mother's house from me. So I end up with all of it. It doesn't seem fair, does it?"

"So Rick bought that house. Where is Michelle's dad living now?"

"He moved over into the house where Michelle and I used to live."

"George, years back when your dad walked out and your mother was working as a waitress, did you ever dream your life would turn out like this?

"You knew my mother?" George's jaw dropped.

"I remember her well. My husband and I often ate in the restaurant where she worked. She was such a kind person. She really seemed to enjoy serving others. I knew she had dire financial needs of her own. But she gave others what she had in her heart, and that was pure gold." George pressed his lips together and nodded, unable to say a word.

"But, honey," Michelle said, hoping George would tell his story, "you didn't answer her question. Did you ever dream your life would turn out like this?"

"Did I ever dream?" George smiled and leaned forward, resting his elbows on his knees. "It's amazing what we dream, isn't it? A few weeks before we found Michelle, I dreamed I met Dr. Martin

Luther King. In the dream, he promised me that good things would come to me if I kept serving others. I didn't know if that really meant anything or not. But I took it as a sign from God. So, yes, I dreamed that good things would happen to me."

"And your friend Roger, he never saw God's hand in any of this?" Eva glanced from George to Michelle.

"If he did, he never admitted it," Michelle replied.

"I told you about how a skunk came out of the woods and protected him from the German shepherd." George raised his eyebrows. "Just coincidence, as far as he was concerned."

Eva shook her head as Michelle picked up the story. "And he thought it was just coincidence that he had a dream about me on the very morning that Jasper was bitten by a rattlesnake."

"And the four freak deaths?"

"That!" George struck the air with his index finger. "That, he believed, someone must have planned."

"But not God," Michelle added. "He could see evidence of a plan in the four freak deaths, but not in the origin of life. He saw no evidence of a plan in the natural world around us."

"It seems so clear to us, doesn't it?" Eva shook her head slowly.

"We think he didn't see things clearly because he didn't want to believe." Michelle rubbed her chin as she remembered sitting in a tent on a rainy day, discussing this with Roger. "But he thought we didn't see things correctly because we have a preconceived belief that God is real."

"It seems we always have someone asking that question, don't we?" Eva took a deep breath. "Is there any real evidence of God, or isn't there?"

"Or," Michelle paused in thought, "is it simply a matter of where we choose to put our faith?"